HEXED IN SHOW

SONOMA WITCHES
BOOK SIX

GRETCHEN GALWAY

ETON FIELD

CHAPTER

ONE

"You're not leaving forever, right?" I asked.

The changeling and I stood beside the garden between our two houses, under a beam of early-June sunshine. Most people would be glad to see the last of a fairy who had permanently stolen the body of a human being, but he was my boyfriend. I'd grown more than a little fond of him.

Seth grinned at me, reaching forward to brush hair out of my eyes. His touch was as soft as milkweed floss. "You wish, demon's daughter."

I didn't take the bait. He loved to tease me about the many fun facets of my identity: part demon, all witch, daughter of a criminal, bead artist, secret agent for the Protectorate, gnome wrangler, terrible cook, unreliable gardener. "Seriously," I said. "How long will you be gone?"

We lived in a remote town about two hours north of San Francisco, but he was originally from Minnesota and had a flight to return that afternoon.

He kissed me on the forehead. "Too long, Alma. Too long."

"You don't have to go."

He flinched a little and turned away. "You read the

1

email. My mother is up to her tricks again. I can't let her ruin another life."

His kind, the lake fae, were difficult to appreciate—ruthless, amoral, and often cruel. His fae mother had exchanged his spirit with that of a human baby boy, allowing Seth to be raised with love and comfort. Unlike the little human who'd become a fairy. Unhappy life, unhappy death.

"What will you do if it's too late?" I asked.

He played with the car keys in his hand. "I don't know," he said finally, his eyes downcast.

"You're worrying me," I said. It wasn't like Seth to brood. He often teased me for even thinking about the future. Live in the moment, enjoy the warmth of the sun—or chill in the rain—and always be grateful for what you have. To see him so uncharacteristically anxious made me reach for the strong magical beads on my wrist and cast a protective spell around him.

Amused by my unnecessary effort—in ways I didn't understand, he had more magic than I did—he seemed to shake off his gloom and become my lighthearted, wise-cracking fairy again. "You like worrying," he replied, pulling me into a hug. "Don't get into too much trouble while I'm away. Then again, go ahead. Trouble makes you happy."

I sighed happily against his chest. We understood each other. "Text me while you're away," I said. He was naturally secretive, but I was working on him. "More than once. With more than a few words. Actually tell me what's going on."

"Hm," he mumbled into my hair. It wasn't a promise.

I pinched him where he'd notice. After he yelped, I repeated, "Text me."

"Fine, fine," he said, rubbing the sore spot. "You'll get tired of hearing from me. You'll end up blocking me on your phone."

"Good." I broke away from him and pushed him toward the SUV he was taking to the airport. The Ford had been a gift—well, a payment, really—for my helping a friend out of a deadly family situation. But although the electric SUV was smooth and shiny, I hadn't been able to give up my Jeep. Seth ended up driving the new one most of the time. "Please go before I try to stop you," I said.

He flashed another grin. "That game sounds like fun. We should try it. Will you sprinkle blueberry leaves on me like last week?"

My heart squeezed. A romance between a demon-stained witch and a changeling shouldn't have felt so good. So right.

I kissed him; he kissed me back. Too soon, he was driving away.

Fighting tears, I turned back to my house. Because I was so emotional, I almost didn't notice the break in my protective boundary spells along the driveway.

I got a grip on myself—and the most powerful redwood bead on my necklace—and followed the sense of wrongness into the shade of the redwood trees in the backyard.

～

MY BACKYARD CONTAINED A DETACHED GARAGE, a small patio, overgrown weeds, and a towering redwood tree. Almost as wide as my one-car garage, the ancient redwood rose up from my backyard like a giant's leg without a foot.

Or maybe there *was* a foot, and it was underground where Willy the Gnome lived. Sometimes he appeared in front of a magical little door at the base of the trunk to talk to me. Although we'd been friendly neighbors for several years, I was still careful to use my best manners with Willy. Gnomes were sticklers for protocol. He protected me, my house, my dog, my interests. In return, I brought him baked goods, burritos, and plenty of compliments.

His power was vast and mysterious, but today something was wrong. The broken boundary spell and the wrongness that had invaded my property were leading directly to the base of his tree. Instead of a miniature, shimmering front door, there was a rotted hole.

My stomach sank. "Willy?" I pulled more power from my redwood-bead necklace and surrounded myself with it. As I moved closer to the tree, my sandals crunched in the gravel along my cracked, weedy driveway. I was always meaning to clean up the yard—both Willy and Seth pressured me all the time—but I never got around to it. "Willy?"

There was no response. My heart began to pound. If something had been able to break my boundary spells and hurt Willy, it had to be very powerful—more powerful than me.

And Seth and I had just been standing in the road a minute ago. We'd spent the night together at his place, my going-away present to my fae boyfriend, who could still struggle to relax under the many witchy enchantments in my home.

For a split second, feeling a stab of fear, I considered calling him and asking him to come back to help me look for Willy. But the gnome didn't like Seth because he was a changeling. He called him the "impostor" or "wrong one." Whatever was going on in my backyard, introducing another magical force to the party might backfire. Seth had protected and cared for me, but I still had the winning score for saving lives, in particular his.

I'd have to go on protecting him. Willy had once lifted the most powerful witch and demon killer in the Protectorate into the air and dumped him into the middle of the street. If he'd been hurt by an assailant, then...

Then Seth and I might not stand a chance. If I let Seth continue to the airport, at least one of us would live.

I'd faced death before, but now I had so much more to lose. Love made me more afraid of danger and loss, but also braver. I'd fight to protect him. I'd fight to protect our life together.

"Willy," I called out, more loudly but unsteadily.

I waited for a sign in the silence, ignoring the pounding of my heart.

CHAPTER

TWO

Over the course of the next sixty seconds, I
stretched out all my senses, magical and physical. I scanned the ground, the trees and
branches, the small patio, and the woodland around my
house.

The small wood sprites and flower fairies that usually
gathered near my house were still there, assuring me there
wasn't a demon nearby. And I couldn't feel any other
witch's hex or spell residues. Nothing stood out except for
the magical trail of wrongness that had swooped in
through the road, broken my boundary spell, and blasted
the base of the tree.

Where it ended. And seemed to be fading with each
breath.

After I gathered the guts to move closer to the tree and
crept around it, I concluded that the force had struck
viciously but was no longer there.

I let out a long breath. The danger had passed—for me,
anyway. But I couldn't just let Willy suffer. He'd saved my
life and my dignity more than once. We were allies, we were
neighbors, and we were friends.

After hurrying down the driveway to reestablish my
boundary spells, I called my friend Birdie.

She picked up immediately. "What's wrong? Are you OK? I knew I shouldn't have taken Random overnight. Seth's probably gone and now you're alone and don't have a dog to protect you. Are you bleeding? Sorry—dumb question, we're witches. I keep forgetting that if you're calling me, it's probably something magic—"

"Birdie, listen to me," I said. She had trouble, especially at the beginning of a conversation, to stop talking. It usually slowed down on its own, but I didn't have time. "I'm not hurt, but Willy's missing. Can you come? Bring Random and whatever magic you've got to protect yourself."

"You think he left because Random was with me?" Birdie asked. "I know Willy likes him, but I don't think he'd just leave because Random did. I mean, I take Random all the time when you and your babe need alone time."

Despite the urgency of the situation, I felt myself blushing. "No, I think something attacked him. There's... There's something bad. I'm not sure what it is."

Birdie hesitated only a second. "I'll be there. I just have to close the store and get Random's leash. I guess I can put a sign on the door. Do you think I'll be back today? Or, I guess, ever? I'm not saying I'm complaining about being a witch, but sometimes it makes planning difficult."

Birdie hadn't known she was a witch until I'd told her. Since then, in the midst of a few life-threatening but educational situations, she'd been able to start training and had opened a bookstore with a specialty in the supernatural.

Books, I thought suddenly. "Birdie, could you please bring any books you've got about gnomes? I don't think there's much written down, but maybe we can find something useful."

Birdie's voice expressed the joy my request had given her. She loved to help me and show her growing skills. "Totally," she said, sounding as if she was already rushing around. "See you in a minute!"

"Thanks." I ended the call and used my phone to take a

picture of the hole at the base of the tree. Then I knelt on the ground and, gripping my beads in one hand, gingerly touched the dark, shredded bark.

Now that I was studying the hole from close up, I decided it was an old, natural injury to the tree. Willy must've used it as some kind of entrance and then camouflaged it.

I was still pacing around the backyard, looking for clues, when Birdie arrived with Random. My boundary spells were attuned to her, and she was able to walk in unhindered with a small stack of books in her arms. Random broke away with the leash dangling and ran to sniff a dandelion growing through a crack in the patio.

"There wasn't much about gnomes, but I got what there was even though some of what I've read in here isn't even true," she said. "I mean, we know Willy would never kill anybody just because they had bad manners."

I wasn't so sure. I took the books out of her hands. "Thanks. See the weird hole?" I gestured at the base of the redwood.

Birdie frowned at it. "I don't remember that being there."

"Exactly. But there was some magic residue, not good, coming from the road. And he's gone."

"Oh no." She looked around, hands up and fingers splayed in a defensive stance. "Should we go inside?"

"I think it's safe now." I hugged the books against my chest. "But yeah. Let's."

Inside at my kitchen table, I spread out the five books and cast a quick seeking spell to see if my subconscious or the mysteries of the universe would give me a hint.

None. Five was a good number though, so maybe I'd get lucky.

"What are we looking for?" Birdie picked up the smallest book. About the size of a sandwich, it had a bright yellow cover and the title, *Gnomes and Their Ways,* in a feminine script. I was unable to read the author's name under

Birdie's hand, but I doubted it would mean anything to me. Witches seldom wrote under their real names. "Who would want to hurt Willy anyway?" she added.

"Who *could* is my question," I said. "But you've got the right idea to look for potential enemies. I know—"

Against my will, my teeth clamped together. The movement was sudden and slightly painful, reminding me with a shock that there were some topics I could absolutely not discuss.

I know genies hate gnomes. To utter those words aloud would've come too close to revealing the existence of a genie nearby who granted wishes if adequate payment was provided. As part of one of those deals, I'd once agreed to a magical nondisclosure agreement that was strong enough to impress even the most ruthless entrepreneurs in Silicon Valley. Whenever a topic ventured near the existence of Jen Bardak, owner of Cypress Hardware on Main Street, I would completely lose the ability to communicate.

And the topic of gnome enemies was inevitably going to lead me to the jinn. They hated each other. I didn't know why—what human could understand such ancient, supernatural personalities?—but I knew it was true. And not many others did, so I couldn't even talk about it in a theoretical way with Birdie.

I waited for my verbal paralysis to pass. Birdie, her attention fixed on the book, didn't seem to notice my sudden silence—but that was another facet of the magic. The scope of Jen's powers terrified me. The only other creature I'd ever met who could compare was Willy.

"This book is terrible," Birdie said, making a face as she flipped the pages. "I'm embarrassed I even have it in the shop."

"What's wrong with it?" I asked slowly, testing the flexibility of my lips. They were still a little stiff.

"Listen to this," she began. "'Gnomes are as tall as the house they are cursed to haunt. Contrary to myth, all gnomes are quite large. Were a human able to ever see one'"—she emphasized this last phrase with meaningful mockery—"'he would surely faint from the shock of sharing the company of a giant that he had, until then, assumed to be quite diminutive.'" She stared at me with her mouth open.

I sighed. "Yeah, not all books about magic or magical beings are written by people who actually know anything." I opened a thick, nondescript book titled *Magical Beings*. Again, no author. It had a tattered spine, and I searched the table of contents for gnomes.

"Hold on, it gets better," Birdie said, back to hate-reading the yellow book. "Listen to this—'All gnomes are covered nose to toe in long white fur.'"

I laughed, but Birdie seemed more angry than amused.

"Seriously?" she demanded. "Seriously? They're basically Bigfoot of the North Pole? The Abominable Snowman?"

"I know," I said soothingly, returning to my own unhelpful text. "This one says gnomes are little fairies that like human gardens but don't really do much of anything."

"That's way better than this," Birdie said, flinging the little book across the table. "Were they on drugs or what?"

"Probably," I said. "Springwater can give witches some really nice hallucinations sometimes."

Water from a wellspring—like the one in Silverpool—had magical properties.

"But not to you, right?" Birdie asked. "I had too much of it after the floods last winter, and I swear I saw an elephant driving a unicycle past my store. I almost called you."

"It doesn't affect me very much," I admitted. "Probably something to do with my, uh, heritage."

Birdie shot a thoughtful glance at me. "You don't usually talk about the demon thing."

My stomach clenched involuntarily. It was bad enough that my biological mother had been possessed by a demon but even worse that other people knew about it.

Birdie, however, had become my best friend. I valued

her warmth, her curiosity, her instincts. Maybe it was time to tell her some of my darkest, deepest thoughts.

"I don't usually like to even think about it. But with Willy missing, I can't pretend demons might not be involved." I swallowed over a lump in my throat, suddenly anxious about revealing so much of myself. But she deserved to know what I was thinking—and I deserved to have a friend who knew what I was thinking. What I was *feeling*. My voice fell to a whisper. "Maybe it's something to do with me. Maybe something hurt him because of me."

THREE

Birdie stared at me a moment, frowning, clearly confused. "What? Why?"

Pushing the useless book aside—and my feelings—I picked up another one. "I have no idea," I said roughly. The new book had a larger section on gnomes, complete with a photo that looked as if it had been taken from a website selling cheap garden statuary. I set it aside and looked through the others, finding not much better. "And these books aren't helping."

"Sorry," Birdie said. "I should have better ones."

I touched her arm, softening my tone. "No, no. It's not your fault. You've got what's available. Not everything can be learned in books."

Birdie smiled. "Hey, take that back."

"I'm probably going to have to do some field research." It would be just like the old days when I was a trainee agent for the Protectorate, sent out to do the grunt work. "I need to find somebody who actually knows about gnomes."

"Good idea. You can always leave Random with me." Birdie gave me her open look of complete trust that made me uncomfortable. I'd been her teacher once, but I'd rather now that we could just be peers. Friends.

"The only expert I can think of is a gnome herself," I said. "She lived in the garden at Hawk Ranch."

We'd been up there a previous summer for a house party that had led to more than one death. Birdie had been discovering her own powers for the first time, and I'd learned about my demon ancestry.

"Oh right, you told me about her," Birdie said. "What was her name...? Bark something?"

"Barkfoot," I said.

"I wonder if she stayed after the nonmagical owners took over. It's a bed-and-breakfast again."

I stared at her. Apparently she knew more than I did. "Where did you hear that?"

She blushed and began gathering the books together into a pile. "Raynor," she said quietly.

"You talk to Raynor?" The admission shocked me. He was Director of the Protectorate in San Francisco. The two of us had become uneasy allies who shared the secret trait of demon-stained ancestry. He'd also convinced me to work for him on a freelance basis—and that had almost gotten me killed more than once. If he was trying to hire Birdie to do more dirty work, I'd have to set him straight.

"Every once in a while," she said. "No big deal." Her flush deepened.

My surprise sank into dread.

I knew what that blush meant. She was an incorrigible matchmaker, in part because she was a natural romantic who longed for a partner of her own. Unfortunately, her usual awkwardness hit pathological levels when she was with men she was attracted to.

"You're blushing," I said, feeling queasy.

She opened her mouth, then closed it. A rare bubble of silence formed around her.

"It wasn't a work assignment you talked about," I said.

Almost everyone found Raynor attractive. He looked like the Rock, for Brightness's sake. He was single and powerful. He was even, I hated to admit, a fairly good guy. But with Birdie?

No way.

"He's way too old for you," I said.

"You slept with my dad," she said, lifting her chin, "and you're the same age I am."

Direct hit. Sadly, she was right. Before either of us had known that Tristan Price was her biological father, I'd had a brief fling with him. But so had a significant percentage of all women in Sonoma County. Birdie's link to him had only come out after his death.

I closed my gaping mouth with effort and got to my feet, more uncomfortable in Birdie's company than I'd ever been before.

What could I tell her? That she was too sweet and innocent to get romantically involved with a ruthless, ambitious demon killer who was now the most powerful witch on the West Coast? That he'd had a string of girlfriends and would never settle down? Or that I didn't believe he'd ever think about *her* that way, having seen the last woman Raynor had dated? That witch had been as ruthless and driven as he was.

It was none of my business.

I made a pathetic effort to look relaxed as I poured myself a glass of water.

It was none of my business.

I wanted to ask her so many questions: Had they gone on a date? Was it just phone calls?

Was she in love?

I wanted her to be happy. I even wanted Raynor to be happy. But—obviously—it could never happen. Never.

Birdie deserved to be happy. I'd kill him if he hurt her.

The thought knocked some sense into me. I'd been fired from the Protectorate because of my Incurable Inability to kill anything, even a demon, and now I was considering murder because my friend blushed over a phone call? No. Birdie's love life, or lack of it, was *none of my business.*

"Anyway," I said finally, trying to overcome the awkward silence that had stretched on too long. "Raynor's probably the man I should talk to as well. He might know a gnome expert."

Birdie nodded and smiled, as eager as I was to clear the air. "Great idea. I bet he does. It's his job to know things like that."

"Right," I said.

"It's a great idea," she repeated.

We smiled at each other.

If he hurts her, I'll kill him, I thought again.

FOUR

Although I knew he'd be busy in the middle of the workday, I called Raynor immediately after Birdie left for home.

I stayed in my kitchen, where my magic was at its strongest. Sometimes Raynor pretended I was still a Flint agent who needed routine safety tests—that is, he attacked without warning, then said it was good for me.

He started speaking without saying hello. "Your boyfriend is making our agents in Minneapolis nervous."

I looked at the clock. Seth's flight wasn't even due to land in Minnesota until evening. "How did you know—?"

"Please. We all know. As soon as he crossed the Golden Gate Bridge in that new car of yours, an agent came to tell me."

I rolled my eyes. I'd put shielding spells on my Jeep, but obviously the Escape needed an upgrade. "He's just visiting family."

"His family has the nasty habit of possessing nonmagical human beings."

Seth wouldn't want me telling the Protectorate about his mission. "He has human family," I said.

"His parents are dead."

"Extended family. Don't worry about it," I said. "The reason I'm calling—"

"Is he trying to contact the lake fae? The human family that raised him is dead. Why visit?"

I bit my lip and stared at the photo of Seth I kept on my fridge. Dark hair, blue eyes, dimple on his chin. I focused on his good looks to prevent Raynor from removing any secrets out of my head. He had the delusion that his job gave him the right to know everything.

But I also had to get him and anxious Protectorate agents in Minneapolis to leave Seth alone.

Raynor had kept his silence about Seth before, so maybe it was a risk I'd have to take. "If I tell you, you have to keep it to yourself," I said. "With a binding vow."

"No vow will hold if the protection of humanity is at stake."

I rolled my eyes. "So much drama. Demon's balls, Raynor. He's a good guy. A *great* guy. There's much more Shadow in my soul than there is in his."

He scoffed. "Knowing what I know, that's not saying much."

I was tempted to hang up, but Willy was in trouble, and now I had Seth out there to protect as well. "Like I was saying. Promise to keep what I tell you to yourself, including an exemption for the fate of humanity, and I'll explain."

"Am I going to be angry at you if I do this?" he asked.

I looked into Seth's smiling sapphire-blue eyes in the photo. He was as Bright as any creature I'd ever met. He'd been willing to die to return his human body to its original soul. He'd ended up paying a different kind of price, to be trapped in an undefined state of existence, not even knowing if his life would be as short as mine or as long as a gnome's.

"No," I said. "You won't be angry. You'll be relieved."

That was a bit of an exaggeration, but I wanted to prime the pump of his emotional reaction.

"I'd be relieved if he rejoined his kind under the water and stayed there," Raynor said.

"No, you wouldn't. I wouldn't be any use to you anymore because I'd be so sad. And you'd miss him too." Fear of losing my man washed over me. What if he didn't come back to me? My eyes started to burn. "He's"—my voice cracked—"unique."

There was a long silence. "You're hooked bad," he said.

I wiped my eyes. Cleared my throat. "Promise you won't tell?"

He let out a long, exasperated sigh. "Fine." I heard him inhale sharply, a familiar sound when talking to Raynor. He had a habit of snorting a blend of magical herbs up his nose. "With a strong humanity-welfare exemption. What's he doing?"

"He's going to prevent his fae mother from changing another human baby."

Raynor growled. "You said I wouldn't be angry."

"You want his fae mother to—"

"I want her fae son to leave the protection of humanity to the Protectorate," he said. "It's right there in the name. *Protect*."

"Witches can't stop fae from anything," I said. Demons were the enemy we'd been trained to fight, not fairies or other supernatural beings. "Agents won't do anything except kill the baby after it's been possessed by the fae spirit. Is that what you want?"

He growled again but said nothing, so I continued.

"When the baby is safe, Seth will return to Silverpool, where he's never caused any trouble," I said. "What are you afraid of?"

"I'm not afraid of him, but those Minnesotan witches have a long history with this strain of lake fae." Although he was still griping, his tone had softened. He was satisfied. "You'll keep me posted."

"Sure, sure. Of course." I walked over to the back door off the kitchen and looked out the window at the wide base of the redwood tree. "I called you to ask about gnomes."

"I'd have thought you're the expert, not me."

"Remember when we were at Hawk Ranch? There was a gnome in the garden—"

"Barkfoot," he said.

"Yes," I said. "You really seemed to connect with her. I wondered how much you know about gnomes."

"Gnomes? You ratted out your changeling boyfriend to ask me about gnomes?"

I flushed, angry. "You were going to sic the Minneapolis Protectorate on him."

He scoffed. "Ooh, scary. Minnesotans."

There wasn't much about the phone conversation I wasn't regretting. "Just tell me what you know about gnomes."

"You have an expert ten, twenty feet from your own witchy kitchen," he said. "Ask him for help satisfying your newest and probably dangerous obsession."

"I would, but he's in some kind of trouble. That's the point," I snapped. "I'm trying to help him."

"Somebody put him into trouble?"

"I think so, yes," I said. "Broke through my boundary spells."

"That's very bad."

"Oh really?" I asked flatly.

"You should've told me about the violation of your boundaries from the start," he said. "That gnome is a menace. If somebody could hurt him, they could hurt you."

I gritted my teeth. Raynor could be insufferable. "I had no idea. Thanks so much for pointing that out."

"Barkfoot probably moved away after the nonmags took over Hawk Ranch," he said. "What you need is a witch who's an expert on gnomes."

I rolled my eyes hard enough to hurt. I didn't trust myself to speak.

Eventually, as my silence stretched out, he got the

message. "Yeah, yeah," he said. "What I mean is, I'm not the expert. But I do know where one is."

I sighed in relief. "Great. Where?" Flying to New York or Boston, where Raynor had spent much of his career, wasn't something I enjoyed doing, but I'd do it for Willy.

"Elwin," he said. "Humboldt coast."

That region was only several hours north by car—much better than the East Coast. I tried to remember if I'd heard of Elwin. "Is there something about plants there?"

"Elwin Flower Show," he said. "I'm surprised you don't know about the place. It's one of the hot new places for witches escaping San Francisco."

"I've already escaped San Francisco," I said. Mostly.

"Well, you're not the only one," he said. "With all the working from home the past few years, witches are leaving the city for places with cheaper housing, ocean views, lots of hiking, fresh air, starry skies, all that jazz. If the Protectorate wasn't paranoid about Silverpool, you'd be getting overrun there too."

The wellspring was enchanted to keep it secret. Only the powers of the solstice were strong enough to draw strangers to town. "I had heard about city witches moving to places like Montana. I hadn't heard about Elwin."

"Witches have taken over the village government, downtown, and even the schools," he said. "Percival Tuff is a teacher there. I gave him a rec."

"Percy?" He'd been an apprentice in Silverpool for a brief period over the winter solstice. After a murder or two and the invasion of Silverpool by demon-summoning witches, he'd given up his job in the Protectorate for a new career. "I thought he'd gone to a school in Oregon."

"Guess he didn't make it that far." Raynor sounded bored. Percy hadn't impressed him, and although he kept track of Percy as he probably did all former Protectorate agents, that was the end of his interest. "I'd have thought you'd know all about Elwin because of the show and your plant-magic thing."

"Hey," I said. "I've been busy." He knew that better than anyone since he was the one who usually kept me that way.

"Still. You rely on those wood beads of yours," he said. "Your staff, your little baggies of strange leaves, the weird tea you make…"

"I'm a witch. There's nothing weird about any of it." Because of the mild climate, the witches of the Bay Area were more into gardening than most modern witches, but most still looked down on botanical magic, venerating gold and stone as much as any New Yorker. It came at a cost, however: gnomes were partial to the homes of witches who followed the old-fashioned ways. "Is the gnome expert going to be at the flower show?"

"I imagine she'll avoid it," he said. "She lives there year-round. Has since… Well, since we used to spend a lot of time together."

I knew what that meant. As I'd tried to tell Birdie, Raynor had a lot of women in his past—and would in his future, too. "What's her name?"

He took a moment to snort more herbs up into his nose. "Clematis Mallory. Everyone calls her Clem. Clemmie." His tone became a little wistful. Maybe she'd been a favorite. "Anyway, she's really the expert on gnomes. Does the name sound familiar?"

It didn't. "Can you call her and tell her I'd like to talk—"

"She doesn't touch nonmagical technology," he said. "At least nothing to do with communication or computers."

"So texting is out. Landlines—"

"Nope."

"Snail mail?" I asked. But I was already imagining the days a letter would take to reach her and the poor chance an eccentric witch would respond, if she ever did. Meanwhile, Willy was in danger, and possibly so was I.

"I doubt it," Raynor said. "She threatens anyone who comes to her gate with armpit boils. Even postal carriers."

"If she's that crazy and hostile, then what use could she be to me?" I went outside and walked over to the tree. There was still no sign of Willy's door. "You must know lots of people. Isn't there somebody else who knows about gnomes? I mean, come on. Didn't you learn things when you were Protector? Secret things they only tell you when you get up in the ranks?"

Raynor scoffed. "Gnomes don't pose a threat to humanity the way demonkind does."

I could see where this was headed. Or rather, where *I* was headed.

"You're going to have to go up there in person," he went on. "We parted on good terms, so tell her I sent you. Besides, you two should have a lot in common. Hearth witches, living alone in the middle of nowhere? If she'll talk to anybody, it'll be you."

FIVE

The next morning, I made the four-hour drive north to the coastal village of Elwin. I would've liked more time to explore the area with its redwood forests, rivers, and geological resources, but I was in a hurry. Maybe another time.

As soon as I parked my car, I called Seth.

Other than a quick text message when he'd landed in Minneapolis, he and I hadn't spoken. It had occurred to me that if I'd told him about Willy and my planned trip to Elwin while he was still near the Minneapolis airport, he might've rushed back—and I didn't want him to. Therefore, I'd decided to wait to tell him about Willy until today. When I was parked outside Clematis Mallory's house.

I licked my lips, still nervous about telling him about Willy and my trip even though he was now hours away from an airport. His magic had mysterious abilities to reach far beyond his physical location. I didn't want him to worry too much about me, but I also didn't want him to try to stop me. But we'd promised to be honest and open with each other.

"How's it going?" I asked, the cheer in my voice sounding false even to me.

"I miss you. But you'd love it here," he said. "Lots of trees."

My heart squeezed. Not letting on that I wasn't home, I quickly told him about Willy.

He wasn't concerned. "The old creature can take care of himself," he said, laughing. "And you, I bet."

After a pause and a deep breath, I told him about Raynor's gnome-expert connection and my drive to Elwin to meet her.

He stopped laughing. "You went to Humboldt by yourself? To ask a hostile witch for a favor?"

I stared out the window, flinching at the hint of anger in his voice. Clematis Mallory's house felt important somehow. I'd just have to explain it to him.

The street was wider than it needed to be for such a tiny town. Sunnier and windier, too. Maybe the fact that Elwin was surrounded on three sides by redwood forest had seemed like more than enough trees for the town's founders back in the nineteenth century. Or maybe it was all the gardeners hoping to grow tomatoes despite the dense coastal fog rolling off the shore. Whatever the reason, most of the old houses dotting the neighborhood lacked anything taller than an evergreen shrub out front.

Except for the house I was visiting. That one, a purple bungalow, was almost hidden by vegetation. There was a tall tree—possibly a bay, but I'd only glimpsed it—in the backyard, plum and citrus in the front garden, and an espaliered apple tree half-smothered by a rambling pink rose along the driveway. And that was just what I'd noticed on my drive by.

The house was unnumbered, but I could deduce from its neighbors that it bore the address Raynor had given me. Even without that intel, however, the garden gave it away. A gnome expert wouldn't tolerate a manicured lawn.

"She's an old friend of Raynor's," I said. "I need to help Willy, and she's the only lead I've got. Unless you've got a better idea?"

"My idea is to let Willy figure out his own problems," Seth replied. "He's survived who-knows-how-many centuries by now. He doesn't need your help."

I wasn't going to argue about that; Seth and Willy had never been friends. My own safety would be more likely to convince him. "Whatever could scare Willy might be able to kill me," I said. "I have to find him so I know what to look out for."

Seth fell silent. "Why couldn't Raynor just ask her himself?" he asked finally.

I explained again. If it weren't for my own slight qualms about danger, I wouldn't have told Seth about my trip until after I'd finished it. But it would be more considerate and, I admitted, safer to tell him beforehand. On the rare occasion, I did benefit from a modest amount of rescuing.

"I should come home," he said. "I should be there with you."

"You're doing something you have to do. I'm doing something I have to do. It'll be fine." I looked down the street at the purple house overshadowed by its garden. "Listen to us. You're the one who's supposed to be telling *me* not to worry." His change in personality worried me more than the witch behind the fortress of rambling roses.

"You're right. Nothing like visiting your family of origin to erase decades of personal growth." His playful tone was back. "My fairy mother is pretending I'm not here, but I heard her singing in my dreams last night."

I was glad to hear he'd slept. Once I found him watching me in the middle of the night, a soft smile on his face, and he'd said I was the best insomnia treatment a "fairy slash human" could have.

"Where are you staying? Airbnb?" I asked.

He laughed softly. "I'm lake fae. I slept near the lake."

"On the ground?"

"As if." There was a long, worrying pause. "I made a bed of cattails."

The image of Seth sleeping rough, alone, made my heart

squeeze. He loved human comforts and company and had only returned to his home out of a sense of compassion and responsibility.

I closed my eyes, tempted to drive to the nearest airport and join him. "Seth..."

"Mom says hello, by the way," he said. "In the singing dream."

"You're kidding," I said.

There was a long pause. "She wants to be a grandmother."

Ugh. The idea of a lake fairy thousands of miles away wanting me to be impregnated by her changeling son made me queasy.

I didn't know what to say. Talk about problematic grandmothers. A demon on one side and a fairy on the other.

"Sorry," he said. "I shouldn't joke. Don't worry, she doesn't know about you. The reason she put me in Launt's body as a baby was to contaminate a human bloodline. It's instinct. It was always there and always will be. If I hadn't tried to undo the damage, leaving me in the undefined state that I am, she'd probably see me as a great success."

My churning guts calmed slightly. "Why wouldn't she think so now? You're alive, you're human," I said. "Ish."

"With my fairy body dead, I'm invisible to her. She can touch my dreams, but when I'm awake, I'm just another human adult to her."

I liked the sound of that. "So you're safe. She can't hurt you."

He chuckled. "I will return to you, fear not. It may be that I bear another psychic scar from my aggressively amoral fairy mama, but my strange not-quite-human life will continue."

"You bet it will," I said.

"As will yours," he said. "Say the word, and I'll be there."

I sighed, pleased by the offer. "Will I need to use a

phone, or can you hear me without it?" There had been moments when he'd seemed to be connected to me from miles away.

"Please use a phone," he said. "My little gifts will be busy with the situation here."

I resisted making a joke about his gifts, some of which I was already missing. "Don't let her take that baby."

"I won't. But there's a puppy here that might not be so lucky."

I gasped. "A puppy?"

"The parents got him to grow up with the baby," Seth said. "He can sense my mother is out here, and it's making him really, really clingy with the woman."

"The woman?"

"The baby's human mother. She's in her third trimester."

"Seth," I said, exasperated. "You didn't tell me the baby wasn't even born yet." Sometimes his secrecy wore me out. I'd thought he'd be gone for a week or so, but now I realized it could be a month. Or more.

"I thought that was obvious. She always goes for the newborns. First three days." His voice didn't change, but I sensed a tension in him when he added, "That's when she switched me with Launt."

It was hard to ever stay angry with him for long. He was the product of a childhood I couldn't imagine. "Do you think your mother would kill a dog to get to the baby?"

"Like I said, I need to keep on top of things here," he said.

I regretted involving him in my own situation. He had an important mission of his own. "Yes, of course. I'm so glad you're there."

"You wound me. I was just feeling bereft without you, but there you are, celebrating my absence."

The midday sun was coming in through the windshield. The car was getting uncomfortably hot inside, and I was sweating. It was time to get moving. "I love you," I said. "Call me tonight? Text?"

He was quiet again for a moment. "I have a weird feeling. Are you with new witches right now?"

"I'm down the street from the one I came to meet."

"I sense more than one," he said. "A lot more."

I hadn't told him about the town attracting a large witch population. He had enough to worry about. When too many witches got together, people tended to get hurt. "Focus on fairies. Witches are my problem."

After a bit more banter and sweet talk, we finally ended the call. I got out, telling myself to erase the dumb smile on my face, and went to the back to get the gift I'd brought for Clem. She might prefer money as payment, so I'd brought that as well.

I walked down the street and stood in front of the garden gate.

Once painted white, the picket fence and arbor were now a mottled gray, mostly invisible under the twining vines of roses, jasmine, morning glory, and red trumpet flowers. The arbor, smothered under a mountain of thorny roses, arched over a hip-high gate with a rusty iron latch that gave off a sharp, acrid magical odor.

Boundary spells. Stronger and more hostile than mine. They encompassed the property from all sides—sidewalk, fence, earth, sky. I suspected a tunnel would have to go twenty feet underground to avoid the enchantments there. A hot-air balloon might be able to approach from above, but the hexes broadcasting into the sky would probably puncture it before it reached the roof.

Although it was June, there was smoke rising from the chimney. I smelled cedar logs and dried sage burning amid the sweet, slightly fecund smell of too many roses.

I waited, feeling exposed, and glanced at my watch. It was pushing three now.

"Hello?" I called aloud. My hands holding the small velvet gift bag had started to sweat. Nothing could've made me reach out for the iron latch and try to walk through the gate. The magical residue of the owner's boundary spells was as thick as saltwater taffy. I spoke louder. "My name is Alma Bellrose. I'm here to ask for your help. I humbly request an audience."

I rolled my eyes at my own archaic language. Maybe it was the overgrown roses covering the front of the house that made me think of Sleeping Beauty's castle. Instead of a princess inside, however, there was a witch.

But where was she?

I considered throwing the present over the gate and coming back later. Nobody would steal anything from that yard.

There was the soft ring of a bell behind me.

CHAPTER

SIX

I turned to see a woman approaching on a baby-blue bicycle, the upright kind with a big basket between the front handlebars. She weaved over the cracks in the sidewalk, biting her lips with concentration as if she'd just learned how to ride.

I waited for her to come to a stop in front of me. I knew instantly this was Clem, although she was not at all what I'd expected. Raynor's last girlfriend had been athletic, sophisticated, fashionable, and self-composed. This woman was unkempt and awkward, wearing baggy men's cargo shorts and a tie-dyed T-shirt that was so large it could've been belted and worn as a dress.

She was a petite woman in her forties or fifties, short and round, her small stature emphasized by her oversized clothing. Ash-blond with blue eyes, her fair skin had turned pink and sweaty from her ride. Her overall impression was that of a woman who had specialized in gnomes because she herself resembled one.

I knew appearances could be—usually were—deceiving, so I pulled up a second protective boundary around myself. She stopped a few feet away, leaned her bike against the fence, and regarded me with her helmet half-askew.

"Yes?" she asked, nervously playing with an amulet at her throat. It was silver, but the string holding it around her neck was made out of human hair. Not her own.

"My name is Alma Bellrose," I said. "Raynor told me you know about gnomes. I'm trying to help one. I'll pay you for your trouble." Belatedly I held out my gift.

She looked at the velvet bag with disinterest, not even bothering to scan it, then shot a longing glance at her house. As her awkwardness increased, she fumbled with a leather pouch clipped to her cargo shorts, took out a pinch of herbs, and snorted them up into her nose. A second later, her tension easing, her shoulders softened, and she let out a deep breath. The herbs had done their magic.

I wondered if it was Raynor who had gotten her hooked on the magic snuff or the other way around.

"OK," she said slowly, glancing again at her house. "But we'll have to talk out here. I've got so many boundary spells on the house, I think it would be uncomfortable for you."

"Sure."

"Just a minute. Let me put this away." She turned and pushed the bike up the driveway. Halfway up, her arm caught on one of the arching, thorny canes of one of her own rosebushes. She tugged her arm free, rolled her bike into a bush, and cast a locking spell over it.

Totally unnecessary last step. Nobody would be able to walk within ten feet, let alone steal it.

After she'd tried to smooth down her wild blond hair, she snorted another pinch of the herbs and returned to me on the sidewalk. She lifted one hand politely in the air— fingers up, palm out. A welcome without threat of physical contact.

"Clematis Mallory," she said.

"Nice to meet you," I said, mirroring the gesture. "I really appreciate your time."

"I don't see how I can help you," she said.

She wasn't exactly friendly, but at least she wasn't trying to turn my organs inside out. "The gnome is important to me," I said, holding out the gift bag again. "He lives in my backyard."

She frowned at the gift. After a second, she reached out and took it. She didn't open it, but I could finally feel her pass a magical scan over it. A small smile teased her lips. "You follow the old ways?"

"Is it that obvious?"

"The three-year-old who lives in that house over there wears more metal than you do," she said. Her smile broadened. The aversion that had been so obvious upon first contact was melting away. Maybe she was so hostile to visitors because they were contemptuous of her and her old-fashioned magic. I certainly knew what that was like.

I looked over at the freshly painted yellow bungalow across the street. The fence looked new, with modern horizontal slats using an excess of galvanized steel nails. There were brass pucks of solar lighting on each copper-capped post. The twin hip-high planters flanking the front door were plated with shimmering bronze.

Even without being told, I knew the residents had to be newcomers. Everything about the place gave the impression of metal magic and money. She was eyeing the house with distaste.

"I hear a lot of witches have moved up here over the past few years with everyone working from home," I said.

"It actually began about five or six years ago when witches took over our school. Before that, the town got flooded with visitors once a year for the flower show but otherwise was nice and quiet." Grimacing, she put her hand on the small of her back. "Do you mind if we take a walk? My joints hurt if I stand for too long."

"Of course. I'd like that."

It was a relief to get away from the magic broadcasting off her property. As we walked up the street past the tidy bungalows and Victorians, I eyed her neighbors with curiosity, wondering what they thought of her.

Clem snorted another pinch of herbs, making me

wonder about them. Were they the same as Raynor's or different?

"At first I thought the school was a great idea," Clem said, wiping her nose. "A witch charter school? About time. Finally, a free, magic-centered public education for witch families of modest means."

"But?"

"Then the town changed. Too many people from the Bay Area moved up here. Elwin just isn't the same." She gestured at the driveway we were walking by that held two Teslas. Across the street, the house was in the middle of gaining a second floor with a rooftop deck. Its front yard held nine stone spheres—I could feel a silver chain connecting them along the ground—laid out in a spiral pattern. "They might not be superrich, but they have more money than anyone here. But it's not just that. They're such... *strivers*. You know how metal witches are. Every-thing's about status and getting ahead. It's just not my thing."

"Me either," I said. "My thing is wood." I gestured at the necklace inside the gift bag she held, glad I'd brought it. She might actually be able to appreciate it.

We walked past a yard with perfectly smooth green grass. It took me several seconds to realize it was synthetic. A witch had put plastic grass over their own soil.

Clem noticed my shocked gaze and nodded with shared disapproval. Then she said, "I'm surprised Raynor would even speak to you. When I knew him, he wasn't exactly impressed with botanicals."

I laughed. "He's still not."

She watched me, a twinkle in her eye. "Maybe he was impressed with you personally," she said. "And vice versa."

Unlike Birdie, my body didn't react with a full-body flush. Aside from one brief, misguided second, I'd never been attracted to Raynor. "Not like that," I said. "I was an agent once. Briefly. You can probably imagine how well that went, given my woodsy ways. Now I live in Silverpool." If she was the type of witch to be an expert on any supernatural subject, she probably knew about the secret wellspring in my hometown.

"Ah," she said. "That explains your gnome friend."

"Willy," I said. "He lives in my backyard. An entity broke through my boundary spells and did something to him." I explained the visible changes to the tree, the sense of wrongness, my debt to and fondness for Willy.

She frowned. "That's not good." She looked around as if the menace might have followed me to her neighborhood. It was hard to believe any supernatural enemy would risk coming into an enclave of powerful metal witches who protected their tidy flowerbeds with iron fences. "No wonder you're worried."

"Have you ever heard of a gnome being attacked? Something that left a hole in the tree like that?"

"No. No. I'm sorry." Clem touched the amulet on her belt, muttering a good luck spell. "I have no idea what could be stronger than a gnome in their own home."

My optimism took a serious hit. I tried not to show my disappointment, which might insult her, but my thoughts were already racing ahead to what I could do next, who else I could ask. We'd walked to the end of the block and were now standing near my Jeep. If I got on the road within the hour, I'd be home before it got too dark. I avoided driving through the forest leading into Silverpool at night because the fairies always tried to run drivers off the road with their songs and mesmerizing lights.

But then who would I ask? Helen in San Francisco, I supposed, though she'd never seemed interested in Willy before. I doubted she knew more about gnomes than I did.

The genie?

I shuddered. Jen Bardak always demanded a high price for her services.

"But I know somebody who might," Clem said.

CHAPTER

SEVEN

I started to feel hopeful again. "Oh?" I said casually, trying not to pressure her.

"I'll have to be careful though. She takes offense easily." She spoke quietly, under her breath, as if the potential helper could hear her.

"A witch?" I asked.

Clem shook her head. "Brightness no."

A supernatural creature then. One who might help Willy but was easily offended.

"Is she another gnome?" I saw the confirmation on Clem's face. "What's her name?"

"I wish I knew," she said. "She's never shared it, though she's honored me with her presence for over twenty years now. Actually, I should say she's indulged me with *my* presence. She was here before I was."

"Same," I said, feeling a rush of kinship. "How do you address her when you see her?"

Her eyebrows rose. "You *see* your gnome?"

For a moment, panic ran through me. It wasn't safe for anyone to know I could see the fae. But I quickly relaxed; Willy made himself visible to many of my visitors, not just the demon marked. "He's friendly with witches," I said. "Yours isn't?"

"She's more friendly than I am," Clem said, cracking a grin, "but she doesn't choose to show herself. Her way of making contact is by singing. Her voice is amazing. People think it's a mockingbird when they hear it."

I was trying to see how a gnome whose only form of socializing with humans was through song was going to be able to help me. "She sounds fascinating."

"She's the reason I've studied gnomes all these years," Clem said, coming to a stop. She looked back toward her home, as if the short distance we'd traveled was as far as she wanted to go. "If I'd known about your Willy, I would've requested an introduction. Naturally, I would've respected your refusal if that's how you feel."

"Of course I wouldn't refuse," I said, even if that's exactly what she herself would've done. "When he's back safe at home, you're welcome to visit. I'll introduce you."

Her face softened, giving me a glimpse of what she must've looked like as a young girl. "Would you really? That would be fantastic. I've seen other gnomes in my research, but I'm always thrilled to meet a new one."

"Of course."

She nodded. "I'll talk to her tonight. She only communicates after dark. She seems to prefer singing when the birds are quiet." She gave me an apologetic look. "Sorry that you'll have to wait."

"No, that's great. I appreciate it."

With another nod, she began walking back home. "Raynor probably told you I don't use any tech," she said, wrinkling her nose at the word, "so I won't be able to contact you after I talk to her. It can take me hours to interpret her songs. Can you come back in the morning?"

I groaned inwardly. Spending the night in the witch town was unappealing. Unlike Seth, I wouldn't sleep outside on a bed of cattails, but a motel would cost money and still not be as comfortable as home.

She saw I didn't like that. "Well, if you must, you could

come by around midnight. Given your craft, I expect you're often up with the moon."

I didn't enjoy driving at night, but I could use herbs to push through my fatigue. If she gave me something to help Willy, I'd want to hurry home. "You're right. Thank you. I'll be here," I said. "I'll call out from the gate again."

"That's probably a good idea. Sorry, but I don't have many visitors."

As if I didn't already know that. I bowed my head, hand over my heart, and sent out a magical puff of gratitude. "Thank you so much."

With a small smile, she turned abruptly away and hurried home. I stood on the sidewalk, still a few houses down, watching her disappear into her garden.

It was only early afternoon, so I'd need somewhere other than the sidewalk in front of Clem's fortress of roses to wait until midnight. Eager to stretch my legs after the long drive, I left my Jeep where it was and walked the half mile to the business district.

Like Clem's street, the rest of tiny Elwin seemed to have a high population of luxury vehicles. Protectorate agents always drove black SUVs, and I saw a few hand-me-downs dotted between the rainbow of vehicles by BMW, Audi, Tesla, Lexus, Porsche, Land Rover, Ferrari. It reminded me of rich enclaves south of San Francisco where the one percent of one percent lived.

The newcomers really had taken over. Witches didn't usually go for flashy cars, needing to lie low to avoid detection. Maybe the influx of people to Elwin hadn't exclusively been witches but also venture capitalists, professional sports figures, celebrities, socialites. The nonmagical moneyed class.

But by the time I reached the small downtown, the smell of magic had begun to give me a headache. The vehicles seemed like the type rich nonmag people would drive, but these definitely belonged to witches. I could sense the magical residue on the pavement, the sidewalk, even the curb in front of the liquor store that was freshly painted green to limit parking to short visits.

Larry's Liquors looked as if it was far older than any of the drivers of the cars lining the street. Given its peeling paint and midcentury sign font, Larry's hadn't joined in with Elwin's gentrification.

I put my hand on the redwood beads at my throat to block the overpowering sensation of so much metal magic. Elwin might have been famous among most witches for its flower show, but my impression was that the newcomers were not the type to spend a lifetime developing a new California poppy hybrid. Unless there was a fortune to be made doing it.

These were mainstream witches who wore gold, platinum, silver, and steel. Their cars were unusual, but the charms hanging from their rearview mirrors were not. I spied shiny chains and pendants dangling above the dash of each car I saw. I tasted the sour tang of protective spells around each electric SUV, each Italian sports car.

I was trying not to look too obvious about scanning the interior of a huge, extended-cab pickup when I heard a scream—just before a body coming at an impossible speed struck mine and knocked me off my feet.

"Balls!" a girl screeched in my ear. The sound hurt me almost as much as the impact with the pavement.

A skateboard went flying—literally, it was five feet off the ground—over our heads.

My hip and elbow seemed to take the brunt of the fall. Gasping with pain, I rolled to one side, cursing myself for only using protective spells against magical attacks. I hadn't considered tween witches on wheels.

"Demon's balls," I muttered. "Stop touching me."

The girl removed her hands from my torso, which she'd been patting and trying to improve with a pitiful healing spell. "Sorry. Sorry. Sorry."

"You'd better get your skateboard before a nonmag sees

it flying around," I snapped, staggering to my feet and scowling at her.

The girl was maybe eleven or twelve. She had long reddish-brown braids pulled back in a ponytail, and woven between the curls in her hair was a thin gold chain studded with emeralds.

I felt the power wafting around her head and suddenly understood how such a young witch had managed to levitate her skateboard. Her hair jewelry alone was worth a fortune. If my thieving father had been there, I would've warned him to not even *think* about stealing it.

And that wasn't all she was wearing; her neck and wrists were also encrusted with gold and precious stones.

Her parents were obviously loaded. Too bad they hadn't paid for skateboard lessons.

"Sorry," she said again.

I rubbed my elbow. I was glad I didn't have to drive anymore for a few hours. "What's your name?" It was rude to ask so directly, but she'd attacked me first.

"Marta," she said. "You're here to see Clem?"

"None of your business." I was still annoyed about being in throbbing pain. But then she looked so stricken, making me feel like a mean old lady, I sighed and softened my tone. "Yes," I said.

"Nobody ever visits Clem. What did you talk about?"

"You're nosy," I said.

"My mom says I'm very old school that way." She flashed a grin at me and loped off to collect her skateboard, which had crashed to the ground next to a bike rack. She brushed it off, dropped a kiss on the board, and returned to me, hugging it to her chest.

I found myself liking her even though she might have ensured my need for hip-replacement surgery in several decades. We'd all be robots by then anyway, right? Witch robots?

"You look like you're going to pass out," Marta said. "Maybe you should sit down."

I rubbed my forehead. Driving through mountains and rough coastline had already worn me out. The stress of meeting Clem, the potency of all the magic flying around, and then a heavy blow to my already-bruised body had nearly finished me off.

"I'm fi—" I stopped. If she was nosy, she'd have good gossip to share with me. I had hours to pass until midnight, and the two city blocks of booming Elwin probably wouldn't have much to offer. "Actually, I do feel a little weird. Will you stay with me a minute to make sure I don't pass out?"

"My dad's been teaching me a restorative spell," she said, aiming a finger at me. "First I draw a circle—"

"No." I blocked her magic and gently pushed her hand away. "Safer just to let me do it myself."

"Are you sure? It works better if you do it right away."

"I'm sure." I felt the slightly distorted sizzle of her magic around her hands and was certain it would be unhealthy to let it get through my personal boundary spells. "Do you live here?"

"Yes. *Tragically.*"

"Don't you like it? It seems nice."

"Nice." She rolled her eyes. "Boring."

"Where did you live before?"

"How did you know I'm not from here?"

"Just a hunch," I said.

"Did you scan me? I felt it but thought I blocked you."

I had scanned her but hadn't noticed any blocking spells. "You might want to practice that a little bit more," I said. "Instead of levitating your skateboard. And it really is dangerous for nonmags to see us floating around."

"They just think it's a new hoverboard or a drone or something." She scratched her nose. Each finger had at least one ring on it, each with a precious stone. "The kids from school do much worse."

Of course—she would be in school. But was she too old to be at the charter school I'd heard about? I wondered if she knew Percy. I didn't want him to hear I was in town, which might make him seek me out. Clem might change her mind about giving me any help if she saw me with a fellow ex-Protectorate agent. I wasn't sure why I thought that, but it felt right. She was the paranoid type.

"You're in high school, right?" I asked. She was clearly too young, but she might warm to a compliment that aged her upward.

"I wish. All we have here is the school for the Little Weirdos on the Prairie."

"One school for everyone?"

She nodded. "K through twelve." Her brown eyes fixed on mine. "What kind of school did you go to?"

I paused, but I wanted to keep the conversation going. "Boarding schools, mostly."

She made a face. "Typical. I don't know why Mom is so sure this is better. She and Dad went to a real witch school too. And, of course, Auntie did."

I stopped myself from arguing with her, wanting to invite her confidence. "Elwin looks OK to me," I said, looking around. "But I just got here."

"I've been here two *years*," she said. "Believe me, it's not OK. They hate us."

"Nonmags?"

"Nah, they're OK," she said. "It's the old witches who were already here. Mom says they'll come around, but they won't. They're crazy."

"Are there a lot of them?"

"Too many. All they care about is plants. Clem is the worst."

I could imagine Clem had encouraged a terrifying reputation among the kids in town. "How do you know her?"

"We live next door. Such a nightmare." Marta hugged her skateboard. "She put a hex on the bushes. It makes your stomach hurt if you get too close. And she likes weeds."

The northern coast of California was famous for a particular weed, but I didn't think that was what she was talking about. "Do you mean the stuff she sniffs up her nose?"

"Probably. The old Elwin witches use all that creepy stuff. They forage for berries, leaves, random stuff from their yards. From *our* yard. From the side of the road." Marta stuck out her tongue. "I hate hearth witches."

"Too bad," I said, giving her an expression I hoped was both playful, apologetic, and oh-so-slightly threatening.

She stared at me. A cloud of defensive magic formed around her head as she took a step back. "Forgive me, Witch," she said formally, dropping her eyes.

Somebody had obviously taught her at least a few formal manners. I decided to let her be scared for a minute; it would be good for her to learn to be more careful with strangers.

"What do your parents do?" I asked. "I hear lots of new people here work remotely for jobs somewhere else."

Still behind her protective cloud, she glanced to either side as if looking for a rescuing adult or friend. Cars were driving by, but nobody on foot was close enough to pay us any attention. "My mom and dad work at home, but my aunt works at the school. She'll be coming by any second. With her dog. A big dog. And probably a few other really powerful witches."

I suppressed a smile. "Nice of them," I said. Too nice to torture her any longer, I dropped my menacing grip on my beaded necklace and sent out a friendship spell to reassure her. "Is your aunt a teacher?"

Her shoulders relaxed a little. "No, she's..." Her voice dropped to a low mumble. "The principal." The situation apparently embarrassed her.

It was obvious she didn't want to talk to me anymore. Given her aunt was probably Percy's boss, I felt the same way. Under the softer effects of my friendship spell, she mumbled a goodbye and rolled away on her skateboard. This time her wheels contacted the pavement.

I wondered if she'd tell her family about meeting me.

I hate hearth witches.

A shiver ran through me. I decided to drive south to Arcata to wait until midnight. There was a state university there and lots of activity to disappear into. My Jeep's back seat could be an excellent spot for a nap.

Another shiver struck me. This wasn't psychological, but magical. A premonition.

Forget the nap. Until I'd left Elwin for good, I'd be sure to stay wide-awake.

EIGHT

After escaping south for the rest of the day, I returned to Clem's garden gate promptly at midnight.

"I'm here," I said softly. Given the potency of boundary magic around her property, I thought she'd hear me.

The night was much colder than the day had been. I zipped up my fleece jacket and cast my gaze over the neighboring houses. The metal witches certainly loved their porch lights and landscaping lanterns; it was as well lit as a big city.

The only fae I saw were tiny flower fairies sitting in a billowing mass of orange poppies tumbling out of Clem's yard into the sidewalk. Preferring natural light, the fae were hiding from the newcomers' bright technology like a dog hiding under the bed during a fireworks display.

"Hello," Clem said, appearing before me without warning. She looked at the poppies. "Did you see something?"

I didn't think she suspected I could hear fairies—she probably wasn't sure they were there—but wanted to be sure her own security measures were working. "No, just admiring your garden."

She paused. I couldn't see her face in the shadows of her

arbor. "If you were one of my neighbors," she said, "I'd say you were being sarcastic."

I smiled. "No. Mine is a lot like yours. Maybe in twenty years I can hope to have a garden as amazing as yours."

She laughed—a deep, satisfying sound. "I do too," she said, sounding a little surprised. "Well, I've got good news. The honorable gnome who graces me with her presence has given me something that might help Willy. And with his help, you just might get a jungle like mine."

My heart leaped. "Oh, thank Brightness. Thank you. Thank *her*," I said. "What is it?"

She held up a long, thin item. "This."

I couldn't see well in the shadows, and I was unable to magically scan anything inside her boundary spells. "What is it?"

"It's a stick from my apple tree. I believe she said it will point the way to him. It was a long song with lots of traveling in it, but I believe that's what she was saying." When I was silent, she continued. "Sorry I can't be more certain. A gnome in distress is a terrible thing."

Her vagueness was disappointing, but it was better than anything I'd come up with so far. "Thank you." I bowed. "Really. What do I owe you?"

I'd considered not offering payment, which might offend her, then concluded that it would be worse not to.

"You've already paid. A necklace of redwood beads carved under a full moon is plenty," she said. "Really cool magic. I'm impressed."

I felt my face get warm with the compliment. "Thanks."

She handed me the stick, which just felt like an ordinary twig to me since I couldn't risk a magical scan until I was farther away. After we expressed mutual good wishes and appreciation again, I turned to go, fighting a yawn. I hadn't let myself take a nap, and it was past my bedtime. Several long hours of driving through remote mountain terrain lay ahead of me.

I reached into my pocket and took out a small velvet

pouch stuffed with enchanted feverfew flowers and dried serrano peppers. It was a new herbal spell I'd created to help me stay awake and alive on long drives at night. I still had nightmares from the time the fae had run me off the road into a ravine. If I had to drive through there again, I'd be prepared.

Unlike Clem and Raynor, I had no desire to snort the spicy mixture into my delicate nasal cavity, so I gulped down three pinches with a mouthful of water from a bottle I'd filled at home. Even the small amount of wellspring magic in the Silverpool tap water might help the spell's potency.

As I continued walking to my Jeep, feeling my tongue burn from the serranos, I noticed an upstairs light turn on in one of the houses.

Marta's? No—she said she lived next door. This was several houses down.

I sensed the sharp tang of an intrusive magical scan coming from the copper landscape lanterns. I had no idea how it worked, but the spell made me feel like a child again, a student eager to please, work hard, do what I was told. It was just the kind of magic I'd expect a school principal to use.

By the time I was opening the door of my Jeep, I realized several more windows up and down the street were now lit. The bitter taste of metal magic was like smoke in the air, getting in my mouth and trying to snake my throat.

I pinched another helping of my new botanical mixture and set it on my tongue. Within three seconds, the unpleasant residue of metal magic faded away.

Proud to see proof of my new concoction working even better than I'd hoped, I climbed inside my car, locked the door, and started the engine.

There was something strange about Elwin. When I'd arrived, it had been Clem's house that had scared me. Now it was the rest of them.

I hoped I never had to come back.

IT WAS dawn when I got back to Silverpool. Thanks to my botanical spells—as well as a fortifying cheeseburger and energy drink at a truck stop—I'd been able to make it past the forest fairies outside Silverpool without careening to my death. Yawning, I parked in my driveway and looked up at my redwood tree, bathed in the first morning rays of sunlight. The lack of fog suggested it was going to be a relatively warm day.

Holding the stick Clem had given me, I strode immediately to my backyard and squatted down at the base of the tree. The hole was still there, and Willy still wasn't.

I propped the stick on the ground in front of the hole and sat back to watch.

Nothing.

I picked it up, rolled it between my palms, bathing it in an energy spell, then set it down again.

It just lay there.

Frowning, I waited a little while longer, then picked it up and waved it around like a wand. I felt a little ridiculous. It was another witch's magic, and I felt nothing coming from it.

Why hadn't I asked her to come with me and use it herself? She might've agreed if I'd offered to introduce her to Willy. Years of isolation and rejection had made her put up boundaries, but she might've been open to a fair exchange.

That gave me an idea. I picked up the stick and thought of Clem's purple bungalow, the wild fortress of roses and trumpet vines, imagining the image was a solid thing that could move down my arms and into my fingers.

It began to wiggle. I squeezed my eyes shut and tried to remember more details of Clem's house. The bike. The fairies. The scent of sage smoke.

The stick became rigid in my hand. I tried to move it— and couldn't. It levitated, locked in place, pointing upward.

I opened my eyes and followed the direction of the narrow tip.

Straight up the tree trunk.

Really? Willy was up there?

With my declining focus, the stick began to slide down toward the ground, but its angle stayed the same. It was clearly pointing up into the branches far above the ground.

"Willy?" I called out. After a pause, I repeated it, louder. "Willy!"

There was no answer.

If he was so close, why hadn't he replied? Or was I unable to offer the help he needed?

The thought came to me of going to Cypress Hardware and renting a genie-provided cherry picker. But I dismissed it. I had no idea how to operate one and didn't want my elderly nonmag neighbors to ask questions.

I had to act now, on my own. Which meant I needed to eat an owl pellet as soon as possible. Birdie had Random, so the house was quiet when I went in.

The owl pellets were in my file cabinet with most of my most powerful magic. After chanting the passwords and casting a series of spells, the bottom drawer popped open.

Inside were several objects that would shock even Raynor, who knew more of my secrets than anyone except Seth. But today all I wanted was the magical antihistamine that allowed me to shape-shift into a cat without triggering an allergy attack.

I found the vial of mouse bones—once inside the gut of its predator, the owl—and immediately emptied it into my mouth. Crunching the little pieces between my teeth wasn't pleasant, but I'd gotten used to it. I went to the kitchen and washed it down with tap water. As I had earlier, I hoped the municipal water supply might carry a magical enhancement.

I cracked open the kitchen door and undressed right there in the kitchen. Shifting into a cat left my brain scrambled for hours; better get started as soon as possible.

The pain was immediate and comprehensive. I'd gotten used to that too, but it still made me gasp and start to cry as my face shrank down to a feline shape, sprouting fur, whiskers, and pointy little teeth.

As was unfortunately always the case, I forgot myself as soon as my front paws hit the ground. It was risky to leave my door open, but it was the best way to guarantee I could get back inside quickly.

CHAPTER

NINE

It was hours later before I regained my human consciousness. Licking sticky blood—I didn't want to know from what—off my paw, I glanced up at the moon, saw it had sunk in the sky, and remembered my mission.

Luckily I was still in my own yard. Sometimes I went down to the river when I was a cat, but it hadn't rained in a few months now, and so its dry bed hadn't promised the hunting grounds to lure my feline self down the hill.

I slinked over to the base of the redwood tree, sniffed the dark spot at the bottom that had been Willy's door, then the stick—sensing nothing—and leaped onto the trunk. Sinking my claws into the shaggy redwood bark, I climbed upward.

In my cat shape, I had the grace and athleticism I normally lacked, but it took a few minutes for me to reach the first horizontal branches. They were thin, dwarfed by the massive trunk rising up to the sky.

I paused and meowed to let Willy know I was there, then waited.

Was that a scrambling rodent up above? A bird?

My teeth felt wonderfully sharp in my mouth at the thought of another delicious snack.

With effort, my human brain dragged my attention back to searching for a hiding, possibly injured gnome. I continued climbing until I was in the top third of the tree, the branches coming thicker now, and meowed again.

"Well, this is a welcome morning visit, I am thinking," said a voice overhead. "I would be saying it is too early, but very truthfully it is quite the best there is for me on this fine day."

Willy! I meowed louder and resumed climbing.

"There will be singing about this sad story, but I am thinking it will not be the singing that I will be doing," Willy said. "I am knowing that the laughing will be from the others of my kind and not myself, as you will know."

He was still a climb above me, and the skinny horizontal branches had become thicker and harder to climb past. The redwood was hundreds of years old, tall even by local standards. I knew it would be a bad idea to look down before I had to.

My progress was slow, but it wasn't too long before I was looking into the eyes of a little man sucking on a pipe. He was from the Old World—I wasn't sure which region in Europe, but he still wore the traditional red velvet coat— and enjoyed smoking all kinds of herbs, flowers, and leaves.

"It is sure that you are wondering how it is that my home is not where I am being," he said, reaching out and grabbing fistfuls of fur on my back. "How delightful for me and you as well that your mouth cannot be asking the questions. I will be enjoying very much your smaller voice saying hello and goodbye as soon as it is we are back on the earth, paws and feet. We are both happy to be there soon, I am thinking, definitely."

I meowed, crouching tightly against the trunk so he could climb the rest of the way onto my back. It was true that if I'd had my human voice, I would've asked why he needed my physical help, given his ability to blink in and out of existence the rest of the time. He was a gnome, not a toddler. Normal rules of physics had never applied to him, so why was he squeezing handfuls of my fur as if he'd die if he fell?

"Your little mouth noises are full of questions, I am knowing," Willy said. His voice was altered by the pipe he clenched between his teeth. "Please be telling yourself when you are back in your big smooth shape that it is not able to be answering you now or possibly ever, I am thinking this is definitely the case."

At that moment, I lost any interest in asking him questions because the top of the tree was swaying. Maneuvering around so that I could climb down the tree without killing us both was my priority now.

If he *could* die, which I'd thought from his previous statements wasn't the case.

Glimpsing the roof of my house from far above, I felt a wave of nausea roll through my feline stomach and disembodied human consciousness. I began to tremble.

"It is too bad, I am thinking, that you are not the strong bird with golden feathers and very nice large wings," he said. "Although I detect the owl is inside you, part of what it left behind, which I am hoping will help us get down to the soft earth where I am belonging, as you are."

He wished I could shift into a golden eagle? Yeah, me too. But the cat thing had never been my choice. Just something I'd been born with, like my father's knack to apparate and steal treasure from strangers.

I crept downward with my eyes closed, repeatedly bumping into branches, inspiring more speeches from Willy that became increasingly incomprehensible. It would be interesting to see where the bruises from his fierce grip on my back would appear after I'd resumed human shape.

After what felt like hours, we finally reached the base of the trunk. I jumped down into the thick carpet of fallen redwood needles.

"Ah, my dear Alma with the ears like triangles and a mouth that I am so happy is not talking to me at this time," he said. "We are home. Please remember I am hoping the songs about tonight are not heard by me, at least not until I have consumed a large vessel of the good water."

He rolled off me and staggered—still as if his body was affected by gravity—toward the hole at the base of the tree. It was too dark to see him clearly, but his shadowy figure settled there on the ground, covering the hole.

A moment later, he was gone.

I meowed, a complaint and a goodbye. It was bad enough he wasn't going to explain what had happened to him, but he could've said thank you.

So much for good manners.

Well, he'd saved my life and my pride at least once, so I'd forgive him.

Perhaps there was something I could give him to entice him to explain what had happened to him. Any threat that was strong enough to cast him out of his home might do the same to me. It would bother me forever if I couldn't find out what it was.

CHAPTER
TEN

Willy continued to refuse to discuss what had happened to him. The day after I'd rescued him, I saw him at the base of the tree, appearing to paint the restored door with a coat of yellow paint, but he ignored me. Even after I baked him a loaf of springwater-laced banana bread. The fact that he was showing himself to me was a good sign, however—he alone among the fae seemed to have the ability to hide himself regardless of my demon ancestry—but he wouldn't tell me what had been powerful enough to break through my boundary spells and send him hiding, humiliated, up in the tree.

Seth was frustrated to be so far away. In our nightly phone calls, he made me promise I'd tell him the instant I sensed any danger.

"I'd be there now, but I'm making progress," he told me one night, after he'd been gone six nights—which, yes, I'd been counting. "I'm holding a little thing around the mother and baby to protect him."

"A little thing?" I asked.

He didn't answer. He still avoided talking about his fairy powers.

"Physical or spiritual?" I prompted.

A pause. "Both and neither," he said.

"Seth," I said with a sigh. "Please. You can do better than that."

He lowered his voice to a sexy purr. "If I were with you right now, I'd do a lot better."

"Only to change the subject. Luckily, I'm somewhat immune this far away."

He chuckled, and the sound sent tendrils of pleasure down my spine. "I'll let you believe that," he said.

I'd walked right into that. More than once, I'd suspected he held his powers back so I didn't get spooked and break up with him. "Seth, for my peace of mind, would you please, in human terms, tell me a little more about what you've done to protect the baby?"

"Mm. In human terms, I splashed water on him." He paused. "Well, on the mother. She was strolling down the sidewalk, and I ran past and squirted my water bottle on her."

"Ew," I said.

"I admit she didn't seem to enjoy it."

"What was in the water?"

He fell silent again. Then cleared his throat. "I'd rather not say."

"Tell me it wasn't your pee," I said.

"Of course not," he said.

"Thank Brightness."

"It was yours," he said.

I choked out a sound of outrage—disgusted, furious—then heard him stifling a laugh.

Closing my eyes, I shook my head. That Shadowed changeling...

"It was springwater with a twist of fae," he said. "I brought some from home. It's why I had to check my bags. They don't like gallons of liquid in carry-ons these days."

"Gallons? How much did you bring?"

"As much as I could carry," he said. "I might need to persuade all kinds of creatures to help me. You know how it is, being a hero. Out here saving the world. As one does."

I smiled. Warmth spread through my chest. "I miss you."

"As I miss you, darling demon babe."

After another minute or two of that sort of thing, we hung up, leaving me with my original dilemma: What had happened to Willy?

Once again, I reinforced my boundary spells and slept with my redwood staff by my bed. Random, although a wonderful dog, was too likely to confront an intruder with his tail wagging.

A few days later, as I was walking Random along the river after dinner, my phone chimed with the sound I'd given to Darius Ironford, my former partner at the Protectorate. Although our initial professional arrangement had been unpleasant for both of us, our relationship had improved since I'd been fired as an agent. I might've said we'd even become friends.

You around? his text asked.

Instead of texting back, I called him. "Hey," I said. "What's up?"

He sounded annoyed to have to actually speak to me. "Something wrong with your fingers?"

"I'm holding Random's leash. Is something the matter?" Darius never called just to chat.

"When's the next time you planned on being in San Francisco?" he asked.

"I'm not," I said. Unless I was forcibly summoned by Darius's current and my former employer, I avoided the city. "Why?"

"I don't get why you insist on staying in that backwater," he said, sounding annoyed. He often did with me, though not as often as he used to.

I didn't answer. I didn't have to explain myself to Darius. He could still put me on the defensive sometimes, in large part because he'd been thrown off the Golden Gate Bridge because of me—at the hands of the Protectorate target who was now my boyfriend, though he had definitely not been so at the time. Seth would never have let him get hurt, but theoretically it was a fatal fall into the San Francisco Bay from the middle of the span.

"I like it," I said finally.

"I just don't understand," he said. "There's nothing to do there until somebody starts killing things. Which isn't my idea of a good time. Funny how it's yours."

I considered hanging up. There was no reason to put up with his attitude anymore. "Brightness me, I can barely hear you. The connection is fading. I'll hang up and we can talk some other time. Or not."

He sighed. "I was hoping you'd be in civilization soon. But I guess I can make the trip."

"Trip?"

"Up to that delightful metropolis of yours," he said. "But I'll have to wait until morning. I hate making that forest drive on the bike in the dark, anyway. I swear the road changes every time I visit Silverpool."

"Why do you want to see me? What's going on?" Although I got tired of him hating on Silverpool, I was bored and lonely with Seth away. The baby still hadn't arrived, and I was desperate for a distraction. "Does Raynor have a job for me?"

"Since when does he talk to me about that?" Darius snorted. He was the ambitious agent who followed the rules and worked hard on his way up to Emerald. I was the fired troublemaker who got plum secret assignments. "Be glad it's not Raynor. He would've ignored your privacy before handing it over, if he ever did."

"Hand what over?" I asked.

"A couple of letters. They came here to the Diamond Street office. Addressed to you."

I paused, thinking about what that might mean. If Darius thought it was important enough to hand deliver personally, and he knew Raynor would've wanted to read it himself, then the envelope had to have a magical residue.

Although the letters were probably just junk. Over the

past year, I'd been involved in a few high-profile incidents. Random witches of all sorts had suddenly started reaching out to me, wanting information or introductions. But like nonmagical humans, they'd used the easy way to reach out —text or email.

"There are two of them?"

"Yes, and I can tell they're from the same person," he said. "The first one got lost at the front desk. I found it when the second came. I just happened to be at the door when it was delivered and saw your name."

To make sure I was alone, I looked around the empty lot above the riverbank where Random and I were walking. It was a popular spot for locals to park to visit the narrow beach below. "How does something get lost? Everything is scanned and tracked so carefully."

"There was a Flint with a bad attitude," he said. "He's gone now. They found a month's worth of mail and filing in a storage closet."

I frowned, skeptical that kind of incompetence could be accidental. Not everyone liked the Protectorate. The guy might have been intentionally trying to sabotage it from within.

"Any idea who they're from?" I asked. If there had been a return address, he would've said so. But he might have run a quick magical scan to guess.

"A witch. That's all I can tell. But it's somebody who doesn't know you well enough to have your home address."

"Or maybe whoever it is knows half the mail sent to Silverpool never makes it." I pulled Random away from a patch of foxtails along the trail. Like humans, he loved to eat things that weren't good for him. "I'll be here tomorrow. Text me when you're on the road."

"It'll be early," he said. "Before noon. Like I said, I'd rather avoid taking that ride through the forest after nightfall."

His urgency confused me. "It's probably not important," I said. "Lots of weird people try to talk to me lately."

I expected him to make a joke about like attracting like, but he was quiet for a long moment. Then he said, "I think this might be important. I don't know why, but I trust my instincts."

A shiver ran down my spine. I trusted his instincts too.

"I'll be here," I said.

ELEVEN

Birdie shook me awake late that night.

"Alma? It's Birdie. Could you please wake up?"

I was aware of a dog climbing over my legs, then his hot breath on my cheek.

I cracked open an eye. My bedroom was dark, but a light was on in the kitchen.

Birdie wasn't the only one in the room.

Grabbing my staff, I sat up with a start. "What's the matter?"

"Sorry," Birdie said. "I knocked on the door, but—"

"I'm not going to come near this house without an escort." Darius's voice came from behind Birdie. "You didn't reply to my texts."

I took a deep breath and waited for my heart to stop pounding. I picked up my phone and glanced at the notifications. "I was *asleep*. You said you were coming in the morning."

"I changed my mind," he said. "I didn't realize you went to bed so early."

"It's almost midnight," I said.

"It's just after ten," he said. "Are you feeling OK?"

Seth hadn't called me or answered my message, so I'd taken a new potion that had been, in hindsight, a wee bit too strong. I'd aimed for a light cocktail, but apparently... it had been a bit stronger. I had no memory of finishing the small drink. My throat felt raw, as if I'd been snoring. Or swallowing foxtails.

"He came and got me at the store," Birdie said. "I had to cancel quiz night."

I stroked Random's muzzle, grateful at least somebody wasn't angry at me. "Sorry," I muttered, fighting a wave of exhaustion. "I-I made a new potion. Wiped me out."

"You hardly ever go to bed early," Birdie said, looking around the bedroom. "I had the crazy thought you were cheating on Seth. I was worried you were going to ask me to keep it a secret from him, which I know I'd never be able to do, and then you'd think I wasn't really your friend even though friends should be honest and stand up for—"

"I'm alone," I said, cutting off her nightmare scenario that I filed away for reference. Not that I would cheat on anyone, but it was good to know Birdie wouldn't lie for me about everything. "And I wish I still was."

"I'll make you tea," Birdie said, moving away from the bed.

"Put wellspring water in it," Darius said.

I made a noise of protest.

Darius passed Birdie and came into the room. "Don't tell me it doesn't do anything to you. I've seen it help you at least a little bit sometimes." He found my robe on a chair and handed it to me, reminding me I was, in fact, only wearing a camisole and underwear under the loose sheet I held to my chest.

"Thanks," I muttered. Why should I feel embarrassed for being half-naked in my own bed in my own home at a perfectly reasonable time to be sleeping?

"So the gnome is all right?" he asked, turning his back to me. "Raynor just told me he'd been attacked. I decided to bring you your mail tonight. That was another reason I wasn't coming near your house by myself."

"I think he's fine now." I pulled on the robe and got out

of bed. "Although the fact that you were able to come into the house without me letting you in does worry me a little bit." There had been past visits when Willy had forcibly expelled him.

"Birdie told him it was OK," he said. "And I brought him a donut from the food truck outside the hardware store. Weird it was open so late."

He didn't know there was a genie who granted the wishes of all shoppers who came on her property.

"Smart of you," I said. "You've got the letters?"

He turned and began walking toward the kitchen. "Have the tea first. Send Birdie home. Then we'll talk."

I rolled my eyes at his request. He was such a stickler for secrecy.

Deciding the robe put me at a social disadvantage with Darius's judgy ways, I got fully dressed and sat down in the kitchen with the mug of tea that Birdie had made for me.

"I'm really sorry about quiz night," I told her. "When did you start doing those?"

"It's the second one," she said. "Every other week. I was afraid you'd be mad."

"Mad? Why?" I asked.

"Exposing our world, magic and everything," she said. "Most of our topics end up being something paranormal."

"Most of the books you sell are paranormal. And the crafts and cards and games and little sweaters and my jewelry and those little baby socks with the stars on them and—"

"So you don't mind?" she asked.

"It's your store. You don't need my permission."

Birdie stared at me, her brow furrowed. "I was afraid that you might think it was dangerous. Is it?"

I brought the tea to my lips and inhaled the steam, feeling a loosening as well as fresh energy inside me. Well-spring water did have a nice, though small, effect on me when I was at my weakest.

I'd been overprotective of Birdie and—I'd never admit it

aloud—underprotective of myself. She had to explore and try things, just as I did. "I'd be a hypocrite if I told you not to follow your interests. You're curious and social—a quiz night about magical topics sounds fun."

"Fun enough for *you* to go?" Darius asked.

I sipped the tea and shot him eye daggers over the rim. Just the idea gave me the urge to become a cat and climb the tree in the backyard again. And stay there.

"Of course Alma would never want to actually play with the group"—she ignored Darius snickering into his fist—"but I was hoping you might help me come up with some of the questions. Not today, but sometime." Birdie walked over and gave Random a pat. "I'm going now, Randobananapup. Such a good boy."

I thanked her again, and she left with a smile, obviously relieved her secret had been exposed without any negative fallout.

Darius went to the door and checked it was locked. Then he watched to make sure I reestablished a boundary spell before saying, "Raynor is going to flip out if he hears she's throwing magic-themed parties in public less than a mile from the most powerful—and ideally secret—wellspring on the West Coast."

I wasn't going to tell Darius about any possible romance budding between the two. I already had a headache. "It's Silverpool. How many people could actually attend something like that? What few people live here tend to keep to themselves."

"I hope you're right." Joining me at the table, he took two envelopes out of his bag and set them in front of me. He must've had the bag under a hiding spell because I hadn't noticed him carrying one. "Go on. Show me I'm an idiot for thinking there's anything to this so I can get back to the real world."

TWELVE

I studied them without picking them up. One was a thin, business-sized white envelope without a return address, postmarked three weeks earlier. My name and the Protectorate office address were on a computer-printed label. The other was thicker and dated just a week ago—the day after I'd been in Elwin.

I stroked the beads at my throat and cast a quick scanning spell over them. Darius would've already done so, but it was reasonable to think there might be something aimed at me personally.

Nothing sinister struck me. There was, however, a hint of something—somebody—familiar.

"I think I know who sent this," I said.

"Who?" Darius asked warily. "Is Raynor going to kick me out of Diamond Street for not giving these to him first?"

"I'm surprised you didn't," I said, looking at him. "Especially since you just heard about Willy being attacked. Why didn't you give them to him after that?"

He scowled, chewing his lip. As if sensing his mood, Random let out a loud sigh beneath the table.

"He's been a bit of a tyrant lately," Darius said finally. "As bad as a Sapphire mage from New York. High on his own supply of herbs, if you know what I mean. Telling everyone what to do, micromanaging every little thing. I knew he'd just tear open your mail without respecting your privacy, thinking his position gave him the right. If there's something important in those letters, it's for you to decide what to do about it."

Being friends with Darius entailed putting up with his Silverpool insults, but he was loyal and honorable, and I was grateful to have him on my side. "Thank you," I said, hearing the emotion in my voice.

He brushed aside my sappy smile and pointed at the letters. "You're welcome. Who sent them?"

I looked down, preparing myself for more magical effort. "It's somebody I've met before." Running my beads through the fingers of my left hand, I picked up the thin envelope with my right.

"Friend or foe?" Darius asked.

The scent of familiarity grew stronger. A man's face flashed in my memory—dark hair, eyebrow and nose studs. Reassured, I tore open the letter and scanned to the bottom signature. "Percival Tuff," I said, nodding.

"Kurt Bosko's old app?" Letting out a sigh of disgust, Darius leaned back in his chair. "What a waste of time. What's he want, a job reference? Jewelry advice?"

Ignoring Darius, I read the letter. It was short, only a paragraph, typed and printed on copy paper.

"Why didn't he just text like a normal person?" Darius leaned over the table and grabbed the second, thicker letter. "This one feels like there's something in it. What does that one say?"

I handed it to him to read for himself.

Dear Alma,

I hope this letter finds you Bright. Forgive me for writing you, but I don't know who else to ask. Do you remember when I told you I hoped we'd never meet again because I thought you were scary? I apologize for saying that. Now I think scary is just what I need. What this whole town needs. Is there any way

I could tempt you to visit? Forgive me for not saying more. It's just too dangerous. Not for you, but for me. Please consider it. I can show you a grove of redwoods that are truly ancient. You could collect materials for your craft, perhaps?

Brightness be upon you,
Percival Tuff

Darius frowned as he read, then tossed it down with a snort. "Percy always was annoying."

If I'd known about the first letter, I would've found a way to talk to him. But I hadn't.

I picked up the thicker letter. "This one's from last week."

"Maybe he slipped a few hundred bucks in there to sweeten the oh-so-appealing offer." Shaking his head, Darius got up and went to the fridge. Having a low opinion of Percy, he'd lost interest in the whole thing.

I opened the second letter, surprised to find a brochure tucked between some official forms of some kind. Attached to those was a yellow sticky note with a single handwritten word.

Please.

The forms were for the Elwin Flower Show. Did he hope I'd want to sell my jewelry there? It didn't look as if there was an arts and crafts section, just flower and plant exhibits.

I gasped.

"What?" Darius turned away from the fridge with an expensive bottle of my favorite ginger kombucha in his hand. It was nice he'd made the trip, but I wished he wouldn't consume all the goodies I was saving.

I waved the forms at him. "He's entered me in a big garden show. He even paid the entry fee."

Darius almost snorted the kombucha out his nose. He

set the bottle down and took the forms from me. "You? Has he *seen* your garden?"

"Hey," I said. "It's not supposed to look inviting. It's a working witch's garden."

"Yeah, right. It's all part of your plan to let everything grow wild and die," he said. "He must have had his concerns because he's entered you in the Cottage Hearth category. That's code for crazy old lady."

"What was he thinking? I never agreed to anything. So far as he knows, I totally ignored his first letter. I even came to town without seeing him." I was concerned earlier, but now I was angry. I'd barely known Percy. I certainly didn't owe him anything like making a long, difficult trip into something dangerous—while also having to provide some kind of stupid, embarrassing plant exhibit.

I'd disliked Elwin and did *not* want to return.

Darius took another swig of the kombucha, then burped discreetly into his fist. "Maybe he thought you'd find it more tempting this way." He came over and pointed at the bottom of the submission form in my hand. "Yeah, look at that. Not cheap. He thought he was bribing you with something valuable."

It wasn't a month's rent. It was three. "He wasted his money," I said.

"I could've warned him," Darius said. "Your place has gotten a little nicer since the—since Seth has joined the frame, but it's still a mess."

"Hey," I said.

"You can't even use your front door because of the weeds."

"It's not weeds," I said. "It's rosemary. And other things. Good things."

Darius raised a mocking eyebrow as he finished the expensive bottled drink I hadn't told him he could have. He was the one with a paying, salaried job, not me.

"Well, it would be a quick setup if you did exhibit," he

said. "Just dump random plants here and there, dead or alive, and call it authentic. You'll win first place."

"Enough." I dropped the papers on the table and stood up. "Thanks for bringing me my mail. Now I think it's time you went home."

He heard the seriousness in my tone and stopped smirking. When a witch—especially me, who was quite powerful in her kitchen—told a visitor he was no longer welcome, she could be dangerous.

"I'm not saying I'll call Willy to help send you on your way," I continued, "but I might call Willy to help send you on your way."

He held up his hands in a defensive pose. "Easy, Alma. I was just kidding."

The sight of genuine fear in his eyes drained the fight out of me. I glanced longingly toward my bedroom. I was still dazed from the potion, and the delights of sleep were calling to me.

"I know," I said, sighing. "Relax. I'm not going to hex you."

"Tell the gnome how much you like me," he said.

"Willy will let you go," I said. "You're my friend."

He turned a skeptical look toward the backyard. "Maybe you could walk me to my bike."

"If it gets you to leave," I muttered, looking around the floor for a matching pair of flip-flops.

Part of me was tempted to gather up Percy's letters and give them back to Darius. If they stayed with me, I'd be reminded of both my irritation and my guilt.

What if he really needed my help?

"Could you bring these to Raynor and ask him what he thinks?" I heard myself asking. "There must've been a reason he didn't just text me. Maybe somebody is monitoring his phone." Communication tech was usually immune from witch spells, but anything was possible with magic. Especially, for instance, if a large group of witches from Silicon Valley had suddenly moved to a remote coastal town, got bored, and invented a new type of hex.

There had definitely been something wrong about Elwin.

Darius, tying his shoes, looked up at me in surprise. "The whole point in me bringing it to you in person was so that he wouldn't know about it. You always complain about having no privacy. I was trying to give you some."

"And I appreciate it. In general. But this time... Maybe he could send an agent," I said. "Percy was trained by the Protectorate. Maybe he noticed there's something Shadowed going on. Raynor might want to know."

Darius shook his head. "He's busy. He'd just tell you to go yourself." He gestured around, as if at the world outside my house. "He's been trying to recruit somebody decent to be Protector of Silverpool. After Bosko, they're giving him time to find somebody who isn't a springwater-addicted, trigger-happy fanatic."

"Glad to hear that. But—"

"And if Percy wanted to get the Protectorate involved, he would've asked us," Darius continued. "He went out of his way to get you instead."

I groaned. He was right. But Percy hadn't given me enough to go on. "You said you felt something when you touched the envelopes that made you uncomfortable," I said. "Can you be more specific? Percy was a mind mage. Could it have been a spell he put on the paper? Maybe it compelled you to bring it to me?"

Shaking his head, Darius opened the door to the back door. "I don't think he's that powerful. It's gone now. And here in your house, I can't use much magic anyway. You're too potent."

I smiled, liking how that sounded. As if I was a rare, powerful potion.

At his request, I escorted him to his motorcycle parked on the road. After he had roared away, I walked back and was happy to notice Willy's yellow door was visible in my backyard lamplight. He didn't answer my call, but that wasn't unusual. The door told me he was OK for now.

I went back inside and folded up Percy's letters, including the sketch of a hearth witch's garden, telling myself it wasn't my responsibility to respond to every call for help.

But even after drinking a strong blueberry leaf tea I brewed as an antidote to my earlier potion, I couldn't forget that simple word.

Please.

THIRTEEN

The next morning, after taking Random for a long walk, I went out to return the gnome books to Birdie at her store on Main Street. I'd forgotten I still had them, having shoved them in a pile under an unfinished crochet project, and she'd been too nice to ask for them back.

Silverpool's quaint, picturesque business district ran parallel to the river. Just about a block long, it supported Cypress Hardware at one end and a few humble places to eat—a café, a taqueria, and a rotating-owner Thai restaurant.

Birdie didn't technically open her bookstore until ten, but I knew she was an early riser. I also had a small gift for her for having unintentionally ruined her trivia night.

She came to the shop door in a bright yellow sundress with appliquéd daisies on its camisole straps. Her wavy auburn hair was down, her eyes carefully lined, her lips a glossy dark rose. I glanced down at my muddy feet, suddenly aware of the contrast between us. I was the wild forest witch; Birdie was the customer-facing professional.

As Random thrashed his tail in hello and bounded into the store ahead of me, I held up the books. "Just bringing these back. I hope this isn't a bad time?"

"Of course not! I was just—getting ready." She pulled the door open for me.

"You look great." I wiped my hiking sandals on the mat before stepping inside. Random and I had made a detour to the riverbank to collect a fresh selection of magical stones —mostly jasper and agate—in sizes small enough to use in my jewelry.

"I feel bad about selling those books, knowing how wrong they are," Birdie said.

"If you only sold books that had accurate information about magic, you wouldn't have any store at all," I said. "More like one of those little free libraries on a fence post with only two books in it."

She looked stricken. "There are only two accurate books about magic?"

I thought about the two I had in my own possession and regretted my comment. If anyone knew about one of them—an infamous book I'd collected the previous year— Willy wouldn't be the only one hiding up in the redwood tree.

"Sorry, ignore me," I said. "It's all useful in its own way. I'm sure there are bits and pieces of good stuff even in these books."

"Even the one with the giant North Pole Bigfoot claims?"

"Sure. Who knows? Maybe they exist too."

Birdie looked thoughtful. "I've always wanted to see the Aurora Borealis. Raynor said the first time he was in Norway, he—" She cut herself off and turned red.

Pressing my lips together, I set the books on the checkout counter near a spinning rack of my magic jewelry she let me sell on consignment. The pull-on bracelets were surprisingly popular, and I'd been spending hours in my garage making new redwood beads to meet the demand.

She was my friend—my best friend—and now my business partner. I was determined not to make the same mistake I had earlier and flip out about her and Raynor.

"I've always wanted to see it too," I said. "Maybe we could go someday."

Random trotted over and sat on my feet. The word *go* was one of his favorites as long as he was the one going.

Birdie grabbed the books and hugged them to her chest. "Could we really? I'd have to get somebody to watch the store." She walked over to the shelf along the far wall and began putting the gnome books back. "Or I could close it for a week or two during the slow times, which unfortunately seems to be always. Since the equinox, there's been hardly any foot traffic. I'm hoping the summer solstice brings some witches to town. Or even nonmagicals. Nonmags. So funny to call them that when it's basically everyone I used to know."

I knew she was rambling because she was nervous. It had been a long time since I'd made her so anxious to be with me, and the setback made me sad.

"I brought you something." I took out the gift I'd made in my garage studio the night before. "It's a good luck charm."

The only thing that worried me about her and Raynor having a relationship—if there was one, and I told myself it was unlikely—was her getting hurt.

The charm was from the oxalis in my backyard. Instead of transforming the leaves into a lucky four-leaf clover shape, I'd put them in a pot with springwater, simmered it down to a paste, and filled a tiny bottle that she could carry or even wear around her neck. To all that I'd added a pinch of polished jasper sand I'd just collected at the beach.

She took the pinky-sized item from me and let out an appreciative "*Ooooh,*" that made me feel warm all over.

"It's a new concoction," I said. "I hope it works."

"Of course it will." She brought it to her face and peered through the clear glass at the murky gray-green liquid. "I can feel it."

"I was going to make a chain for it, but I think it'll be

stronger if you make it yourself. Hair, jute, maybe copper wire." I cleared my throat. "So you like it?"

She hugged it to her chest, smiling. A second later, her gaze turned thoughtful. "Could you make a few more and see if they sell?"

I laughed. "You want me to commercialize this unique gift of my heart so you can make a few bucks?"

She grinned at me. "So *you* can make a few bucks. I'm rich already. You're not."

"Ouch." I stared at her, impressed at how much she'd changed since learning what she was. "You... witch."

We both laughed. She broke off and put a hand over her mouth.

"I hope you're not mad," she said.

"If you didn't have any Shadow in you, we wouldn't be friends," I reassured her. "Anyway, thanks for always dog-sitting. I don't know what I'd do without—"

Both my watch and my phone chimed with the sound reserved for Raynor.

For a moment, I had the crazy thought it was Birdie's good luck already kicking in. She wanted him; there he was.

But if that was the case, he would've called her, not me.

"Excuse me," I said to Birdie, not telling her who it was. I didn't want to see her hopeful, blushing face. For Brightness's sake, having a crush on Director Raynor was as big a curse as being possessed by my demon mother. At least that had been a spell I'd been able to break.

Out on the sidewalk, I drew upon my beads for a protective shield before taking the call.

"You alone?" Raynor asked.

"Almost." Gesturing apologetically at Birdie through the window, I turned my back to her. More experienced witches could listen in on a nearby conversation even after it had happened, but she wasn't there yet. "Yes."

"Darius told me about the letters," he said. "He should've given them to me."

I muttered another protective spell. He could hex me

through the phone if he felt like it. "They had my name on them."

"They were sent to the Protectorate. My office. The one they gave me the fancy title for. *Director*. Perhaps you've heard of it?"

Anyone in the Diamond Street office could probably hear him shouting. Demon's balls, even Helen next door could probably make out the words.

I stroked the big redwood bead at my throat and began weaving a thicker guarding spell around my head. Just muffling his voice would ease the pain in my eardrums.

"Is Darius OK?" I asked. At least I was a hundred miles away. Darius was—hopefully—breathing the same air as he was.

"What, you think I killed him? Transformed him into something?"

It wasn't impossible. "You've locked me up in that attic room more than once," I said.

"You're different. You're impossible." Raynor let out a noise that was half growl, half sigh. "He did what he thought was right, bringing you documents marked with your name."

"Then what are you so angry about?"

"You should've told me! Once you'd opened them, you should've told me!"

I looked up at the sun peeking out from behind an overcast sky. Although it was June, it was still chilly so near the coast until the coastal fog burned off in the afternoon. "That's what I told Darius, not that it's any of your business. Listen, just because I've done a few consulting gigs for you, I'm still a free person. I don't work for the Protectorate anymore." I glanced over my shoulder at Birdie, who was watching me through the window with her brow furrowed. "And neither does Percy."

"And he never will again," Raynor said. "Because he's dead."

FOURTEEN

Even with my protective magical earmuffs, Raynor's words took the breath out of me.

"Dead," I whispered. "How?"

"Natural causes. Which of course means it wasn't." Raynor sniffed loudly, then continued in a slightly mellower tone. "Even without those letters, the Protectorate would be suspicious. He was recently a Protectorate agent. We never die of natural causes."

He didn't need to tell me. "What was the official story?"

"Heart condition. Got him while he was driving. Died in the crash," he said. "I'm sure the death certificate will say that he had some unknown congenital disorder that he's had all his life and could've struck at any time." He let out a disbelieving snort.

"When?" I asked.

"Four days ago. We kept it quiet until now. I wouldn't be telling you at all yet if Darius hadn't come to me—finally —about those letters. This is why we don't keep secrets."

"You're the one keeping secrets," I said. "Four days? He wasn't a stranger. I *knew* him. You should've told me."

My mind swam with the memory of his letter.

That one word.

Please.

I took in a deep breath and rubbed my eyes. They were wet, prickling with emotion.

Please.

"He asked me for help." My throat tightened. "He was afraid."

"Yeah," Raynor said. "Darius told me. Eventually. Too late."

More tears fell. It wasn't guilt; the letters hadn't found me in time.

I'd related to Percy. He'd left the Protectorate because, like me, he'd felt he'd lacked the killer instinct for the job.

Well. Now that Raynor was involved, he could do something about finding justice for him. It was too late for me to prevent disaster, but Raynor could root out the Shadow that had ended the life of a witch not much older than I was.

I wiped my face and cleared my throat. "Are you sending Darius up there? Or would that be too obvious?" Darius and I had both known Percy during the same troubles over the winter solstice. "You probably want to send an agent that never met him. To investigate undercover."

"Nice try," Raynor said.

"What do you mean?"

I heard the clicks and tapping of his hands on the computer. "It's not until next week," he said. "That's plenty of time. You're already signed up."

"No," I said.

"Yes."

I closed my eyes. He was completely ignorant about anything botanical. Like most modern witches, he used metal for his magic—steel, gold, silver, brass, copper, even silicone. And he probably hadn't watched all the TV from the UK showing how crazy people got about garden shows.

"You have no idea," I said. "People spend years planning for these things."

"It's not like you have to win. You just need an excuse to be there."

"It will be painfully obvious I don't belong," I said. "The excuse won't hold."

I heard him tapping at his computer. "There's a hearth-witch subcategory. That's perfect. How would you not belong? That's exactly what you are. You have herbs, right? And a kitchen?"

It wasn't worth explaining that other hearth witches were more like Helen, obsessively developing their gardens and greenhouses into financially magical enterprises. Many brilliant mail-order nurseries and famous hybridizing programs were run by witches—not that he'd know that.

"Why don't you want to send a real agent?" I asked. "Percy apprenticed with the former Protector of Silverpool. There's probably a link to something there you'll want to know about."

"And you'll tell me," he said.

"Raynor," I argued. "Why not do this the official way? There's no reason to be sneaky by using me off the books. Send one of your people. Or more than one."

The phone went quiet. My stomach clenched with uneasiness.

"What are you not telling me?" I asked.

He cleared his throat. "I'm sure Percival Tuff was a perfectly nice guy, but his master was widely loathed. His demise has not improved his standing. In fact, his reputation has only grown more Shadowed as more have suddenly found the courage to speak openly about him."

"You're not going to investigate his murder because people didn't like his boss?" I demanded.

"There is more than one way to investigate, as you well know."

I could feel Birdie growing increasingly curious as she watched me through the window. If I didn't want to inspire her to learn new spying spells, I should wrap up the call. "You should send your people. It's the right thing to do."

"Alma." Raynor sniffed again, then coughed. I still didn't know what the herbs did for him. Stimulant? Relaxant? Antihistamine? "You're going to go anyway. Don't pretend you're not."

"What do you mean? The only reason I'd go up to Elwin is if you're too callous or—or afraid—to use Protectorate resources."

"Look, I'm a busy man. I'm trying to find a new Protector, which won't be helped by word getting out that his last app was just killed." There was a click and a change in Raynor's voice, telling me he'd put me on speaker and had started to do something else—something he thought was more important. "You have a whole week to dig up some weeds and rent a truck. We both know you're going. Let's not waste time."

Feeling my temper spike, I moved the phone away from my ear. He wasn't the only one who could hex somebody over the phone.

He was such a manipulative toad. There had been several occasions when my life had almost come to a messy, premature end because he had pressured me into taking on dangerous activities. My curiosity and compulsion to do the right thing were factors in some of my risky adventures, but not all.

"I'm not going," I said.

He didn't reply. I checked my screen to see if he was still there.

The connection was fine. It was the Director who was a problem.

"I'm not," I said again.

"Of course you're not," he said sarcastically. "But if you did, which of course you won't, you could utilize a small fund I've set aside for jobs like this one."

"Even a large fund wouldn't tempt me."

"No, absolutely it wouldn't," he said. "If you were financially motivated, you'd be an Emerald in the Protectorate by now. Instead of scraping together rent money from crafts your nice friend buys off you. With all your intelligence, family connections, and seemingly unlimited powers, why not live in poverty?"

I tightened my grip on the phone, more insulted than flattered by his assessment. "Birdie doesn't buy them off me," I said tightly. "I sell them on consignment."

"Are you sure about that? Are you aware of how many customers she actually gets in the bookstore these days? Do you think the numbers add up?"

My blood rushed to my toes. Suddenly dizzy, I put a hand on the cold concrete storefront to stay upright.

I had wondered how so many of my bracelets had sold last month when she'd had so little foot traffic.

"I apologize for providing the harsh truths," Raynor continued.

"Oh, be quiet." I pushed away from the wall and drew upon my deep well of inner resources to defend myself. "What are your intentions toward Birdie? If you hurt her, I don't care how many Flints and Emeralds you hide behind, I will find you and I will destroy you."

He only laughed. "We'll talk later," he said. Then he did end the call.

I stood on the sidewalk, aware my entire body was shaking. I had to calm down.

Random was sitting on the other side of the door, watching me with his tongue out, his hot breath steaming the glass. Birdie was just behind him, pretending to be busy even though she was just as attentive as Random.

I'd have to explain. But I was angry about her lying to me about the jewelry sales.

I didn't want to be angry.

I couldn't go home without Random or saying goodbye. I had to just chill out. Get a grip.

Demon's balls. Did she think I was that pathetic that she needed to lie to me about a few bracelets? Rent kept going up, not to mention the heating bill, and a loaf of bread now cost enough that I'd started making my own, but still.

I took a few deep breaths and looked across the street at a crow walking proudly along the sidewalk. It was obvious the bird didn't worry what others thought about anything. Excellent attitude. I watched, trying to absorb its mojo, gain some perspective.

I had to admit to myself that what really angered me about the jewelry sales was that Raynor knew. Not that Birdie had done something sweet, albeit sneaky, but that she'd allowed Raynor to extract the secret out of her.

My pride was wounded; my weaknesses exposed. And now he was trying to use my vulnerability against me for his own aims.

My phone vibrated with a text notification. Inhaling deeply first, I looked down at the screen. It was Birdie. I glanced inside, where I saw her holding her phone, watching me anxiously.

Did somebody die again?

FIFTEEN

After resorting to a relaxation spell, I went back into the store with a calm smile.

"Hey," I said, fighting a yawn. "What were we talking about?"

"Who was that?" Birdie stopped pretending to dust the window display and came over. "Was it Seth? Is he OK? You looked so upset I almost came out there, but I knew you'd hate that."

"He's fine," I said. "That was Raynor."

Birdie immediately turned pink again. "Oh," she whispered.

Now that I'd found out Raynor had knowledge of her business conditions, I was suspicious of today's styled hair, careful makeup, and daisy-studded sundress.

"Are you having video chats with him?" I asked. "Did you have one planned for today?"

Her blush deepened. She lifted her chin. "His family owned a store when he was a kid. He has... insights."

Too many thoughts were churning inside me to deal with that right now. Percy was dead, and I'd been too late (although unintentionally) to help. Whatever was going on between Birdie and Raynor would have to wait.

"OK," I managed to say. "Anyway, he was calling to tell

me that yes, somebody died. Again." Witches tempted death too often—or willfully inflicted it.

"I thought so," she said, eyes wide. "I could tell. Who?"

I sighed. "Percival Tuff. He was the apprentice to Bosko, remember him?"

"Of course I remember."

"Well, he left the Protectorate and became a teacher at a school up in Humboldt County," I said.

"And Raynor wants you to find out who killed him?"

"Who said he was murdered?"

Birdie frowned. "Wasn't he?"

"Yes, we assume so," I said. "But why do you?"

"Well, I mean, you're always telling me witches are killing one another, aren't you?" She picked up a fuzzy pink cardigan off the chair behind the counter and pulled it around herself. "All the early magic you taught me was in self-defense, which was totally the right thing to do, given how many people die around you. No offense."

I nodded. "None taken." It had been a rough year or two. I crouched down to stroke Random's silky ears, taking comfort in his warmth. "You're right."

"So he was murdered?"

"Probably," I said. I suddenly remembered his face, the metal piercings, the anxiety in his eyes, the unhappiness. He'd reached out to me of all people, and I'd let him down. "I'm going to have to go up there and see what I can find out."

"I figured," she said.

I looked up at her. "You did?"

"Well, aren't you?"

I held Random's narrow head between both hands and looked into his deep brown eyes. "Yes," I said with a sigh, dropping my forehead to his.

"I like having Random here with me," she said. "Don't worry about that."

I gave Random a kiss on his muzzle and stood up. "I'm

going to need to buy a few books on gardening," I said. "As many as you have."

~

THAT NIGHT, I sat at my kitchen table with a stack of garden design books, bags of junk food, and an empty bottle of local pinot noir. The paperwork assured me that category of hearth witch had a lot of flexibility, but I would have to fill hundreds of square feet of empty dirt with plants, hard-scaping, water features, and demons knew what else.

With a groan, I flopped forward and let my head thump on the table.

"This is never going to work," I mumbled. But it was my best cover story. Going as an attendee would only make sense for me being there a day or two. I might need longer. Meeting Clem and the girl next door had given me a sense of how small Elwin was, filled with curious, gossiping, and possibly—probably—dangerous witches. I needed a solid reason to be there again so I could find out what had happened to Percy.

What had he been so worried about?

Random licked my hands that had fallen low on my sides. It wasn't only his kindness; I had Cheeto dust on my fingers. Overwhelmed by loneliness for Seth as well as the challenge ahead of me, I'd taken comfort anywhere I could. At least Cheetos didn't knock me out like my experimental potion had.

"They'll see right through me," I said. "They'll see I'm a phony."

Random continued licking. It was as good a response as any. Sighing deeply, I got up to wash my hands at the sink.

I was going to have to ask Helen for help. It was a last resort, but I'd tried to do it myself, tried to get Seth to help remotely, but it was no use. If I was going to put on a pass-able garden exhibition at the most prestigious witch garden show on the West Coast, I'd need help. Then I'd be able to focus on finding out whatever had happened to Percy.

But what could I bribe her with this time? Helen was a mercenary old witch. She'd never just help me out of the goodness of her heart. I'd have to pay her.

Springwater? No, she'd said she had enough. Jewelry? She didn't seem to want what I made unless it had a special history.

I didn't want to offer my magic staff again. It was too valuable, too personal.

Information? Living next door to the Protectorate office on Diamond Street, she seemed able to learn about everything before I did. What did I know that she didn't—that wasn't too personal? I wasn't going to tell her about my love life with a changeling, no matter how eager she was to hear about it.

I reached under the sink for another bottle of pinot. It was from the winery on the other side of the river, bottled when Tristan Price was still Protector of Silverpool.

Slightly drunk, I regarded it with blurry eyes, wondering if Helen would find something useful in it. When I concluded that she would not, I had an excuse to uncork it and pour myself another glass.

Sipping it as I walked, I wandered out into the backyard with Random at my heels. The sun had set hours earlier, and the moon was too low to make much light. Too inebriated and lazy to find my LED lantern, I tapped into my magic to create a ball of light in front of me. Floating around the level of my knees, it illuminated the sorry state of my current garden.

How was I going to impress strangers with my botanical acumen? Even at the height of spring, the California poppies had abandoned me to thrive in front of Seth's house. Most of my blueberry bush was still bare, apparently too depressed to put on leaves for yet another disappointing year. There was magic in my garden, plenty of it, but I didn't know how to move and arrange it to a show known for metal, stone, and sophisticated design.

Seeking inspiration, I walked around with my knee-high ball of light. There was an impressive number of rare pink fairy slippers—calypso orchids—peeking out from under the ferny undergrowth under the trees along the driveway. They were rare and special, but they would never tolerate transplantation. Their dried petals were powerful in my latest healing sachets, but an appearance-focused flower show wouldn't appreciate that.

I wandered into the front yard. In a spot that would be sunny during the day, I'd allowed several clumps of gray-green *Salvia apiana* to run wild. A famous witch garden competition, however, would hardly be impressed with white sage. Even nonmagicals grew it for its powers against Shadow. The other plants in my front garden—lavender, several more salvias, thymes, oleander, star jasmine, a deadly *Datura*, mint, juniper, yarrow, mallow, gooseberry—were useful to me but either too wild or sensitive to trans-plantation to be used next week in an exhibition.

I returned to the backyard and leaned over a glossy-leafed plant that had flowers shaped like white umbrellas. My beloved angelica. Its roots healed menstrual pain better than a bottle of pills from the drugstore, but I could hardly showcase a mug of steaming tea as a landscape design.

No, the truth was that I'd developed my most powerful magic from Willy's redwood. My beads, even the largest ones, wouldn't make much of a garden installation. Even a hundred-foot tree planted in the middle of my plot wouldn't be enough. Elwin demanded fancy, unique complexity.

I held the light up to the base of the redwood, hoping to see Willy. He didn't appear, but his door looked good. I sensed the long history of his benevolent, wise presence under the earth.

"Willy?" I asked aloud. "Are you doing OK?"

He didn't answer. I waited, watching the base of the tree, hoping he'd flash into sight and tell me exactly what to do with a garden demonstration—sometimes he surprised me with advice—but he did not.

The loss of him made my chest ache. I felt a void behind my ribs that mirrored the hole where Willy's door had been. In the past, whenever I'd considered moving away from Silverpool, I always thought of Willy. I knew I could never leave him voluntarily. We were bonded some way. A Bright way.

I gulped my wine and thought about Percy's letter. He hadn't been a close friend, but he'd been a good person. A Bright witch who'd survived a difficult trauma and made the best of it.

Starting a new life, he'd sensed danger. He'd written me. Before I could reply, he'd been killed.

But why hadn't he reached out to the Protectorate? He'd worked there for years and had to have known a witch more useful than me.

Unless he'd feared the threat came from somebody with ties in the Protectorate. But so far north in Humboldt, infamous among witches and nonmag alike for its antiestablishment vibe, who would have connections to the Protectorate?

I'd have to learn more about Elwin.

I tripped over something in the grass. An abandoned trowel. The handle was broken.

There weren't enough bottles of pinot noir in the entire state of California to make me feel confident about the challenges ahead. I'd been proud of myself for unraveling mysteries in the past, for uncovering Shadow, for saving a life or two. But what Percy needed from me felt beyond my abilities. I prided myself on my independence, but it had also gotten me into trouble. I wasn't always able to work alone.

But my options were terrible.

I went inside, miserable. Eventually, shoulders hunched, earbuds installed to keep my hands free, I called Helen.

SIXTEEN

"Finally," Helen said, without saying hello first.

"How is it you know everything?" I asked. "I thought Raynor had blocked you from spying on him through the walls."

"Don't insult me," Helen said. She was old enough to be my grandmother, but nobody would ever expect her to bake cookies for free—unless they were laced with pickled ant legs.

"I need help," I said, "but I can't afford to pay for it."

"Perhaps we could establish a consignment plan," she said. "But I won't credit you unless your work pays off in the end."

"Demon's balls," I said. "Does everyone know my business?"

"Lack of business, it sounds like," Helen said. "I could've told you the life of a freelance hearth witch isn't easy."

"You told me all the time," I said. "That's why you said you had to charge me so much just to sleep in your basement."

Back when I'd been a new Flint agent at the Protectorate, she'd been my informal landlord. Rent was too high for agents to afford a real apartment, so most slept at work under their desks. A few, like me, paid Helen for the luxuries of a sleeping bag on her concrete floor.

"Look out for yourself," she said now, "because nobody else will."

"If you don't look out for anyone but yourself," I replied, "nobody else will either."

She snorted. We seldom agreed on the softer points of humanity. "You just want something for nothing. I don't work that way."

"As if I didn't know that." I took another long sip of my wine. "What do you want, Helen? I need to come up with something to display at a garden show that isn't completely embarrassing."

"You ask the impossible. You've barely got a week. I've had friends start working *years* in advance to prepare for that show."

I burped. Fine. She was going to play dirty. I considered hanging up. Let her think I was giving up so she'd meet me a little closer.

"I guess you're right," I said, letting my words slur. Or maybe it had been unintentional. "Too bad. Sorry to bother you."

"Drinking isn't going to help," she said.

I lifted the wineglass and studied the dark red liquid. I could probably get some more from the local winery. It was pretty good, and the genie liked it. "I don't suppose a few bottles of fine wine would tempt you?"

"Not unless it came from oak barrels in France."

"Some of the language on the label might be French," I said. "So it can be exported to Canada."

"No dice," she said.

"I don't have time for a proper negotiation," I said. "Can't we just skip ahead to the part where you tell me what to do and extract a promise from me to receive an excessively valuable object that ultimately I'm unable to provide through no fault of my own?"

"That's exactly what I want to avoid this time!"

I burped again. "Sometimes we get what we need. Not what we want."

"Tell me something you know I want to know," she said. "I want secrets. Your objects seem to get lost or waylaid or stolen. I'm not going to make that mistake again, expecting payment that way. This time I want something that you can't take back."

I didn't like the sound of that. A witch demanding an open guarantee was a very dangerous creature. "What *specifically* did you have in mind?"

"Information."

I waited. When she didn't elaborate, I took another drink. She wasn't going to trick me into suggesting things she didn't know enough to ask about.

"We both know you wouldn't be able to set up a folding table of vegetable seedlings without help," Helen said. "It's simply beyond your abilities to install a credible display garden at the Elwin Flower Show. This isn't the Podunk farmers' market, you know. It's the big time."

"I don't need to win first place," I said. "I just need an excuse to be in town for a little while."

"If you show up with your pitiful excuse for a garden in Elwin, your laziness and incompetence will make it obvious you're not there for the show," Helen said. "You might as well wear a hat that says Here to Find Out Who Killed the Former Protectorate Agent."

"That wouldn't fit on a hat," I mumbled. She was only telling me what I already knew. It was the reason I'd called her.

"You need me. You have no choice but to tell me something I don't know."

I walked over to the sink and rinsed out the empty glass, feeling my head swim. I shouldn't have had so much to drink before negotiating with Helen. "Which is what?"

"If I knew, it wouldn't be valuable enough to justify my time, expertise, and materials to help you."

I began to worry Helen couldn't be the help I needed.

"Maybe I'll just pretend I'm on vacation. I can just be there to enjoy the show, not participate in it."

"That would only give you a reason to be there for a day or two," she said. "How are you going to explain why you need to stay for longer? I'm not a fancy Protectorate agent like you once were, but I know witches. When they kill somebody, they're a lot smarter than a nonmag at covering it up. You'll need plenty of time."

I stifled a groan. Again, she saw my challenges the same way I did. I had a good track record at finding murderers, but it had always taken more than forty-eight hours.

"I'm not going to volunteer information randomly just to find out after the fact if it's good enough for you." Turning away from the sink, I began walking to my filing cabinet in the other room. Maybe there was an amulet or magical memento I'd forgotten about that I could tempt her with.

"I can narrow it down a little," she said. "Make it something about Silverpool. Tell me something I don't know about—"

Without warning, I lost the use of my legs. One second I was stepping on the rug in the hallway, the next I was toppling to the floor.

I twisted to the side just in time to avoid landing on my face. As I took the fall on my elbow, pain shot through my arm, my shoulder, my hip. With a groan, I rolled onto my back. My earbuds, dislodged by the fall, had popped out, skittering somewhere into the shadows of my cluttered little house.

Furious with being assaulted in my own home, I cursed at the ceiling. But when I tried cursing Jennifer Bardak, the genie of Silverpool, my mouth clamped shut.

It confirmed it was *she* who had ended my chat with Helen.

My anger, locked inside my rigid mouth, had nowhere to go.

I could do nothing but wait for my anger, pain, and

paralysis to fade. Random rushed over and licked my face, which was sweet of him even if his breath smelled nasty.

What kind of *power* that genie must have, I thought with reluctant awe. Jen was unable to walk into my house without my permission, but somehow the magic that held my promise of silence was strong enough to cause me physical injury when, even in an abstract conversation, somebody had approached the concept of her existence.

"Demon's balls," I whispered. That was all I could say for another long minute. The phone on the kitchen table, I assumed, had disconnected the call with Helen even before my elbow had struck the floor. I was careful not to even think about calling her back, although I was curious—Brightness, I was curious—to learn what Helen remembered about the interaction. More than a small part of me hoped that the mercenary old lady had also been knocked to the floor.

Then I felt guilty. She was a senior citizen. Even a powerful witch could break her hip.

It wasn't wrong to hope she took a small tumble. Onto a padded surface. And bumping her elbow wouldn't have killed her.

Still on my back, I rubbed my own throbbing limb. Random demanded comfort, so I patted him through the pain.

So now what? I refused to go to Jen for help. I couldn't risk getting caught in another binding with that genie. Too dangerous. My next fall could be down an abandoned well.

Percy deserved justice. But who else could help me find it for him?

CHAPTER

SEVENTEEN

During my shower the next morning, I saw how collapsing on the floor had left me with a purple bruise on my hip. It wasn't worth using my energy to heal myself, which would be like trying to make a piece of string longer by cutting off one end and tying it to the other, so I just patted it dry and tried not to bump it. After I was dressed and sitting in the kitchen with the garden books again, determined to figure out the design by myself, I found it painful to prop my banged-up elbows on the table.

That genie had really done a number on me. More than ever, I loathed making another deal with her.

Without using my existing well of power, I lit a juniper-and-rosemary healing candle I'd made months earlier and propped it next to the garden books. Hopefully I wouldn't set anything on fire; Willy might not rescue me as he'd done in the past.

Coughing on the acrid smoke—Helen had sold me the recipe a year earlier, and I was skeptical—I flattened out a piece of paper and sketched out the general shape of my plot. Rectangular. In real life, it wouldn't be much bigger than my kitchen. Should've been easy to figure out how to arrange some witchy plants, a fountain, a rock or two.

94

I stared at the blank paper, my pencil hovering uselessly as my thoughts kept drifting to Percy.

He'd been a mind mage, able to read the surface thoughts of most and the deeper, hidden thoughts of many. That seemed like the most likely reason he might be killed. Somebody up in Elwin had secrets that he'd discovered that were worth killing over.

Had he left me any clues in the letter? I hadn't noticed any. Yet. I needed to get up to Elwin again.

I shoved the garden books aside. It was a waste of my time and energy to cram a lifetime of magical landscape architecture expertise into my brain when I should be researching Percy's life and the culture and history of that town.

Somebody else had to do the design, and I'd just pretend it was mine. It would be expensive though. Who did I know that had unlimited cash and resources?

Ah, right. Zoe Thornton, my billionaire widow friend. But she'd already done so much for me. Could I ask her for another—

My phone vibrated with an incoming call. I stared at it, weirded out.

Zoe's name was on the screen.

Suspicious—the genie could be anywhere—I cast a protective spell before picking up. "Hello?" I asked.

"Phil said you need help," she said.

Phil was dead. I'd seen his smoking husk of a corpse myself. But life—and death—worked in mysterious ways. Zoe was convinced he was an angel who had taken corporeal form (when he was her husband) and was now back to his spiritual shape, looking over her as a benevolent guardian. She'd even written a book about it. Other witches thought she'd lost her mind—angels didn't exist, only demons—but her having unlimited wealth kept most from saying so to her face.

I wasn't sure what to believe. I tried not to think about

it. Which was very incurious and therefore un-witchy of me.

"Alma?" she asked, after my prolonged silence.

"I'm surprised to hear from you," I said finally. She'd helped me recently with another problem, and I hesitated to rely on her too often. Billionaires weren't thick on the ground, even amid the magical community, and I wanted to protect our relationship for real emergencies. "I... You see..."

After another pause, she prompted, "Yes? Please. I called you because I want to help."

"Well," I said. "You see, I think a witch was murdered..."

AFTER I'D TOLD Zoe about poor Percy and the flower show, she was quick to help me. Although she was a genealogist and not a gardener, she was still an influential, connected member of Protectorate high society. She put out the word, and by the end of the day, I had talked to three witch garden designers about coming up with an installation that I could pretend was my own. The first two didn't seem like they'd be able to keep quiet about their role in the project—big witchy egos—but the third, a retired designer named Rupert, seemed a perfect fit.

He wasn't even one of Zoe's contacts; he'd heard from one of the other witches that I was looking to hire somebody and reached out to me himself.

"I've already enjoyed enough accolades for a lifetime," he said. "I'm going to be in Elwin anyway. Can't stay away. It would be lovely to have something to do with myself."

"It's just a small plot," I said. "A kitchen garden. Hearth-witch magic. Have you ever done that sort of thing before?"

"Well, I admit my career was focused on metals and stone. My clients, you see, had the money to make that happen," he said. "*Personally* though, I love to design with the old magic. It's how I garden at home in Napa."

His voice was quite raspy with age, and I wondered just

how old he was. Could he do the manual labor I'd need for the garden? I didn't want to be stuck with it all myself. I needed all my strength for investigating.

"I won't be able to do much, uh, lifting and digging and all that." I tried to think of a good excuse. Bad back? Carpal tunnel? Perhaps it was best to be honest. "I'd rather not hurt myself. Can you work around that?"

"Of course! I have a crew of guys I've known for years."

I flinched at the idea of labor costs, then remembered it was Zoe picking up the bill. She had bottomless funds and was glad to help, but I'd have to find some way to thank her.

"And they'll be available on such short notice?"

"With the Thornton name behind you, absolutely," he said.

I sighed. Money talked. "Then... yes. Thank you. Sounds good."

"It'll be interesting to see if I win a gold without my name on the installation," Rupert said. "People have been saying for years I was winning on reputation alone. Hah."

His competitive spirit gave me a pang of worry. "Please don't make it too good," I said. "People would never believe it was my doing."

"This is the Elwin Flower Show," he replied. "Nobody does this on their own. The winners always have other professionals behind them. Most usually start preparation a year in advance, sometimes more than one. Get working on the potions in the water feature, start developing enchantments for the granite hardscape, begin strategizing the fae fertilizers—"

"Hold on," I said quickly, my stomach tightening. "Some witches are using fairies as... *fertilizer*?" My garden books hadn't mentioned any of that, but most had been written by nonmags. What was I getting into? I wasn't going to let anyone hurt fairies for a flower show, not even to find a murderer.

Rupert chuckled. "Don't worry," he said. "It's all super-stition. I don't bother with it."

"Good," I said, still upset. "But what do you mean by fertilizer?"

"It's just an expression," Rupert said. "Some plants are thought to be attractive to the fae, so a witch will use masses of those in the hopes the fae will flock to it during the competition. Nobody will know they're there, of course, unless odds and ends start going missing, or somebody's pet gets hurt, but it's one of the enduring beliefs of the trade."

I was relieved to hear witches weren't somehow consuming fairies the way demons did. That could've been the reason Percy had been alarmed enough to reach out to me.

"Having lots of fairies in your garden is supposed to help you win?" I asked. My competitive juices started to flow in spite of myself. I'd certainly have an advantage, given my rare ability to see the fae and therefore be able to do more to ensure their presence.

"More superstition," Rupert said. "I've never paid any attention to fae, and I did pretty well."

"It sounds like you're a legend."

"Ah, I had a few good years," he said, sounding embar-rassed. "I just love gardening. And people, too. Even witches. The show is a good way to get both at once."

I warmed to him, even though I didn't identify with loving gardening or people, then wanting more of both. I did love plants for what they could do but wasn't motivated to make the combination of them in my yard look pretty. "I'm sorry there's so little time," I said. He knew only the basic situation of me needing to be in town for personal reasons and using the show as an excuse. "It really doesn't have to be incredible. Just passable."

"I hear you," Rupert said. "Hearth witchery. A lovely tradition. Send me photos of gardens you like, give me a general idea of what you're looking for, and I'll take care of the rest. I already have my bed-and-breakfast booked. It'll be fun to use a new spell or two to create a good disguise."

"Although I myself won't be able to offer cash payment, which will be provided through our benefactor, my beaded necklaces are well-known and quite powerful—"

"No talk of that. Mrs. Thornton is known to be very generous."

I cringed, feeling like a charity case. "Still, I'd like to thank you personally if I could, in my own way."

"Whatever floats your boat," he said, "but it's not necessary. I like to keep busy. Antiaging spells work great for the wrinkles, but they aren't so useful on the brain. And just between you and me, I think my husband will be glad to get me out from underfoot for a little while this time of year. He says I take over his corner of the garden when I'm supposed to butt out and leave him to make his own mistakes." He laughed.

We talked another few minutes about logistics and then had a long conversation about hearth magic, the limitations of metal, and the challenges of a creative life in a cutthroat world. When we finally ended the call, I was smiling. Rupert was going to be a lot more fun to rely on than Helen.

Now that the alarming likelihood of me embarrassing myself in front of witch society yet again had passed, I could turn my full attention to what truly mattered.

Percy's murder.

EIGHTEEN

I left for Elwin the next morning after several hours of restless sleep. As part of my investigative strategy, I'd been up late cutting and coloring my hair.

I couldn't wait for a salon appointment to get the look I wanted. Every hour that passed since Percy's death could make any evidence harder to find. Magical residues would've begun to fade within seconds after any hex was cast, but if I got up to Elwin fast enough, I might find something, anything to guide me.

My Jeep was filled with (I hoped) useful magic, Random was safely back in Birdie's welcoming embrace, and my house's boundary spells were as strong as I could make them.

And although Raynor, Birdie, and Darius knew where I was going, Seth did not.

As I drove across the Silverpool bridge, I looked at the thin bracelet on my left wrist that he'd given me. It was barely noticeable, just a narrow band of braided jute, but it held a strand of his dark hair, given freely to me under a full moon. I brought my wrist to my mouth, brushing my lips across its rough surface.

A sense of him flooded me. He was alive. In good spirits. And wet.

I smiled. It wouldn't be a kindness to tell him about my upcoming adventure when he couldn't do anything to help. Why make him worry? Even if he said he didn't, I knew he did.

And, I had to admit, I didn't want him to stop me. When he was motivated, his magic could do surprising things, especially with me. Without me, Percy's death would never be explained. Maybe Percy would be stuck in an alternative state of being, haunting all of us. Me in particular for ignoring his plea for help.

Maybe I was just rationalizing. The fact was, I really wanted to go, so I was going to go. That was basically it.

Seth didn't often get angry, but this might push him over the edge.

Yet another reason to act quickly.

I TIMED my arrival in Elwin to match the check-in time for the motel where I'd booked a last-minute room. With the flower show just around the corner, I'd been lucky to find anything at all.

It wasn't fancy even by off-brand motel standards. Its pictures online had suggested they would be no-frills, budget accommodations—and they were right. It was one story, U-shaped, beige, and had absolutely no landscaping. The outdoor pool was exposed in the middle of the parking lot with a black metal fence around it. From the look of the scraggly brown plant matter clinging to the slats, I guessed there had once been a flowering vine to provide privacy, shade, and beauty. It had died a long time ago.

Strange for a small town that was famous internationally for its flower show. There had to be some reason nothing was growing in any of the patches of exposed earth in the Elwin Garden Motel.

I parked near the reception office but didn't get out of

my car right away. The uneasy feeling in my gut demanded my attention.

I reached under the front seat and drew out my emergency magic stash. The old handbag held extra beads, small metal charms, bottled potions, seashells, dried kelp, various land botanicals, and trail mix. The whole package was getting too big to fit under the seat; I'd have to weed it down one of these days.

Or I could just get a second bag and put it under the passenger seat. It was so hard not to squirrel everything away, just in case. There was never a way to know what I'd need someday.

I raked through the stash for the cheap tin bracelet I'd earned years ago collecting game tickets at an arcade. My memories told me I'd been about Marta's age at the time, which made me think the item would be a good choice today. Other than Clem, she'd been the only person in Elwin I'd talked to on my previous visit. I didn't generally choose metal, but the dearth of plant matter around the building suggested the witch owners had cast killing spells on anything botanical.

I pulled out the tarnished bangle and brought it to my lips.

Nickel. I inhaled the weak, steady magic into my body and turned my gaze toward the motel office door. There hadn't been any other vacancies in town, but if the management was Shadowed, I might be better off sleeping rough, just as Seth was doing in Minnesota.

My first scan was inconclusive. There was somebody inside, but I didn't sense danger, just... something I couldn't describe.

Fatigue? Illness? A sleeping enchantment?

There wasn't enough danger to stop me from at least going inside. Even the nearby campgrounds were booked solid for a month.

Slipping the bangle on my wrist, I got out. Not sensing

any hostile spells, I peeked through a dirty window into the office.

My fears subsided immediately. It was just a woman playing something on her phone. She was hunched over, stabbing the keys, eyes fixed on the screen.

I cast a quick defensive spell and went in. She didn't look up, but her muttering stopped, and she even blinked once. A small woman of about forty, she wore her black hair tightly pulled back in a bun that was secured with beaded clips.

Out of habit, I scanned the beads to see what magic they held, realizing belatedly they were plastic.

She wasn't a witch.

I walked over to the counter, impressed she still hadn't looked up. After waiting a long moment, I cleared my throat. "Hi. I'm here to check in."

She frowned and made a face. After tapping the screen a few more times, she finally lifted her gaze. Her shimmering eyeshadow was copper-colored, but she wore no actual metal anywhere on her body—no earrings or necklace, not even a smartwatch.

"Alma Bellrose," I said.

Now I had her full attention. The look she gave me was one I recognized in nonmagicals who knew about us: she was wary but curious, disgusted but jealous.

As if she were a robot whose correct button had been pushed, she turned to a computer, tapped a few keys, and in a few efficient minutes I had a key card and a small piece of paper with useless information such as the lock code to the pool. Even if there was water in it, which I wasn't positive there was, I wouldn't be dipping any of my body parts into it. At least not unless I had to. Such as if I were on fire, and even then I'd try a quenching spell first.

"Thanks," I said.

She stared at me. I could feel her urge to go back to her game, but she was waiting until after I left.

A man burst through a door behind her. "Babe, have you seen the wrench set? The table in 102 is wobbly again." He put his hand on the woman's shoulder, started to bend closer for a kiss, then saw me. Smile tightening, he straightened and maneuvered himself to stand between me and the woman.

Now *this* guy was a witch. Muscular and blond, he wore a single gold chain around his neck that was as thick as my pinkie finger.

He and I gave each other a magical once-over, running scanning spells that were well hidden enough to be polite but strong enough to be useful.

A sizzling between my shoulder blades told me he was powerful. More than I would've expected from a man behind the desk in a budget motel.

"What brings you to Elwin?" he asked, moving to completely block my view of the woman.

I thought it was a funny question, given throngs of visitors would be arriving for the flower show. "Kitchen gardens," I said.

"First time at the show, is it?" he asked.

The woman laughed as if he'd made a hilarious joke.

Apparently the motel I had chosen because it had been the only vacancy in a hundred miles was vacant for a reason. "Is there a problem?" I asked. "If there's something I should know, I'd appreciate it if you just told me."

He stared at me. "You don't mind?"

The tingling between my shoulder blades became painful. There was a lot about the motel I minded, starting with the creepy customer service. "Mind what, exactly?" I asked, careful to keep my voice light.

He raised his eyebrow, slow and high, a smirk tugging at the corner of his lips as he studied me. "No Shadowed *plants*," he said. "I don't let any grow here. Aren't you here for the show?"

The woman got to her feet with a sigh and walked out the door he'd come through earlier. As a nonmag running a motel in a witch enclave, all their power plays had to get tedious.

Or was she being careful, giving the man space to hex me?

Time to get serious about why I was in Elwin. "What's your name?" I put the force of an interrogation command into my words.

Eyes blazing, he tried to resist me at first. But I was a visitor to his home, although a paying one, and they had welcomed me in. The balance of power was on my side.

He grunted, unable to stop himself from answering. "You'd call me Frost," he said in a rush.

I froze. My heart lurched and began to pound.

If this was the Frost I'd heard of, I suddenly understood why a witch might drive a hundred miles instead of sleeping in a room to which he had a key. And why there weren't any climbing roses out front.

A witch, nicknamed Frost, was widely believed to have killed nine witches between Florida and Maine during the spring break season of 1999. As I had been taught by both my father and the Protectorate, the only clue he'd left behind was a frozen flower rose clamped between the teeth of each corpse. Otherwise there had been no trace, no way to stop him or bring him to justice.

And now here he was, just an ordinary motel guy. Was this where witches checked in but didn't check out?

I could run, but then I'd always wonder. And wasn't I there to find a murderer?

"Are the stories true?" I asked. My voice wavered slightly.

His eyes widened with surprise. After a long moment, he shook his head. "No," he said, with almost as much reluctance as when he'd told me his name.

I clasped my beads, not breathing. His voice had been steady but raw, not a hint of magic in it, like a single-ingredient meal without salt or spice. He'd given me one pure word that I could analyze with all the craft of a Protectorate agent.

Some of my terror eased. Maybe—maybe—he wasn't the monster everyone said he was.

"What's your real name?" I continued.

His jaw clenched, still trying to fight me, but he ground out, "Lacoste."

It didn't ring any bells. "Funny how it kind of sounds like 'Frost,'" I said.

"I was set up."

My truth spell told me he believed what he was saying. The magic wasn't always reliable, but that was a huge thing to lie about.

I gestured at the door behind him. "And her name?"

Leaning forward, he planted two strong hands on the counter and glared at me. For her, he'd risk more than he would for himself. "None of your business."

It would be easy enough to learn her name if it was important. Pushing him further now would be dangerous.

The interaction was making me dizzy. I needed to get away from him so I could reflect in solitude. But first...

First I had to help him forget what I'd just done. I had nowhere else to stay, and could hardly sleep under his roof when he hated me.

I put my hands on the counter, palms flat, and felt the particles of old wood that had been glued together to make it years earlier. He was still leaning forward, his skin close to mine. There was enough of my favorite material to send a current of magic through the material and into his palms. It would filter up to his brain and rub out the memories he didn't like—namely of me overpowering him. It was much easier to use a subtle hex like that on a man like this guy than it would be to erase the encounter entirely. He didn't *want* to remember that a young woman with a dumb smile had gotten him to talk, and I'd use his own wishes against him.

He frowned and blinked at me. When I was done, I lifted my hands and pretended to look through my bag while his thoughts morphed into ones he himself would be proud of.

Luckily, we'd been alone. The woman who had been at the front desk wasn't a witch, and he himself wouldn't think to scan himself for my interference. If he did later, he'd find nothing. My forgetting enchantment would dissipate within five minutes.

"Thank you," I said, waving the key as I turned to leave.

Lacoste nodded, still dazed. "Did Serafina tell you about the coffee?" He pointed at a machine and disposable cups on a small table near the door. "Fresh until ten. No guarantees after that."

I made a mental note of Serafina's name. "I won't need it. Thanks." I walked outside and held my breath as the door closed behind me.

Muttering silent curses at myself for having walked right into an unnecessarily dangerous as well as awkward situation—I could never, ever let Raynor learn I'd booked a motel room without researching the owners first—I went out to my Jeep. I didn't even pretend not to hurry. It took me a few seconds for my hands to stop shaking enough to open the door. Casting every calming spell I knew, I drove through the parking lot to the other side of the pool.

I pulled into a spot near my room but didn't turn off the engine. Thinking hard, I wiped my sweaty palms on my jeans. Should I stay in the Serial Killer Motel? Would I even be able to fall asleep?

I shut down the engine.

He believed he'd been set up—and I felt myself believing him in return. He hadn't seemed capable of being a serial killer. The man I'd just seen, my senses told me, abhorred killing.

I could feel a weird kinship with him on that point. My gut told me that whatever the stories were about him, the witch I'd just met wasn't going to steal my life and stick a frozen rose in my mouth.

So then why was my skin still crawling?

CHAPTER

NINETEEN

M y room was on the opposite end of the motel's U shape from the office. Its proximity to the street wasn't ideal for noise, but it was good to have the fastest escape route in an emergency.

As I brought in my bags, I was relieved to notice there was a healthy population of fairies in the parking lot and around the low roof of the motel, despite the lack of plants, trees, or fresh water. They were an unusual type, about the size of a hummingbird but with wings like a butterfly. Each was dark and bald except for a white beard. I'd seen them in cities, but they weren't the type to gather in a small town. Did they like the concrete?

Thinking about Lacoste, I corrected myself. He had to be feeding them something. Plants weren't welcome, but obviously fairies were. Bread with honey was historically a favorite treat to leave out if you wanted to draw them closer.

How bad could he be if the fairies loved him?

I snorted to myself. He could be completely Shadowed. The fairies could be bringing him the hearts of tortured puppies to get extra honey on their sourdough.

When all my stuff was in the room, I bolted the door.

Maybe Darius could tell me something about him without getting involved or telling Raynor.

I snorted again. Darius would tell Raynor about the infamous Frost if I mentioned him, and neither would support my staying on his property. I'd have to learn about him on my own.

I brought one of my bags into the bathroom and sized up the small sink and shower. There was a faint magical residue from a cleaning spell—either Lacoste cast it himself or there was a witch on the housekeeping crew—but otherwise the bathroom had no enchantments.

Even a nonmag could see that—the tile floor was uneven, the fixtures were outdated, and the bulky fluorescent bulb over the sink made a high-pitched buzzing sound.

But it was private and didn't have another witch's heavy-handed spells everywhere, and that was what I cared about.

I needed both to touch up my disguise.

Changing my appearance with magic had never been easy for me, but every witch learned a few basic tricks as a kid—usually around Marta's age or a few years later—to make their social lives a little more tolerable. Big changes took more power than most witches had, so it would be little things that could be just as easily done with makeup or a trip to the salon. By adulthood, most just used those easier means, preferring to use their magic for bigger goals. Usually that involved the basics: love, money, and power.

I regarded my pink hair in the mirror. To make the color change easier, I'd had it cut into a chin-length bob, which made the curls fluff up and form a cloud around my face. A bright one. I'd fit right in with all the flowers.

The vibrant fuchsia didn't feel true to my personality, but the color would give people the impression I was a free-spirited gardener, a fun-loving artist—not a conservative Protectorate lackey. I couldn't avoid using my real name, which had only become more widely known over the years, but I could emphasize my (infamous) Incurable Inability.

I wanted a disguise that told the world that I'd never belonged in the Protectorate. I wanted to look like a witch who would never get ahead by sending a bad witch to the Protectorate prison in Death Valley. I was harmless. All I cared about was flowers. My gig selling magic beads was just a way to fund my true passion for gardening. Which was totally why I was in Elwin. To go to the show. I was so, so excited.

It had nothing to do with wondering why a witch friend of mine had recently met a suspiciously violent death.

The hair had been a product of bleach and dye, but the changes to my face were drawing continuously from the well of magical power deep inside me. The effect was subtle, I hoped, suggesting I wasn't fully paying attention, or if I was, that I'd quickly forget anything told to me. I'd put a film over my eyes that made them seem out of focus, as if I'd forgotten to wear my glasses or was just generally absent-minded. My mouth would always appear friendly, a smile always lurking, just so happy to come out and meet you. I wasn't the suspicious type. And naturally, I loved everyone. Of *course* I'd been kicked out of the Protectorate. I was just so *nice*.

Those were the main changes. I was also going to keep wearing the copper ring that Raynor had given me—on a long chain around my neck, out of sight—that hid my demon ancestry. A powerful old witch named Lionel had told me the ring would also hide other details about me that I'd like to keep hidden, but I hadn't tested it enough to bet my life on it. And with Percy already dead, the stakes were high.

To complete the disguise, I wore decoy beaded jewelry in highly visible places: big chunky necklaces and bracelets that were handmade and stylish but created by nonmag artists. Witches who scanned me would determine the wood beads had no magic in them and think I was harmless. The truly powerful beads from my collection would be under my clothes or under a powerful hiding spell.

That left the tattoos. I had six dark lines, similar to tree rings, encircling my left wrist. Each had appeared after a life-threatening magical conflict, usually resulting in the death of my opponent—which of course had never been my intention. The last thing I wanted was to give the impression I was some kind of powerful secret Protectorate agent who left a trail of dead bodies behind me. Even if it was maybe sometimes kind of true, perhaps just a teeny, little bit.

I couldn't rely on long sleeves. I had a tendency of pushing those up subconsciously, which could expose the marks at a bad moment. Something more secure was necessary. A spell on only that part of my skin would draw too much attention to what I was trying to hide; a witch who was curious, and most were, would use a spell of their own to see through it.

But if I used magic to cover *all* my skin, as many did to look younger or prettier or whatever, then I'd fit right in. Nobody would think anything of it in a community of wealthy exurbanite witches.

Given the reaction of Lacoste in the motel office, the spell I'd cast at home wasn't strong enough. He'd clocked me as a witch—a threatening one—right away. I'd have to enhance the effect. Regretting the effort it would entail, I took a bottle of murky liquid out of my makeup bag. It contained Silverpool springwater blended with redbud and ceanothus pollen, California poppy petals, redwood bark, and oxalis leaf from my own yard.

To work its best here, I'd have to mix it with local water before I drank it. Tap water wouldn't do—it had to be unfiltered, guaranteed to be from nearby. During droughts, water was sometimes brought to the coast from inland. I couldn't risk that. It had to be touched by the soil in Elwin.

With all the risks of bacteria, nastiness, and social exposure that might entail.

I had to go out and find some. And then, my stomach hoped, I could get something to eat while I met more citizens of the booming witch enclave of Elwin.

TWENTY

The creek ran along the Elwin RV Camp in a redwood grove. It seemed the safest location where I could get out of the car and collect some water. Surrounded by other visitors, I wouldn't draw as much attention.

I drove down the narrow lane through the trees, jealous of everyone who got to sleep in such a lovely place filled with lush greenery, the quiet hush of the forest, and a high population of contented wood sprites. Before I'd booked the motel, I'd considered tent camping. Thirty seconds later, I'd thought better of it. Sharing a communal shower and sleeping on dirt was OK for one night—maybe—but not more than that, even with ground-softening spells.

Besides, the park had been fully booked for the show next week. It wasn't filled yet—there were still empty sites in between the long-term RV residents with their canopies and outdoor furniture—but it would be soon. In fact, there already seemed to be a lot of vehicles lined up at the ranger's office, checking in.

I rolled down the windows of my Jeep and inhaled the rich, damp scent of the coastal rainforest. As I drove, a wood sprite in a light-brown tunic flitted over and perched on my driver's side rearview mirror. It stared at me for a long minute, even after I parked near the creek. Knowing a tropical treat would be a rare pleasure for a local fairy, I reached down, dug a strip of dried coconut out of a bag of trail mix in the center console, and balanced it on the edge of the open window without making eye contact. It wasn't necessary to let them know they weren't invisible to me, but it could be useful to have allies.

The fairy didn't hesitate. Wings flapping, it swooped closer, grabbed the coconut in its bare toes, and darted away, its flight off-balanced by the weight. I got out and walked down the access trail to the creek—another benefit of being at a commercial park—and watched as more sprites began gathering in the trees above me.

The coconut had been a success.

Kneeling on the rocky shore, I dipped my stainless-steel thermos into the cold water and muttered a pathogen-killing spell to enhance the enchantment I'd already put on the metal. Killing all living matter might make the water less powerful, magic-wise, but I wouldn't be any use if I was doubled up over the toilet with giardia. Unfortunately, my skin spell might need to be strengthened daily, so I filled the bottle and returned to my Jeep.

When I was back behind the wheel, I balanced the bottle from home on my lap and added a few drops of the creek water. I shook it to blend, paused for a second to prepare myself for the taste, then chugged it as quickly as I could.

Blah. It certainly wouldn't ever be a bestselling recipe at the juice shop. The poppy petals weren't too bad, but the splinters of redwood bark stuck to my tongue. And it was hard to swallow the lumps all the way down.

Coughing and gagging, I vowed to save up enough money to buy one of those expensive blenders that could pulverize rocks.

When I'd choked down what I hoped was an effective dose, I unscrewed the cap from a bottle of iced tea and indulged in a small mouthful to wash it down. Hopefully the dilution wouldn't affect the potion's strength.

Leaning back in my seat, I held out my arm and watched my skin slowly transform from a normal, splotchy, imperfect human witch into the blemish-free complexion of a model in an ad for aging cream. Even the enchanted tattoos disappeared.

It made me uneasy. I felt as if I were now wearing a stranger's skin suit.

My stomach growled. Hunger was giving me weird thoughts. All I'd eaten since dinner the night before was trail mix. Unlike the tree sprites, I wasn't interested in eating any more coconut flakes.

I drove out of the RV park and back down the winding two-lane road to the business district. The ocean and a small harbor were visible between gaps in the nineteenth-century brick buildings lining the main street. I parked in front of the run-down bar I remembered from my previous visit and pulled down the visor to look at myself in the mirror. My nose had been tingling, and I wanted to make sure it hadn't grown four inches and sprouted pink fur or something.

I stared at myself. Even I could see the difference. It was wonderfully subtle. *Imperceptible*, I realized proudly. A Hollywood makeup artist couldn't have done better. My skin didn't *look* as if it was coated with foundation, creams, and powders, but the result was the same. I leaned closer to the mirror, amazed by my impossibly healthy, ridiculously uniform complexion.

Shaking my head, I slammed the visor back up. It was dangerous to get attached to the idea of looking perfect. Some witches used all their power in the pursuit and neglected everything else. Even I felt the temptation.

Luckily my hunger was stronger than my vanity. There weren't many places to eat in Elwin, so I'd have to try a place called Krog's Grog if I didn't want to leave town. I was grateful to see it was open for breakfast as well as dinner.

It was a little shabby and cramped, but clean, with black-vinyl booths lining the walls and small tables on the floor in between. The server, a nonmag guy around twenty, brought me to a table and handed me a tablet with the digital menu. "Uh, there isn't any soup left, but the roast chicken is good. The only reason we still have that is because we got a lot of vegans tonight."

I was too tired and hungry to look over the menu. "I'll have that. Thanks. With fries and ice water."

"Tap OK?"

I nodded. After what I'd been drinking, I obviously wasn't picky.

After he left, I turned my full attention to my surroundings. I'd chosen a chair facing the door out of habit, although walking in and ordering without scanning the place properly had been careless. There were only a handful of other people sitting inside, spread over three or four tables. All were witches. They glanced at me, did quick scans, but didn't pursue beyond that. I relaxed, relieved my enchantment wasn't so strong it attracted stares.

The server brought me my water and a basket of fresh brown bread. I tore off a slice, slapped a hunk of butter on it, and popped it in my mouth.

I closed my eyes a moment to enjoy it. The other witches' disinterest and the warm, seeded bread were lifting my mood. It was good to be out having an adventure. As much as I loved my house in Silverpool, it did get a little boring sometimes—something I'd never admit to Raynor. He'd have to bring in a crew of Sapphire witches from New York with advanced interrogation spells to get that out of me.

My meal arrived a few minutes later. Only after I'd eaten half the chicken and most of the fries did I search the other witches with a deeper scan that I now had the strength to camouflage.

Ah. These must be the local, long-term residents. Their magic was rough and botanical—no surprise, given the setting—and they enhanced their power with steel, copper, and iron. Urbanite witches used gold and platinum if they could afford it, or silver if they couldn't, not the odds and ends the locals wore.

None was from a jeweler. I sensed reclaimed materials from the local community, a jumble of various, unfamiliar objects.

I popped another fry in my mouth and pretended to read the label on the ketchup bottle.

First I detected the fragment of a rusty saw in a lumber mill. It was powerful, painful to scan. There was also fishing tackle, bolts from a bridge, and the turn-signal knob from an old sky-blue Chevy pickup.

I wasn't sure how I had such a clear vision of what truck it had been, but then I decided it must've been cherished by its witch owner, who was now sending out its beloved essence to the world like a radio station playing only one song.

Sustaining that kind of steady hum would take considerable power. It would be stupid to assume the locals with their scrap-heap magic were harmless yokels, especially since I was on my own, far away from home and possible rescue, in a possibly hostile environment.

I extinguished my scanning spells and returned to eating. On my plate between the fries and chicken was a small mound of wilted kale. Skeptical, I poked it, telling myself it would be good for me. On a whim, I cast a scanning spell over it, probably hoping to learn it was toxic and therefore best to leave untouched.

Instead, I found a hint of springwater. Potent and fresh. Interesting.

"It's for my kids," a man said above me.

I looked up to see a muscular man in an apron. Around forty, he was bald but had the coloring of a redhead. Bright blue eyes, full-sleeve tattoos on both arms, and a tag on his tight black T-shirt reading Bruce in all caps.

The man was a witch, a powerful one, and given the air of command around him, this was clearly his restaurant.

"Do they eat it?" I asked, conscious of my pulse starting to accelerate.

I hoped my disguise would hold. He'd just caught me scanning the food he'd given me, which some hosts would find insulting. On his turf, I was at a disadvantage. I glanced at the door, estimating how many seconds it would take me to get outside.

"Relax," Bruce said. "You shoveled the rest of my food into your pie hole quickly enough."

I clutched the napkin under the table. Was he looking for a fight? Tired of outsiders in his precious town?

Before I lost my temper and flung a mind-your-manners hex at him—it was his joint, but I thought I could take him—I remembered my mission. I was supposed to be harmless, too stupid to realize I was being insulted.

"I was really hungry," I said. Tapping into the bracelet I'd braided out of Random's fur, I drew out the essence of his canine personality and flung it at the man's face. What better friendly, harmless impression could I aspire to than a dog's?

Bruce grunted. Blinked a few times. "Right," he said. "Of course."

"The chicken was great." I tapped the edge of the plate.

His expression softened. His shoulders slumped, his eyes widened, and his voice rose to the higher, softer pitch big men used with small children and, yes, dogs. "You should eat your veggies," he said. "They're good for you."

I picked up my fork with genuine hesitation and speared the soggy mound. "I know you're right."

"Go on. It'll make you strong. You'll see."

I made myself take a bite and felt the springwater hit my magical taste buds. As I often did, I wished it worked on me as well as it did other witches. Moaning with feigned surprise, I smiled at him. Then, as he would expect me to, I lowered my shovel and put another load into my pie hole.

I had to pretend to enjoy all of it. Then, careful to hide how I drew from the beaded necklace under my shirt, I cast a spell to appear completely restored by his slimy springwater-laced greens.

"See?" he said.

I nodded. How was I going to survive multiple days of putting on the stupid act? Just one serving of vegetables and I already wanted to puke.

The bells on the front door chimed. Both of us looked over to see a tall woman walk in. Bruce visibly tensed.

She was a witch of the modern sort: well-dressed, lots of jewelry, spells to look younger than she was. Her long, straight hair appeared to be a shade of dark red, but I could feel her magic from across the room and doubted anything she let people see was natural. Right behind her was the girl who'd run me over in her flying skateboard, Marta. Tonight she held a small but chunky dog with protruding eyes. Contrary to the big dog she'd mentioned, this one was about the size, shape, and color of a loaf of sandwich bread. I tried to imagine the pug working as an effective guard dog, but I didn't think it was possible even with supernatural intervention. It was adorable.

Bruce pursed his lips and walked away to greet the woman who I assumed was Marta's aunt, the principal of the school. He'd mentioned his kids, which made me curious about if they went to the public school and their possible connection to Percy. Bruce's posture—and a puff of defensive magic around him—suggested he didn't like her.

I watched carefully from behind my enchanted blank face.

"No, no, we don't need a table," the woman said dismissively, striding past him. "I'm not here to eat."

Bruce turned a hot-pink color. Jaw clenched, he glanced at the table where the knob-from-the-pickup-truck man sat. I saw them share a look I couldn't read.

I didn't have time to further investigate the exchange

because the woman was rapidly approaching my table with her gaze fixed on me. I felt her examine my clothes, my hair, my body, my shoes, my empty plate, my visible jewelry—even my half-empty glass of tap water.

The scan was quick and efficient with little effort to hide its scope, as if she was used to dominating people and didn't mind causing offense.

"Is that the woman, Marta?" she asked, not looking away from me.

Marta gave me a worried—no, terrified—look. She nodded.

"Marta?" the woman demanded.

Marta nuzzled the loaf of dog in her arms. "I think so," she mumbled. "Yeah."

The woman reached my table and looked down her nose at me.

Since it would support my disguise, I indulged in a little panic—really, she was scary—and shrank lower in the vinyl seat.

TWENTY-ONE

Everyone in the restaurant was staring at her—and now me, her target—but she didn't seem to notice. Her air of self-assurance had blasted through the restaurant like a high-pressure washer, wiping away whatever conversations or introspective musings had been going on before she entered the restaurant. All that remained was her, her goals, and the distinctly crisp aura of metal.

A fortune in it. From what I could see, all of it was highly polished silver—a comb in her hair, a stud in her nose, piercings in her ears, and then down to all the necklaces, pins, and bracelets below her chin.

I stayed in my cowed position, genuinely overwhelmed. She was a force. A deafening, blinding force. Even her perfume was too strong.

"Excuse me," I said in a small voice. "Can I help you with something?"

She indulged me with an answer. "Nerissa Pike. Marta is my niece."

I sat up a little taller. "Oh hi. Sure. Nice to meet you."

She took a chair and sat down. "I can't stay long," she said, as if I'd asked her to. "Marta didn't get your name."

If I weren't trying to appear to be unsophisticated and defenseless, I wouldn't have answered. But I was. "Alma," I said. "I'm here for the garden show. My first time. I'm so excited. I know I have no chance of winning a gold, but it's just an honor to be here. It was nice to meet Marta. And now you, of course."

Subconsciously, I was babbling like Birdie would. Imitating her mannerisms was a good disguise, but it would probably be better for our relationship if I didn't ever tell her about it. She was genuinely smart and talented, and I didn't want her to think I believed otherwise.

"You're a hearth witch," Nerissa said.

I smiled as if I was embarrassed and dropped my gaze. She wouldn't expect me to be defiant about it, so I wasn't.

While I stared at my empty plate, my mind sifted through the reasons why this dominating witch had come to confront me. Seeing Marta's panicked face, I decided it was probably because I'd scared the girl when she'd insulted hearth magic.

That had been careless of me. Hopefully my enhanced disguise and meeting me personally would downgrade my importance in her aunt's mind.

I looked up at Marta and smiled. "Brightness," I said. "Your dog is so cute. What's its name? Here, have a seat." I pushed out a chair.

Her aunt looked over at Marta and pointed at the door. "Why don't you wait outside? Beryl might scare people."

Marta nodded, shot me a curious look, then reluctantly left the restaurant. I saw her loiter just outside, watching through the glass.

"Beryl's an interesting name for a dog," I said.

Nerissa flinched slightly, a show of discomfort that had to be rare for her. "My brother thought it would be funny to give an Emerald name to a pet. She's not even a familiar. Doesn't have a drop of magic in her. Just a funny little dog."

I smiled. "I have one of those. They're the best."

With a dismissive lift of her eyebrow, Nerissa lifted her wrist and tapped her watch a few times. The show of vulnerability was over. "I apologize for interrupting your meal," she said brusquely. She gave the watch a final tap, then looked at me. "Marta clearly got the wrong idea. She led me to believe you'd nearly hexed her, which is obviously not the case."

I bet Nerissa Pike didn't apologize very often. I hesitated, glad my disguise was having its effect while scrambling to think of how to use the situation to my advantage. "Oh no! That's terrible." I was careful not to apologize myself, which would neutralize my leverage too quickly.

"She shouldn't have insulted hearth magic to a witch she'd just met."

I bit back the temptation to ask her if it would be cool to insult witches she'd known a long time. "I really like using the old ways in my garden," I said instead, "but please tell her I'd never hurt anyone." I touched the beads under my sleeve and used a hit of magic to bring a flush to my face. "Just ask them at the Protectorate."

She frowned. "The Protectorate? But—" Her expression froze. For a split second, I saw her arrogance waver. "What do you mean?"

"Oh, I thought everybody knew." Slumping in my seat, I let my mostly-healed-by-now embarrassment show on my face. "I used to work there. It wasn't a good fit."

"Alma," she said, realization dawning. "You're Alma *Bellrose*."

I shrugged. "See? Even up here you've heard of me."

As she smiled at me, her arrogance on full display, she brought her hands together and began caressing the many rings on her fingers. A cluster of interrogation spells wafted over the table and surrounded me in a heavy, slightly damp cloud. "Perhaps. Are you the one who couldn't bring herself to kill a demon?"

Although I'd planned to look harmless, that didn't mean I wanted anyone to think I couldn't defend myself. That would only bring trouble. Pretending it took great effort—I gripped my stainless-steel fork and panted a little

—I cast a boundary spell around me from head to toe to block her magic.

She nodded, a grudging show of respect, and made a show of looking behind her to wave at Marta. The girl was still watching through the window, but now Beryl the dog was out of sight.

Now was a chance to ask my own questions. "Marta said you're the principal at her school," I said. "I heard recently—well, I wonder if you might have known—a colleague of mine."

Her face gave nothing away. "Why would you wonder that?" She managed to seem both helpful and terrifying at the same time. No wonder she'd gone into education.

"Well, because he was a teacher," I said. "I didn't know him well, but he used to work in the Protectorate too. He's the one who encouraged me to give the garden show a shot. But..." I tweaked my disguise to look especially confused. "He just... died."

"You mean Percival Tuff. Yes, of course. He taught the upper elementary cohort. Now that you mention it, he was probably why I've heard your name before." Nerissa gave me a cool, professional nod. "A tragedy. The children are still grieving."

My pulse had spiked. I was on the right track. "I heard it was something with his heart."

"It gave out while he was driving," she said. "Not his fault, but he could be careless about safety."

It took a special kind of personality to blame a man for crashing his car during a heart attack. "Kind of hard to control the car if you're unconscious," I said.

She gave me a sharp look, as if trying to decide if I'd criticized her. When I stared back with dumb innocence, she said with a sigh, "I was just angry to lose him. Maybe if he'd had a strong enchantment on the car—I never drive without one—he would've survived the crash. But he 'didn't want to live like a paranoid Protectorate agent anymore'—his words. And then he died. I *warned* him to be careful about dropping his self-defense magic. Just because we're far from the city doesn't mean there aren't dangers to look out for."

I held my breath. If I asked too many questions, she'd get suspicious—but I might not get another chance like this. "What kind of dangers? Drunk drivers? Fairies?"

"Those and others. As I tell my kids, demons never sleep."

"You think there are *demons* here?" I made my voice quiver a little.

"This should be a very attractive region for the fairy kind. It's logical to believe demons would be drawn here to consume the fae."

Any time the topic of demons and fae arose, I had to work to hide my discomfort. It had been a while now since I'd learned my ability to see fairies was because I had demon ancestry, but I was still sensitive about it. I picked up my water glass and sipped with exaggerated relief. "At least you haven't seen any though, right?"

"We can never be too careful. The flower show is such an unnecessary risk," she went on. "All these strange witches coming from all over the world. Their exotic plants, their potions, familiars, spells, stones, metal—it's reckless."

There was that word again. *Reckless.* Nerissa wanted her world to be as safe as she could make it. Considering her strong personality, I wondered how far she would go to protect herself and her community.

The answer came to me immediately: as far as she thought necessary.

I remembered Percy's letter. How he'd unearthed something that scared him. Was it something about his boss? His last one had been Shadowed. Had the pattern continued? Was the woman sitting across from me a cold-blooded killer?

TWENTY-TWO

I lifted my water glass and took a sip, unable to muster any true fear. Nerissa didn't seem the type to kill anyone; she'd be above that sort of thing. "What grade did Percy teach?" I asked. "Was he instructing the witch kids on magic or everybody on something like math and reading?"

"It's a charter, so technically we answer to the State of California." She gave a smug smile. "I put him down as an art teacher. But it doesn't matter. We make sure Sacramento never asks too many questions."

I waited a moment before giving her a knowing smile, as if it had taken my slow brain more time to figure out she was admitting to using magic to cut through the red tape. "It's awesome witch families can get a public education. Not everyone can afford it."

"Surely *you* were educated," she said. "Bellrose is an illustrious name."

I nodded. "I went to some of the best schools. The Protectorate recruited me right after graduation. But I wasn't cut out to be an agent." I gave a self-deprecating shrug. Let her think it was nepotism that got me that far and that only harsh reality put me in my proper place. It's what most people had thought for years now.

"As I tell the children, everyone has to find their own path." She pushed to her feet, looked at her watch again, then gave me a we're-done-here nod. "Best wishes with the show. I've never had time for gardening. Maybe when I'm too old to do anything else."

It wasn't easy to keep a bland, stupid smile on my face as she walked away. I wasn't one to spend hours digging and weeding either, but her attitude offended me. One reason I didn't garden enough was because it was hard work. Being older wasn't going to make it easier.

After Nerissa had left, the atmosphere in the restaurant became noticeably more relaxed. Conversation resumed, plates rattled again, and Bruce came over with the check.

"A friend of yours?" he asked me.

I gave him a worried smile. "She's nicer than I expected. I heard she was pretty tough."

"Heard from who? You look too young to have kids." He eyed me more carefully, long enough to make me worry about my disguise. "And too old to be a student in her time here."

"My friend was a teacher there," I said. "But he..." I looked down and let genuine grief hit me. I'd kept pushing it out of my mind, but Percy, a peer of mine, had just died.

"Ah," Bruce said. "You knew Mr. Tuff. He seemed nice enough. The kids walked all over him, but you know how witch kids can be. He had to learn a lot of new defensive spells. They kept messing with him."

Bruce laughed, but I wondered if it had been as funny for Percy as it had been for his kids. The school went through twelfth grade, which included eighteen-year-olds. Some of them would be training to be Protectorate agents —or being captured by them—within a year. Had one or more of them gotten into serious Shadow, and Percy had needed help dealing with it? As a teacher in a remote witch enclave, the politics of coming down hard on one of his pupils could get him into trouble. Parents would be defensive, offended, angry—not to mention the kids themselves.

"What kind of things did they do to him?" I asked.

"Oh, it was nothing, really," Bruce said, still looking amused. "Turning his shirts inside out, sticking his phone on the ceiling... You know how kids are. It really was nothing. Tuff took care of it without making too big a deal of it. He was all right."

Wanting to keep him talking, I gave him a sad but reassuring smile. "Yeah, I know what it's like. I'm sure they didn't mean any harm," I said. "He... I'm hearing mixed stories about how he died. First I heard he died in a car accident, then I heard it was a heart attack. Do you know what the real story is?"

Bruce looked away for a moment, then turned back to me with a shrug. "Both, is what they said." He touched a thick gold chain around his wrist and muttered a blessing for the dead. "One caused the other. Seemed young to me to have his heart just kaput like that, but you never know, do you? Something made him give up his big job in the Protectorate and come here. Maybe it was that. The stress got to him."

It was true that Percy had burned out under the stress of being an agent, but it hadn't been enough to kill him.

Not wanting Bruce to have my credit card—a physical object which he could enchant to reveal more about me than I wanted—I placed cash on the table. It hadn't been possible to do the same at the motel, but I'd avoid handing over plastic again. Even with all the Silicon Valley expats, Elwin apparently hadn't updated to high-tech methods.

"I need to go pay my respects," I said, wriggling out of my seat. "Do you know where the accident was?"

It was polite of me to imply he hadn't already been there himself. I bet every witch in fifty miles—and the fae too—had gone to the scene. A witch's corpse could leave behind usable magic.

"Just down the coastal road." He touched his gold bracelet again. "Well, below it. On the rocks. Half mile south."

I thanked him and left the restaurant, aware of a dozen witches' gazes following me out. Once on the sidewalk, I maintained my harmless-little-me disguise for another block before finally letting it down. Keeping it at full blast was tiring, and I'd need to pace myself.

As I strolled south, I glimpsed the ocean to my right between gaps in the two-story, nineteenth-century buildings that made up downtown Elwin. There wasn't much; four jewelers, the old bar, a café, a couple of gift and antique shops that must've also sold witch supplies under the counter, a tax preparer, and a few hair and beauty salons. Soon there was only the road winding along the cliff face. If I wanted to continue, I'd have to walk on a narrow shoulder along traffic next to a fatal drop over the cliff.

I didn't like those odds, so I turned back. Eventually I found a well-worn path down to the beach. Cold and windy, the spot wouldn't attract many honeymooners, but there was a wide stretch of sand that would be tolerable for a short visit under a warm blanket. Off in the distance was a pier marking the shallow harbor. Although Elwin might have been a fishing port once, it seemed to only have a handful of boats that looked recreational moored there now.

I took off my boots and walked down to the flat, damp sand above the waves. The tide was out, giving me access to the southern stretch of beach that became narrower as I approached the cliffs ahead.

Even from a distance, I could feel where Percy had met his death. It took me a few more minutes to reach the end of the beach. Rocky pools gave way to a slope of impenetrable boulders.

Well, they would've been if witches and nonmag people hadn't worked to make the crash site accessible. Now there was a clear path through the rocks to a shadowy depression, strangely free of the pooling seawater and critters that occupied its surroundings.

His car had been removed, in part by magical means. All that remained now was the psychic scar of a lost life.

I stood several feet away, the wind blowing hair into my face, struck by the loneliness of the spot. I hoped Percy had loved the sea and that that had been one of the reasons he'd moved there, because part of his spirit would always be on this beach, striding over the sand, dipping his toes in the tide pools with the crabs and anemone.

I wiped a tear from my cheek. He didn't deserve this.

I looked up. The road was over twenty feet above. It must've been terrifying to feel his wheels roll over the edge, feel the sickening drop—

But maybe he'd been dead already. Maybe he'd already been killed, his heart stopped, before his driverless car took him all the way down to this damp, sea-swept grave.

There wasn't anything left to tell me otherwise. His body had obviously been taken by the authorities, but neither was there a car or even a scrap of metal or glass. Every piece had been scavenged by the unsentimental witches—and Brightness knew what else—who populated the area.

Without a clue to guide my next steps, I whispered a respectful spell for the dead.

I didn't make a formal vow to avenge his death, which would've been too dangerous (since failure could make my life forfeit). But silently, with my heart, I promised to find out who had killed him.

And fight to have justice done.

TWENTY-THREE

Although I survived my first night under the probably-not-a-serial-killer's roof, I wasn't tempted to sleep late. Just after seven, when coastal Elwin was still gloomy under the fog, I walked to a café downtown where I could have breakfast. Like Bruce's restaurant, it was filled with witches; this one, however, held more of the recent arrivals. They all had laptops out, wore earbuds, and ignored me.

After eating my avocado toast and tepid tea, I tore my paper napkin into pieces and arranged them on my empty plate, pondering my situation. Without anyone watching me, I risked a little prophecy spell and stared at the napkin fragments for insight.

Nothing.

I was frustrated, afraid I hadn't learned anything useful yet. And I was feeling lonely, having had to cancel my video chat with Seth the night before to protect my secret about where I was.

"There you are. Did you get me anything?"

I heard the man's voice, recognized it, but just couldn't believe it.

I looked up. No, it wasn't Darius after all. This guy was clearly one of the original, eccentric witches who'd been living in Elwin before the urban witch invasion. His style shouted antiestablishment: faded, stained sweatshirt; baggy jeans, Birkenstocks. Shells, copper amulets, and wood beads were attached to his body in various forms.

My wood beads.

"Da—?" The word caught in my throat. He'd cast a silence spell on me.

"Don't say it." He sat in the chair next to me and clamped a hand over my knee. His grinning smile paired with an unblinking stare pinned me to my seat.

Darius, I thought silently. It really was him.

I nodded to show I understood the need for secrecy. In fact, his presence was a disaster. I was immediately thinking of who I should blame. Raynor could've sent him *instead* of me—why put me in danger like this by risking my cover?

"It's awesome to get away, isn't it?" Darius asked. Releasing the spell on my throat, he moved his hand to mine on the table and patted it. He wore a bracelet made of braided jute and redwood beads—one of my cheaper creations that I sold at Birdie's bookstore. When he left his hand over mine, continuing the stupid grin, I began to have a very unpleasant feeling about what *his* cover story was going to be.

"Where are you staying?" I asked quietly.

He held my gaze. "I wasn't able to find us a better place," he said. "Sorry, baby. We'll just have to make the motel work."

Pulling my hand free, I stood up and brought my dishes to the tub by the counter. The witch barista glanced at me, ran a scan over my used cup—sometimes witches left a residue of usable power, which I hadn't—then dismissed me as too boring to look at again.

But I had the uneasy sensation that there was somebody who was interested in looking at me. I scanned the café but saw only the same indifference as before. Then I peered through the doorway behind the counter into a back room.

Bruce stood just inside, staring at me. When he saw me recognize him, he saluted me with his mug and turned away.

It seemed Bruce was the kingpin of eating establishments in Elwin. As a witch, I didn't like the idea another witch was controlling what so many other witches were consuming. A potion witch could command a lot of power from that position.

As I began to walk back to Darius, I sensed the essence of the Chevy truck tattoo I'd felt the night before. I glanced over at a nearby table and saw a man with shoulder-length white hair reading an actual newspaper.

When it came to privacy, Elwin seemed to be worse than Silverpool. Darius was going to explain himself but not with so many witches around.

I strode out the door, knowing he'd follow. I considered my options—Jeep, motel—then walked to the corner and stabbed the button to change the light. The harbor was just a block away; I'd find a place to talk privately on the beach.

Down the street, heading toward me, I was surprised to see Clem walking a small gray dog with pointy ears. Wearing dark glasses, a black beanie, and bulky noise-canceling headphones, Clem gave off powerful don't-talk-to-me vibes—possibly enhanced with magic—so I didn't. But to my surprise, when she spotted me standing at the corner, she gave me a wave and a faint smile before turning around and hurrying away.

I smiled, feeling more kinship with her than most would.

As I'd expected, Darius followed me outside. I allowed him to take my hand and kiss my cheek, taking reluctant comfort in the warm touch of another human being.

While we walked across the street, I pictured Seth's loving face, felt his kiss on my cheek, his deft touch—

"Demon's balls," I cursed under my breath. *Seth* had been the one to summon Darius. I felt his fae fingerprints.

We kept walking until we reached the end of the street where it met the ocean. I took the rocky path down to the beach again.

"Come on, darling," Darius said. "The tide is out. You can collect some shells and beach glass. And those rocks you like."

Now that I'd realized he wasn't acting on Protectorate orders or by his own heroic motives, it was impossible to be angry. For Darius to come to Elwin because a changeling had pressured him had to be more unpleasant for him than it was for me.

"Sorry," I said.

Darius scrambled down to the beach and held out his hand to assist me with the last few steps of the steep descent. "It gets worse," he said. "I'm on leave. I asked to use my vacation time."

"Demon's balls," I said again.

"I share the sentiment."

We stood on the sand, looking at each other.

"Sorry," I said again. "How did Seth make you do it?"

"I'm not sure," Darius said. "One minute I was on the bus heading home, the next I was packing to come here. I was on the road within an hour."

"You must've been up all night," I said.

"Most of it."

It was at least a five-hour drive. "You must be exhausted."

"I am," he said. "It took me a while to find you. Your disguise is pretty effective. I don't feel that same scary buzz coming off you I usually do."

I grinned. I really did like being called scary.

Talk about scary—how had Seth known I was here, that it might be dangerous? I thought back to yesterday. I'd arrived, met the creepy Lacoste, gone to the river...

"The river," I said to myself. When I'd dipped my hand

into it to collect the water for my spell, I must've triggered some lake fairy magic Seth had connected to me.

"I told Raynor how I'll be spending my leave," he said. "I didn't even try to come up with a cover story for him. At least your boyfriend doesn't have the power to stop me from doing that."

Or he wanted Raynor to know as a backup. Seth and Raynor shared a weird truce to work together on keeping me alive. "Raynor better pay you for this. He's a big reason I had to come. He told me he didn't have the resources to send an agent." I looked out at the waves, wondering if Seth would feel me if I put my feet in the water or if his powers only worked in fresh water on land. "It wouldn't be right for you to lose your vacation time over me."

"It would be on brand, though," he said. "You can't claim your existence has been exactly great for my career."

"Hey, you're doing pretty good for a Flint—excuse me, a Quartz." He'd just been promoted, largely because of the accomplishments he'd displayed in adventures with me. "You got the confidence of the Director of Diamond Street to give you this juicy undercover assignment."

"Unofficial and unpaid. Not very juicy."

"Better than tracking down Shadow market goods in a strip mall in Livermore," I said.

"My sister made Quartz and they sent her to Paris," he said.

"Rochelle's in Paris?" I smiled. Last I'd heard, after taking a leave from the Protectorate, his sister had been living in Berkeley on an assignment caring for an old witch. "They probably didn't want her to quit again. She's too good to lose."

"Unlike me," he said.

I grinned. Finally, I had an opportunity to point at his outfit. "Well, look at you. It's hardly professional."

He glared at me and said nothing.

"Who came up with the disguise?" I asked. "Was it Seth?"

"Please, I've got skills. He was smart enough to let me go home first." He held out his arms in a flourish. "This isn't Dash's first assignment. He's had time to get perfected."

"Dash?" I asked, laughing. "That's your name?"

"That way if I slip up, or somebody else does, I can pretend it's just a nickname for Darius," he said.

He was actually enjoying this. The man needed to have more fun outside of work.

I bent down and picked up a small reddish rock, rolled it between my fingers with a scanning spell, then handed it to him. The rock was jasper, useful with interrogation spells.

He made a pretense of loving the gift—clutching it to his chest, embracing me—then put it into his pocket.

I rolled my eyes at his mockery. The real Darius would never utilize a rock he found on the beach. The closest would be a lost diamond earring.

"Does Dash ride an old VW bus he bought off a dude in Berkeley?" I asked.

"I hitched a ride," he said. "Because my *girlfriend* is going to give me a ride home."

"Hitched? With whom?" I felt a twinge of unease in my stomach. "Who just happened to be driving from San Francisco to Elwin in the middle of the night?"

"He was an old guy. A landscaper or something," he said. "Coming up here for the garden show."

My stomach tightened. There were small odds of magical beings like Seth relying on coincidences.

"What was the old guy's name?" I asked.

Darius took a small, black leather notebook out of his tie-dyed sweatshirt pocket and flipped it open. The business item was incongruous with his bohemian disguise.

I could feel the name coming off the page even before he spoke.

"Rupert," he read.

TWENTY-FOUR

I bit my lip. What did it mean? Maybe Seth had simply found somebody trustworthy who was already on his way.

"What is it?" Darius asked sharply.

After a pause, I told him about hiring a garden designer named Rupert.

"Big ears, lots of stone jewelry?" he asked. "Like that pebble you just handed me?"

"I didn't meet him, so I don't know."

"And I didn't get his last name," Darius said. He made a note in the book, shaking his head and muttering with disgust.

"That's not like you," I said.

"Of course it's not like me," he said. "It was obviously part of the hex that got me here."

"Fairies can't hex," I said.

"Seth's not really a fairy anymore though, is he?"

"I don't know what he is, but he didn't mean any harm. He was just..."

"Protecting you," Darius said.

"Yeah."

"Obviously Raynor didn't mind, or he wouldn't have let me be here with you." Out of habit, he started to adjust his clothes, straightening his sweatshirt and pulling up his jeans. Then, seeming to realize what he was doing, he stopped and scowled.

Raynor did always like to have his herb-snorting fingers in the pie.

I saw a shimmering stone on the beach that was giving off a powerful buzz of energy. I bent down and picked up a lovely round agate with beautiful banding. "You can go home after you've had something to eat," I said, handing him that rock too. It wasn't payment enough for the magical kidnapping, and he didn't appreciate its value, but it was a start. "I'll call Seth and tell him to leave you alone. Raynor, too."

"You're giving me *permission*, are you?"

"I don't need you," I said. "It just complicates things to have you here. The last thing I want is to look like some dangerous Protectorate agent out for blood."

Pocketing the agate, Darius gave me an amused once-over. "Is that why you've made yourself look like Birdie?"

I stared at him. "I haven't."

"You have. Even your hair looks like hers." He frowned at me. "It's not bad. You should consider wearing it like that all the time."

"I'm not *wearing* it like hers," I said, tugging at the long, silky waves. "It's an enchantment. My real hair is nothing like this." Its natural state was chin-length and frizzy.

"Obviously."

He was trolling me. "Look, I'm sorry you were dragged here in the middle of the night. I didn't ask him to do that." I looked inland toward Main Street. If Seth could get a strong Protectorate agent to the Humboldt coast within six hours, he could get me another vehicle. "Tell you what. Take my Jeep home. I'll find another way to get around." I took out my keys and held them out.

"Are you crazy? You just told me the garden designer who called you out of the blue just happened to be the same guy who drove me up here last night."

"He didn't call me—" I stopped. It *had* been him to call me. But he had to be connected in the garden design world to have heard about my project within a few hours. "We don't know if it was the same guy," I finished lamely.

"It was the same guy. This is the witch world. Come on."

I knew he was right. "It doesn't mean he's dangerous," I said weakly.

Darius just sighed and shook his head. The beads dangling from his earlobes bounced back and forth.

I wagged the Jeep keys at him again. "Go on. You know you want to leave."

"No," he said. "I'm already here. Somebody's killed an ex-Protectorate witch. One you knew. You need backup."

I pointed at my enchanted necklaces. "Me?"

"Your disguise is fair," he said, "but it can't compare with mine. Other than changing into a cat or a turtle or something, it's the best you've ever seen. Admit it."

"It's fine until you open your mouth," I said, "and then it's obvious you're not what you look like. Laid-back dudes off the grid shouldn't talk like chief financial officers."

He took out his notebook and began to jot something down.

"What are you writing?" I asked.

"Making a reminder for myself. You're right. I forgot about my voice." He clicked the end of his pen and shut the notebook. "I've got a steel cartilage piercing that might be strong enough to consistently affect my vocal cords. I'll try out some spells when we get to the motel."

I stared at him, not sure if he was kidding. "It's not just your voice. It's the way you use it."

He rubbed his mouth, regarding me. After a moment he said, "You think I sound too authoritative?"

"Yeah, and you use words like *authoritative*," I said. "It doesn't fit with the persona."

He sighed. "I guess you've got a point. I'll try to work on that." He tucked his notebook in his front jean pocket and began walking toward land. "Let's go find this Rupert and interrogate the Brightness out of him."

"He's probably a pawn just as much as you are," I said. "I'll talk to him alone. The minute he sees you, he'll know you're part of the investigation."

He stopped. "Why? I'm just your quirky boyfriend joining you at your garden thing."

"He knows I'm here because of Percy."

"Why did you tell him that?"

"Because I needed a reason to explain everything. He already knew about Zoe paying for it." I took a deep breath. "He doesn't know I'm here to investigate or anything. I told him that Percy invited me right before he died, kind of as a joke, betting me I couldn't do it, and now I wanted to honor his memory."

He stared at me with an uncomfortably paternal look— more disappointed than angry. "How was it possible you were ever trained as an agent? I'm starting to think that disguise is revealing the true you."

It was true I'd been careless, but I held his gaze. "I needed to explain why I was hiring somebody to do all the work for me."

"People hire professionals all the time," Darius said. "I'm sure most of the displays are paid for by witches just trying to look good."

"Yes, but not on such short notice." I sighed. "Look, there's no point arguing the point. It's too late. He knows I'm here because of Percy, and he knows Zoe Thornton is paying for it."

"Let's go talk to him together anyway," he said. "At least you owe me that."

"I don't—" I cut myself off. Maybe I did owe him a little bit, given there was no guarantee he'd get his vacation time back. "Fine. Do you know where he's staying?"

"Don't you?" he asked.

I took out my phone. "I'll ask him. He mentioned a bed-and-breakfast. We planned on meeting today anyway."

After I'd sent Rupert a quick text, I climbed up the path to the road.

When I got to the top, I saw another rock that was even cooler than the two on the beach. Peeking out from under the fleshy pale green leaves of a dudleya was a smooth white rock. A moonstone. I picked it up, pleased with the good luck of moonstone and dudleya—more commonly known as liveforever—found together.

Reaching the top of the path behind me with a poorly contained yawn, Darius tripped over his feet as he joined me on the sidewalk.

He was suffering for my sake, so I offered him the moonstone.

"Oh, I couldn't," he said sarcastically. "You've already done so much."

I took his hand in mine, set the stone in his palm, and gave him an apologetic look. "I insist. You're here because of me. It's the best I can do right now."

He rolled his eyes but put it in his pocket. "You texted him?" he asked.

"Yes."

"Demon's balls. He should've gotten right back to you." He scowled at me. "I don't like it."

"It's only been a minute. And it's early. He's probably taking a quick nap." *Like you should be doing*, I added silently.

Feeling Darius grow increasingly irritable beside me, we headed south on a narrow sidewalk along the coastal road. To my relief, he didn't demand we hold hands again.

There was a lot of traffic for such a small community, but since most vehicles were pickups and vans marked with landscaping and garden businesses, I figured most were there for the show.

The phone in my pocket was quiet. I, too, was becoming alarmed by Rupert's silence but didn't let on.

A few minutes went by. The fog was giving way to warm sunshine, and I pulled on my sunglasses. It almost felt like the summer it was. It might even be warm enough later to take off my sweatshirt.

"Still hasn't gotten back to you," Darius said, his tone low and cold.

"No, but I'm sure—"

Obviously assuming the worst, he took my arm and used a hidden diamond cuff link to cast a protective charm around me.

"I can do my own defensive spells," I said, pulling free.

Darius only raised an eyebrow and waved a palm in front of my face to cast another one.

"While we're waiting for him to get back to me," I said, "and he *will*, we can go to the school. Percy was officially an art teacher, Nerissa said. She's the principal. I've already talked to her—and her niece, a kid named Marta— and written up some notes. Oh, and I talked to another parent, Bruce. He owns the restaurant and I think the café, too. He said Percy was a pushover. The kids gave him a hard time." I was eager to earn back his respect for my agenting skills.

"It's Summer vacation. And a Saturday. You want to go to the school?"

He had a point. "It's next to the fairgrounds. Maybe Rupert is there."

"This isn't amateur hour," he said. "I don't need to wander around blind. I can trace old Rupert with this book I took from his back seat." He pulled something out of his rear jeans pocket and held it up: a thin yellow paperback held together with packing tape. *Magic Bees of the West*, the title read, its font very 1980s.

"You stole his book before you knew there might be something sketchy about him?"

He waved it at me. "Unlike some people, I plan ahead for unknown contingencies. Have you forgotten everything you learned at the Protectorate? Take samples. *Always*. It horrifying you're out here doing agent work without using agent skills. Do you *want* to die?"

"Tell you what," I said. "If Rupert doesn't text me back within two hours, then—"

"Two? He could create a massive Summoning Circle before then."

"What herbs have you been sniffing? Why would he want to call demons here?"

Darius crossed his arms over his chest. "I don't guess why Shadowed witches do what they do," he said, "I just stop them from doing it."

I started to believe Darius really, really needed a nap. Like a toddler, he'd need to be redirected. If I kept trying to argue with him, he'd just push harder. Throw a big-boy tantrum.

"OK, you win," I said. "We'll track him down. But first, since we're really close, how about we go to the crime scene? The crash on the beach has been picked clean, but maybe there's something we can pick up on the road where he went over."

When I'd been alone, it had been unsafe to explore the narrow road above the cliff, but with two it would be possible to do a proper scan.

"You know where he went over?" Darius asked.

I knew mentioning the site of Percy's death would be too tempting for him to resist. "It did occur to me that a crime scene might have useful information, you know. It's just up here. He was driving to school." I pointed ahead. "That's another reason I was walking this way."

"At least you haven't forgotten everything," he said, bringing his hand up to his mouth. He made the funny face people do when they're trying to stifle a yawn.

"You need to sleep."

He shook his head. "No time. Let's look at the scene."

CHAPTER

TWENTY-FIVE

We walked on the sidewalk until it ended, leaving us to make our way cautiously on the narrow shoulder between the road and the cliff.

On the other side of the road inland was a grassy slope topped with cedar and cypress. To our right was a sheer drop down to the rocks where Percy's car had landed.

"You're sure he'd been driving south?" Darius asked me. We stood together near the edge, each protecting the other with interlinking boundary spells. Rock fairies that only I could see were looking up at us curiously from the boulders below.

I nodded. I could already feel the wheels going over and knew Percy had been headed toward the school. Inhaling deeply through my mouth, I tried to detect the residue of any hex. Sometimes a witch cast a spell that tasted sour, which I associated with negative emotions such as jealousy, spite, anger, hatred. Emotions themselves weren't Shadowed, so it didn't mean a crime had been committed if the air was sour.

The only emotion I could taste, however, was fear. Like a drop of blood, it stained the ground where we stood.

"He went over right here," I said. "I can feel him, but... I'm not sure what else."

Darius squatted down and scooped up a handful of dirt and gravel. He whispered a few words into it, licked a finger, then drew a triangle shape through it. A moment later, he looked up at me with an expression I recognized.

A thirst for justice. The blazing fury in his eyes made me take a step backward.

"Yeah," I whispered. "Right there with you."

His hands were fisted. "He was alive when he went over the edge."

"I'd hoped he'd died before that," I said, swallowing hard, "but I agree. I can taste his fear."

"Terror," Darius said. "The man knew he was breathing his last breath."

My own emotions welled up inside me. Through the flush of anger and grief, I suddenly saw a different type of fae presence around us. It wasn't embodied like the rock fairies, with wings and faces, but simply streaks of glowing energy. They were vaguely familiar. Perhaps they weren't fae after all but... I tried to study them from the corners of my vision, which was often more revealing than head-on.

But then I blinked, and the images disappeared.

Darius waited in silence, knowing I could see things he couldn't. Finally I looked at him and shook my head. "I almost saw something, but I'm not sure."

"Something? Sure of what?"

"It might just be my imagination," I said.

"Alma, you might be a terrible agent, but I'd never doubt your Sight. What did you think you saw?"

I rubbed my eyes. They hurt from the strain of staring into the fae realm. "It wasn't human. At first I thought it was fairy, but not quite."

Darius's voice dropped to a growl. "Demon?"

"No, no, nothing like that." I shrugged, smiled. "Gnome. Maybe?"

"A *gnome* killed him?"

"I told you, I don't know."

"Demon's balls," Darius said. "That's just what we need. Homicidal gnomes."

Given what had just happened to Willy, I couldn't help but shudder. Demons and witches killing each other were bad enough, but what if a gnome had turned to Shadow? We'd already had a lake fairy start an uprising. I wasn't sure humans would survive another supernatural battle if a creature as mysteriously powerful as Willy got in the game. The only thing worse I could think of would be a genie.

"I don't like this at all," I said.

I expected Darius to make a sarcastic comment, something like *Not me, I love it*, but instead, he took my hand. I felt another diamond cuff link protective spell settle over me. It was stronger than any I'd ever felt Darius create before. He was an expert at surveillance and, with demons, *killing until a smoking husk*, but the enchantment he'd settled around me was beautifully defensive.

"Seth was right to send for me," he said, closing his eyes. He swayed slightly on his feet with the drain on his energies both magical and physical.

I squeezed his hand and released it. It was too soon for me to say I was glad he was there, though I was grateful for his presence. If anything happened to him, I'd feel responsible.

Maybe he was right about finding Rupert as soon as possible. I took out my phone to try calling him, then was cheerfully surprised to see he'd sent an email.

I didn't tell Darius, who still looked as if he needed a few minutes to recover from the protective spells he'd put around me. And if Rupert said something suspicious or annoying, I didn't want to be standing two feet from a fatal drop down a sea cliff when I shared it with Darius.

"Do you feel anything else?" Darius demanded.

"No. Just the faint gnome residue and... and Percy's fear."

"Then let's get out of here," Darius said, grabbing my

arm. Another jolt of energy—his magic, connecting with mine—ran up my shoulder.

"Agreed."

When there was a gap in the traffic, we ran across the road to the safety of the other side. We scrambled up a grassy slope and hiked to the top of a hill that separated the town of Elwin with its shops, homes, and surrounding forest from a flat, sprawling plot of land with several industrial-looking buildings and a large parking lot. It was buzzing with activity—trucks, vans, cars, trailers, cement trucks, sledgehammers, front loaders, even a cherry picker.

"That's the fairgrounds," I said. "Site of the garden show. Obviously."

"Seems early for all this," Darius said. "Isn't the show next week?"

"Opening day is Wednesday. That's in only four days. Even with magic, it takes time to set up." As I watched the frenzied work underway, I began to feel performance anxiety. All that energy was contagious. "I'm learning witches take the Elwin Flower Show very, very seriously."

Cramped in a corner near the fairgrounds was a U-shaped building with a small sports field. Typical of California schools, it was a squat, rectangular single story with its individual classrooms opening to the outdoors.

"*That's* the school that attracted all these Bay Area witches up here?" Darius asked. "I've seen nicer public storage facilities."

"Maybe it looks better from up close," I said. Some of the boarding schools I'd gone to had been quite luxurious—one had been a converted ski resort, another had been an elaborate estate confiscated from witches convicted of Shadow crimes. But even when I'd been with nonmag kids, the schools had been in larger communities that could afford a nicer campus.

Darius had pulled out compact birding binoculars and was looking more closely at the scene below us. "Ah," Darius said. "It's enchanted. Not bad—I bet one of the witches used to be Protectorate. You barely see it. Like a crime scene with a forgetting spell around it."

"Sad how everything reminds us of a crime scene," I said.

"If we're around, it usually is."

While he was busy with the binoculars, I used the opportunity to take out my phone and read the email from Rupert.

Because of poor internet service, the images didn't load, but the text came through right away. It was just a quick note with the name of his bed-and-breakfast followed by the design he planned with photo attachments.

"Rupert got back to me," I said. "He said he'd be down there all day. At the fairgrounds. He's started working on my garden."

Darius put down the binoculars and frowned at me. "He drove all night. What charm is *he* using to stay awake?"

"You're determined to be suspicious of him."

"I'm determined to do my job," he said, shoving the binoculars under his shirt, "which is being suspicious of everyone and everything. You should be the same. After everything you've been through, Alma—"

"Yes. Yes, I know. Let's go meet him, scan him, get this over with."

Darius had seen a paved path that led from the fairgrounds and school to the rest of town. We hiked across the hill until we met up with it, then walked the rest of the way with the bikes, dog walkers, kids on scooters, and two witches pulling a wagon filled with shrubs and flowers.

"Doesn't anybody have a job?" Darius grumbled under his breath.

"It's Saturday," I said. "And I bet for lots of these folks, the show *is* their job."

Darius scoffed, shaking his head. He kept rubbing his eyes and scowling, looking more like a burned-out toddler than ever.

I reached through my pockets until I found a sachet I'd

made at home. Filled with dried calypso orchid petals and the tiny white blossoms of native *yerba buena*, as well as a fragment of an iron nail—all of it then soaked in Silverpool springwater—it could give him relief from his discomfort. "Take this," I said, holding it out to him.

He gave it the side-eye and shook his head.

"If I'm going to accept your help," I said, "you should take mine."

His eyes blazed above his tight jaw, making him look as if he wanted to break something. For a split second, I felt afraid.

But then he turned and scrubbed his face with his hands. I noticed now that he wore a ring on each finger—more than usual, and these looked like low-grade silver instead of the gold and platinum they actually were beneath their enchantment. I sensed a tremendous wave of magical power moving through him, and when he lowered his hands, his face was calm, cheerful, and slightly dopey. "Sure, baby. Whatever makes you happy."

Concerned with his powerful mood, I swallowed hard. "It's a healing sachet," I said carefully. "It'll help you feel better."

"I'm not sick."

"You're sleep-deprived. I'm guessing it's not just last night, either. Have you been having trouble sleeping lately?"

He looked over my shoulder and scowled at a passing wagon filled with Dachshund puppies. They were only a witch mother's enchantment for her child—a toddler was sitting with them, giggling as her imaginary friends crawled over her—but any normal person would've still found it impossible not to smile.

He didn't.

"How much sleep did you get the night before last?" I asked.

He rubbed his face again. "I haven't slept more than

four hours a night for a month. And what hours I get aren't consecutive. I just can't sleep."

No wonder he wasn't himself. I myself felt deprived with three times that. "Clearly, then, your body isn't getting what it needs. That's a health issue." I pushed the sachet under his nose. "It'll help you be more productive."

I'd hit the workaholic's bull's-eye. With a sigh, he finally took the sachet and sniffed it. "What's in it?"

"Iron, herbs, and springwater," I said.

"That's it?"

"Scan it yourself."

I could feel him begin to create an inspection spell, but then he muttered, "Oh, to Shadow with it" and shoved it in his jeans pocket without looking at it again.

We resumed walking. I counted our steps, eager to see how long it would take to kick in.

One... Two... Three... Fo—

"Hey, I can feel it," he said.

I smirked. "Don't sound so surprised."

"My head doesn't hurt anymore."

"I'm glad to hear that."

He took the sachet out of his pocket and held it up to his temple. "I can feel the iron. I didn't realize it could be used for healing."

I bit back a retort. Healing and feeling good wasn't something they emphasized in the Protectorate. "It also has herbs."

He waved that aside. "I bet it's the springwater on the iron that really gives it a kick."

Botanical magic had never impressed him, and I'd given up trying to change his mind. "It'll work better if you wear it against your chest," I said. "Closer to your heart."

With a nod, he pulled the binoculars out from under his T-shirt, tied the sachet to it, then tucked the bundle back down out of sight. Under the garish tie-dye swirls of his shirt and the subtle techniques of his magical disguise, the lump was invisible.

As we resumed walking toward the fairgrounds, his walk became peppier, his comments less gloomy. By the time we reached the edge of the fairgrounds, he was actually smiling.

TWENTY-SIX

Rupert's email had included the location for my future exhibit. After walking around for fifteen minutes—dodging the landscapers who were hauling plants, gravel, sod, boulders, fountains, and metal ornamentation—we finally found my assigned section at a far corner near the school.

Unlike some of the other installations, the gardens in the hearth-witch category didn't have a building, path, or natural feature to work around—other than old tree roots that made the ground uneven and undoubtedly difficult to plant into.

On the other side of the school's chain-link fence, wedged between the playground and the stump of an old tree, was the students' poorly maintained compost pile. There were flies, and it smelled.

"Perfect, I'm right next to the garbage dump," I said. Even though the garden show was just a cover story, I was offended on behalf of all hearth witches.

Darius pointed at a gray-haired man lying face down on the ground. "That's him. Rupert." He sounded pleased. "Ha. He *did* need to take a nap."

A woman approached from behind us, carrying a ladder. Around thirty, she had bronze-toned skin and braids arranged above a straw sun visor. "He's not napping," she said in a businesslike tone. "He's surveying."

Darius turned to look at her. "Oh." He reached up to adjust his shirt—an old habit—but finding only the sweatshirt, he pulled at the neckline. "Right. Sorry."

Seeing Darius's unusually meek reply, I was afraid she'd flung a hex at him—until I saw the look in his eyes. They gleamed with the intensity of a man, not a Protectorate agent.

I myself was fascinated by her jewelry, which was half metal and half botanical. I had the impression if I were to count each piece, there would be an exact fifty-fifty split.

"I'm Alma Bellrose. This"—I waved around the sad little plot of earth—"is my exhibit. Or it's going to be."

The woman's chilly expression warmed a little. "Oh, of course. Rupe told me about you." She held up a hand in a witch's polite no-contact salute. "Holly."

"Your name or your favorite plant?" Darius asked.

We both turned to look at him. His smile became awkward.

Taking pity, I put my hand on his arm. "This is Dash, my honey," I said. "The man, not the bee vomit."

"Honey isn't bee vomit," Darius said. "While technically the nectar does get regurgitated when the bee returns home, by no means is it in any way a digestive product. Bees have a second organ just for nectar. It's an entirely separate system."

I was alarmed. Maybe my sachet had done something weird to him.

Weird or not, Holly approved. "Exactly right." She gave Darius a closer look. "I can never get people to understand that. Even witches argue with me."

Darius gave her a lopsided grin. "My cousin's son set me straight. The family keeps bees."

"Nice." She turned to me. "You probably want to talk to Rupert. He'll be free in a minute."

I looked over at Rupert, who remained prone. A magical

cloud spread around him, seeping into the dry soil under his body. "What's he doing?" I asked quietly, not wanting to disturb him.

"Connecting with the earth. We'll haul in a lot of good soil and plant in raised beds, but he says it's important to feel the deeper world beneath to make a good garden."

Darius eyed Rupert with suspicion, reassuring me he hadn't totally lost his mind. "Have you two worked together a long time?"

"If a project needs it, he calls me up. He can't do the heavy lifting he used to." She went to a bag on a small folding chair and returned with a tablet, tapping on the screen as she walked. "Your original design application was really vague. I'm surprised they approved it, honestly. Elwin usually demands more details. Your 2D sketch doesn't even list the plants by name. And there aren't any specific plants at all. Just a few vague blobs with general categories listed off to the side."

I plastered a smile on my face. I didn't know what Rupert had told her about me and didn't want to contradict his story, so I just shrugged.

"Friends in high places?" As she asked the question, a gold pendant strung from a cotton string around her neck emitted a faint aura of magic.

She might have just been naturally nosy with everyone, but either way, I wasn't going to explain anything until I knew more about her.

An awkward silence grew. I glanced at Rupert, who was getting to his feet.

"Alma was friends with the poor dude who went over the cliff," Darius said, coming to my rescue. "The teacher. He filled out the forms as a..."

Rupert came up behind Holly. "A bet," he said. "I hope you don't mind, Alma, but I told Holly about him. Everyone was talking about the witch from the school who'd just died, and she guessed I knew something about it. It's hard to hide things from a witch with mind magic."

He and I shared a no-contact salute in greeting. Rupert looked as if he'd once been a fair-skinned man, but years outdoors had left him with mottled, sun-damaged skin. As Darius had said, he did indeed have big ears, more obvious because of the sparseness of his gray hair. The ears were almost as noteworthy as his bright green eyes, which regarded me with curious interest.

"Whoa, mind magic. You too, huh?" Darius asked. "The dead dude had that, didn't he, babe?"

I tried not to roll my eyes. He'd finally remembered to affect a more laid-back drawl as he spoke, but he was overdoing it a little.

"He did," I said. "You too, Holly?"

She looked distressed. "Oh no. Rupert is just kidding, aren't you?" She gave the old man a tight smile.

I gritted my teeth, trying to hide my alarm. Why in Brightness had Rupert hired an associate who might have mind magic? It was going to be hard enough to avoid suspicion.

He gave us all a big smile. "Yes, sorry. Just a joke. My ego is still stinging because she saw right through my antiaging spells."

I hoped that was it. "It's nice to meet you in person," I said. "Thanks again for doing this."

Nodding, Rupert said to Holly, "How could I not help the poor girl? It might have been a playful game when he put her in the show, but now, I'm sure you agree, she's got to do what she can to honor him."

"An expensive game," Holly said. "But maybe ex-Protectorate types get starved for excitement."

Intelligent and curious, she wasn't the type of witch I wanted to have around. I needed to get Rupert away so we could talk. So far he hadn't given any indication he'd ever met Darius before, let alone had just given him a ride from San Francisco the night before. Maybe he could keep a secret.

Holly took off her gloves and set them near the ladder.

"I think I'll go get myself some coffee. Anybody want anything?" She shot me a grin. "Rupert says you're buying."

"That's right," I said. "Not right now, thanks."

Nobody else spoke up, so she strode away. Darius watched her depart with the same intensity as he'd greeted her, then caught himself and turned back to Rupert.

"Hey, dude," Darius said. "Thanks again for the lift last night."

Rupert smiled, glancing at me. "I tried not to give you away. Didn't know if it was a secret, your taking a ride from a stranger."

"Same thought here," Darius said. "Very appreciated, of course, but it did seem risky. Is that something you do often? Give total strangers a ride in the middle of the night?"

His tone was casual, but I knew he'd be analyzing the response with all the tools of the trade.

"No, not at all," Rupert said. "Actually, I've never picked up a hitchhiker before."

"Weird, don't you think?" Darius continued.

"Extremely. I don't know why I was compelled to pick you up." He cast a glance at me. "When I saw you here with Alma, I thought maybe it was *her* doing."

I tensed. If he thought I had that kind of power, what rumors had he heard about me? Was he pretending to be a garden designer as much as I was? Because of the short notice, I hadn't researched him as vigorously as I might have. In fact, barely at all.

Darius laughed. It sounded natural, so I knew he'd used magic to pull it off. "She'd love to have that kind of power, wouldn't you, sweetheart?"

"I didn't even know you were coming," I said. "I told you I'd be fine."

"Last-minute thing." Darius gave me a squeeze that made my shoulder joint pop. "Realized I was going to miss you too much."

"Sounds like fate then." Rupert smiled, his green eyes

twinkling at us. "I don't usually drive at night, but there just wasn't time to wait. I used every stimulant enchantment and herb I could get my hands on to keep my eyes open. Still buzzing, as you can see."

"Don't kill yourself on my account. Whatever you do will be fine." I realized that sounded like faint praise, so I added, "Great, I mean. It's not your fault I didn't give you much time. I really appreciate whatever you do."

"Not complaining, I knew what I was getting into, but I wanted to get up here and see the site before finalizing my design," Rupert said. "Only three full days to set up before previews. I'm going to be leaning hard on magic to get the installation done, but I still want to be sure before I proceed. I always second-guess myself. I'm a perfectionist."

I felt the sincerity in Rupert's statement and hoped Darius did too. If Rupert was lying about anything, it wasn't his eagerness to get working on my garden installation. He kept looking at the sad little plot of land, eyes darting from corner to corner, clearly hungry to literally dig in. He'd sent me a preliminary design plan in the email that I'd have to remember to look at. I doubted I'd want to make any changes. If he wanted to beautify the postage stamp of clay and gravel that would bear my name, I was grateful.

"Do you always lie on the ground like you were a minute ago?" Darius asked. Then he added in a more relaxed tone, "Very cool. Some kind of plant spell thing, right?"

Rupert looked embarrassed. "Ah, you saw that, did you? I bet I looked ridiculous. We do all kinds of tricks to design a successful garden." He ran a hand over his bald scalp. "There was a young gentleman who was on a winning streak a few years ago. Word got out he was doing an earth connection spell. I thought... Well, I thought I'd try it myself."

Many nights, in my backyard under the full moon, I'd created a necklace or focusing string. I usually drew power from above—the sky, stars, and moon—but probably would benefit from focusing downward more often.

"Is there a special herb or object you're using?" I asked. "For the spell?"

"Ah, no. Just..." Rupert waved his hands vaguely. "Just thinking about dirt, worms, sand, clay, that sort of thing. I'm really not the expert, as I said. Trying to do what I saw the young fella do. He didn't share his secrets with me, I'm afraid."

He was flushed, and I wondered why. Witches stole enchantment methods from each other all the time. It was like art; theft led to progress.

Darius gave me another joint-popping squeeze. "Well, baby, I think we better let Rupert here get on with things."

Before I could stop him, he'd spun me around and started walking away.

TWENTY-SEVEN

"**B**ut—" I began.

"I want to catch Holly by herself."

"I bet you do," I muttered.

"Get your mind out of the gutter," he said. "I need to ask her about the old man alone. He seems Bright to me—if your boyfriend could get me up here, why not him too?—but I want to be sure."

We met Holly as she was walking toward us, holding a take-out cup and a paper bag. She smiled when she saw us —at me or at Darius, I wasn't sure—and stopped to greet us.

"Done talking to Rupert already?" Hugging the cup to her chest, she unfurled the bag with the other hand and took out a churro. "I'm surprised. He usually can't stop talking."

"Is he always this intense?" I asked, figuring Darius wouldn't be the best lead for the conversation. "Winning isn't important to me. I just don't want to be too pathetic. I'm glad to have him, but I'm afraid he's working too hard at this. Staying up all night... rolling on the ground... I don't want him to hurt himself. Has he ever pushed himself too hard?"

"Elwin is huge. Everyone loses their mind," she said. "Even me. There's nothing like it, you know? The big time."

She looked like she was eager to get back to work. I made a mental note to return later to talk to her later.

"That's why you guys are here," I said. "No way I could do this by myself."

Holly lifted the churro in its wax paper wrapper toward her lips, then suddenly held it out to us. "I can't eat this by myself. Want to break off the top half? I haven't touched it yet."

I shook my head, but Darius said, "Groovy, thanks," and tore off the protruding end. "Starving."

It wasn't like him to accept food from a strange witch, so I hoped he was either trying to scan her magic or look like a laid-back type who would eat anything—and not sew the first thread in a physical and emotional bond.

"The truck is just around the corner," she said. "Easier than going into town for something. The old witches in Bruce's restaurant tend to give visitors the evil eye."

Avoiding my concerned look, Darius swallowed the churro. "But you go back a long time, it sounds like. Family friends?"

"I've lost count how many years," she said.

I took Darius's hand and began guiding him away. He'd swallowed the food without scanning it. I'd been watching closely, and he hadn't. That was unlike him.

"Hon, I want to go see where Percy worked. The shrine must need refreshing." I caught Holly's eye, who looked amused now. Maybe his obvious personal attraction erased any suspicions about why he was asking so many questions. "There *is* a memorial, isn't there?"

She shrugged. "No idea. Sorry. Just got here this morning like you guys."

I gave her a polite smile and pulled Darius along the chain-link fence toward the school entrance. The enchantment around the fence became obvious as we passed through it onto the campus—a tingling, dizzy sensation struck me. I felt as if I'd stood up too quickly after not eating all day on a ferry in rough water. In fact, the image was so specific I decided the witch must've had that exact experience and put it into the spell.

I touched my beads and drew a hit of magic into my body to wash away the nausea just as Darius rubbed a gold ring over his eyes to do the same.

When we were both recovered, too experienced with such things to even mention it to each other, he said, "We should ask Holly more questions."

"Later. You're coming on too strong. It's suspicious. All anyone has to do is ask a few questions about who my partner was at the Protectorate and draw the obvious conclusion."

"I changed my name."

"You really need to work harder on how you're coming across. The disguise needs to be more than baggy clothes and botanical jewelry."

He dropped my hand and adjusted a thin loop of beads hanging from his left ear. "I ate her food."

"Yeah, what was with that? It was reckless."

"Make up your mind. Am I too professional or too normal?" He looked over at the fairgrounds, a faint smile teasing his lips. "She's obviously got nothing to do with Percy's death. Maybe she could help us out. Keep her ears to the ground, her eyes open. Tell us what she learns."

I stopped in the middle of the school's playground. I knew he found her attractive, but his statement stunned me. The school was only a little better within the enchantment than it had appeared from the hill above, and the asphalt was cracked and weedy. "Excuse me? We don't know her. We don't know anything about her."

"I tried to ask, but you—"

"Darius—"

"Dash. You'd better get used to calling me Dash."

I rolled my eyes. "*Dash*. You're not thinking clearly." My sachet seemed to have given him the energy to act upon his sleep-deprived impulses. "We can't trust a stranger. Any of them. You were *just* telling me that. Repeatedly."

Maybe something else was going on. Could his disguise be so effective that it had somehow seeped into his brain, influencing his personality? It truly was a remarkable enchantment. He'd even changed his teeth, which was brilliant—now they were too large, crowding his mouth, with gold crowns on both incisors.

He kept glancing across the school campus at my garden plot. Holly stood with Rupert, who was gesticulating around the space.

I definitely would come back by myself later to talk to Holly next time. He was obsessed. Maybe she'd hexed him.

I dismissed the thought. She couldn't have done that without my noticing.

Right?

"There's somebody there," he said.

I looked at him, then followed his gaze.

Ah. He *hadn't* been looking at Holly. On the school side of the fence, about ten feet away from my plot, was a woman holding a plastic garden tub.

"Maybe she knew Percy," I said. "Let's go ask her about the shrine."

We approached the woman with our hands hanging away at our sides, visibly not touching any of our jewelry or other objects. With a start, she set down the tub next to the compost pile, then put her hand on a pearl choker and watched us approach.

A pale woman in her thirties, she wore glasses, leggings, sneakers, and a gray hoodie. Other than her large amount of jewelry, she looked no different from a nonmag teacher at a regular school. Behind her, presumably invisible to everyone but me, several goblins the size of house cats were sitting in the compost, pretending to eat the rotting food. One had a stub red nose (with the usual three nostrils) and wore a blackened banana peel as a wig. Two more, cursing at each other, had rushed over to the small tub and were climbing inside.

Consciously tuning out the fae, I held up my hands palms out. "Brightness upon you," I said to the woman. "We mean no harm. Percival Tuff was known to me." Just to be careful, I didn't mention *Dash* had known him as well.

Darius shot me a look, probably wondering why I was speaking with excessive formality. Teachers still made me uncomfortable, maybe because in school I had often been falsely accused of stealing things—just because my father had been rightly accused of stealing things. (They didn't even know that I'd helped him burgle when I was younger. They just *assumed*.)

The woman seemed to relax. "Oh, such a tragedy." She brought a hand and drew a jagged shape in the air. A second later, I tasted a magical sympathy charm, the type a grandmother would use with a child who'd scraped his knee. "I'm Mrs. Andrews." She shook her head. "Jill, that is. Only the kids call me Mrs. Andrews. Are you here to visit the memorial?"

"Yes, that's right," I said quickly, glad to have an excuse. "I'm Alma. This is Dash. Could you show us where it is?"

"Well—" She bit her lip. "Of course. Excuse me a second." She turned away, hauled the tub behind the compost bin, and covered it with a tarp—oblivious to the goblins' howls of outrage at being smothered. "Sorry about the smell. Percy was the compost manager, and since he left, well... It's gotten a bit rank. I volunteered to take care of it over the summer." She escorted us over the playground to a classroom door at the end of the building.

The door was buried under a pile of flowers, notes, and metallic ribbons that gave off a soft hum of magic that grew stronger as we approached. Strong gusts off the shore were blasting the items this way and that, and empty tape on the door showed that several objects had already blown away.

"It looks like he was popular." I felt another pang of sadness. Percy hadn't been a teacher when I'd known him, but I could believe he'd been a good one. He knew how influential a teacher could be in a young witch's life—for Brightness or for Shadow.

Several steps away, Jill held up her arms, heavily encircled with silver bangles, and drew a protective boundary spell around herself.

I looked at her in concern—both for her as well as myself. "Is something wrong?"

TWENTY-EIGHT

J ill drew another spell around her head. "He had mind magic. I've always had a bit of an allergy to that kind of power, and lots of the objects the children have put here came from his class and so are contaminated with it."

I frowned at her, impressed she hadn't left a millimeter gap anywhere in her boundary spell, not even at her feet. "An allergy?" I'd never heard of such a thing.

Safely cocooned, Jill regarded me through her large round glasses. "Yes." She lifted her chin and continued to stare. I imagined it was the same look she gave a difficult child.

"Did you like him?" Darius asked suddenly. "It's cool if you didn't. I didn't much like him myself. Alma was the one who kept in touch."

I turned on him. "D—" I caught myself just in time. "*Dash*. That's inappropriate."

He shrugged. "What? It's not like he can do anything. He's dead."

Jill looked at me. "I really didn't know him very well," she said. "The kids liked him. That's what matters."

Darius took something out of his pocket—a vape pen— and lifted it to his mouth. "And the parents?"

"Please don't smoke here," Jill said. "It's a school."

"It's a Saturday." He sighed loudly at the sky but put it back in his pocket. "I hate mind magic, that's all. Just wondered what it would be like to work with a witch like that. I'd probably quit."

Understanding what he was going for, and appreciating it, I played along. "Dash, you'd quit anyway. When's the last time you actually kept a job for more than three hours?"

"Three is unlucky," he said. "I always stay for five. Then it's cool."

Jill watched the exchange with curiosity, nodding along when Darius expressed his opinion about mind magic. I gave her a warm—and I hoped, dopey and unthreatening —look. "Did it bug you too? I mean, if you've got an allergy, that must've been hard."

"I shouldn't speak ill of the dead," she said. "Especially since you were friends."

I lowered my voice as if it would prevent Percy's spirit from hearing me. "We weren't that close, actually. Maybe not as much as, well, as much as he would've liked." I tried to look embarrassed. "He put me in the garden show as a surprise. Said it was a bet, but..."

Jill gave me a knowing look and nodded. "I get you. I know at least three women he asked out, each more than once. I have a friend who stopped going to the café because she was afraid of running into him."

Interesting. It didn't sound like the Percy I'd met, who despite his unusual mind magic had seemed awkward, even shy, but I made a mental note.

Had Percy pestered a witch who had the personality and power to put an end to it in her own way? Pushing him off a cliff had more guarantees than a restraining order. And less paperwork.

I shook my head. "Not cool."

Jill bit her lip, looked around us, and moved in closer to

whisper, "I mean, he even flirted with Nerissa. The principal." She barked an incredulous laugh.

My mental note got an asterisk. And an underline. "What happened?"

"She shut that down real quick, I'll tell you," Jill said.

Darius was pretending to be bored, casting little smoke ring spells from his inert vape pen, but I knew he was listening closely.

"Well, as long as we're speaking honestly," I said, "I only came because I was afraid of the bad luck if I didn't. When a witch dies in such a horrible way... Well, how could I *not* come? I mean... Having me be in the garden show might've been his last wish. I just couldn't risk ignoring it."

"I completely understand," Jill said. "I would've done the same. It's why I've taken over his garden projects. Who knows how that mind magic might affect his afterlife spirit?"

I nodded in superstitious agreement, though I didn't buy Percy's magic could've outlived him in any way. Mind magic relied on, no surprise, the mind of the witch. If it stopped working, so did the magic. In my opinion, only demons and fae had spirits that could survive the lack of a mortal self.

"Anyway, I'd better get it over with and pay my respects." I gestured at the shrine. "I'm glad to see there's already something set up for him." I turned and took a step toward the door. Bowing my head, I drew a circle in the air and cast a watered-down memorial spell.

Out of the corner of my eye, I saw Jill take a step toward Darius and put her hand on his arm. "I share your opinion about mind magic," she said. "Unfortunately, the principal felt otherwise. She was always asking him to teach it to her. She even was considering teaching it to the children. Can you believe that? Disgusting."

"Totally gross," he said, putting his hand over hers.

I resisted rolling my eyes. His approach was working.

"You're a gardener too?" Jill asked, her tone losing all hint of anyone named *Mrs.* Andrews.

"Nope," he said. "Just here to hang out."

She turned to me after I'd finished my spell. "Where's your garden installation going to be? I'm going to the show on Wednesday. I'll come by and see it."

"Right over there. On the other side of the fence from the compost pile," I said. "Hearth-witch category."

"Oh right." She nodded politely. "Hearth. Like kitchen. You must have a lot of herbs."

"Enough to kill a troll," I said. "Or is it the sea fae who hate herbs, since they're all about water? You know, unless it's kelp."

Now it was Darius's turn to give me a warning look. If he could have fun, so could I.

Jill took that as her cue to leave. "Well, I need to finish the garden chores before the day gets too hot. That compost pile isn't going to turn itself."

"Given its stench, maybe it will," Darius said.

She smiled and gave him the kind of look Percy would've dreamed of.

I cut in. "Thanks so much for talking to us and showing us the memorial. I'd like to stay another few minutes, is that OK?" Even on weekends, schools could be hostile to visitors. I took out a folded piece of paper out of my pocket —it was a receipt for my breakfast, but she couldn't see that—and held it against my heart. "I'd like to read him a few words."

The teacher was already backing away. "Of course. Nobody's here but me." While we watched, she returned to her tub next to the compost pile. The goblins gesticulated at her with rude hand movements, but she moved around them like a human who had no idea they were there.

"Well, she's not demon marked," I said.

Darius rolled the vape pen around his fingers, making me suspect he wasn't kidding about wanting to use it. "Are there lots of fairies around?"

"Yes. Goblins. They seem to love the compost pile." I turned back to the memorial on the door and began to do a proper scan for any clue to why Percy, beloved teacher, had been driven over a cliff to his death.

"Figures," he said. "It reeks."

"It probably means no demons, either," I said, "though I'm not sure goblins are as touchy about being near demons as tree and river fairies are."

Darius put an arm around my shoulders as I finished my probing scan of the flowers, notes, metal pieces, and other shrine offerings. He put his mouth near my ear. "Are you going to break into the room now, or am I?"

"I'll have a better excuse if I get caught. Better be me."

"But I'll look more suspicious standing out here," he said.

We looked at each other.

"Together?" I asked.

He nodded. A moment later, we'd hexed the lock, opened the door, and climbed over the shrine to get into the classroom, all under the cover of one of Darius's best hiding spells.

Inside with the door closed again, I closed my eyes and inhaled. Before I saw the room, I wanted to analyze it from my other senses. What would be my first impression—happiness? Boredom? Fear? Had there been an enemy lurking right there amid the bookshelves, desks, racks of potions, dry-erase boards, and shelves of various metal objects?

Darius grunted. "Demon's balls. I stepped in gum." As he bent over, he bumped into me. "I guess I'll bag it, but I don't sense anything interesting on it."

"Please," I said. "I'm trying to focus."

He scraped the gum off his shoe into a plastic zip-top bag. "There's nothing here. The entire room's been wiped clean."

"You haven't—" I sighed and opened my eyes. Even without using my beads, I had to admit he was right. There wasn't a trace of magical residue in the room—and it had presumably been filled with child witches and a witch teacher learning spells as well as nonmag lessons. The only reason it could be missing now was because somebody cleaned it away.

"It's like a Protectorate office before the Emeralds visit from New York," I said.

"Somebody powerful has been in here. Maybe the principal didn't want anyone finding magical residue from when Mr. Tuff taught her mind magic?"

"Or she didn't want them finding out she'd given him a congenital heart defect to end his sexual harassment," I said. "Let's look around." I went over and studied the bulletin board along the back wall. Although it was summer, student work was still pinned up for display. When Percy had died, they must've just moved the children to another classroom and left it all here as it was. A new teacher would have the pleasure of cleaning up.

"There's nothing in his desk," Darius said from the front. "Not even a paper clip."

I continued to study the bulletin board. The assignment seemed to have been family trees, a vital topic for the witch community, where most held old-fashioned prejudices about blood and inheritance. The students had been at the age to draw people as blobs with sticks coming out of their heads. Most of the blobs had big smiles and googly eyes, but a few were angry. With teeth.

Holding my redwood-bead necklace with one hand, I gently touched a fingertip to the sharp little crayon triangles that filled the mouth of one tall blob. A shiver ran up my arm and exploded behind my eyes.

I jerked back. I recognized the taste of it.

Darius stood beside me. "What did you f—"

I slapped a hand over his mouth. He grunted a complaint but stopped talking.

"Let's go back to the motel, darling," I said.

Frowning, his eyes darted sideways to look at the empty

classroom. "Sure, darling." His voice was muffled under my hand. If anybody was eavesdropping—or would be later, which was my concern—his voice sounded decidedly sarcastic.

Despite his attitude, he knew I'd seen something I wanted to discuss where it was safe to talk. Without another word, we fled the classroom and the school, erasing our trail with all the tricks we'd been taught at Diamond Street.

TWENTY-NINE

We walked to the motel without speaking. There was a lot of foot traffic now, and anything and anyone could be listening to us on the paths and streets of Elwin. When I turned in to the parking lot, quickly checking my Jeep hadn't been interfered with, Darius stayed on the sidewalk.

"This place?" he asked. "This was as good as you could do?"

I took out my room key and opened the door to my—our—room. My magical boundary spell sent a sizzle through me. When I was home, I liked to think of the sensation as equivalent to an affectionate dog licking me after a long day.

Darius followed me inside, his face showing a great deal of disappointment when he saw the spare accommodations. Because of my magic, housekeeping hadn't been able to come to the room—that was my charitable thought anyway—and I hadn't been tidy that morning. The bedspread was the type to be made of such a high percentage of synthetic material that it lacked the friction to stay on the sheets. It was now a twisted pile on the floor.

"At least there are two beds," I said.

"Only because the owner probably cut a real one in

half." He closed the door behind us and locked it, shuddering as the extra spell I'd put on the dead bolt jumped onto his arm and climbed into his brain. "I was going to ask if you think the room is a safe place to talk, but now I'm sure." He rubbed his forehead. "That security spell nearly gave me a lobotomy."

I grinned. In the past year, I'd developed an excellent portfolio of defensive magic. "Thank you."

I had to tell him about what I didn't want to tell him. If I waited, he'd be even angrier than he was going to be now. Better to tell him right away.

But how should I phrase it? *Everyone thinks the owner of this motel is a serial killer, but I don't?*

He saw the look on my face. "What's the matter?"

Well, direct was usually the best way with Darius. "Everyone thinks the owner of this motel is a serial killer, but I don't," I said.

He blinked. "Excuse me?"

I sat on my unmade bed and gave him a detailed summary of my interaction with Lacoste at the front desk the day before. Then, perhaps with a subtle self-protective muffling spell around my ears, I braced myself for his explosion. He was going to point out all the completely logical reasons we shouldn't put ourselves under the roof of a witch who the Protectorate believed had an unhealthy compulsion to kill women my age.

Maybe sleeping in the Jeep wouldn't be too bad. I did wish I'd brought the new SUV, though—if I put the rear seats down, I'd have room to stretch out.

"OK," he said. "That explains the cerebral assault at the doorway."

I waited.

He walked deeper into the room. "There was nowhere else to stay, I take it?"

"Not within a hundred miles," I said. "Even the tent sites are filled. It's the show next week. It's just huge, and with witches coming from all over the country or the world to this tiny—"

"Fine. Got it. We'll reconsider if he starts carrying around frozen roses and giving you hungry looks."

I let out my breath. All my preparatory tension had nowhere to go. "Great. My scan told me he wouldn't kill anyone, and I believe it."

"Yeah, those are usually accurate, I admit," he said, surprising me again. "So what was it you felt back there at the school? One of the drawings seemed to freak you out."

Relieved to move on, I said, "A man. Somebody I've met. His name's Bruce, and I ate in his restaurant last night. The one Holly mentioned. I think his child was in Percy's class. She drew a picture of him with lots of teeth." It was too bad, because I was hungry for lunch, and his restaurant had seemed the best place to eat in town.

"If he owns a restaurant, having teeth makes sense," he said. "What bothered you about it?"

"The feeling it gave me. It was afraid."

"School makes lots of kids anxious," he said.

"The child who drew that picture was terrified of something."

Darius considered. "Maybe the father killed Percy for harming his child."

"I don't know," I said. "It's a clue, though."

Nodding, Darius kicked off his sandals and padded over to the second bed. He pressed his hand on it, scowling when it squeaked, then sighed and flopped down on it. He crawled up to the pillow and fluffed it up. "It's not too bad. Better than a hard floor."

"Hey, that's right," I said. "Where is your bag? You didn't have one when you found me."

His eyes were already closed. Without opening them, he snapped his fingers. A miniature bag the size of a football fell out of the air and landed on the bed. He gave it a smack, and it grew to the size of a sizable duffel bag.

"Ooh," I said. "Teach me that one."

Even with his arm flung over his face, I could see him grin. Then he lowered his arm, sat up, unzipped the bag, and began digging through it until he found a pillowcase, a bag of trail mix, clean socks, a toiletries case, and a metal box that I figured was where he stored his magical jewelry when he slept.

"I wasn't carrying it around with me," he said. "Too heavy. I tucked it behind a bush on the main road before I went looking for you, then picked it up as we walked here."

"You didn't let on at all," I said.

"I wanted to surprise you."

"Show off, you mean," I said, laughing.

"Not me. That's your style." He got to his feet with his duffel in his arms. "I'm going to shower and brush my teeth. Try not to get yourself hexed while I'm gone."

"I'll try."

While he was in the bathroom, I made my bed. I hadn't expected company, and years of boarding schools had made me enjoy my adult freedom to be a slob a little too much.

He came out wearing a fresh tie-dyed T-shirt and put away his duffel in the small closet with his Birkenstocks. He hung the binoculars, still tied to the sachet, on the only hanger on the rod. It wasn't as if I'd packed a ball gown, but he could've *asked* me if I'd need the only hanger.

"How many tie-dyed T-shirts do you have?" I asked. "You were wearing a different one earlier today. One is a disguise, two is a collection."

He sat at the small table—there was only one chair—and glared at me. "What's that supposed to mean?"

My smile fell. "I was just kidding."

He slapped his notebook on the table. "Too much of that. Time to get serious and make a list."

I knew what he meant—write down everyone we'd met and wanted to meet. But his mood seemed frayed. Laughing one minute, snapping at me the next. "Are you OK?"

His eyes flashed. "No, I'm sure as Shadow not OK. I haven't slept, I haven't eaten, there's no hot water, and from what I've seen of Elwin so far, none of those problems are going to resolve themselves satisfactorily until we find out who, if anyone, killed a witch I didn't even like."

"Arcata's not very far," I said. "We can get a decent burrito at least." My toddler comparison came to mind again. Hangry boy needed a snack.

"What if I want a cheeseburger?"

"With dead cow or, like, pretend dead cow?" I asked. "It's a very vegan-friendly environment. College kids, Humboldt coast, health trends—"

He gave me a withering stare. "Later. First the list," he said in a low voice. He took out a pen, clicked it, and opened his journal.

THIRTY

"Right, right. The list." I flopped sideways on the bed and got comfortable. It wobbled and squeaked under me. "Technically, the first person I met in Elwin was Clematis Mallory. You should put her down."

"Fine. She sounds like she'd love an excuse to kill somebody."

"You should go say hi," I said.

Ignoring me, he continued writing. "Then you met the principal."

"Let's use her name. Nerissa Pike."

"She sounds like a fish from Minnesota," he said. "Speaking of which, have you told Seth yet that I'm here and I'm not happy about it, so he might want to just stay where he is forever?"

I cast an uneasy glance at my phone. He hadn't texted me. "No. Don't joke about that."

"I'm not—"

"Then there's Nerissa's niece," I said quickly. "Marta."

"You said she's just a kid."

"Percy was a teacher at her school. She's got a ton of metal that most people don't get until they're in their thirties. Some of it might've taken on a life of its own. She got mad at mean Mr. Tuff, wished him dead, and... off he goes."

"You've got a dark mind."

"I don't actually believe she could do that," I said. "But since you're making a list, let's be comprehensive."

He nodded and kept writing. In some ways, we'd been terrible partners, but our brainstorming sessions had been rewarding. It was satisfying to have somebody to talk to again.

"Who else?" he asked. "Before we get to Rupert and Jill Andrews."

"And Holly," I said.

His lips flattened, but he said, "And Holly" and wrote it down.

"Well, there's Bruce, the school parent and restaurant owner. I saw him in the back at the café, too."

He kept writing. "Last name?"

"No idea."

He looked up at me. "Seriously?"

"It's not like it'll be hard to find out."

With a sigh, he took out his phone, tapped the screen, and set it down. "A Flint at Diamond Street is on call to help me with chores like this."

"Raynor put him on call? That's coo—"

"No, I did. He's ambitious and knows I'm the grateful type."

Striking deals and sucking up to other agents hadn't interested me—another reason my career in the Protectorate had been so brief.

Less than a minute later, Darius's phone chimed. He picked it up, tapped it once, and set it down. "Bruce Krog and Holly Thayer," he said. "And Marta shares her aunt's last name. Pike."

I watched him write the names down. His mouth was in a hard line, disapproving of me. "You know I was never good at the paperwork," I said.

"Take out *paper*, and you've got that right."

I sighed. He wasn't wrong. But why was that a bad thing?

"There was also a man with a truck tattoo," I said. "Old witch, old truck."

"And?"

"He was at the restaurant and the café."

"What's his story? Did you get his name?" Darius asked.

I just looked at him. He made a face.

"What kind of vibes did you get from the teacher?" I asked to move on.

"She's hiding something. There was no reason for her to make physical contact with me. Mrs. Andrews was trying to use her... her wiles."

"Did her wiles work?"

"Hardly."

I resisted teasing about how Holly's wiles would've had much better odds. "No offense, but I don't think you're actually the teacher's type."

"Agreed. Not in this disguise anyway."

"If she had something to hide when an ex-Protectorate agent with mind magic joined the teaching staff," I continued, "suddenly developing a so-called allergy to it would be one way to protect her secret."

"She's not allergic to it," he said. "I used it on her today. Not a sniffle."

"You can do mind magic now?" I clapped my hands together in childish enthusiasm. "What did you get out of her? How did you learn the technique? Will you teach it to me?"

He scoffed. "You are so greedy. Don't you have enough power already?"

"What do you mean? It's good to learn new things."

He put his pen down and looked at me seriously. "Sometimes, Alma, you don't take the time to decide if learning is the best use of your energy."

"Why shouldn't we always be learning as much as we can?"

"Because you might neglect your responsibilities," he said. "You might neglect the people in your life."

"Where is this coming from?"

He frowned and looked down at his notebook. "Forget it," he said roughly. "Just something I've been thinking about since... Forget it."

"Since when?"

He jerked his head up. "Since a changeling who knows he's one wrong move away from having a silver stake shoved into his chest got a Protectorate agent to drop everything and come to a witch town to protect you." He leaned forward, his brown eyes flashing with intense emotion. "Do you know how much he must care about you to do that? To risk *everything* for you? Do you have any idea how *rare* it is to... to... to have somebody like that?"

I felt as if I'd been slapped. "Yes," I said, my voice unsteady. "But what does that have to do with learning new things?"

"You should pause sometimes. Think about other priorities in your life. It's not all about collecting the most stones and sticks, the most books, the most amulets."

"But I'm not like that," I said, my voice rising. It felt as if he was attacking my most core self. "I collect knowledge. Skills. Techniques."

"Like mind magic," he said.

"Exactly!"

"For what?" he asked.

"To protect myself and those I lo—"

"*No*," he said. "That's not why. You just want to know for the sake of knowing."

"What's wrong with that?" I demanded. "That's what Helen says is the most true, pure calling for a witch."

"You're taking life advice from a mercenary who hates everyone, has no friends, and lives alone in a house filled with ancient junk she doesn't even enjoy?"

I was speechless. My heart was pounding so hard I could feel it in my throat.

He glared at me, shook his head roughly, then went back to writing in his notebook.

I sat, frozen, watching him write. My hands were shaking.

"Sorry," he said after a long pause, not looking up. "I don't know what came over me."

I tried to make a joke, but my emotions were too raw. It was taking all my energy and half my magical power to keep my feet from hurrying me out the door.

Over the next long, awkward minute, I managed to get a little control of myself and wonder about why he'd said what he'd said. I'd think about *what* he said later, but why... *why* was important too. And to be honest, easier to handle when I felt so attacked.

Darius had been doing a lot of things today that were out of character. He wasn't usually moody. Irritable and critical, yes, but in a steady, consistent way.

Could he be under the influence of an enchantment? A hex?

There was Seth, of course, but I didn't believe he had the ability to change a witch's personality from a few feet, let alone a few thousand, miles away.

Rupert? He'd been in the man's vehicle for a long drive. Maybe something had seeped into his system there.

"I'm not under the influence of anything," Darius said suddenly.

"I didn't say—"

"I can hear you thinking it," he said.

I bit my lip, tempted to laugh. That felt a lot better than crying. "You aren't acting like yourself."

"To you, maybe." He looked off into the distance. "To me, it feels right. Just saying what I'm feeling."

I was tempted to say *feeling is out of character* but stopped myself. I didn't want to bring on more tears (mine) or a lecture (his).

Could it be the sachet I gave him? It seemed impossible. There wasn't anything unusual in it; it was just a bundle of healing substances. And he'd taken it off.

Maybe it was his own magic that had unbalanced him.

"Is it possible your disguise is a little too good?" I asked. "You wanted to look sensitive and contrary, and maybe... maybe it broke through the brain barrier. It can happen if the witch is really strong and the spell reverb—"

He slammed both hands on the table and got to his feet, his eyes flashing red. "What did you say?"

I recoiled. "Darius, wait. I—"

The journal flew up into the air, its pages flapping over his head like an angry bird. He lifted his hands between us. His fingers, generating power from the metal rings, began shimmering with pale green sparks.

I stared, incredulous and increasingly afraid.

He was going to attack me.

THIRTY-ONE

I jumped to my feet, drawing power from my beads into my chest and preparing a defensive boundary around myself from head to toe. But I'd been relaxed, my guard down, and his power had already grown into a weapon.

"You think I hexed my own brain?" he demanded.

He flung a line of green fire into the air, striking the smoke detector. It gave a loud pop, flashed white, and fell on the carpet between us in a cloud of smoke.

Giving up on my defensive spell for now, I ran for the door. I'd have more resources outside. And a motorized vehicle.

But he grabbed my shoulders, his touch burning, and jerked me back. With a cry, I tripped over his feet and fell to the floor. A green haze filled the air. Gasping for air, I crawled away toward the bathroom on my hands and knees.

Water. Maybe I could lock myself inside and use the water as a shield. The green smoke tasted thick, as bitter as a campfire; water might disperse or at least weaken it.

"Darius, it's me, it's Alma, your friend, your friend," I was saying, over and over, hoping whatever had taken over would snap out of it with a reminder of our bond. It had started rocky, but since then we'd shared dangers and helped each other. Surely he had to remember that.

He grabbed my ankle. His touch was hotter now, burning through my jeans. "My brain is fine."

As he dragged me away from the bathroom door, I caught a glimpse of his face in the mirror on the closet's sliding doors. It was twisted, frenzied, mindless. The eyes looked even more red than they had a second ago.

Red. Not a trick of the light, not my fear. His eyes, usually a warm brown, were now a shimmering blood-red.

He was hexed. And not via his disguise or because of my little healing herbal sachet. Somebody had gotten to him.

And now he was getting to me.

Or he would if I didn't figure out a way to stop him.

I flung a self-defense spell at his alarming red eyes and kicked hard. His grip loosened enough for me to twist and cast another defensive spell around myself, this time enveloping my feet completely.

What had changed from a few minutes ago to his sudden change in mood?

The shower. He'd taken off some things and put others back on.

What hadn't he replaced? The original shirt... the binoculars... the sachet.

My mind raced to remember what his jeans had looked like. They—

He cast a beam of power through the floor and jabbed me in the throat from beneath.

I gagged, breath catching in my chest.

The jeans were the same. The rocks. I'd given him the jasper, the moonstone. He'd put them in his pockets.

"You've been hexed, Darius!" I choked out. "Empty your pockets, empty your—"

He struck again. I slapped at the sliding door and pushed it open. The sachet. Could that have been some kind of—

"My. Brain. Is. Fine." A blast of fire struck the mirror, shattering it.

I gasped and covered my head with my hands. "Stop, Darius, stop!" I got to my feet, jumped into the closet, and pulled the door shut between me and the increasingly frequent blasts of his destructive fire. He'd run out of power soon—I hoped—but I might not survive that long.

I'd let my guard down because it was Darius and I was in my excessively protected motel room. I had my beads, but half of them were fake to provide my disguise. There were more in my bag, but I'd set that down.

I felt the quiet hum of my own magic coming from the sachet. With trembling fingers I separated my little bag of herbs and iron from the binoculars' cord, then clutched it to my chest. It was mine, it was healing and good, it was powerful.

I had to get it back on Darius somehow. Whatever the hex was, the sachet had protected him—and me—from it until he'd taken it off.

I had to think of him as my enemy. What would I do with an opponent if I wanted him to take something from me?

I'd pretend I didn't want him to take it.

His voice came from the other side of the door, more terrifying because of how softly he spoke. "Face me, witch."

Heart pounding, I took off the redwood-bead necklace from my neck and wrapped it over my left palm and around my wrist, keeping it close to my skin but not as visible as my throat. Then I held the sachet against my neck where Darius could see it and assume I was using it as a magical battery.

Withdrawing as much power from my internal magical well as I could afford to lose, I shoved the door open.

"You asked for it," I said, making a show of holding the sachet near my jugular as I erected an offensive hex at his eye level.

It was almost too easy. He reached out and grabbed the

sachet from me. I'd left a gap in my defenses just big enough for his hand to pass through. Dangerous but necessary.

He held it up, goading me with it clutched in his fist. "This iron is the only metal you have on you, isn't it?"

I pulled the door shut again, turned the offensive hex into a power-absorbing curtain, and squatted down in the corner with his Birkenstocks.

They reeked. I wasn't going to mention that to him now, however.

But I would later. Oh yeah. He'd never hear the end of it.

I waited. My breath was loud in the small closet. Out in the room, he wasn't making any noise at all, which was almost worse than him shouting at me.

Where was he? What was he doing?

I forced my breathing to slow down so I could hear better. A sharp pain in my foot drew my attention to a shard of glass stuck in my toe. Flinching, I pulled it out. I must've stepped on it when the mirror shattered.

"Alma?"

Darius sounded less bloodthirsty, but I couldn't be sure, so I waited, counting the seconds.

One... two... three...

"Alma, I don't feel so good."

I didn't move, but I called out, "Watch out for the glass on the floor."

"Too late," he said. "I'm bleeding. But it doesn't hurt. Is that because of this herb bag thing?"

Probably just the blind rage, but I said, "Yes. Don't let go of it. It's keeping the pain away. And you'll heal in... in just a few minutes if you lie down and let it do its work."

"OK," he said, sounding agreeable. "Good thing the carpet already looks like it's welcomed a few corpses before. My blood will blend right in."

There was the squeak of the bedsprings, followed by Darius's long sigh.

I continued to wait. My heart was racing, my power

drained. I hadn't been prepared. I'd let myself get hexed by a Protectorate agent—a Quartz!—out to kill me.

My arm stung, making me wonder if the glass had cut me there as well. But when I explored it gingerly with my other hand, all I found under my sleeves and bracelets was a soreness that reminded me of—

Of the tattoo rings that formed after a magical duel. Now there were seven.

Demon's balls, I'd come close to joining my mother on the other side. Both of them—the biological human one and the currently bodiless demon one.

"Alma, could you bring me a washcloth? I'm dripping. I don't want to lose consciousness, you know? And all my blood here will have to be scrubbed away so I don't give another witch the chance to hex me." His voice sounded more playful with each word. "I'm sure you'd love that though. See me get thrown into the San Francisco Bay again. Am I right?"

He was himself. Well, he was an extremely nice version of himself. Or he sounded like it.

I slid open the closet door.

THIRTY-TWO

I peeked out at him from inside the closet. "If you keep holding on to the sachet," I said, "I'll get you a towel."

"There you go again, striking deals." He was lying on the bed. "You're as bad as Helen. I hope when you're old, you aren't a mercenary like her."

Grimacing at the bad smell, I slid my feet into his sandals and walked slowly across the glass-littered carpet to the bathroom. There was only one towel, because it was that kind of motel, but I brought it out to him—with my left hand clutching my redwood beads, ready to strike.

He rested his head in his cradled hands, staring at the ceiling with his feet sticking over the edge of the bed. The pose was that of a contented man watching lovely cloud formations in a summer sky.

"There's something I want you to do," I said. "I'll explain later. Will you just do it without arguing? Please?"

"Is it something to do with the chunk missing in the ceiling?"

I looked up at where the smoke detector had been. There was a black hole. "Yes," I said.

"Sure. I'm curious. What?"

"Take out whatever's in your pockets and set them in" —I grabbed the pillow from my bed—"inside here." I pulled out the pillow, threw it back on my bed, then held out the empty case.

With a shrug, he reached into his jeans and took out the three rocks from the beach, a crumpled tissue, and a few coins, probably carried for their copper core and not their currency value. "This is all I've got."

I moved closer. "Great. Drop them in."

He did, shaking his head as if I were crazy, then resumed pondering the ceiling. I moved as swiftly across the room as I could in his big sandals, unlocked the door, and set the bundle outside.

Feeling a little better, I came back into the room, closed the door and locked it, muttered the strongest spell I could spare before I turned around.

Darius lay motionless on the bed, his mouth slightly ajar, the sachet gripped in both hands against his chest.

He'd fallen asleep.

I let out a long, ragged breath.

"For Brightness's sake," I whispered. "Who is trying to kill whom?"

And why?

I exchanged his sandals for my own shoes that were next to the door where I'd left them, grabbed my bag, and went outside. Darius's feet were bleeding onto the towel, and we'd have to clean that up, but later. The sachet would help get the healing started. If it was strong enough to neutralize a killing hex, it could mend a few scratches in human skin.

The pillowcase with its unknown Shadow object was just outside the motel room door where I'd dumped it. Until I had Darius's help, I didn't want to touch it again.

I gave it a wide berth, then climbed behind the wheel, locked the door, and put the keys in the ignition. When I was sure that I could drive away instantly if Darius suddenly appeared with glowing red eyes, I called Seth.

It went straight to voice mail. I lowered the phone to make sure it wasn't the middle of the night—of course not, it was Minnesota, not Romania—then gave him a taste of my frustration.

"Seriously?" I demanded. "You're not going to answer? Can't you feel how much I need you?"

I blinked away tears. I knew I was probably in shock. Darius, one of the few witches on the planet I trusted completely, had tried to kill me. That was why Seth had sent my former partner to me, precisely because he was completely trustworthy.

I stared at the motel room door, breathing deeply, trying to prevent myself from giving in to the tears. I'd have to find another way to release the trauma. It wasn't safe to cry in a serial killer's motel's parking lot. A truism if I'd ever heard one. A tourism truism.

I was losing it.

Realizing the phone was still recording my message, I added, "Seth, I need you to call me. As soon as you can. I'm alive. I'm not bleeding. I mean, just a little. Where are you? I'm fine. Never mind. I hope the baby's OK."

Then I hung up and did indulge in a little cry. Hearing Seth's recorded voice on his phone had cut through my tough witch defenses. He should've told me he was sending Darius, and since he hadn't, the least he could do was answer the phone now.

I continued staring at the motel door. It was very closed. Last night I'd felt safe on the inside, and now I felt safe on the outside.

The minutes ticked by. No reply.

A terrible thought occurred to me.

What if Seth *hadn't* been the one to send Darius?

I was just about to call Seth again when I hear the roar of an approaching motorcycle. Tensing, I put the phone away and slid down in my seat.

Any witch, even those who hadn't worked for the Protectorate, had a healthy vigilance regarding the sight or sound of motorcycles. Agents drove them when they were on assignments hunting down demons and Shadow practitioners, but they were also used to summon ordinary civilian witches for Protectorate inquiries. If one showed up and gave you a summons, you had to respond in person, usually by daybreak. Most witches would be taken into custody right away and transported on the back of some agent's bike to the summoning location—here it would be San Francisco, three hundred miles away. When the questioning was complete, if you were lucky, you were allowed to go home, but since they'd transported you on their vehicle with no notice, it would be an inconvenient and usually expensive return journey.

The last thing I wanted was to be summoned to Diamond Street right then. Darius was in a questionable state, some mysterious hex object was in a threadbare pillowcase on the ground of a motel near a major road, and I was *busy*, for Brightness's sake.

The bike's roar got louder. And louder. I put my hands on the wheel, patted it a few times, then started the engine. If the agent didn't give me the summons, they couldn't blame me for not showing up.

But just as I was starting to back up, a Harley without a muffler rolled around the corner from out of nowhere and parked directly behind my rear bumper.

"Demon's balls," I muttered. For a moment, I considered jumping out and making a run for it. But if they got curious and picked up the pillowcase, who knew what would happen? It had made an upstanding friendly agent like Darius try to kill me; a cold, hostile one might succeed.

So I waited. A man wearing a leather vest, jeans, and a half helmet covered with spikes dismounted and came around to the driver's side window. He was in disguise—the Protectorate usually forbade brain buckets and bare arms, though the spikes were useful—but I recognized his cheerful face above the full gray beard.

I rolled down my window, relieved it was Gilbert, a lifetime Flint who everyone liked, but still unhappy he'd caught me. "Hi, Gilbert. Great to see you again, but I'm really busy. Is there a way I could take a rain check?"

He lifted a white padded mailer and slid it through the window. "Don't worry, Witch Alma, it's not a summons." He held up a metal plate. "I'd appreciate a receipt."

I studied the mailer, felt only paper inside, and set it on the seat next to me. Then I lifted my right hand, pressed it against the plate, and let it scan me. Once, when the former Director had disliked me, I'd used spit to prevent a similar zinc plate from working. Now I allowed it.

"Thanks, Alma." Gilbert slipped the plate into a magical pocket inside his leather vest. I noticed now he really was bare-chested; it wasn't just an illusion. "It's nice up here. I've always wanted to come to the flower show myself."

"Aren't you cold?"

He shrugged and patted his belly. "I'm well padded. I'll put on a sweater when I get to Arcata. Job's done."

"Indeed it is." I waved, and he ambled back to the Harley. A moment later, he was roaring away, and I was feeling the envelope for booby traps.

CHAPTER

THIRTY-THREE

My phone chimed. I glanced at it.

It's just paper, Raynor's text said. *Might be useful. Might not. Give my regards to Dash.*

Shaking my head, I set the phone down. He could've warned me. Letting me panic when I saw the bike wasn't nice. I gave the envelope a security scan before opening it and taking out a stack of printer paper.

It was about forty or fifty pages made up of small blocks of text frequently broken up with dates, times, and places. The only images, other than the formal work portrait of Percy on the first page, were simple maps and line diagrams.

It was the Protectorate file on Percival Tuff, former agent. Since it was chronological, I flipped through to the end, but the last year only had a few entries. His girlfriend had left him; he'd left Oregon; he'd gotten the job in Elwin. No known Shadow behaviors or acquaintances. An early withdrawal of his meager Protectorate pension was being sent to his online bank every other Friday.

I set the envelope down. Darius could read the rest of it. Maybe I was carrying a grudge, but Darius would have to admit he was better at enduring boring detail work than I was.

194

Still no reply from Seth. The distraction with the dossier's arrival had helped me shake off the last of my shock. After a soothing hit from some jade beads and a second herbal sachet under my driver's seat, I was ready to face Darius again. First though, I'd get a few fresh towels and a new pillowcase.

I walked to the office, prepared to use magic again to defend myself against Lacoste, but it was just Serafina. Giving me a wary glance, she reached under the counter for exactly two towels and one pillowcase, and set them on the counter without a word.

When I got back to the room, Darius was awake but still lying down, still regarding the ceiling. "Did I really do that?"

I locked the door behind me. "Yes. You were hexed."

He nodded. "I thought it was a bad dream. But I can see that hole is really there."

"Yup. And pieces of the mirror are on the floor."

He lifted a foot and frowned at it. "And in my feet, apparently."

"I think the hex came from one of the rocks we got at the beach," I said. "I've put them outside. When you feel up to it, we'll have to deal with them before housekeeping picks it up and, well, gets hurt."

Seeing the envelope in my hand, he sat up. "What's that?"

I set it on the table and brought the towels to the bathroom. "Percy's file. Raynor sent it up with an agent on a Harley."

"What, just now?"

I came back and put my pillow in a new case. "There's not much there. I couldn't see anything to explain why somebody would kill him, but maybe you'll find something."

Darius stared at me. "A Protectorate agent was just here, right outside the door, and you didn't ask them to help with whatever hexed me?"

"It was Gilbert."

He slumped. Nodded in understanding. "Ah. Right."

Poor Gilbert. Fifty-three and still a Flint. Lovely man, but not the one to call for the big stuff.

Darius turned his attention to his feet. With a hand on something metal under his shirt—I guessed a nipple piercing made out of steel, but we weren't on those terms—he cast a healing spell that was strong enough to make me feel better as well.

I brought him his sandals, glad he was back to himself. "Your shoes stink."

"I'm surprised you don't like it."

"Who likes swamp feet?"

He put them on and stood up. "It's *Salvia clevelandii*. It repels Shadow. I took the sandals off when I came into the room, and I'm sure that's one reason the hex struck me so hard then." He walked over to the table and picked up the envelope. "You've got one growing in your front yard. Didn't you know that's what it was? It's good for blocking hexes."

I nodded, pretending to remember. There were multiple reasons I'd hired Rupert. My memory for plant names was unreliable.

"Don't criticize me for not knowing," I said. "You almost killed me. Be nice."

"I never would've hurt you."

He looked pained, so I decided we'd debate later. Right now we had to deal with the stones. I pointed at the door. "Ready?"

He adjusted his shirt and jeans, checking the bracelets and necklaces and studs and buttons, even the wood beads in his hair, then nodded. "I feel pretty good."

"Where's the sachet?"

To his credit, he didn't dismiss its importance. "In my pocket."

"Keep it close until we know what happened."

He nodded, stern-faced, and we went outside together. The pillowcase was just outside the door where I'd left it.

"Quite a risk, leaving it here. Housekeeping could've picked it up," he said.

"I'm not convinced there is housekeeping. But yes, it wasn't ideal. I was a bit busy not letting you kill me at the time." I picked up the pillowcase.

"I never would've— Wait, what are you doing?"

I peeked inside. There were three stones: the jasper, the agate, and the moonstone. The moonstone had been the last, and I'd found it at the top of the path. If somebody had been watching me and Darius down on the beach, they could've seen me picking up stones. If they had hostile intentions—and obviously one of the witches around did, because the enchantment on Darius could've killed somebody—the moonstone was the most obvious one.

"It was stupid of me to pick up a pretty rock at the top of the path," I said, disgusted with myself. "What an easy trap to spring. Why would there be such a gorgeous moonstone right on a path that probably gets dozens, even hundreds of witches passing by every day?"

Clutching an antique gold watch in his fist, Darius peered inside. I felt a current of magical energy float past my hands holding the pillowcase and envelop the rocks. A tendril of green smoke rose from inside, its color an unpleasant reminder of his earlier attack.

"Yeah, it's the moonstone all right," he said. "It's been booby-trapped with... I'm not sure how to describe it, exactly... There's more than one command wrapped into it. But at its source is anger. Violence. Or maybe vengeance?"

I inhaled the green smoke, trying to sense the same thing he could, but I wasn't holding the gold watch that enhanced his sight. "So whoever picked it up would want to kill somebody? That's a lot more random than what I thought we were dealing with. There's no solid motive, just insanity."

"No, there's a motive. We just don't know what it is."

Darius stepped back and reattached the watch to his belt loops. "The spell's actually brilliant. It would change depending on who held it. Therefore, it probably wouldn't have been dangerous for housekeeping to pick it up. It would just be a rock to them. Only the proximity to the victim would trigger the hex."

"I don't understand. Who was the intended victim? What was the command built into the hex—to kill me? To kill you? How do we know it was intended for either of us?"

Darius took out a small bag I knew contained iron filings. He untied its leather drawstring, enlarged the opening, then sprinkled them over the rocks.

"Whoever set this enchantment wanted to cause damage," he said, "but it's open-ended in how it would happen."

As the green smoke turned to white, the moonstone popped and sizzled.

I was shaking my head. "You can't put that kind of situational magic into just a rock. I mean, metal isn't my favorite, but if I wanted to have something behave like some killer robot drone, I'd use metal, not stone."

"I'm just telling you what I see. The scan strongly implies the hex was activated as soon as I held it." He tied the small bag of iron filings closed and put them in another pocket. "I believe I've neutralized it. Want to test it out?"

"Better me than you, is that your thinking?"

He took a few steps back and held up his hands in a defensive posture. "Better you attack me than the other way around. Yes."

I looked around the motel grounds. It would be better for my serious magic to be unobserved; after all, my goal was to appear harmless.

"I've put a stealth spell around us," Darius said. "Anybody who looks over here won't see anything unusual."

"Thanks." I reached under my shirt and took out a glass vial hanging from a braided jute string. Inside was a nugget of redwood charcoal I'd made under the summer solstice. I unscrewed the cork stopper and dumped the charcoal into my palm. When I brought it to my lips, Darius made a gagging sound.

"There's no way that tastes better than even rusty iron," he said.

Ignoring him, I popped it under my tongue and reached inside the pillowcase for the moonstone.

CHAPTER

THIRTY-FOUR

I lifted the moonstone out and regarded it with both normal vision and my magical intuition. It was just as beautiful as before, even knowing it might've killed me—or even more so for its power.

I'd been an idiot to pick it off the ground earlier. Its purity and smoothness would never be ignored in a witch town; it was bait, pure and simple.

And it was filled with hate. Specifically—I rolled the redwood charcoal around in my mouth, grimacing at the taste—vengeance. Darius's iron had neutralized its ability to affect anything outside of itself, but its atoms retained the witch's Shadow energy.

I dropped the moonstone back into the pillowcase, heard it clack against the other two rocks, and rolled it all together. "It can't hurt anyone, but I'd rather not bring it back into the room."

"How long has it been since Gilbert was here?" Darius asked.

I spit the charcoal back into its vial for later use. "Great idea. He's nice enough to come back, too. Do you have his number?"

Within the hour, Gilbert had driven back up on his bike, placed the bundle in an iron box kept inside the tank case

200

for similar situations, given us both a hurried but cheerful wave, and was gone again.

We went back into the motel room and cleaned up the blood and glass. Everything had to be rolled up in plastic and stored in an enchanted duffel bag; the blood of either one of us would be potent in the wrong hands.

"Maybe now Raynor will take this situation up here seriously," I said. "He can do a proper scan on that moonstone and see there are serious powers at work here."

"Don't hold your breath," Darius replied. "As long as we're here, Raynor doesn't have to do anything but wait. He really doesn't want anything messing up his recruitment for Protector of Silverpool."

It was a very strange turn of events that a once-primo job had become untouchable.

"What will it take?" I asked. "One of us dying?"

"Probably." Darius gave an enormous yawn.

It was now almost seven.

"Let's order a pizza," Darius said. "As much as I'd love to continue our investigations tonight, I should probably sleep first."

I was glad to hear him accept the limits of his body. Also, I wanted him to be unconscious so I could call Seth again.

It was going to be difficult to sleep next to the witch who had, against his will, tried to maim me, and I needed all the reassurance I could get that he hadn't been sent by an adversary.

I woke the next morning to the feel of Darius kicking the end of my mattress with his foot. He was probably afraid to touch me while I was sleeping, knowing I might rise up with my defensive magic on blast before I'd woken up all the way.

"It's almost eight," he said. "Do you always sleep this

late? I went through Tuff's dossier. There wasn't anything that stood out to me other than he's got a problem with the ladies."

I pulled the pillow over my head. Seth hadn't replied to my message from yesterday or the several others I'd left overnight. It had been very late when I'd finally dropped off into an uneasy sleep.

It seemed like yesterday had been wasted. Being hexed hadn't told us anything we hadn't already known: a murderer was out there targeting Protectorate-affiliated witches.

And now Seth had disappeared. What if the Protectorate there had caught up with him?

No, I told myself. Raynor would've told me. There was a lot to worry about, but not that.

"Let's go to that restaurant." I could hear Darius putting on the jewelry from his storage case. "I'll get a chance to meet more of the locals."

Grumbling but knowing he was right, I flung the pillow aside and got ready for the day. After I'd sent another text to Seth, we went out to the Jeep. We could've walked to the restaurant, but it was safer to have a quick getaway on hand.

Just as I was backing up, my thoughts still ruminating on Seth's silence, I noticed two people in my rearview mirror. They were in the parking lot, talking behind a large white van. Two people I didn't expect to see together.

"What's the matter?" Darius asked.

I paused. "Holly is here," I whispered. "Talking to James Lacoste."

He craned around in his seat to look. A second later, he shrugged and turned back around. "She came up on short notice too," he said. "Stuck here just like us."

Holly looked up just then and saw us. I continued backing up, pretended I didn't see her, and pulled out into the street.

"What's the matter?" Darius went on. "You think she's a serial killer too?"

"I'm being suspicious of everyone the way you told me to be."

"Within reason," he said. "It's a motel. You said there wasn't anywhere else to stay. She probably just wants a clean towel."

"I hope she is a serial killer," I said, "and her favorite victim looks just like you."

He laughed in spite of himself. "Noted."

When we got to the restaurant, I immediately saw Nerissa Pike sitting in the largest corner booth with two other women who might have been her friends. Maybe not. They were older than her and appeared quiet and passive while she spoke and gesticulated over the table. Parents? Teachers?

Sunday morning before the garden show, the restaurant was busy; the only empty seats were at the counter. Wanting privacy, we had to wait for the first table to open up, a two-seater in a dim corner near the swinging kitchen door.

I pointed out Bruce, who was serving behind the counter. He smiled at me, gave Darius an amused look, and went back to pouring coffee for a dark-haired woman sitting alone.

"The teacher, Jill," Darius said.

"Popular place." My worry was making me irritable. If Seth was in trouble, how long would it take for the news to reach me?

Our mountain of food arrived. It looked good, but I kept imagining Seth in perilous situations—unconscious in the cattails, impaled with silver by a Protectorate agent, drowned by his fae mother in a lake.

Holly came into the restaurant and sat at the counter next to Jill. They nodded hello, but I couldn't tell if they knew each other.

As I was picking at a blueberry, my phone chimed from

Seth. I tapped the screen so fast I knocked over the saltshaker.

I'm alive and well
more soon
take care
Love
S

I let out a long, relieved breath.

Then the anger hit me. That was all he was going to tell me? I leaned back in my seat, glad to be feeling annoyance instead of anxiety. Only Seth could irritate me in quite that way with a perfect blend of love, caring, and playful avoidance.

Appetite restored, I dug into the waffles, eggs, ham, sausage, pancakes, fruit, yogurt, and oatmeal we'd ordered. Darius had been as hungry as I was and had already eaten more than half. The hex and its aftermath had left us both ravenous.

When we were done, Darius looked around the restaurant with fresh energy. "I can feel the truck tattoo you mentioned." He tucked his used napkin away in his pocket just in case somebody in the back knew how to take discarded spit and skin from people and use it against them. "My grandad had one like that of my grandmother. It's called a memory skin."

"Hm." I took a bite of my scrambled eggs and wondered if Nerissa's companions knew she was using more magical power than most other witches used in a week.

Darius tapped my arm. "If you keep staring at her like that, she'll notice."

I lowered my voice. "I think she's using mind magic."

"What? No. Here in public?"

"Look at the women sitting with her," I said. "They're transfixed."

Darius leaned back in his seat with a coffee mug in front of his face, appearing to be looking at the ceiling. A moment later, he set it down. "Demon's balls. I think you're right."

"Who do you think they are? Teachers?"

"No idea," he said. "But don't overdo it. She's a strong one. Don't let on we know."

I peeked again. Probably not teachers, since Jill wasn't sitting with them. And they were wearing too much jewelry. Fashionable clothes, expensive shoes, trendy haircuts.

But their wealth wasn't enough to protect them from a witch who could read minds. An ambitious woman could do more than run a small school with that kind of power. There were businesses and governments to run, too.

If she'd learned mind magic from Percy, then killed him to hide her tracks, how could we prove it?

Darius started to get to his feet. "I'm going to go say hi to Holly and the teacher, get a closer look at Bruce."

I grabbed his wrist. "I should be the one. You're just my easygoing boyfriend."

He reluctantly agreed. I got up and weaved my way through the narrow space between the tables, stopping at Holly's side.

"Hi, I saw you here and just wanted to say hello. Wasn't Rupert hungry?" I spoke to Holly but offered a cheerful smile to Jill as well. Just like Birdie would do—friendly to everyone.

"He gets breakfast at his fancy bed-and-breakfast. He's got a private hot tub, ocean view, and room service," Holly said. "But I'm stuck at the motel, so here I am."

"I'm surprised he came up alone," I said.

Holly picked up her coffee. "Alone? What do you mean?"

"It sounds nice. I'd think his husband would want to join him."

Holly hesitated, swallowing. "Right." She picked up her napkin and wiped her lips. "Hm."

Her reaction made me wonder if all might not be rosy at home for Rupert. His passion for garden exhibitions might be wearing for anyone.

Jill glanced over to watch the exchange, then went back to scrolling through her phone. Was it possible they were only pretending not to know each other?

"Food here is good, don't you think?" I asked, aware Bruce was only a few feet away and probably listening. "We ate way too much. I can feel a food coma coming on." I was trying to keep up the Birdie act—enthusiastic, unsophisticated, eager to please, harmless—but it was exhausting.

Holly glanced at her plate of eggs. "It's OK."

"Are you... digging and stuff today?" I let myself sound as if I'd never gardened in my life. But the sort of work they were doing, designing and landscaping a plot from scratch in a few days, really was foreign to me. I usually let things just grow on their own. Bare dirt never stayed bare for long.

Bruce came over when he saw Jill waving her card. He took it without a word and went over to an old-fashioned cash register.

"They *really* need to modernize," Jill said loudly.

The blond man sitting past her at the counter turned to face her. "Maybe we don't want to be San Francisco," he said sharply.

We both started. It was Lacoste from the hotel. I hadn't seen him come in, which was remarkable given my interest in everyone—clear evidence of how powerful he was.

Useful for a serial killer, I thought reflexively.

The thick gold chain around his neck sizzled with magical menace.

THIRTY-FIVE

I'd expected the teacher to lecture him to mind his own business, but instead, Jill put her hand on her heart and bowed her head. "I apologize, Witch Lacoste. I spoke with ignorance and impatience."

Bruce came back with Jill's card and paper receipts. She took the pen he offered with a shaking hand, signed one, pushed them both over on the counter at Bruce. "Brightness be with you," she muttered, hurrying away.

I watched her go. A big man on Lacoste's other side got up and walked away—just like a conflict-avoidant cowboy in a Western who'd just seen the black-hat gunslinger come into the saloon.

Bruce seemed to find it necessary to bring coffee to a man on the opposite corner of the restaurant.

Eager to maintain my ignorant-and-harmless persona, I smiled at Lacoste as if I hadn't noticed he was terrifying everyone, including me, then returned to my table.

"What was that about?" Darius asked. "I felt weird energy."

"Let's go," I muttered. "Can't talk here."

"Fine with me."

Nerissa was still talking to the transfixed women at her

table when we left. I overheard words like *just what the world needs*, and *time for a change.*

As we were walking toward the Jeep parked on another street, I felt an urge to walk the long way around.

"The car's that way," Darius said.

"I feel something." I took his hand and led him down a side street, lowering my voice so only he could hear. "Start talking so it doesn't look like we're snooping."

He sighed. "Right." After a moment's pause, he began to speak in a slow drawl that immediately reminded me of an Emerald witch who'd taught us world history at the Protectorate. "Perhaps you're not familiar with the history of the first witch gold hunters to reach California. They came to San Francisco on a ship from Savannah in 1851. All men, mostly Shadow practitioners, they opened a bar along the Sacramento River. They weren't interested in digging for gold. They stole it."

I grinned at him. His impersonation of our old teacher was pretty good. "How terrible," I said.

He lowered his voice. "Maybe one of those dudes was your ancestor."

"Probably." I followed my senses to the alley behind the restaurant. Somebody nearby was smoking.

We exchanged a look. He smelled it too. "The witches took the gold," he continued, more quietly now, "and developed the first pure California magic."

"Metal witch propaganda." I was keeping up the banter in case we were seen, but now it was time to hide. I pulled him behind a dumpster with a plan to cast a stealth enchantment, but Darius was quicker. Putting his hand on the large container, he used the metal energy to create a magical spy bubble around us. We'd be able to see out but nobody—well, few—would be able to see in. It was an exhausting spell, but with four hundred pounds of steel under his palm, he wouldn't have to use much of his own power.

We edged out from behind the dumpster and peered around it to see who was standing at the back door of the restaurant. I felt a little ridiculous, figuring we were probably wasting our efforts on a cook and a waitress enjoying a quick break, but then...

Then we saw who it was. Darius and I exchanged another glance. Why would Bruce and Jill be talking to each other?

More than talking. They were arguing. Passionately. And I didn't think it was about him modernizing his customer billing system.

She was only half his size but was jabbing him in the chest with enough magical power to make him spasm each time her fingertips made contact. Her other hand held a cigarette, which she brought to her mouth for a drag between every thrust.

"Now," she was saying. "Now. Move it now."

He was shaking his head, taking the hits without fighting back.

The door knocked open. One of the waiters stood there. "Bruce, man, we need help with—"

"Later," Jill snapped.

"Right." The waiter closed the door.

"There's going to be a garden just *inches* from the pile," Jill said. "You've got to get it out of there tonight. There are going to be all kinds of witches walking right by there. For *days*."

"You said it was just the hearth-witch gardens," Bruce said. "Nobody cares about those."

Jill gave him a blast with her finger that knocked him against the door. "I care. I'm the one—"

She stopped suddenly. Drawing on her cigarette, she turned and stared at where Darius and I stood under the bubble. Neither of us needed to be told to hold our breath.

My pulse thudded in my ears. I needed air, but she was scanning the area.

Bruce regained his balance and brushed himself off. He seemed strangely calm about having been attacked. "There's an event at the fairgrounds tonight," he said. "Every city witch stuffing their face this morning is talking about it. I'll go at dawn. Unless you want these rusties seeing me?"

Rusties. That was a term I hadn't heard since I was a kid. It was a very old-fashioned term for a witch who relied on the magical efforts of others but never mastered the craft themselves. It had originated centuries ago with hearth witches who looked down on metal, but it had since come to include any witch who was useless without powerful external objects.

Finally turning away from where Darius and I stood, Jill threw down the cigarette and ground it under her snow-white athletic shoe. "She just called a staff meeting for Monday at eight. Summer vacation. Typical." Jill reached up and twisted the sleeve of Bruce's T-shirt between her fingers. "If it's not gone by then, I'm sending this to Diamond Street."

Darius and I exchanged an even-more-interested glance. Sending his personal garment to the Protectorate would be to inform on him. But for what? The agents would arrive to find out—and that wasn't something any witch wanted, even innocent ones.

"It'll be gone," Bruce said.

Shooting magical purple sparks behind her, Jill strode away in the other direction. Bruce watched her calmly, then went inside.

Just in case Jill came back to test her suspicions, we waited five minutes before leaving the protection of Darius's hiding spell, which tethered us to the dumpster. When he finally released it, I walked over, pretending to be calling for a stray kitty, and picked up Jill's discarded cigarette. I put it into a velvet bag for later use or study. Just as Bruce's shirt sweat could be used against him, or Darius's napkin, so could the spit on her cigarette.

Abandoning our gold rush conversation, we walked back to the Jeep and got inside.

"I guess we know what we'll be doing tonight," I said.

THIRTY-SIX

After driving several blocks away, we started talking about what had happened.

"Drugs?" Darius asked. "Something she's growing in the school garden she shouldn't be?"

"Maybe," I said. "Or a weapon. Like an amulet strong enough to stop an ex-agent's heart while he was driving."

He tapped the dash. "Right. Because he uncovered something they were doing. There's a connection between the restaurant and the school."

"But not to the principal," I said. "It was obvious Bruce hates Nerissa."

"They could still be working together. Criminals form alliances with people they hate all the time."

"And then there's the motel guy," I said. "Everyone's terrified of him. Even Bruce and Jill." I told him about the interaction at the counter.

Darius took out his notebook. "Maybe it's just that they know he's accused of being a serial killer but don't have the magic to do what you did and learn it was a false accusation."

We'd reached the northern end of Elwin where the last buildings gave way to redwood forest. I turned around and headed for the residential area where Raynor's ex and Marta lived. "Maybe. Hope so."

"If Percy was a young woman in a bikini, and she'd been found with a frozen rose in her mouth, maybe I'd be interested," he said.

"Yeah," I said, unconvinced. It bothered me to not understand.

"The principal. Now she's the obvious choice."

"Why would she kill Percy though?" I asked. "It's not illegal to learn mind magic."

"A principal in a public school using mind magic would be very bad. She wouldn't want that to get out."

"Don't you think everyone working with kids uses some kind of persuasive magic?" I asked. "It would be impossible to get anything done otherwise."

"But mind magic isn't just persuasion," he said. "It's extraction. Learning what you're not supposed to learn. Uncovering secrets. Look at how Jill talked about it, claiming to have an allergy. And even in the Protectorate, it didn't help Percy make any friends—at any level. Only a Shadowy witch like Bosko wanted him as his apprentice."

I parked the Jeep at the end of a residential street dotted with perfectly manicured houses protected by metal magic —all except for one.

"We've got a lot of ideas," I said, "but no proof of anything."

"We should go to the school and dig up whatever's in the bin. I can put us under another hiding shield."

"It might be better to catch the witch red-handed as he digs it up," I said. "But then we won't be able to do anything about it without blowing our cover. It might not be related to Percy's death."

Darius banged his notebook against the dash. "I hate not having Protectorate authority on this case. It makes everything so messy." With a loud exhale, he looked around. "Are we parked here for a reason?"

"Clem lives a block ahead," I said. "And Marta, Nerissa's

niece. I'm not sure Nerissa lives on this street too, but I kind of feel like she does. Something about the way the windows watched me the last time I was here."

"I took an essence reading on her at the restaurant. I'll see if I can track her."

"Essence reading? From across a crowd?" I was impressed. "Teach me that too, will you?"

"The master stays the master, and the apprentice stays the apprentice," he said, putting his hands together in a prayer pose.

I laughed. "I'm not afraid to admit I don't know something."

"Only because you're so greedy to know everything."

"Are you under that hex again?" I held up my hands in a defensive posture. Mostly kidding.

He rolled his eyes. "You're never going to let me live that down."

"I almost stopped living at all, so yeah."

"I never would've hurt you," he said stiffly, turning a page in his notebook. "If Nerissa is at the restaurant, we can try to get into her house now for a quick look around. And Marta's, too, if they're not home."

"It's broad daylight. People are around."

"Less suspicious than being the only ones." He clicked his pen and made a note. "Isn't that why you drove us here?"

I looked down the street. The tall tree in Clem's backyard was visible from a block away. "Actually, I was thinking about gnomes."

He followed my gaze. "The residue at the crash scene," he said. "Have you ever heard of a gnome hurting a human being before?"

I turned, laughing. "Willy threw you and Raynor—*Raynor*—out of my house by force. You guys were flying through the air."

"But he didn't hurt us. It was embarrassing, but he was"

—he turned back to his notebook, finishing with a mumble —"gentle."

"Because Willy is a good guy," I said. "He likes me and my dog. This gnome in Clem's backyard doesn't like her enough to give her its name after years of living together. She's afraid of it."

He nodded. "So what do you want to do?"

I took a deep breath. "Ask Clem for an introduction to her unnamed gnome and see if its fae fingerprint matches the crime scene."

"Not until we hear back from Raynor about the moonstone."

"You're eager to break into houses right now on a busy Sunday morning, but I can't go ask to say hi to a gnome?"

He nodded. "Gnomes are a complete unknown."

"Not to Clematis Mallory," I said. "If it weren't for her, Willy might still be stuck up in the tree."

Darius gazed thoughtfully down the street. "Hers is the one that looks like a deranged recluse lives there, right?"

On her behalf, I took offense. "It's a hearth witch's garden."

"It's a mess. Worse than yours."

"You just don't respect our flavor of magic," I said.

He made a noncommittal grunt. "Hard to imagine Raynor dating a woman like that."

Again, I felt myself get defensive. "She's a lovely person."

"You told me she gave boils to delivery drivers."

I adjusted the beads on my bracelet, aware my footing in the argument was rather weak. "She threatens to. I don't know that she actually does."

"You're right. Very lovely. I hope you'll introduce me."

"Is it so hard to believe a witch who follows the old ways has actually become difficult and withdrawn because everyone has treated her with so much contempt and disdain her entire life?"

Darius gave me a raised eyebrow. "You identify with her," he said. "Is that wise?"

"I'm just sharing the perspective of somebody who isn't as blinded by prejudice as you are."

"Fine. But we still shouldn't talk to the gnome until we know if that moonstone had any fae signature on it."

I crossed my arms over my chest and stared down the street, brooding for a moment. Without trees, the front yards of the houses were bathed in summer sunshine. A few dogs, both familiars and pets, watched us from behind metal fences. I realized one lump at the end of the driveway wasn't a sack of potting soil or an out-of-place outdoor cushion, but Beryl, the pug Marta had been holding.

Marta had said she and her parents lived next door to Clem, so maybe the dog, and driveway, belonged to her aunt.

"I think that's Nerissa's house," I told Darius, pointing at the property halfway down the block. It was a freshly painted Victorian with a box hedge, trimmed to perfect right angles, lining the property. "I saw her niece with that dog."

"That's a dog?" He peered through the windshield. "It's not moving."

"It's a dog. Not a good time to break into the house."

"I don't think that animal is any threat," Darius said.

I wasn't sure. Even from a distance, I had the impression Beryl's protruding eyes were fixed on us.

"Somebody's probably home if the dog is out," I said. "Let's go to the fairgrounds and hang out at my garden. We can watch the compost pile without drawing any suspicion and make sure nobody takes anything from it."

"Fine. We'll come back after we've got whatever's stashed in the dirt."

"And Raynor gets back to us about the moonstone," I added.

Ten minutes later, we pulled into the fairgrounds parking lot, and I had to park far away because of the trucks and construction. There were boulders being lifted off flatbed trucks, a twenty-foot magnolia in full bloom, and cement mixers pouring concrete. We walked through the fairgrounds to my garden at the quiet, unpopular back edge.

Rupert was there with several men in long-sleeved T-shirts and work pants. They listened to him talk as he gesticulated at the ground, a stack of logs, bags of something that looked heavy, then at papers in his hand. Holly was measuring the ground near the fence.

She had a measuring tape out and was drawing it across the same area, over and over. The goblins were sneering and pointing at her straw hat, miming taking it off and stomping on it.

I kept watching, suspicious. Why was it taking her so long to measure the ground—right across from where the compost pile was?

THIRTY-SEVEN

Darius squeezed my arm. "Rupert wants a word."

I turned toward the old man, busy drawing shapes on the ground with a stick and showing no sign of wanting to talk to me. I gave Darius an inquisitive look.

"You were staring," he mumbled in my ear.

I was going to defend myself but saw Holly's gaze on me. Two goblins had crawled up to the top of the chain-link fence and were scraping their claws along the mesh like a musician playing guitar.

"Oh look, there are paper printouts of the design." I pointed at a folding table. "I'd love to look at those."

Darius shrugged, all laid-back again, and wandered over to Holly while I flipped through the poster-sized sketches.

Rupert walked over, shoulders hunched, limping heavily on one foot. I felt a pang of guilt.

He was smiling, though, as he pointed at the sketches. "What do you think?"

"They look amazing." And they did. Trees, fountains, a gazebo, bamboo trellises, a firepit, all within just over a hundred square feet—they were like garden spreads in *Sunset Magazine*, if the magazine had a staff of witches and a billionaire's deep pockets. I'd given him Zoe's contact number for budget approval, and clearly she'd been generous. Maybe too much so.

"There are only the sketches," he said. "I'm still making changes to the final design. It's part of the magic."

I drew my finger along the drawing where the fence separated the garden from the compost pile. "Holly's working in this section?"

"She asked for it," Rupert said. "Likes the tall things. Climbers. Hollyhocks. Sunflowers."

I shook my head in wonder. "Only a witch could make all that grow in a few days."

A fanatic gleam came to Rupert's eye. "There's nothing like the Elwin Garden Show."

I looked over at Holly, who didn't seem half as passionate as her colleague. At the moment she was leaning against the fence and scrolling through her phone.

"Dash and I will get everyone coffee," I said loudly. "Or soda, iced tea, whatever you want."

Darius guessed I wanted to talk to him privately, so he played along and asked everyone what they wanted. A few minutes later we were walking toward the food truck.

"What's on your mind?" Darius asked.

"You and Holly," I said.

He gave me a wary look. "Just because she's a beautiful woman doesn't mean—"

"Listen. I've got an idea." I squinted up at the sun, wishing I'd remembered my hat. It was going to be hot again. "I studied Rupert's sketches. There isn't a final one, but it looks like for all the potential designs, he's designing the front part of the garden and Holly is going to do the back."

"He wants all the spotlight. Like all divas."

"No. He says she asked for it." I gave him a meaningful look. "Suspicious, don't you think?"

"Maybe."

"Anyway, she's going to be working along that fence all afternoon. You get what I'm saying?"

Darius nodded. "Go on."

"How about you chat her up? We can pretend I'm OK with it, or not OK with it and so we're breaking up, and there's a lot of tension and you complain to her about it."

"That doesn't make me look very good."

I played innocent. "You care about looking good for her?"

"Strategically speaking, she's not going to want me hanging around her if you're over there sulking about it."

"Do I look like the type to sulk?"

He turned and nodded. "You're totally the passive-aggressive type."

"Do you mean me or my disguise?"

He snorted. "The *real* you is aggressive aggressive."

I smiled. "That's right."

We reached the food truck and got in the back of the line. Wood sprites from the neighboring redwood forest had come over to watch the people and investigate the food and drink. I counted five sitting on top of the truck and a few more inside.

"Open relationship and you're cool with it," Darius muttered.

"Actually cool or just pretending?"

"How about you've got another guy yourself. Which you do. He's the one you really care about."

Inside the truck, two fairies were trying to open the flavored syrup bottles next to the coffee machine but had to make do with the drops that fell on the counter.

I thought of Seth and sighed. "Yeah," I said wistfully. "He's the one."

Darius caught the tone. "He's OK, right? You're in touch?"

"He's OK. Thanks."

"Good," he said. "So it's a plan."

It would be a long day for me to sit there looking

cheerful about my boyfriend hitting on other women when there wasn't much for me to do anyway. "I'll find a reason to leave," I said. "So it doesn't cramp your style."

He frowned at first, then agreed. "Gives me a reason to stay since you'll have the car."

When it was finally our turn, Darius ordered a half dozen drinks and a few breakfast burritos.

"Get her a churro," I suggested. "For Operation Woo."

Stifling a grin, he ordered two. When we got back to my garden area, the men were already digging—and Rupert had gone.

"Where'd he go?" I asked, setting the drinks on a folding table.

Darius brought Holly a churro and an iced coffee. She hesitated, then took off her gloves and took them.

"More plants," she said. "He's ordered most of it, but he said he knew a guy with a private nursery on the Mad River who's willing to sell him a few rarities he can't get anywhere else on short notice."

I hopped out of the way of one of the men who was wielding a simple shovel with more force than I'd be able to manage with a gold wand and an excavation spell. According to the design letter he'd emailed me, the garden beds were going to be three overlapping areas with a water feature enchanted with metal fixtures to give the impression of a misty dream.

While Dash shadowed Holly, I went over to Rupert's cooler to see if it needed a refill. Shopping for workers' drinks on a hot day was a good errand for the owner of the garden installation. If it was full, I could use an ice run as my excuse for leaving.

But I couldn't undo the plastic latch on the lid. I wiggled it again and realized it was locked with magic. The plastic cooler with plastic latches had hidden metal inside keeping it shut.

I tried again, running my fingers over the lid, the edges,

using a discreet tap of my magic beads to analyze what was inside.

It was completely blocked to me. I'd played around with boxes in the Protectorate security office that had weaker shields.

Pretending to get distracted by my phone, I sat on the cooler and tapped the screen absently while I turned my magical gaze into the plastic again.

Thick platinum wire. The type jewelry designers used if they could afford it. It crisscrossed the lid and interior, preventing me from detecting even a hint of the material inside.

Why would Rupert lock the drinks cooler with enchanted precious metal?

My phone vibrated. I looked at the screen and saw a message from Raynor.

Moonstone is old hex. Not fae not demon not relevant. Be more careful. R.

I sat stunned for a moment.

He was lecturing me to be more careful?

That was it?

Anger surged through me. I stood up and, very carefully, made myself put my phone away instead of hurling it into the hole the man next to me had just dug. There were too many people around for me to make a scene.

Raynor had the nerve to imply it was all my fault that Darius was hexed. That the moonstone had been abandoned by a nasty witch in the distant past, and I'd been too stupid not to leave it there.

Not relevant? Shards of glass, glowing red eyes, green smoke, Darius's loss of free will. But to Raynor, it wasn't relevant.

I let out my breath. Darius, lost in lovey-dovey land, didn't glance my way. He was listening to Holly describe (and demonstrate with her hands) how high the plants and support structures were going to be along the fence.

I was afraid I was going to lose my temper. Rupert had a

common drinks cooler that was locked with exceptionally advanced magic. A teacher and restaurant owner who used words like "pie hole" and "rusties" were involved in a conspiracy involving a school compost pile surrounded by goblins. And the principal of that school might or might not have been learning mind magic, which probably didn't but might have led her to murder an ex-Protectorate colleague of mine.

But none of this had anything to do with gnomes. The only actual evidence we had so far was that gnome residue was present at the crash scene.

Darius had wanted me to wait to approach Clem's gnome until the moonstone was formally scanned; it had been. Now, I realized, I could go to her house and ask for an introduction.

I could feel my temper subside a little.

I tried to make eye contact with Darius, but he was laughing at something Holly had said. Anyone could see he was smitten.

If I were really Dash's girlfriend, and he was over there neglecting me, it would make perfect sense for me to leave him there without saying goodbye.

Maybe I was still angry about Raynor. But it felt good to wave goodbye at the men with the shovels and mattocks, take one of the iced teas for the road, and walk away.

I was definitely in the mood for another hearth witch's company.

THIRTY-EIGHT

I was angry, but I wasn't stupid. Before I walked up to Clem's garden gate, I called Raynor from my Jeep, using the private line he'd graciously obliged to share with me.

"Hello, Alma," he said. "I knew you'd be unsatisfied with our conclusion about the moonstone."

I wasn't going to give him the satisfaction of letting him know he was right. "Tell me more about the northern coastal edition of your ex-girlfriend catalog," I said. If Clem had a killer gnome in her backyard, I'd need to know if I could rely on her for backup. "How did you two meet? Would you trust her in a crisis? Why did you break up?"

He paused. "Who are you talking about?"

I wished he could see me roll my eyes. "How many ex-girlfriends of yours are there in Elwin?"

"Clem and I weren't that serious. We were kids. You know how it is. We were friends, we fooled around, we went our separate ways."

"So... two other women? Three?"

I heard him snort his herbs. "If you're counting Clem, then one, I suppose," he said.

"Why didn't you just say so? Why did you imply there was somebody else?"

"There's a woman in Crescent City I was close to about twenty years ago." He sniffed again. "Right around when Clem bought the house in Elwin to stay, and I moved to New York."

I exhaled. It was so hard getting basic information out of Raynor. He was like Helen, hoarding his secrets until he was forced to share for his own benefit.

"Did she break your heart?" I asked.

"That's an awfully personal question. Why do you want to know?"

"There's a gnome signature where Percy went off the cliff. I want to ask the creature in Clem's backyard some questions about it."

"I see. What does Darius say?"

"To wait for you to clear the moonstone."

"Which I did," he said.

"So here I am. I'm parked in front of Clem's house."

"Is Darius there for backup?"

"No. He's at the fairgrounds following another lead." I told him about what we'd overheard and seen behind the restaurant.

Raynor was quiet for a long moment. I could feel the gears turning, comparing the advantages to disadvantages of having only me and Darius up in Elwin.

"I'll tell him what you're doing," Raynor said. "And only approach the creature if Clem agrees. After you give her my number. I'm sure she could get it herself, but that would add a delay if there's an emergency. I'll stand by."

I smiled, glad I was finally taking action. "What will you do if she calls?" I began checking my bracelets, necklaces, herbs, and other hidden amulets and beads.

He paused to snort more herbs. Something seemed to go into the wrong hole because he broke off to have a coughing fit. When he recovered, he said, "There's another agent not too far away. Off duty, but they're there."

"In Elwin?"

"Don't count on it," he said. "But within an hour or two. Maybe three."

"Male or female?" I prompted. "From Diamond Street? New York?"

"Let me know how it goes with the gnome." The phone went dead.

Demon's balls. He was hiding *more* things from me. I pulled my hair back into a tight ponytail, cursing his name a few times.

But I had to admit it was a good thing Darius and I weren't the only agents in the area. It was annoying Raynor hadn't been honest upfront, but it was a relief to know we might have help if hexes started flying.

My phone chimed with a text from Darius.

Heard from Raynor. Keep me posted.

It was only midday, hours from when Bruce said he'd go dig up whatever was in the compost. Darius could enjoy the long wait in Holly's lovely company. I responded with a thumbs-up emoji and locked up the car, leaving the phone in my bag inside.

The gnome was hostile to most humans, even witches. So would it be safer to wear more magic or less to meet it?

I thought about Willy's reactions to my magic over the years. He'd once asked me if I was angry with him after I'd loaded up my boundary spells with new herbs and potions.

Less would be better. I unlocked the car, slipped off the phony jewelry and most of the real pieces, then tucked them into my bag. I put a large piece of petrified wood that I'd offer as payment into my pocket.

The item I did not leave behind was an amulet I relied on most and seldom removed, a chunky redwood-bead necklace I'd carved under the full moon in my backyard. The redwood, a difficult wood to work because it splintered so easily, came from a branch in the tree Willy lived in. Clem's gnome would be able to sense his connection to it— and hopefully, to me.

With a glance down the street at Nerissa's driveway,

now absent the dog, I walked up to Clem's garden gate with the petrified wood in my hand.

The sun was directly overhead. Midday in June—a powerful time for witches who paid attention to the celestial bodies more than precious metals or gemstones.

A shiver of power ran through me. I was attuned to the old ways, more every day, and savored the deliciousness of Clem's overgrown lavender, lilac, coyote bush, *Mimulus*, blackberry, *yerba buena*, lupine, yarrow, poppy, and sage...

My senses swam with it all. I was dizzy with all the *potential* living in Clem's front garden. If I were a judge in the Elwin Flower Show, I would've given her gold.

But I certainly wasn't a judge, and the real ones probably wouldn't see it the way I did. The magic was secretive and wild, unwilling to be tamed with a human hand or shovel or even a trellis of bamboo stakes.

What a garden. What a witch Clem must be to have cultivated it.

While I was staring in wonder, she stepped out from behind a multibranching sunflower. "Hi, Alma." She didn't look surprised about my visit, maybe because she'd seen me outside the café earlier. "Has something happened to your gnome again?"

THIRTY-NINE

She wore a red cotton sunhat with her hair tucked up inside, creating a lump at the crown. She wore matching pink overalls with a trowel hanging from a loop at her hip and its pockets visibly overflowing with seed packets, a muddy glove, and twine. Her sunglasses were also pink and studded with tiny crystals.

"No, he's fine," I said. "Thanks to you. The stick worked."

"Thanks to old Whatshername." Clem adjusted her glasses, drawing my attention to the tiny diamonds in the corners of the cat-eye frames. Apparently she wasn't exclusively a user of botanical magic. "Small steps. She wasn't angry at me the other day when I nipped out there for a sprig of parsley."

I tried to imagine what it would be like to share a property with a paranormal being who might give me a hard time for cutting my own herbs. If it were me, I would've moved by now.

"I saw you yesterday walking a dog?" I looked around the yard for any sight of the little animal.

"That's Nemesis." She flinched, shaking her head. "The meanest dog you've ever met. Except it would be better you didn't. She bites. Right now she's enjoying the second bedroom for her nap."

It seemed Clem had a high tolerance for intolerable creatures and none for everyone else. "I love dogs," I said, though probably not hers. "Sorry for bothering you again. I... I wanted your help with something else. I've brought this as a token, but I'd love to get you something bigger and better if you can think of something I might offer you in exchange."

I held out the petrified wood. She adjusted her glasses again and stepped forward to take it, her fingers brushing mine. I realized she was shorter than I'd remembered. The top of her sunhat barely came up to my forehead, and her fingers were as small as Marta's.

Her personality was much larger than the reality.

"Thank you," she said, weighing the object in her hand. "This is remarkable. Where did you find it?"

"There's a petrified forest in Sonoma County, not far from where I live. You're not supposed to take samples, of course, but it followed me home somehow. It... jumped into my pocket."

Clem gave me a sly grin. "Your father teach you that?"

I didn't like the joke, but we were on her property, and I was asking for a favor. "Unfortunately, it was one of the few things he cared about enough to share with me," I said.

She snorted. "Men." Holding the object to her temple, she paused, nodded slowly, then lowered her hand. "Well, I would like to keep this piece of an ancient sequoia. Millions of years old, my senses tell me. Before I commit, however, I'll need to hear your request."

"Of course." I swallowed, nervous. "I'd like you to introduce me to your backyard gnome."

Clem's mouth dropped open. For once, she seemed unsure of herself.

I rushed on. "I understand it's dangerous. I know she might refuse to talk to me. But I believe she might be able to"—this is where I was most afraid of offending both Clem and the gnome—"tell me something about Percy's death."

Clem frowned. "Percival Tuff. The teacher."

"Yes. He drove off the cliff." I'd decided to avoid telling the complete truth. "I'd like to know why. My gnome shares information about the world with me—I have no idea how he knows everything he knows—but I thought yours might be the same. Maybe there's a gift or payment I could offer her. I could get food. Or magic. I'll do my best to make a fair trade. Do you think you'd let me do that?"

"I heard he had a heart attack," Clem said, her face giving nothing away.

"He was a witch. It seems too coincidental for it to have happened at the most dangerous spot in town."

She said nothing, gazing at me from behind her pink sunglasses for several long, tense seconds. "I wondered the same," she said finally. "Of course I'll let you try to talk to her. I can't promise anything."

I let out a long breath. Asking her to talk to the gnome had made me more nervous than I'd realized. "Thank you."

"As far as gifts, she might value this even more than I do." She held up the petrified sequoia.

I hesitated, unsure if she was offering to give it to her. "I'm sorry, that's the only piece I have."

The breeze caught the edge of her hat and pushed it down over her eyes. "Perhaps we can agree that, if she helps you, you'll acquire another." She lowered her sunglasses and peered at me with her bright blue eyes. "And see that I get it."

"Yes. Absolutely. No problem." The nonmag administration of the petrified forest park didn't have a chance against a witch raised by the best thief in the magical world.

"Then we have a deal." With a small nod, she folded her sunglasses, put them in the chest pocket of her overalls, and gestured at a path that ran along the side of the house. "I trust you won't struggle against the defensive magic of my property as we walk through? It would only backfire."

"I understand." It would be the same at my house.

I followed her through the gate, bracing myself for the sizzle of sensation that covered me from nose to toe, then dove under my skin and wrapped around my bones like electric wire. It was unpleasant, but I paused to let it happen.

Nodding her satisfaction when it was done, she led me around the overgrown shrubs and perennials through a gate in the tall redwood fence.

The small backyard was as thick with greenery as the front. Towering above it was a large tree in the far-right corner, similar to my redwood. Unlike my property, however, there was no hint of open space beneath it that might pretend to be a lawn.

Before getting any closer to the tree, I reached into my pocket and took out the scrap of paper where I'd written Raynor's phone number.

"If anything happens to me, please call Raynor's direct line." Only as I was handing it to her did I remember she didn't use telephones. Swearing, I retracted my arm. "Sorry. I forgot you don't—"

She held out her hand, palm up. "It's OK. You'd better give it to me." Her lips curved in a self-deprecating smile. "I can't always indulge my eccentric little preferences, especially when a life is at stake."

Relieved, I handed her the yellow note. "Hopefully you won't have to use it."

She became serious. "It's important to see justice done."

For a moment, we regarded each other. Over twenty years separated us, but I felt a kinship with her. "I agree."

She handed me the petrified wood. "I'd give you advice, but I think it would be better for you to follow your instincts." She smiled faintly. "After all, your gnome has trusted you with his name while mine continues to withhold hers."

I took the hunk of stone, once part of an ancient tree, and felt its ancient life force tingle in my palm. When Clem put her pink sunglasses back on and strode away through the shrubs and flowers, I turned toward the tree.

"Hello, honorable gnome," I began, subconsciously imitating Willy's odd turns of phrase as I held out my gift and took a step closer. "I am being most appreciative of your lovely garden. Please, if you have the patience, I would be deeply grateful if—"

I was struck by a magical blast more painful than any I'd ever felt in my life. It swallowed my gasp, locking me in a silent scream, and propelled me through the air.

FORTY

The magical strike felt like a current of fire laced with rocks, nails, and poisonous snake's teeth. It tore through my defenses as if they were tissue paper, ripping away my boundary spells, clothing, skin, bones, and muscle until my blood and soul were bare.

My external body, a minor concern at that moment, landed in a rosebush with arching canes and long, piercing thorns.

The worst thing—well, it was one of the bad things, maybe not the worst—was that I couldn't even see the gnome. Unlike other fae, gnomes could control if I saw them or not. This one wasn't showing herself. She was going to destroy me without ever letting me glimpse her little hateful self.

No. She was trying to. But one of the advantages of extreme, blinding pain was how quickly it brought out a witch's strongest powers. Without thought, I'd already begun to defend myself.

There was no reason to try to negotiate, to beg. Any creature that would attack a peaceful visitor who approached with a gift and respectful language—attacking with killing strength—wasn't a creature worth talking to.

Without conscious thought, I began to shape-shift into

a cat. My clothes were tangled up in the caning rosebush, but my smaller feline body, emerging within seconds from my human frame, had more flexibility. I was able to wriggle through the bottom of the shirt, kick off the pants, and dart, screeching with fury, into the undergrowth. My necklace, by my design, was the right size to fit both my human and cat bodies.

I'd never shifted so fast. The pain of the transformation was nothing compared to the gnome's continuous super-natural assault.

What a monster.

For a moment I became trapped between a raised bed and a jumble of ceramic pots, which allowed the violent energy to strike me, at full concentration, in my left ribs for two solid seconds. But then, howling with pain, I leaped over the pots, knocking over a glass ball on a spike, and scrambled under and through a summer vegetable patch that hadn't yet grown mature enough to slow me down.

The decorative glass ball, taking the force of the blast, exploded behind me into tiny pieces. There was then a pause in the magical blast, allowing me to duck under a lemon tree, over a mound of crawling rosemary, and onto an arching trellis. I climbed it and then jumped with grace I'd never have in my human form to the top of a shed. Then, finally, I was trotting along the fence, and from there, piercing the boundary spell that was aimed more at keeping visitors out than holding them in, I slipped across the property line onto the neighbor's fence.

The survival instinct had allowed me to keep my human wits about me long enough to escape, but now I was feeling them dissolve the way a dream quickly fades with the first light of day.

There was no use fighting it. For the next few hours, I'd have to trust my cat self to keep me alive.

It was doing a better job of it than I had. Had Clem known how dangerous her gnome was? Was there something about me, my magic, possibly Willy, that had triggered her?

My human consciousness splintered into a collection of feline urges for other things.

The last thing I remembered was leaping off the fence into a plot of green plastic turf that would never, ever attract a gnome.

WHEN I REGAINED MY AWARENESS, I found myself licking my paws on the windowsill of an old house that smelled like burning lasagna.

With my human intelligence restored, I looked more closely at my paws to see any sign of having raided somebody's meal, but they were already clean. The smell was coming from inside the house.

I was next to a window that overlooked a tidy and sterile backyard—all gravel, potted succulents, and decking —so I knew I hadn't returned to Clem's house. Thank Brightness.

Not much of a view for the person inside the house. I turned and looked through the window to see an enormous modern kitchen with slate-gray cabinets, white granite counters, and stainless-steel appliances.

Again, clearly not Clem's house. The blinding countertops were empty of canisters holding herbs, dried flowers, owl pellets, fur, rodent bones, or similar hearth-witch valuables. There was a knife block and an expensive blender, but nothing else.

The burning smell came from the smoke coming out of the oven.

Had I come here because I was hungry or because I'd sensed something I knew my human brain needed to deal with?

First I needed to know where I was. I brushed against the house, then licked my paw.

It tasted like Nerissa Pike. This was her house.

She'd forgotten her dinner in the oven. Was it possible, in a fit of altruism, my cat self had wanted to find her and warn her about it?

I jumped down and crossed the patio to the sliding patio doors. There was a flap for—I wrinkled my nose in disgust—a dog.

Well, Darius had wanted to break in. Might as well take advantage of my shape. Once I told him about how dangerous the gnome was in Clem's backyard, maybe the Protectorate would finally take an interest.

I climbed through the flap and walked proudly into the house. My brain was ruling the head now, but my body was still a cat.

The unpleasant odor of burning tomatoes and pasta made me want to run away and find a lovely goldfinch to eat instead. And I might have were it not for the other scent in the house. One that was much worse.

A dead body.

FORTY-ONE

I padded across the hardwood floors until I found her. Slumped over a desk facing the street, Nerissa Pike stared over my head with empty eyes.

It wasn't good for me to be there. I didn't want to be seen, as a cat or a human, which would only confuse the investigation.

With a second witch to die suddenly in a short time, the Protectorate would be there as soon as they heard of it.

And I'd have to be the one to sound the alarm.

I turned and trotted out the way I'd come, following my path as closely as possible. Before I was five, my father had taught me how to step in the same place and use magic both to avoid making any impressions or erase the ones I did.

Out the flap in the door—I hadn't observed any sign of the pug—and then over the fence to the street.

As I walked to my Jeep, I scanned the area for clues. People, magical footprints, amulets, herbs, anything. But it was just me and the acrid smoke rising from Nerissa's house.

At the Jeep, I wasn't surprised to find Darius sitting in the passenger seat. A year ago I'd started leaving openings in my boundary spells just for him and a few others I trusted. After he'd attacked me in the motel, I'd reconsidered changing that, but now was glad I hadn't.

He got out when he saw me trot up the sidewalk. After looking around to see if we were being observed, he opened the door for me.

Since my clothes were in Clem's rosebush, I curled up on the floorboards in the back seat and meowed as loudly and urgently as I could, aiming to express the importance of getting me back to the hotel where my clothes were so I could tell him what I'd just seen and experienced.

Had the gnome killed Nerissa in her hunt for me? Or was there some other motive for wanting her dead?

Darius proved himself a brilliant agent and beloved human being by driving immediately to the motel. I was grateful he had both magical and nonmag tools to utilize a car that wasn't his. I was also grateful I'd brought a bottle of antihistamines, because as soon as I shifted back into my human body, I was going to be hit with a crippling allergic reaction.

He parked in front of our motel room and sighed. "Well. At least you're alive." He craned around to look down at me on the floorboards. "I assume you can understand me?"

I meowed.

"The serial killer is sunbathing right over there next to the pool," he continued. "He's got a towel over his face, but I bet he's going to watch me go in. And you. How would you feel about climbing into a bag? Is that something you'll try to claw my eyes out about?"

I didn't deign to reply. Turning away from him, I began licking my right paw.

Scoffing, he left the Jeep, went into the room, and returned with his magical bag. He opened it on the back seat and said, "Please be reasonable."

I had been offended by his suggestion that I would be irrational, but now I was tempted to jump out the door and walk out in the open like a queen.

"I had to leave the compost bin unattended," he said.

"Raynor got a call from his ex when you disappeared. He told me to get over there ASAP. Now I want to get back. But I need to hear what happened." His tone sharpened. "Please, Alma. There's no time."

My human intelligence overrode my feline pettiness, so I stopped licking myself and got into the bag.

Less than a minute later I climbed out in the bathroom. Darius brought me clothes, closed the door, and I shifted back into my human form.

Without the adrenaline of an attack to distract me, the sudden awareness of pain made me cry out. Bones and flesh, suddenly transforming into its proper shape, brought both physical and emotional agony. But it was quick, and as soon as I had use of my fingers, I clutched the bead necklace that I'd designed to survive a shift and used the redwood to soothe myself.

Ah. I exhaled, doubled over. My first thought was that the grout on the tile was disgusting. The second was that Darius didn't know Nerissa Pike was dead.

The third was blasted away by the first sneeze. Then another.

I tore through my toiletries bag and found the mouse bones. Better than a pill from the pharmacy, mouse bones that had passed through the interior of its predator, the owl, had marvelous restorative power.

I crunched them between my teeth and washed them down with tap water that tasted like rust and chlorine.

But it worked.

"Darius?" I pushed away from the sink and hurried out into the room, afraid he'd been so eager to get back to the stupid compost pile that he'd left already.

He stood by the door, wearing more silver, platinum, and gold than I'd ever seen him wear before—and he'd always enjoyed a lot of metal. The hippy disguise had been dropped, replaced with a formfitting black T-shirt and slim jeans. He held an official Protectorate "silver jacket" in his hand. His hair was back to normal—short twists over a mid fade. His eyes gleamed with hard, sharp intelligence.

"But—" I began, wondering if he already knew about the dead principal. "Did you—?"

"Raynor agrees there's no longer a justification for disguise. A gnome of some Shadowed type we didn't know about before has attacked you, a Bright witch in the light of day, in front of a witness." He adjusted the platinum chain at his throat. "I'm allowed now to discourage further insults."

He still didn't know. I sneezed. The owl pellet worked best if I took it beforehand. Being allergic to cats was so ridiculous and annoying. "Nerissa Pike"—I sneezed—"is dead. I saw her"—another sneeze—"dead in her h— slumped at—her desk." With a curse, I covered my face and sneezed five more times in a row.

"Demon's balls." Darius immediately pulled on the silver jacket. It was black leather, adorned with zippers, buttons, studs, hooks, chains, and other hardware all made out of silver. To a witch, the official silver jacket would declare the Protectorate was on duty, and everyone was under suspicion, vulnerable to interrogation, and had better behave themselves.

"I'll call—Ray—nor." I ran for the bathroom and grabbed a handful of tissues.

While I was helplessly wiping up snot, I heard Darius talking to someone. He appeared a moment later in the bathroom doorway, holding the phone. "Raynor."

I was too weak to use a screening spell before putting Darius's phone against my cheek. The fatigue of the shift was rapidly catching up to me. First the sneezing, then the nap. Often I'd need to sleep around the clock.

"Hello," I said. My eyelids were pulling down. Only magic was keeping me from falling over. In a hurried, semi-coherent series of words, I told him exactly what I'd seen and sensed in Nerissa's house.

"Too bad you walked through the crime scene, leaving

your traces," he said. "But it's good I told you to give Clem my number. She actually called me. A team's on their way up."

I handed the phone to Darius and staggered over to the bed. "Clem's backyard. Was like a firehose of... of... needles and iron pokers. With nails and thorns in it. Hurt. Don't... recommend."

Darius pulled the blanket over me. "Got it. I can't really hear what you're saying, but I get the idea."

"Sorry... about... compost. Watching. Things. Bin." The tide of exhaustion was sucking me out to the sea of sleep. Should I tell him about the goblins?

"Raynor will get another agent on that and see if they're connected."

As I was reflecting on goblins, realizing how they weren't too physically unlike gnomes if you ignored the sneering and extra nostril and sharp teeth, I lost consciousness.

FORTY-TWO

I t was light outside when I woke, which suggested a day had passed. Hopefully not two.

As my memory of earlier events kicked in, I sat up with a start. I looked around for Darius, but the motel room was empty. I grabbed my phone off the side table and checked messages.

It was Monday—but already six thirty in the evening, meaning I'd been asleep almost twenty-four hours.

I had a text from Seth. He said he was fine, baby was born and is fine, puppy is fine, hopes I'm fine. It was completely inadequate as far as detailed information or anxiety regarding my well-being, but I was relieved.

For a moment, I considered calling him, wanting to hear his voice, be comforted a little. But I read between the lines about the baby being born and decided he'd been through trials of his own. I didn't want to add to his burdens.

There was one from Raynor, charming and respectful as always: *Stay away from that street.*

And finally, a short text from Darius. He'd been starting a magical scan of Nerissa's body when the nonmag cops arrived, forcing him to hurry away.

Now he and the rest of the Protectorate would have to

lie low until it was safe to go back into the house. He was maintaining the enchantments that hid the Protectorate SUVs on the street outside.

I called him, muttering a persuasive charm under my breath to make him answer.

"Hey," he said. I heard voices, beeps, and buzzing behind him. "Did you use magic to make me answer?"

Easier to apologize than ask permission. "Sorry. I'm desperate. Just woke up. What's happening?"

He exhaled loudly, and I heard the slam of a car door. The beeping and voices went quiet, replaced with road noise.

"Are you outside her house?" I asked.

"Hold on, hold on," he muttered. "Demon's balls."

I could hear him walking, a car going past, birds chirping—then nothing. It was better than high-end noise-canceling headphones.

"I've got three minutes max. In a bubble," he said. "Are you OK?"

"Fine. Hey, thanks for being there for me yesterday."

"Of course," he said, sounding affronted at the implication he wouldn't be.

"Clem actually called Raynor?"

"You gave her his number," he said. "Why wouldn't she?"

I scoffed. "Because she's totally antisocial and doesn't touch anything invented before World War I?"

"Raynor didn't say anything about that."

"Maybe that's why the gnome tolerates her and nobody else," I said. "A shared hate of modern technology."

"I don't know," he said. "And we might not get the chance to find out. We've been told to figure out what happened to Nerissa Pike. She was connected to powerful people, apparently. Old family, old money, East Coast, blah blah blah. Probably related to you."

I ignored the family dig. "What happened to me in that backyard and Nerissa's death have to be related." The supernatural world was dangerous, but witches didn't usually have to fight off multiple killers within a block in the same afternoon.

"Blaming it on a gnome is too incredible for them to believe. They want an answer that's within their experience."

I flung myself in a chair and slapped the table. Of course the attacks were related. They had to be. "What's the official cause of death?"

"Suicide," he said.

I paused, not believing my ears. "Excuse me?"

"There's a note."

"The nonmag cops think it's suicide, or the Protectorate does?"

"Both, possibly. I scanned the note. It felt real."

I shook my head. "What'd it say?" I didn't think Nerissa, who valued herself so highly, would ever remove herself from the world.

"I wasn't able to read it. I was just preparing a spell to open it without leaving a trace when the nonmag police car pulled up outside."

"Any gnome signature around the body? Maybe she lashed out at Nerissa after I escaped."

"No trace. Just Nerissa and the dog," he said. "By the way, I also wasn't able to detect a fake cat who'd just been there."

I grinned. "Yeah. I learned that trick as a kid."

"How—Right. Your illustrious family taught you."

"Don't be jealous," I said. "Did you find Beryl?"

"Who's Beryl?"

I rolled my eyes. "The *dog*." After I spent time as a cat, people could get on my nerves more. But Darius was also being particularly difficult, probably because he was back in the bosom of an official Protectorate operation.

"Oh yeah, it's with Nerissa's niece, Marta. Apparently it goes where it likes. Wanders the neighborhood."

"So Beryl might know something," I said. "Is there a dog

expert on the team? One of them should sit down with her and—"

"Already underway. We have done this before, you know," Darius said. "Diamond Street didn't collapse when you were let go."

I almost meowed at him. "Who's on the team that Raynor sent up?"

He listed the names of five agents who had arrived to screen Nerissa's house. I hadn't worked with any of them before.

"They don't know you're here, and Raynor wants to keep it that way," he said. "He doesn't want them interviewing you. The official story is that I'm here because he sent me up earlier under cover to investigate Percy's death."

"He's just covering his—"

"If any agent does recognize you, just tell them you're here for the flower show," he said. "Your reputation fits with that."

"Yes, I am a sad little hearth witch with an Incurable Inability," I said. "Maybe I can crawl out of my shame hole with a big prize at a flower show."

"Oh, don't complain. You like being underestimated."

I bit back a smile. Maybe I did. "What does Clem say about the attack on me?"

Silence.

"You *did* talk to her, right?" I asked.

"She won't come out of her house."

I imagined two Protectorate dudes with their chests out and chin up, sneering at her rose arbor and front yard jungle, demanding she heed their summons to account for herself.

"You should be the one to go talk to her," I said. "With head bowed. Show respect."

"I did," he said. "I could feel those rose vines getting thicker and thornier, blocking anyone out."

"Then I'll go," I said, knowing this time Raynor wouldn't allow it.

He actually laughed. "As if. This is out of your hands now, and you know it," he said. "You're here for the Elwin Flower Show. Enjoy it. Recuperate from the attack."

Well. I had mixed feelings about standing aside. A few days ago I'd been annoyed to be expected to investigate, but now...

Now it was personal. I'd been attacked with more spiteful magic than I'd ever felt before, and I'd been hexed by a lot of powerful witches over the years.

"What about the teacher and the restaurant guy? What's in the compost pile?"

"We might have missed our chance," Darius said. "I had to leave it and rescue you. Besides, all the plants Holly put up—seriously fast, like snapping her fingers or something —made it impossible for me to watch the school anymore. The plants were too thick."

"Do I have permission to—?"

"Don't talk to me about anything," he said quickly. "For Brightness's sake, don't tell me what you're going to do."

FORTY-THREE

I was pleased Darius wasn't going to rat on me. "All right. I won't tell you."

"The bubble's three seconds away—stay safe—two—keep Seth informed—one. Goodbye." He clicked off.

My stomach growled, reminding me I'd slept through several meals. I ordered a pizza before I took a shower, got dressed, and recast the spells on my disguise. When dinner came, I gobbled it down with a few more mouse bones to knock out the last of my allergies, then went out.

The summer sun was still bright in the sky, which would be convenient for an evening visit to the fairgrounds. I was a little tempted to go to the restaurant to listen to the gossip and see if Bruce was there, but I decided it was more urgent to talk to the goblins on the compost bin. The fairy who lived under the bridge in Silverpool was relatively talkative with me, especially when a Protector was on duty nearby, but most fae were not. Maybe a murder would loosen the goblins' tongues.

Even as the sun was sinking low in the sky and there was an exciting local murder to distract the curious, the labor at the fairgrounds continued at full throttle. More than one crane was placing car-sized boulders, statuary, or trees in my—no, Rupert's—competitors' gardens. Magic lanterns enhanced the nonmag floodlights, making me squint as I walked through the installations. The stone and metal witches also used a lot of hard, shiny materials that reflected the light. Many people I passed were wearing sunglasses.

Two days to go.

At first I walked right by my own designated garden plot because I didn't recognize it. I reached the end of the row and turned around, surprised I hadn't been able to identify it from the other gardens.

In the hearth-witch area, all the gardens were as miraculously—magically—elaborate as the modern witches' but in a natural way. Mixed in with the herb knot and kitchen gardens were jungles and forests and native meadows that were enchanted to seem as if they'd been growing there, twelve feet apart from each other, for centuries.

I had to take out my phone for a reminder of which plot address was mine. Little aluminum tags floated at chin level along the walkway, identifying my competitors by category and entry number. I found mine—H9—and stopped to stare.

The back fence and the compost pile behind it were completely hidden by sunflowers, morning glory, hollyhock, jasmine, roses, and honeysuckle—as well as edibles such as vertically trained cucumber, tomato, squash, and beans.

And that was just the very back of the garden. The middle section contained an ancient-looking wishing well in a meadow of wildflowers. And the very front boasted a wide walkway of circular stepping stones made of petrified wood.

Incredible. So much petrified wood gave off a powerfully ancient, intriguing earth power that made my knees weak. My soul wanted to drop to the ground and press my forehead to each individual fossil so I could soak it deep into my bones.

How had Rupert done it? It wasn't hard to get so much

petrified wood if money was no object, but these pieces had the special aura of very local, very ancient redwood.

Clem had been grateful for one small piece of petrified redwood, and this garden—the one with my name on it—made the material look as common as a cardboard shipping box.

But as amazing as the pathway was, or the towering vertical garden behind it, the wishing well was what made me stare, mouth open, wondering if I was going to faint.

It was real. There truly was a deep well with a bucket and pulley that could retrieve water from deep below.

And it didn't feel like ordinary water.

"What do you think?" Rupert asked.

He stood at my elbow, drinking out of a low-carb, high-caffeine drink. His gnarled fingers holding the can were scratched and worn with dirt under the nails, and his bright eyes blazed with energy that hadn't come from his beverage. It was the gleam of a creative genius who was proud of his work and was desperate for it to be recognized—enhanced with synthetic, biological, and supernatural consumables.

"It's incredible," I whispered. "How did you create the illusion of a wellspring like that?"

Because even to me, the water in the bottom of his brick garden creation gave off the magical scent of powerful springwater.

"How long did it take for you to realize it wasn't real?" he asked.

"Took me longer than I'd like to admit," I said. "I've… I've seen a real wellspring. Nobody should be able to fool me on that."

He sipped his drink, smiling around the can. The aluminum connected with the stones in his earrings to make the hairs of his thick white eyebrows stand on end.

The man was wired. He probably hadn't slept since he'd gotten here, maybe even before that.

In all the distractions, I'd forgotten about his weird

enchantment-protected cooler. But seeing his manic energy and the outrageous magical well he'd installed in a stony coastline, I suspected the cooler contained organic substances the Protectorate had banned for all uses, foreign or domestic. And this week he was using all of them.

"You need to sleep," I said gently, terrified I'd pushed him to an extreme he could never come back from. He was vibrating hard enough to make his teeth chatter.

"I'm not tired," he said, laughing. "Don't worry. I'll catch my winks after I've won the gold."

I took a step back. The buzz was affecting me from just a few feet away. "Where's Holly?"

"No idea." He sipped his drink. The shimmer over his skin grew brighter.

"When's the last time you saw her?"

"When the Armenian cucumber went in."

"When was that?" I asked, losing my temper. "Last night? This morning?"

He drained the can, shook his head. "Oh no, she was done with the rear border yesterday. Not long after Dash left—sorry about any drama there, by the way. I needed the moon and the sun to be in the proper position to install the well enchantment, so I encouraged her to work quickly." He looked sheepish. "I may have been unpleasant about it. But don't worry, I gave her a little extra when I paid her."

"She's gone? You don't expect to see her again?"

His gaze returned to the garden. "It's done," he said softly. "Look at it. What else is there to do? Nothing. There's nothing more to be done. It's *perfect*."

So Holly had left and wasn't coming back. I'd never realized a garden could be installed so quickly. Was landscape design her biggest talent, however, or could she have been using it as a front for smuggling illegal magic?

I stared at the back wall of sunflowers, cucumbers, tomato, and morning glory, trying to see through the thicket. Whatever had been hidden in the compost must be long gone by now.

But the goblins would still be there.

"Thank you, Rupert," I said. "I hope you win the gold. You deserve it."

He smiled at me, unblinking. "I do. I really do. That is, *you* do. It's your garden."

I shook my head. "No, this is definitely yours. You should tell everyone. Put your name on it. This is your masterpiece, not mine."

After all, I'd done absolutely nothing. And Raynor wanted me out of sight, which would be hard to maintain if I won a huge, famous competition.

Rupert's eyes became glossy with emotion. "Maybe I'll reveal myself later," he said. "Thank you. Thank you so much."

I flashed a peace sign—enhanced with a dash of magical serenity—and hurried away from Rupert and his wired self to charm some goblins.

CHAPTER

FORTY-FOUR

After a quick detour to my Jeep, I went to the school.
And discovered the Protectorate had gotten there first.

I shouldn't have been surprised they were there—Nerissa had been the principal, and she'd been important enough to draw serious scrutiny—but my brain was still fuzzy from sleeping twenty-four hours on heavy doses of antihistamines.

The two agents were dressed as utility company workers and carried boxes and tools enchanted to appear nonmagical. But as soon as I crossed out of the fairgrounds onto campus property, I became aware of the familiar hum of standard screening magic the Protectorate used in their investigations.

As part of the screening, they'd sprinkled iron filings on the pavement in front of the school office, which was at the end of the wing of the building closest to the street, and then linked it to a "utility" truck parked in the loading zone. One man stood with his back to me inside the Circle, which was the same size as his arms would reach, muttering a spell to feel magical fingerprints. Not all witches used words, but some couldn't do magic without them. I myself wasn't so impaired.

252

The other agent stood outside the truck, watching me.

"The school is closed right now," he said, using a phony wrench to fling a repulsion beam at me. "We're doing some dangerous electrical work."

I reflected the spell but tried to look distracted as I did it so he'd think I'd only been able to overpower him through some sort of freak good fortune.

He frowned at his wrench, put it down, got another.

"Oh, I'm in the flower show," I exclaimed. "I won't go anywhere near the school. Just over there where my garden backs up against the fence." I pointed across the playground.

"You'll have to come back later." He waved the new wrench.

I dodged it by holding up my hands in a begging position, which placed my redwood-bead bracelet directly in the hex's path, repelling it. "I can't! The show starts the day after tomorrow," I said. "Please? I'll be way over there. Some of my... my sunflowers, which are totally important for my installation, they are leaning too far over the fence into the school, and you can barely see them. I just need to push them back. It won't take more than a minute or two."

While he frowned at the second wrench for failing to send me away, I tilted my wrists to aim the redwood beads at him. Inspired by the other agent's use of spell words, I whispered, "Please" as I tapped into my wood magic.

He looked up at me and frowned, his mouth falling open. I waited a moment for him to give permission, but he just kept staring.

"Thank you!" With a wave, I jogged past as if he'd agreed.

Falling back against the truck, he watched me run by without a word.

I might have struck too hard. I was confident he wouldn't tell the other agent, however—his pride wouldn't let him.

The compost pile was around the corner from the office,

and when the agent in the Circle didn't call out for me to stop, I let out a relieved breath.

Now the goblins.

They were in the same place they'd been before, sitting on the bin or the overflowing scraps, making rude gestures and pulling faces at me.

I walked up to the pile, pretending I couldn't see them, and wrapped my fingers around my largest redwood bead for my scan.

It took a moment for me to separate all the personalities in my mind.

There were the traces of Jill...

A few children...

Four or five other adults, but in the distant past...

And Bruce. His traces were the most recent, within the past twenty-four hours, confirming my fear that he'd come and dug up whatever had been buried there. It was the most logical explanation for why his essence covered the ground, the scattered cardboard, the planks of wood forming the bin, and the compost itself.

Wait. His wasn't the most recent. It was...

I sighed, frustrated and regretful, guilty and annoyed.

Holly. She'd done a good track-erasing spell, but since I'd learned those at such a young age, I was able to recognize it. Eventually.

Well, it seemed the pile of rotting kitchen scraps and shredded cardboard was the most irresistible place in Elwin. I was surprised I couldn't also detect Rupert, Lacoste, his wife, Clem, Marta, and Nerissa. For Brightness's sake, maybe I'd find Beryl's signature too.

The goblins were doing clumsy aerial dances around my head. They didn't need solid materials to support their weight since they didn't actually have any.

Dropping the pretense of not seeing them, I took the trail mix out of my pocket and held it up. If the local river fae had enjoyed the coconut, maybe the goblins would too. "Hi, guys, this is for you. Let's talk."

While gnomes enjoyed formality and long sentences, goblins were less wordy and certainly never let good manners slow them down.

"Witch, witch, witch, witch, witch," one said. Goblins loved prime numbers.

The other sang a different word, rhyming the first, and they burst into cackles as they somersaulted through the air.

I closed the trail mix bag and started to put it back in my pocket.

"Eat, eat, eat," the first goblin said, with slightly less hostility. It was almost an apology.

They really did look like gnomes. Ones with green skin who hadn't eaten for months, never indulged in clean clothes or bathing, and filed their teeth to points sharp enough to pierce cowhide.

"The witch who was here and dug something up," I said. "The man. What was it that he took away?"

They hovered but said nothing. I held up the bag, and each took pieces of walnut, cashew, or coconut.

"Witch drink, witch drink, witchy," said the goblin.

A drink. Interesting. "Was it what we'd call a potion?"

"Yes, yes, potion." He glared at me out of green eyes.

I gave him more of the bag. All were listening, but only one was talking. He deserved the best share. "Do you know what the potion had inside it? The witches were hiding it here, which means it was probably something witches don't usually have."

He clawed a handful of trail mix out of the bag, pushed it into his mouth, and said nothing.

"Maybe you don't have the power to know what was in the potion," I said. "Maybe you're not strong enough."

The goblin threw up the cashews, only the cashews, on my head. "Strong enough, me."

I wiped them off and flung them into the compost. As a witch, I'd had worse things in my hair. "Tell me what was in the potion, and I'll believe you."

"Juice of the small ones," he said.

The tiny hairs across my body jolted to attention. I hesitated. "Small what?"

"Small witch ones, like you," he said.

"Juice?" I whispered.

"Witch juices, witch juices, witch juices...," they chanted.

I fell back a step. Then I turned away from the fetid compost and flies and goblins to find a mouthful of clean air.

Small witch ones. I'd imagined black-market botanicals of some kind. Or at the worst, insects, reptiles, or spiders that had been poached from the protected forest land.

But they'd been taking something from the children.

Juice.

When I'd recovered myself, I unfurled the trail mix bag and poured a large pile in my palm. "What color was the juice?" I raked through the trail mix and held up a cranberry. "This?"

The talkative goblin spat on another goblin, who caught the green goo as if it were a game, proud and grinning.

"Not like that nasty one," the goblin said. He looked truly disgusted, and I remembered how much Willy despised dried cranberries.

I held up a hazelnut, hoping to Brightness it wasn't the one. "Was it this color?"

A small goblin who hadn't seemed interested in me until now suddenly pounced on my hand and brushed everything away except a thin sheet of dried coconut.

It made a series of high-pitched whistling sounds, then brushed the coconut away too.

I stared at my empty palm. Then I looked at the small goblin. It was staring intently at me.

"Something almost white?" I spat in my palm. "Like this?"

It nodded its narrow green head.

So they'd collected the witch children's spit. Lovely. No wonder Jill was—

Before I could stop it, the goblin came at my face and stuck a finger in my eye. It wasn't a solid being, but the energy flowing through my flesh hurt enough to make me cry out.

FORTY-FIVE

The goblin nodded more enthusiastically and flapped its fingers on my cheek where a tear had fallen.

"Tears," I said. "They collected the children's tears." What monsters. Goblins were green and bony and had teeth like razor blades, but they weren't as monstrous as humans.

The goblin lunged at me again, but this time I swatted it away with a defensive spell. I got the idea. They hadn't collected blood from the students at Elwin School, but they'd gone for the clear stuff—saliva, tears, and probably sweat.

All the biomatter from a witch held power. For centuries, the tears of a child witch, if properly distilled, had been used as an antidepressant. The taker of the potion was reported to feel an immediate lifting of mood with no side effects—other than guilt, shame, and (if I was on the jury) incarceration.

I wanted to hit somebody. How dare they? How could a teacher at the school and a parent do such a thing? Had Holly been the middleman to buy it and deliver the potions elsewhere?

The goblins ran to the fence, scrambled up to the top,

and watched me from wary green eyes. They must've sensed my shift in mood.

I looked down at my hands. Ah. Not subtle. I'd created a ball of blue light that sizzled with righteous rage.

I spun around and stalked off school property before I flung my hex at Jill's classroom.

There was nothing else I could do there tonight. The evidence had been removed, and my conversation with goblins wasn't admissible in Protectorate criminal trials. My ability to communicate with the fae was a secret I couldn't afford to expose, even if Protectorate higher-ups believed the goblins' story, which they wouldn't.

I got into the Jeep, furious and cursing under my breath.

I'd tell Raynor. He'd believe me and get agents up here to gather enough evidence. First I'd tell Darius. I took a deep breath, knowing he didn't like hearing me be emotional.

When I was calm enough, I called him using another persuasion spell.

He picked up with a sigh. "Not again. If you keep this up, I'll have to put a special filter on my phone to block you."

"I know what was in the compost pile."

He let out a breath. "Just a second." Again I heard him leave a vehicle, walk a ways, then fall quiet within a bubble. "Yes? You're safe?"

"Yes. I talked to some creatures that humans aren't supposed to be able to talk to."

He knew about my power. "And?"

I told him what I'd learned. His reaction was more restrained than mine, but I did feel my phone get hot as his magical anger floated through digital space.

"And they got away with it," he said.

"Just this time. Raynor can send up—"

"They'll be careful now. Nerissa is dead, agents are crawling everywhere—no. They'll lie low."

I was afraid of the same thing. "If Raynor's hands are tied, that doesn't mean mine have to be."

He let out an appreciative whistle. "Listen to you, Witch of the Incurable Inability."

"I didn't say I was going to kill them."

"I would," he said. "Children's tears? You know they must've gone out of their way to make them cry, right?"

"Why didn't they tell their parents?"

Darius scoffed. "Witches. Teachers. Parents. Small town. Lots of traditions, grateful to have a school—"

"And a lot of nasty Shadow magic to prevent talk, I bet."

"No doubt," he said. "I'll tell Raynor. We have a call scheduled in a few minutes."

I looked out the windshield across the parking lot. The sun was low in the west, casting bright, happy colors into the sky above the ocean.

"There's something else," I said. "Somebody else."

His tone sharpened. "Yes?"

"Holly was the last witch to visit the compost pile. She cast a pretty good erasure spell to cover her tracks, but I broke it."

"She could've been working on the installation," he said. "She went over there to reach the plants better."

"Then why cover her tracks?"

He fell silent. I didn't push; I trusted him to choose the Bright path whenever there was a choice to make. And his love life was none of my bus—

"I had a bad breakup once," he said. "Really bad. I didn't think I'd ever get over it. My relationships since... They don't last."

There was an awkward pause. Stunned by his revelation, I waited for him to change the subject or end the call the way he usually did when topics became too personal, but then he continued.

"When I met Holly, I felt something inside me break. It was like—don't laugh, Alma, or I'll hex you, swear to

Brightness—as if the sun had come out after months of rain."

I held my breath. I believed he would hex me. "I'm not laughing," I said finally.

"I don't know why she was at that compost pile, but it wasn't because she's using the biomatter of tortured children to get rich."

I wouldn't remind him now that right after he'd met Holly, he'd nearly killed me in the motel room. We didn't always have control over what we did.

Time for a topic change. "Any information about Nerissa?"

He sighed as if he'd rather keep talking about Holly, which maybe he did. But eventually whatever spell was at work on him would fade and he'd see the truth of his feelings for the woman he'd barely met.

"The suicide theory looks solid," he said. "The note is hers, expressing deep remorse for something she doesn't explain." He paused. "Demon's balls."

The thought struck us both at the same time. "Maybe she was the mastermind of the child torture trade?" I asked. "But why kill herself now?"

"Fear of exposure. She saw me here. I thought my disguise was good, but word got out."

I didn't buy it. "She would've run away. She doesn't have kids of her own. There was just her and the dog in that house. She's probably got plenty of money if she's been selling on the Shadow market."

"If Percy had gotten the secret out of her, that would've been a great motive for killing him," he said.

"Except then why kill herself? He was dead. She seemed the type to fight."

"Perhaps she couldn't bear the thought of being caught," he said. "She wouldn't be the first witch to think Death Valley would be worse than death itself."

FORTY-SIX

The next day was the eve of the Elwin Flower Show. Because Darius had relocated to an undisclosed Protectorate location—probably a camper van parked next to the river—I woke early and went to the restaurant alone. I wanted to look into Bruce's eyes for myself, knowing what I knew now, and see if Shadow like that left a mark. I'd always thought it must, but maybe I was wrong. It was a humbling thought.

The restaurant was busy, but the atmosphere wasn't festive as it had been over the weekend; people were eating and rushing out without lingering over their food. The show had everyone on edge.

I sat at the counter nearest the kitchen in the back, watching people come in, scanning the tables, and looking out for Bruce.

But he never appeared. When it took the server fifteen minutes to bring me my check, I saw the stressed expression on his face. "Short-staffed today?" I asked.

He wiped his brow with the back of his forearm. "Bruce didn't come in. Totally weird."

"That's not like him?"

"He's always here for breakfast. Always. But not yesterday and not today." The server glanced at the table behind me, where a man was shouting for the check. "We were kind of thinking about calling the cops."

The piercings and chains as well as aura of magic told me the server was a witch. "You mean the nonmag police?" I asked.

"Yeah. Maybe he drove off the cliff like that teacher, you know?" He rushed away.

Out on the street, I paused and looked up and down the sidewalk, remembering seeing Clem walking her dog. Of course she wouldn't—

Wait. She *was* there, less than a block away, walking away from me. She had the dog with her again and seemed to be hurrying.

I gave myself a full second to decide, then ran after her.

I was convinced the gnome was the clue to everything, but I couldn't see how to pursue it without help. I needed to ask her what she'd seen when I'd been attacked. Any detail might help.

I had to convince Clem it would be better to cooperate with me and Darius discreetly before the gnome did something else and the Protectorate was forced to apply all the oppressive magic they had. She probably wanted to protect her fae neighbor who provided the magic for her fantastic garden, and maintain her quiet life of isolation, but once the Protectorate was involved, she might lose everything. Even her freedom.

"Clem!" I jogged across the street, dodging a metal witch driving a huge yellow pickup. If he was trying to fit in with the locals, he was failing. The hubcaps were made of pure silver. "Wait up!"

Clem seemed to walk a little faster for a moment, but then she turned, gave me a phony look of surprise, and waved. "Oh, it's you."

I caught up to her, short of breath, and eyed the little dog. The leash was tight, and it was yapping at me.

"Do you have a moment?" I asked.

"Um, sure. Of course." She fidgeted with the herb pouch

on her belt but didn't take anything out. The dog continued to bark.

"I need to talk to you about yesterday," I said. "I've got a few questions."

Clem nodded. "I better pick up Nemesis before she tries something." She bent over and picked up the dog, stroking her little head until she quieted. "I'm a little embarrassed about what happened to you. I should've stopped it."

"It was my decision. I knew the risks."

She shot me a skeptical look from under her red sun hat, which I noticed now was emitting a subtle stealth charm. If I hadn't been thinking about her on the sidewalk at just the moment she'd been in my line of sight, I didn't think I would've seen her.

"If I'd ever thought she'd attack somebody like that," Clem said, "I never would've let you through the gate."

"I know," I said.

"You're ex-Protectorate," she continued. "If you'd been seriously hurt on my property, the great Raynor the Director would've come up here personally to get even."

I had to laugh a little at that. "I'm not sure about that."

"Oh, come on. You might not be sleeping together, but he cares about you. You're special to him."

"What makes you think that?"

She eyed me shrewdly. "Let's call it a feeling." A truth spell unexpectedly wafted over me. "Do you deny the two of you have some kind of special bond?"

I let the interrogation magic do its work and answered honestly. "I don't deny it." But her spell wasn't strong enough to make me tell her why that was. Being demon stained wasn't a safe secret for either of us to share. No matter how high Raynor climbed in the ranks of the Protectorate, he'd always have to hide his demon ancestry and the odd powers it gave him.

She clapped a hand over her mouth. "Demon's balls, I can't believe I did that. I don't have any right to force you to talk about him."

I smiled politely, but I completely agreed. "Anyway, about yesterday—"

"It's just, well, I still care about him." She scowled, but her cheeks were pink. "I can't help but be curious."

It had already been awkward, but now it became truly painful. "I'm sorry."

My apology only made it worse. She looked down at the sidewalk as if contemplating an earth-swallowing spell.

Suddenly she unhooked a chain from around her neck and held it out. "What do you think of this?"

It was metal, which didn't fit her botanical vibe. But then I realized the dark beads on the chain were tarnished copper.

I met her gaze. Raynor had a copper ring with unique properties: it hid his demon stain from other witches' curiosity. It was so unusual that he'd had it melted down and made into two rings so I could also have its protection.

Did Clem also have the Sight? Was she demon stained as well?

"I used to dabble in copper," she said. "I gave Raynor a ring when we were, Brightness, sixteen? Seventeen? Just kids. It was just a junky thing I made out of a pipe in the school bathroom. Romantic, huh?"

I felt I was on unsteady ground. Telling her he still wore it might give her false hope. "Nice of you," I said lamely.

She thrust the chain toward me. "Take it. It's yours."

"Oh no. I couldn't—"

"Yes, you can. It's a powerful piece. You've got the talent to wipe away any of my fingerprints." Her tone became insistent. "You must. You gave me the petrified wood right before the fae on my property attacked you."

"But I gave it to the gnome—"

"We made a deal for you to get me another. The attack on you, right after I accepted payment for the introduction, has brought me bad luck. The worst. Just a few hours later, who showed up but a crew of Raynor's dumbest minions? I'll have no peace until they're gone, which might be never at the rate they're going." She picked up my hand and thrust the necklace into my palm. "You've got to take it. Please. For Brightness's sake, accept my apology so we can call it even."

Her skin was cold, but her eyes blazed. I closed my fingers around the chain and nodded. There wasn't much magic in the metal that I could feel. "OK. Of course. Thank you."

She let out a sigh of relief. Her posture visibly relaxed. "Thank you."

"But you have to tell me—what did the attack look like to you from the outside? You knew it was the gnome?"

"Of course. What else has that kind of power?"

She was a gnome expert, but she didn't part easily with what she knew. Typical of a witch. "Do you have any ideas about how she might be restrained? To stop her from hurting people?" I thought of young Marta next door. "Kids?"

"The literature has never mentioned a witch having power over a gnome," she said. "Never."

"There's never been a story about them attacking us either," I said.

"They defend their territory. I believe that must be what she was doing to you and meant you no harm."

I could still remember the sensation of red-hot nails piercing my skin. "I'm not sure about that."

We stared at each other. Nemesis, sensing conflict, began to bark and thrash in Clem's arms.

Stressed about the dog, I hurriedly agreed that I accepted her apology and let them go on her way. She disappeared before she turned the corner, suggesting she'd enhanced the stealth charm on her hat to ease the awkwardness of our goodbye.

When I was alone, I looked at the necklace in my fist and scanned it more completely than I had at first. The chain was made of gold, which not only resisted tarnishing but the magic of another witch as well. I couldn't detect any of Clem's personality on it. The copper beads, however, felt like a young, eager witch holding a soldering iron. I could almost see her long blond hair getting singed as she bent over her work.

It was sweet. It reminded me of a birthday card I'd made for my father one year out of leaves. I'd saved them up from the autumn the year before, pressing them between the pages of valuable books in the school library until they were perfectly flat and dry. I'd presented it proudly, but his response had crushed me:

"I would've rather had the books."

I put the chain in a spare leather pouch I kept on me and slipped it into my pocket.

I was walking to my Jeep to return to the school for another look around when Darius called me.

"Nerissa Pike was the mastermind," he said. "We've got proof."

FORTY-SEVEN

"I don't care if you've got proof," I said. "She didn't kill herself."

"Listen to you. You don't care about proof? You're the one who thinks a demon deserves a warrant, a lawyer, and a jury trial."

"Exactly," I said. "The evidence isn't good enough to let the real killer off the hook."

"You think that gnome somehow broke out of Clem's backyard after attacking you but got distracted, broke into Nerissa's house, wrote a suicide note, and killed her?"

It didn't sound right the way he said it. "That gnome is behind this somehow." I remembered the compost pile. "And maybe the goblins as well."

"And it doesn't matter that we found the actual lab in the attic of Nerissa's house where she distilled the biomatter of witch children?"

"I believe she was a Shadowed person who tortured children and made money from it," I said. "But why would she kill herself?"

"Because they'd just gotten the evidence out of the compost pile."

I stopped in the middle of the sidewalk. "*Who* did?"

"Special ops out of New York."

"When?"

"While you were sleeping. There was a team watching that compost pile."

"A *team*?"

He grunted.

"Why didn't Raynor tell us?" I caught myself starting to shout and turned in to an alley. Downtown Elwin wasn't San Francisco, but its population was ten times its usual size at the moment, and people were walking, driving, and cycling all over the place. "I was there last night. Those guys were *not* special ops."

"You wouldn't have seen special ops," he said. "That's why they're special."

I scoffed.

"Yeah, I'm kidding," he said. "But they got in and out very quickly. Raynor found out about it after it happened." He sounded remarkably calm about it.

I shook my head. "That's cold."

"He's not pleased."

I heard the faint smugness in his tone. Frowning at some fairies eating out of a dumpster in the alley, I gave my brain a moment to mull over the facts.

Darius was cheerful. Raynor hadn't told us because he hadn't known. That meant...

"Holly was on the team," I said. "Holly is special ops."

"Yup."

I smiled. "Too bad. I was hoping you'd date a criminal so I could tease you about it."

"I'd never associate with anyone who would participate in crimes against children."

"I know," I said soothingly, "but maybe she was just an innocent helper criminal, like I was when I was five."

"She's an agent. She's not a criminal."

He really had it bad. I worried she might have used a romance enchantment on him as part of her disguise. Eventually it would wear off and he'd be left with just an embarrassing memory.

"Did they get both Bruce and Jill?" I asked, reminding myself I couldn't tease him.

"Yeah. Jill couldn't flip on Nerissa fast enough. They're taking her to LA."

"What about Bruce?"

"He's gone home."

"Already?" I asked. "Did he make a deal?"

"I don't know."

I couldn't help myself. "Maybe Holly has the hots for him," I said. "All those muscles. Nice dad type."

"This ends now," Darius said. "And I told Raynor it's possible the man had been influenced. He wasn't acting right when we saw the teacher yell at him. Much too calm."

I thought about that. Maybe he was right. When I'd met him, Bruce had been hostile until I'd increased my innocent-little-me disguise. The fact that my magic had changed his behavior so dramatically suggested he wasn't the strongest witch in town.

And then I remembered how he'd behaved toward Nerissa.

"He hated Nerissa," I said. "But I thought that was just because she was a bossy newcomer who ran his kids' school."

"Maybe there was more to it."

I walked out of the alley and peered around the corner at the restaurant a few doors down. "We need to know. Maybe he killed Nerissa so he could claim to be a victim of the whole thing. When word gets out what they were smuggling, nobody involved will be able to keep living in this town. Or anywhere. They'll be hunted down. These are *witch* parents."

"Does Bruce really seem strong enough to you to create a credible suicide note? I only felt Nerissa's essence on it." He paused. "And he certainly wouldn't have been strong enough to kill her."

I chewed my lip, thinking. The witch I'd met in the restaurant wouldn't have been powerful enough to kill

Nerissa, but Darius and I had both been hiding our powers; maybe he was too. "There's something going on with Bruce. I don't know what, but it's there."

"Leave it to Holly," he said. "It's her case."

I bit back a laugh. Never in Darius Ironford's professional history had he been so confident in another agent's ability.

Or so obtuse about seeing how biased he was.

"Can we talk to him?" I asked.

"Of course not."

"I don't mean me," I said, although I had. "I meant *you*. The real agent."

He didn't answer. That was as good as I was going to get.

"I'm going to the fairgrounds," I said. "Maybe I'll talk to the goblins again. Dig around a little. Get in trouble."

"Go ahead," he said. "The Protectorate is starting to feel like they've got a wrap on Elwin. Dead mastermind, dead victim, evidence of wrongdoing pointing directly at the bad guys."

"None of those people tried to kill me."

"I did apologize," Darius said.

I'd been thinking of Clem's gnome, but Darius reminded me of another outstanding problem.

"Why do you think you attacked me?" I asked.

"Alma, surely you know I never would've without that hex."

"Yes, I do. But why were you hexed?"

"Raynor said it was an old rock. Been lying there like a land mine for Brightness knows how long."

"That's impossible. Raynor's imagining a cliff in the middle of nowhere. But this place is packed. And that rock was right in my path."

He paused. "Maybe that's it."

"What?"

"The rock was in *your* path. Beings do seem to like trying to kill you. Look at those rings on your arm."

They were under a disguise charm, so I couldn't see them now, but I never forgot they were there. Like fairies on the winter solstice, each ring glimmered in the corner of my mind's eye.

"You think somebody tried to kill me because I was investigating Percy's death?"

"I don't know, but it does lead to an obvious conclusion if so."

"I'm not going to be elected mayor of Elwin?"

"Nerissa," he said. "You were on Nerissa's tail. She saw you getting closer. She tried to take you out and failed. Then you overheard Bruce and Jill—"

"How would she know that? We were hiding under a good spell," I said. "And what about that attack at Clem's? That gnome just happened to try to kill me right then too?"

"Maybe it wasn't the gnome," he said. "Maybe Nerissa was the one to attack you. Her niece lives next door. She could've slipped back there. You didn't hide the Jeep. It was right there in front of her house! She saw you go to Clem's, then used the gnome as a scapegoat to attack."

I knew he had to be wrong, but my brain was too crowded to explain why. I needed to sit down with a notebook and my beads, block out the world, write everything out, and think.

"That can't be right," I said.

"I need to go. They've put me in charge of collecting all that monster's lab equipment. I've got two Flints with no brains and a van with no decent safe in it."

It was an agent's typical complaint of the daily grind, but breaking into homes and collecting valuable evidence had been my favorite part of the job. Born to it, I supposed. "Good luck."

"Think about what I said. It makes sense."

I ended the call, shaking my head.

It made sense, but it wasn't right.

Or it was right, but didn't make sense.

I just wasn't sure which.

CHAPTER

FORTY-EIGHT

I never walked around with another witch's amulet without giving it a proper cleansing first, which meant I'd have to go back to the motel to drop off Clem's necklace before returning to the fairgrounds.

After I'd put away the necklace in a second velvet bag in the motel room and was walking back to my Jeep, I checked my phone for messages.

Nothing new from Seth. I typed a quick text to him asking for an update, assuring him I was well, hoping that was true, then looked up as I put my phone in my pocket.

Lacoste was at the pool again, sweeping this time instead of sunbathing. He wore one of those hiking hats that was like a nylon baseball cap with a floppy curtain that covered the back of his neck. As serial-killer fashion went, it seemed uncharacteristically nerdy.

Hand on the door of my Jeep, I paused, suddenly remembering how I'd seen him talking to Holly.

I relocked my car and walked over to the pool. Lacoste glanced up—was I imagining the slight wince?—and resumed sweeping. I noticed he kept moving the broom over the same spot, inefficient and pointless. He'd been watching me.

"Morning," I called out.

He took his time as if he was just too engrossed in his work to even realize I was there. If he was a secret agent, as I now suspect he was, he needed to work on his people skills.

"Morning," he mumbled.

I opened the gate with my key card and joined him next to the pool. It would be a good cover, being a famous serial killer who'd avoided conviction.

Holding a jute bag containing cedar chips soaked in peppermint and Earl Grey tea (I'd needed the bergamot), I cast a thick truth spell around him, the strongest I could make. It wouldn't last long but it would compel him to speak.

"Are you working for the Protectorate?" I asked.

His head jerked up to scan the bubble I'd cast around his head. Eyebrows arching, he turned his gaze on me. "Are you?"

I paused. My spell had barely affected him. He must be wearing something powerful to repel my magic.

I'd have to use another approach—a fair trade of information. "Sometimes," I said.

He said nothing.

"I know about Holly," I continued.

"Congratulations."

I decided he was a very unhappy person—but not dangerous. I watched his rough hands holding the aluminum handle. It was a modern broom: all metal, plastic, and nylon. Far behind him, off his property, I could see a street tree with a dozen or so wood sprites perched on the branches in the shade of the canopy.

In the days I'd been at the motel, I hadn't seen many fairies, but there'd been enough to reassure me he wasn't a demon. A demon would be more charming and have a thriving business. And a demon wouldn't work for the Protectorate.

But it was notable that there was absolutely nothing botanical living around the motel. The fae wouldn't have much interest in loitering in such a place. It had to be intentional.

"Why don't you have any plants on your property?" I asked. "There's nothing growing here, not even tiny weeds in the cracks of the parking lot." The air next to the pool smelled especially chlorinated, too, as if he'd dumped extra chemicals in the water.

"I like things clean and tidy," he said. "Plants make a mess."

My truth spell was clearly not working.

"Plants attract the fae." I watched him closely, using a magical scan to help me interpret his reaction. A demon might jump involuntarily at the mention of the fae, just as I'd perk up at the words *fudge brownie*.

"Serafina has allergies." He swept the debris into a pan, dumped it in the garbage, and gestured at the office. "Speaking of which, she needs me to take over the front desk. If there's anything else you need, don't hesitate to ask." His tone was sarcastic.

Giving up on my bag of herbs, I clutched my necklace and slid my finger across the silver chain holding the wood beads. Sometimes only metal would do.

"Why do you let people think you're a serial killer?"

His jaw tensed. A hollow, despairing look came into his eyes. "Because I am," he said. Then, as if a cord had been severed, he let out a long breath, and his entire body sagged with the release of tension. "I used to be."

A chill slid over my skin. He dropped the broom and walked away, his gait uneven and his shoulders hunched as if he were carrying a heavy weight.

I stared after him, feeling disgusted with what he'd admitted as well as with myself for forcing it out of him.

There were different states of possession, as I'd learned personally, and different kinds of supernatural beings.

I used to be.

I bent over and picked up the broom, scanning it, smelling it, opening myself to it.

A wounded man, I sensed, but one who detested killing. His aversion was even greater than mine.

Something had made him that way. A powerful, lightless Shadow had once engulfed him.

A demon.

I used to be.

With a shudder, I propped the broom against the fence. A demon had committed horrific acts with his body, staining his name and his soul. Then it had left him to live on. Lacoste hadn't voluntarily killed people, but somehow he'd remained on in his body when another, possibly a better person, would've died or fled.

Now he had the ability to see and hear the fae. Perhaps hating the reminder, he'd banished anything that might attract them to his property.

The Protectorate must know about the demon. It explained why Lacoste was still alive, running a motel, married to a nonmag woman, and not locked up in Death Valley. If he was working with special ops out of New York, it wasn't by choice.

No wonder he was bitter.

As I drove to the fairgrounds, I noticed an increase in traffic. The construction equipment was gone, replaced with smaller SUVs and cars. Up on the hill, where Darius and I had walked, I could see a few people on foot and small wheels heading to the fairgrounds.

With a start, I looked at my phone. Had I gotten the day wrong? Was today the opening day of the show? I did have an unfortunate tendency of sleeping around the clock.

No, it was still Tuesday. Preview day.

I parked and walked up to the school as I'd done before. This time, however, the Protectorate agents blasted me away with an enchantment that wiped my memory for a solid ten minutes. When I came to, I found myself sitting in gravel on the edge of the lot, playing with a ladybug that I realized was a tiny flower fairy.

Since only I could see it, other witches must've thought I was out of my mind.

I got up and brushed dirt off my jeans, offering a smile to a white-haired woman wearing a platinum tiara who'd been staring at me. She turned to her companion, another woman in a tiara, and they turned away from me, whispering.

My head hurt. There had clearly been an upgrade of the Protectorate agents at the school. The two guys from yesterday were probably combing through Nerissa's garbage now. Their replacements were... stronger.

It only made me more determined to slip past them and talk to the goblins. I should've prepared myself better, but the weakness of the previous agents had made me over-confident.

I was carrying all my magic enhancers except for the emergency stash I kept in the car. Bracelets, anklets, neck-laces, earrings made of wood; pouches of herbs and dried flowers; my best redwood-bead focus string; and all the metal jewelry I didn't usually wear.

With so much support, it didn't take much of my own power to erase my appearance and replace it with what was just a few inches next to me. As I walked onto the campus now, none of the three agents camped out there could see me.

They were pretty good, but not as good as me.

Grinning, I sauntered over to the compost pile. The goblins wouldn't be fooled by any invisibility spell; that was only for human eyes. I took a new bag of trail mix out of my pocket and tore it open, expecting them to jump up from the rotting kitchen scraps to get a fresh snack.

But they fled. Each of the dozen goblins looked at me, recoiled, and climbed or jumped up the chain-link fence to hide under the leaves of the towering sunflower—even the one who had spoken to me earlier.

"What's wrong?" I asked, holding the bag up. "This is for you. Won't you talk to me again?"

They scrambled farther away. One by one, they moved behind leaves or flowers or jogged along the top of the fence. A few of them started to climb away into my garden on the other side, but something seemed to block them. They turned back, quivering like trapped animals, watching me with shining green eyes.

I looked at the bag. It was a duplicate of the trail mix I'd brought the first time. That wasn't the problem.

I was the problem. Me or my magic.

Or... something or someone I'd encountered since then. Demon's balls. In Elwin, it would be impossible to isolate the variables. I'd had breakfast at the restaurant, eating food that had been handled by several people. There had been the check, the table, the cutlery, the mug, the glass, the plates.

After, I'd taken the necklace from Clem, but I'd isolated it in a protective bag and stored it at the motel.

Where I'd met Lacoste... and had touched the broom he'd been using.

I just didn't know which of those interactions had left me contaminated by something that terrified the goblins.

With a sigh, I turned and headed back to the parking lot. Because of the additional attendees, it took me a little longer to reach my garden plot than it had before. More witches were dressed up today. There were lots of fancy dresses, suits, costumes, makeup, and, of course, jewelry. Some were elegant, some were Goth, most were just eccentric.

When I got to my garden, Rupert jumped off his folding chair and shouted my name. "Where have you been?"

He still looked as if he hadn't slept and was relying on external stimuli. Even his white nose hairs were standing to attention.

"Opening day is tomorrow," I said. "I didn't realize today would be important."

"It's previews! This is the true judging day. The judges make a show of looking at it as per the schedule, but this—*this*—is the real day. This is the real, real, real day." His eyes stared unblinkingly at me.

FORTY-NINE

I was genuinely concerned for his health. "Rupert, I think you should sit down." I gestured at the chair.

"No, that's for you. Don't worry about the civilians. They're just here because admission is free today. Focus on the judges. You need to chat up the judges." He looked at his watch, an old analog with a leather strap. "At least you got here for our official window. It starts at eleven. Goes until four. Then they let us rest until the opening tomorrow at nine."

I hadn't realized I'd be stuck in place all day. "I'm not sure I can stay the entire—"

"You must. That's your chair," he said again. "Mine is over there." He pointed at another chair near the cooler and a table loaded with sliced fruit, cookies, bottled water, and cut flowers. There was a clipboard and pen for the curious to join a mailing list.

I hoped he didn't think I was going to start a garden newsletter. It was hard enough for me to promote my bead jewelry.

He continued to insist I take the chair, so I sat. Most visitors were clustered in the metal gardens, but a few people had wandered over and were now looking with curiosity at the well.

One was a witch in her thirties carrying a baby in a sling. "Is that... *wellspring* water in there?" she asked me.

The possession of wellspring water was technically illegal, so I said, "It would spoil the enchantment to explain its mysteries." The baby, finding me more interesting than the plants, stared at me with eyes almost as unblinking as Rupert's.

"It's cool," the mom said, somewhat grudgingly. Both her ears were studded with stainless-steel piercings, and her nose and eyebrow held gold.

"Thanks. My designer, Rupert—"

She'd already moved on.

The next person to talk to me was a young man wearing a judge's pin. His was a flat, donut-shaped piece of aluminum about palm-width. I'd learned that aluminum indicated his vote during the final tallies and counted for one point. A copper judge got two; a zinc judge got three; a gold, four; and platinum, five.

"Remarkable," he said, stepping into the garden and wandering around for several minutes.

I got up and followed him. "Rupert Ray—see him over there?—he's the designer."

The judge glanced at him, nodded. "It's remarkable." He jotted a note on his tablet and wandered away.

Rupert was flushed and beaming but said nothing.

Two more judges visited; a copper and a gold. These were older witches, both women in their fifties. They expressed concern about the costs entailed in digging such a well but were clearly impressed. I tried to get Rupert involved in the conversation to explain the enchantments and accept his accolades, but he stayed back and just drank it in silently. I decided he was just too nervous to talk to anyone until the gold he coveted had been given to him.

As the hours went by, I began to feel as if I was failing the investigation by lounging under a warm sun, surrounded by flowers and friendly witches who offered a steady stream of compliments I didn't deserve. Darius reassured me in a text that they preferred me to stay out of it. They had their story—Nerissa had tortured children, killed Percy to hide her crime, then committed suicide to escape justice—and there was no reason to complicate it with weird gnome anecdotes.

Around two, I overcame Rupert's protests—it wouldn't kill him to talk to the judges by himself for a while—and left to find a toilet. Then I went to the food truck for lunch.

It ended up taking almost an hour because the line was so long, but the first bite of my hot dog—witches were generally carnivorous—really hit the spot. I ate it while I walked and explored a few of the metal witch gardens. A crowd had formed ahead of me, blocking the path, so I suddenly turned around to walk the other direction.

Lacoste was ten steps behind me. A moment too late for me not to see him, he turned around and ducked into the crowd.

I finished the last bite of my hot dog, shaking my head. If he really was a secret agent with the Protectorate, they hadn't trained him very well.

My phone vibrated. It was a text from Rupert, anxious to know where I was.

I'll be there in five minutes, I replied.

Lacoste had been following me. Why else would a man who hated plants and fairies come to a flower show?

I hurried after him, using a stealth and tracking spell that he obviously hadn't been taught. Within three minutes, I was trailing Lacoste as he walked past an "Energizing Fountain" made from vehicle parts. Twenty feet high, it contained reclaimed metals from cars, trucks, bicycles, and a single San Francisco municipal subway car standing on its tail. Water poured out of its windows and squirted from its sky-pointing headlights.

Perhaps thinking he could hide in the crowd that had stopped to gawk at it, Lacoste stopped and watched as well. Water sprites, drawn by the magical fountain, were swarming the heads of the gathered witches, not that they noticed.

Except for one. When a cloud of thumb-sized sprites encircled Lacoste's head, he reached up a big hand and tried to swat them away. Like gnats, they weren't deterred, and he finally ducked and hurried away.

I'd been right. Lacoste was demon marked. When Rupert texted me three more times in quick succession, begging me to return, I took pity and went back to my garden. I didn't know Lacoste's complete story, but he didn't scare me anymore.

When I got to my plot, I took out my phone and texted Darius. I asked him to reach out to Holly and see if Lacoste really was working with her or if my guess was off base.

"There you are," Rupert exclaimed, flushed and wild-eyed. "Two judges came by while you were gone. One was platinum. *Platinum.*"

I took the chair he held out for me. "Did they like it?"

"Of course they liked it. They loved it. They'd never seen such a thing. A subterranean installation at Elwin? Totally new. They were speechless."

"There must be some old friends of yours here, right?" I looked at the men and women walking past; many looked about his age. "Have you had fun catching up? What do they think of it?"

He waved my words aside. "All that matters is what the judges think." He looked at his watch. "Final two hours. This is make-or-break. Please don't leave again."

I sank into my chair with a sigh. The small talk was exhausting to me, and I felt like the real work, the important investigation, was elsewhere.

I managed to resist the urge to take out my phone and play a game or two. It had been four hours already of smiling and nodding, talking about back borders and water features, prehistoric redwood powers.

If my garden didn't win a gold, I didn't know if Rupert would ever recover. I'd never seen a witch so invested in a competition, and I'd gone to the top boarding schools on the West Coast. There had literally been murders done to get the top score on a test.

Maybe I was cynical, but I didn't think what we said would make any difference. I expected the judges to give the top awards to their friends. It was that kind of community. That's why I'd expected Rupert to mingle more, lean on his old connections.

More judges came by. More locals. More tourists. All were witches. Prompted by Rupert's begging, I kept my phone in my pocket and talked, gestured, and evangelized about the wonders of earth magic until my throat hurt.

Finally, it was over. At four o'clock, I collapsed in my chair and vowed to never participate in the show again, no matter which ex-Protectorate agent associate of mine drove off a cliff.

I saw I'd received a text from Seth about an hour earlier.

Boarding the plane. Home tonight. Have a surprise for you, demon darling.

I stared at it, thrilled but frustrated. I tapped his number to talk to him, but he didn't pick up.

Home tonight? Maybe I would be too if the Protectorate insisted on wrapping things up. Rupert could enjoy the show without me. It was his achievement, not mine.

Too many witches were nearby, so I didn't leave Seth a voice message.

Tonight. He had a surprise—which, knowing him, was probably edible.

I couldn't wait to hold him and be held. Tell him my stories and listen to his.

I sighed, realizing I was terribly thirsty and had been for a while. I looked over at the table, but all the snacks and bottled waters had been consumed. About an hour earlier, I'd heard from disgruntled attendees that the food truck had run out of everything and driven away.

I glanced under the table at Rupert's cooler. He'd been pounding energy drinks all afternoon. Something like that, even if he'd spiked it with extra magical stimulants, was suddenly very appealing.

I watched Rupert nod silently to another judge, an old man in his seventies who was wearing the same style of cargo pants.

Something about Rupert wasn't right, and it wasn't just his unhealthy obsession with garden design. I realized I hadn't seen him go near the cooler all day.

So why did he always have it around? Just what did he have in there?

"Rupert, do you have an extra one of those?" I pointed at the can in his hand and made a move toward the cooler.

He jumped up. "It's empty. I'll go get you something."

"But the food truck has run out—"

Rupert strode away before I'd finished my sentence. The bounce in his step was that of a man fifty years younger.

My suspicion grew. It had been bothering me all afternoon that he hadn't seemed to connect socially with any of the judges. He'd withdrawn to a chair in the back and left it to me. His nerves had only gotten worse as the hours went by.

What was his secret?

I got out of my chair and squatted down next to the cooler. It was just an ordinary, old-fashioned blue-and-white plastic cooler with a broken handle. With a magical metal locking mechanism, but I had enough power to break that.

Running my left thumb across my necklace, I reached out and touched the latch.

And all Shadow broke loose.

CHAPTER

FIFTY

I was quite sure I hadn't opened the cooler, but something burst out of it and caught me in a sphere of white, burning steam.

I was flung into the air like a pinwheel, my limbs flung out helplessly as I spun and spun.

Spinning too fast to see, I closed my eyes and tried not to vomit.

What had I triggered?

Who had I triggered?

I reached for my power, but there was nothing but steam, hot steam. Breathing became my only thought. Air in. Air out. Air in, please, give me air.

My feet were pulled downward, and then I was being spun like a top with my legs together and arms flying helplessly outward. I tried opening my eyes to see my assailant, gauge what I was up against, but the vertigo was too overwhelming. Everything was a sickening blur.

And then my clothes disappeared. Now the steam was burning my entire body. But worse was what was taken next.

My jewelry. All my bracelets, my rings, my strongest redwood-bead necklace. Even the tiny gold studs from my childhood that I still wore in my earlobes—I felt them pop out and fly away.

No! I tried to shout, but steam filled my mouth. I pulled my arms in to protect myself. There was magic inside me, the well of power I was born with, but it took calm and focus to access. I had neither at the moment.

The spinning slowed. I was falling. Feet first, arms overhead, like a child jumping off a diving board.

As I descended, the white steam became black. It was getting darker. I opened my eyes and looked up at the retreating circle of light.

My feet touched something cold and soft. It swallowed me to the knees.

Liquid. Water.

My body came to a stop, but my mind and stomach were still spinning, sickened by the journey.

I reached out to stop myself from falling over and felt damp, slimy bricks. I was in the bottom of the well.

I cursed. Cursed again. I wanted to cry. I'd been so easily fooled, so deftly deceived. And I didn't even know by what or by whom.

I gazed up at the distant circle of light.

Something moved to block part of the light. Rupert's voice trickled down.

"Hi, Alma," he said, his words reaching me too clearly to be natural. "I'm really sorry about this, but you'll be able to get out of there soon. You just have to do one thing."

It was an absurd impulse, but I wrapped my arms over my chest for privacy. As if he could see me over a hundred feet down in the darkness. As if I'd care if the Shadowed stain of demon spit could.

I said nothing, however. Let him do all the talking. I wasn't going to make it easier for him.

"Watch out," he called. "I'm dropping something down to you now. Get ready. I don't want it to hit you on the head."

How considerate of him. I flattened my back against the

slimy bricks and let the object ricochet off the walls and splash into the water.

I didn't reach for it. It bobbed toward me and bumped against my shins.

Whatever it was, it seemed to have been surrounded in bubble wrap.

"Don't worry, it's not hexed," Rupert said. "Nobody wants to hurt you. You just need to do one thing and then you can go."

I still didn't answer.

"I know you're alive. I can hear you breathing. I'm attuned to the enchantment that made the well, so there's no point in you trying to hide or play dead. I know you're listening."

Fine, so he knew. I kept my mouth clamped shut, but gingerly poked the floating package. It was about the size of a large baked potato.

"It's a phone," Rupert said. "You just have to make one phone call."

My mind raced through the reasons Rupert might want me to make a phone call. To the judges? To Zoe Thornton, the billionaire's widow?

"What do you want?" To test the enchantment, I didn't bother to raise my voice.

"Great!" he exclaimed. "I'm glad you're going to be reasonable. All you have to do is call a friend of yours. The number's already plugged in. It's the only one, actually. You can only call one number. That took a little mixing nonmag and real magic, but it works."

I knew instantly there wasn't any friend I would pull into whatever mess I'd literally fallen into. But I needed to understand what was happening.

"Which friend?" I asked. "Why?"

"I can't explain why. Just call the Director. In San Francisco."

"You want me to call Raynor?"

I could hear his soft chuckle. "You *are* friends with him."

His tone suggested he hadn't completely believed it until now.

"What am I supposed to say to him?"

"Just tell him where you are," Rupert said. "Tell him how you got there."

"That's it?"

"Well, you have to explain that he has to come personally to help get you out. That's the only way. And he has to come before midnight."

I pushed the floating phone away from me. "Why?"

"Otherwise, you die. I'm sorry about that, I really am. You seem very nice. But it's the only way."

The man was insane. As far as I knew, the package contained an empty tube of mascara. "Just how will I die? I want to make sure I understand."

"The enchantment will end. Everything in the garden will disappear. The plants, the stones, the well itself. Everything. If you're down there... I'm honestly not sure what will happen. You could be stuck in a magic limbo until your body gives out, or you could be crushed instantly—not sure."

He wasn't sure? "Isn't this your enchantment?" I asked.

"Of course. Yes." He sounded irritated. "Every stone, every plant, every drop of water was my idea."

I held my tongue. It was time to think, not talk.

It was all his idea, but the enchantment couldn't possibly be his.

"You're a Bright witch," he went on. "Do what you're told, and you can go home with your boyfriend."

So he didn't know Darius wasn't actually my boyfriend. That was interesting. Who would know, so I could rule them out?

Holly probably knew now that Darius was a Protectorate agent. If Lacoste was working with her, which I believed he was, then he would know too. He would've noticed "Dash" wasn't staying in the room anymore, anyway.

I couldn't assume anyone else would know. Bruce and Jill might, if agents had talked loosely in their presence. It was unlikely, but I found it was best to keep my expectations low regarding my former colleagues.

"Just call him. You've got to call him."

I'd clearly misjudged Rupert Ray. He was a fanatic, certainly, but I'd never sensed malice in him. His magic was all aimed at life, at growing plants and attracting wild things, not at killing and Shadow.

"Why?" I asked.

"If he doesn't get here in time, the enchantment disappears. Back to dirt and weeds." He snapped his fingers. "Like that. And you'll be stuck down there forever."

FIFTY-ONE

The brick walls of the well seemed to move toward me, eager to crush me as soon as possible.

I reached for a necklace that wasn't there. "At midnight?" My voice caught. I swallowed and tried again. "Tonight?"

"Yes!" His word reverberated against the bricks. "Time's running out. It's at least a five-hour drive from San Francisco. He needs to leave right away."

I tried to think. Nothing made sense. I didn't know why Rupert was willing to kill me, but it had to have something to do with winning the garden competition. Any negotiations with him would have to do with that. "You're saying if the garden disappears tonight," I asked, "you'll be disqualified?"

I was naked in a well and had no focus string or silver chain or redwood bead, but my questions held innate power from my training in the Protectorate.

"You," he said. "*You* will be disqualified. It's your garden."

"But it's really your garden," I said. "Don't you think the prize and honor should go to you?"

He was silent a moment. "Yes. It is my garden. Nobody could do it better."

The plot didn't make sense.

"If it's destroyed," I pointed out, "you won't be able to win."

He snapped back, irritated. "It won't be destroyed if you just make one call to save your life. It's an easy choice."

I covered my face with my hands, trying to think, trying to forget where I was, trying to evade panic.

Why would Rupert want to have Raynor come? Maybe his ego craved the most powerful witch on the West Coast to witness his glorious victory at a flower show.

It seemed excessive, even for him. And the power to make the deep well and stick me inside it would've been too demanding for one old man by himself.

But maybe he wasn't just one old man by himself. I fixed my gaze on the shadow in the light above. "What is your name?" Again, I wrapped it in a command.

He laughed. "Nice try. I heard you'd try that. But I've still got the— The enchantment is still active."

He'd heard? From whom?

And if his name really were Rupert Ray, he would've said so. It explained why he hadn't socialized with any of the judges; he *wasn't* the nice old, retired guy with lots of connections. But who was he? And who was he working with?

Was anybody in Elwin who they'd claimed to be?

"What harm is there in telling me your name now?" I asked. "I'm stuck down here."

"You'll be free after Raynor rescues you."

"I'm not going to call Raynor," I said.

"If you don't, you're going to die a horrible death at midnight."

"Then your glory will die with me." I had to play to his ego. I was naked at the bottom of a well, and he might be my only way out. "Don't you want me to know the real name of the genius who designed my garden? Who created this masterpiece?"

He drew back for several long seconds, then reappeared.

"Promise you won't tell the judges. You're right. You deserve to know. But they can't."

Of all the people I would reach out to for rescue and justice, the judges of a flower show were at the bottom of my list. "I promise I won't tell the judges," I said.

He leaned down into the well as if trying to get closer to me. His voice was excited. Proud. "You aren't going to believe it," he said. "You, Alma Bellrose, have had the unlikely good fortune of being associated with a Jake Barber creation."

The name might have been slightly familiar, but I had to lay it on thick. "Jake Barber?" My voice echoed. *Jake Barber, Jake Barber, Jake Barber.* It was probably the song of his dreams. "I don't believe it. Wow."

"Yes." He paused for emphasis. "The greatest gardener who has ever lived. The only witch to have won gold at the Elwin Flower Show ten years in a row. From his very first year, Jake Barber won nothing else."

Talking about yourself in the third person was never a sign of a well-balanced disposition. I remembered him talking about a *young gentleman who was on a winning streak*, the one who'd cast earth magic by lying on the ground.

"You're a great witch," I said. "Why did you hide yourself? It's a crime for me to take credit for your brilliance." I hoped his ego didn't allow him to register sarcasm.

"Hidebound traditionalism," he said. "The fossils didn't appreciate my diverse magical palette."

Diverse had to mean *illegal.*

"Like what?" I asked.

He muttered something under his breath, then launched into an overly detailed description of soil composition. Filtered sunlight near the summer solstice. And something about sea mist affected by local kelp. As he droned on, I decided he didn't understand it himself.

Somebody must've helped him. An accomplice. Somebody with lots of power who wanted to trap Raynor and knew I had a connection to him. Somebody who'd made a deal with him—their magic in exchange for this enchantment.

A gnome would be powerful enough. But a gnome wouldn't care about Raynor.

The truth struck me like a hex to the brain.

Clematis Mallory.

Shivering in the dark, up to my shins in frigid water, it all came to me in a rush.

The gnome fingerprint. The schoolgirl romance. The bitter isolation.

Raynor had moved on and had a famous career. She'd been drowning in resentment, soured on humanity, plotting revenge ever since.

Her dog was named Nemesis, for Brightness's sake.

I'd thought her whole misanthropic persona had just been her reclaiming a witch stereotype. I'd thought there had been humor in it, some tongue-in-cheek.

I'd been wrong. She'd always been deadly serious.

I began to shiver, overwhelmed by the extent of my stupidity. I'd gone to her house *alone, voluntarily,* and put myself in her power. Amazed by her good fortune, she'd struck immediately. Like me and other hearth witches, her power at home would be immense.

Maybe there was no gnome. It was all a lie, a scapegoat, a distraction. She heard about me from Percy, then I showed up...

No, there had been gnome residue at Percy's crash site. And Willy had been driven out of his home. It had been the stick from Clem's gnome that had rescued him from humiliating exile.

I also couldn't forget the agonizing assault at her house, the one that had driven me into my cat shape. It hadn't felt like a witch's hex. It must've been the gnome—and I'd actually asked for an introduction to her, to the only power great enough to have enabled Clem's vengeance.

I rubbed my arms, furious, cold, wanting to punch something.

Why had a gnome agreed to such human depravity? I'd been looking for fae motivation to kill a human, but the reasons weren't fae at all. They were human. Always human.

Clem had killed Percy. Clem must've killed Nerissa as well. And now here I was, in the bottom of a well, cheese in her trap.

Her trap to catch Raynor.

The bubble-wrapped package bobbed against my leg again. I leaned over and picked it up, using what power I had now through the prism of my memory of Clem.

I felt it. I saw it. The phone inside the plastic wrapping had Clem's fingerprint.

Seeing me finally pick up the phone, Rupert called out cheerfully, "Great. Just remember not to mention my name."

I looked up at his silhouette in the light above. With such a big head, I was amazed any light got through at all.

I flung the package back down into the water, regretting having touched it at all. My shivering grew more violent.

"I'm not going to call him," I said.

"But you have to!" His voice echoed. *To... to... to...*

I put my hands over my ears. *Think, Alma. Think.*

Now I was the one using the third person.

It had to be inside the cooler. Gnome magic. Yes. It had killed Percy. It had made the garden. It had cast me into the well.

But why? What had Clem given the creature to act against its nature? Gnomes rarely participated in human affairs. When they did, it was to assist in the garden or the kitchen. Willy was a very odd exception.

Had Clem taken something from the gnome and now strung it along as payment?

A thought struck me, too horrible to accept. But it was the only explanation that made sense.

Somehow, against nature and all that was Bright, Clem had taken the gnome's freedom.

Could it... Could there be a gnome *inside* the cooler?

I didn't know how, but that had to be it. She'd imprisoned one of the most powerful, mysterious creatures we knew of and had weaponized its magic.

My shivering intensified.

Disgusting. Shadowed. Unforgivable.

I had to get out and free the poor thing.

But I absolutely could not call Raynor. The power would kill him. He wouldn't have a chance. And I doubted she'd free me, no matter what Rupert said.

FIFTY-TWO

I had to act quickly. Right now Rupert was alone, but Clem might arrive any moment, making my odds of survival much less. I had a better chance of overpowering a fanatical gardener of unknown magical ability than I did dueling with an experienced witch who had already proven she had great power to go with her vengeful heart.

Finally I was seeing all the connections, the clues. Just that morning, after pretending to be reluctant to be seen—I flinched to realize how easily I'd been fooled—Clem had made a point of giving me jewelry. Copper beads on a gold chain. Powerful elements, especially when it had been crafted so long ago. Although I'd followed standard operating procedure and put the necklace in a bag, then unloaded it in the motel, its magic could've been strong enough to affect me for the minutes I'd held it. I could only imagine how powerless I would've been had I kept it on me.

It was made from the same copper as the ring Raynor used to hide his demon mark. The metal contained stealth powers. It had hidden her motives, its danger.

I thought of the goblins, running away and then trapped between me and Rupert's garden installation. Maybe they'd felt the necklace's residue on me. It had terrified them, and something about the garden had blocked them from fleeing into it to get away from me.

The flower border at the back. It could act as high walls in a fortress. A magical barrier.

I had to tell somebody my theories. I had to warn Raynor. But how?

The fae. They'd be my best chance of getting a message out, possibly my only one. Rupert wouldn't let any people get near the well, and Darius was busy with Protectorate business. Nobody else knew I'd come to the fairgrounds, but hopefully they'd come here when they realized I was missing.

They. Who would *they* be? Darius? Holly? The special ops I'd never seen or the hostile agents at the school?

It was some small consolation that for as slow as I'd been to see the truth, the Protectorate was even worse.

My thoughts were scattered, panicky. I needed to calm down and be smart. Better late than never.

I arched back and looked up at the distant light above. Rupert's head wasn't visible, but maybe—

Yes. A shimmering of wings. Water sprites, the same ones I'd seen swarming around Lacoste's head. They flitted at the opening, perhaps drawn by the illusion of magical wellspring water. I bent down and scooped up a handful, drawing a memory of the real thing into my mind. It had a particular flavor, clean and sharp, a tangy essence in the back of one's sinuses that could lift even the most insensitive, broken soul.

I glanced up. The wings were flapping closer. A silhouette sank closer, then rose up, fell again.

I called up the memory again and drew on my innate power to project it upward.

Two more fairies joined the first. Then five, six, ten.

A moment later, my hands were surrounded by sparkling, hungry fae.

"Water, is it? Is it? Is it? Is it?" one fairy sang softly.

"No, maybe, yes, no," said another.

"Forgive me," I said. "It's not real springwater. But I'll get you some if you help me. Please. As much as you want."

They flapped their wings in my face.

"Talking witch, talking witch, talking," a fairy said, sounding angry.

"No, no, no," said the other. "Not the water."

But a smaller one perched on my shoulder and pushed an ephemeral foot into my ear. "Much. Want."

"Yes, I'll get you as much as you want," I said. "Just help me. Tell the goblins there's a... a cousin of theirs trapped in a box up there. A gnome. I think she's inside, and if they get together and break it open, then the gnome will be free, and I can go get you as much wellspring water as you want..."

I trailed off. Too complicated, too difficult, and they might not even care about the gnome. To me, the gnomes and goblins looked like family, but maybe they hated each other.

I needed a person. I needed a witch.

Lacoste!

"There's a man," I said instead. "One like me. A witch. He can hear you. He can see you. He's near—"

"Angry witch," a sprite said.

"Funny witch," another said. "Sun hair."

"Sad, angry, shake, wave." A chorus of high-pitched bells rang around my head.

They seemed to be laughing. They were like children who enjoyed tormenting the old man by running across his lawn.

"Him!" I gasped. "Yes, him. His name is Lacoste—"

"La la la la la la," they sang, laughing again.

I waited for them to get bored with their own joke, then held up a fresh handful of water. There was just enough wellspring water essence, although fake, to get their attention again.

"Tell him a witch is in the well," I said. "Tell him Alma is in the well. Then I'll get you real wellspring water. As much as you can drink."

Their laughter faded away, and after a moment, they settled on my head and shoulders like birds on a line.

I waited. Water sprites weren't the most intellectual of the fae. They weren't gnomes.

"We drink," one said. "When?"

I let out a careful breath. Time for them would be celestial. "At the full moon," I said. "I'll bring enough for all of you."

"Now," several sang.

"I can't get it while I'm down here," I said. "I have to go to the Silverpool wellspring and bring it back."

The word Silverpool had an immediate effect. They flew into the air, bodiless voices humming together.

"Moon, water, witch, la, la, la," the voices whispered, as each flickering spirit rose up the shaft of the well and disappeared into the white light.

I leaned against the mossy bricks and let out my breath. An unwelcome thought struck me. Why should Lacoste help me? He hated fae, he hated me—now he's supposed to come running into danger to save my life from a powerful enemy?

I should've told the fae to promise something for him, too. I might be able to get Raynor to help him somehow.

Minutes, then lots of minutes, ticked by. An hour, maybe two. The sunlight above began to dim without any sign of Lacoste or even other fairies. My legs ached, even with strengthening spells.

I was truly captured. My sympathy for the gnome in the cooler became more intense, more personal. A shared pain. Both prisoners of a deranged mind.

What would I feel when the air I breathed morphed back into solid earth? Would it be a sudden crushing of my flesh, or would there be some kind of magical, extended torture as I hung on for a while in a physical and spiritual limbo?

Rupert's voice startled me from above. "Alma!"

I looked up, aware my feet had gone completely numb

in the icy water. To prevent permanent damage—optimistic of me to think I'd have a future use for my toes—I used some of my limited magic to warm them.

"Alma!" he shouted again. "Time's running out! It's seven o'clock. Tell him there's still time to make this easy. I know he can find a plane to get him up here faster, but that means more people are going to get involved, and I think he'd rather keep this on the down-low."

I put my hand on the wall and squinted up at him. "How considerate of you to worry about his feelings," I said. "How do you think he'd feel about being murdered?"

"Just call him, Alma," he said. "Better him than you, don't you think?"

FIFTY-THREE

I was too disgusted to reply. Wrapping my arms around myself, I hunched over and pulled on my magic stores again to stay not only warm but sane. It would be too easy to give in to panic.

I lost track of time as the afternoon faded to night. The fairies might have reached Lacoste, but I had dwindling hope it would lead to my rescue.

Rupert appeared every so often to beg me to phone Raynor so "my" garden wouldn't be prematurely destroyed. At eleven, when the hours before midnight shrank to minutes, he became frantic, alternating between shouting and weeping.

It only made me angry, and anger helped me stay strong.

"I'm not going to call him," I said. "Let me out, and maybe you won't have to spend the rest of your life in a Death Valley jail. How many plants do you think can live in the hottest place on earth? Is that really where you want to do your gardening from now on? You're actually young, right? So that's a lot of years you've got ahead of you."

He made a noise that was either a cry or a laugh; I couldn't tell the difference. "You have no idea how much power she has. It has. You don't know. She—"

There was a flash of light. Rupert's head disappeared. It was several seconds before I saw a new silhouette in front of a bright, artificial light.

"Alma?" asked a familiar voice.

"Darius!" For a split second, my relief brought up the emotion I'd been roughly suppressing. Tears burned in my eyes. "Did you get Rupert? His real name's Jack Barber. I think—"

"I hexed him. Hope you don't mind. He's floating in an interrogation cage."

I smiled, suddenly optimistic enough to worry about being naked. I'd need clothes, a heated blanket, a spell to ease the ache in my legs and back...

"You need to get me out of here. Hex strikes at midnight."

He grunted. "Right."

"What time is it?"

He didn't answer. That worried me.

"I think he's working with Clem," I said in a rush. If I died, I wanted somebody to know what I knew, suspect what I suspected. "I think she's trapped the gnome. She was trying to get Raynor up here to kill—"

"Hold on, explain more when I get you out of there. I'll get a r—" His words ended on a cry.

There was another flash of light. Another cry.

"Darius?" My heart lurched. *"Darius!"*

Silence above. Several long, agonizing minutes passed. I braced myself, pressing my back against the slippery brick wall in case Rupert or Clem or another unknown enemy flung down an attack.

I was shaking all over, especially my hands. Maybe the cold was going to kill me before the getting-crushed-underground thing happened at midnight. How many minutes were left—fifty? Five?

Darius was here because of me. I'd been so brave about not calling Raynor, and then I'd had the fairies tell Lacoste to get me help, not considering he'd be most likely to go to Darius. If he'd been hurt or killed, I'd never forgive myself.

Of course, never for me might be a matter of minutes.

"Darius!" My emotional control of the past hours broke. I picked up the bubble-wrapped phone and flung it against the wall. It fell back into the water and bobbed cheerfully against my leg as if mocking my throwing arm.

"Hey, sorry." Darius was back, his breathing labored. "Prisoner is secured. Again. I didn't expect him to be able to break out of an arrest spell."

He sounded so casual, so confident. My old partner was OK. I let out a long breath. My legs were trembling.

"The power is coming from the cooler." I was talking and crying at the same time. "I think Clem has the gnome inside. Trapped. Do you see it?"

"Yeah. It's here."

"Stay away from it. It put me down here."

"Nasty magic," Darius said. "You OK down there? I can't see anything in the dark."

I wiped my face. "I'm fine. I'm naked."

He hesitated. "You must be freezing."

"I am."

"OK, let me try to find something to get you out of there," he said. "Lacoste told Holly you needed help. Didn't say how."

"He didn't know himself," I said. "Come on, hurry. I've got to get out of here *now*. The enchantment ends at midnight. What time *is* it?"

He didn't answer.

"Darius?"

"We'll get you out," he said finally. "Holly's bringing backup, but I didn't know… about the deadline."

I paced through the water, sending splashes up my numb calves. "I've been thinking. You could put a spell on the sunflowers. Make them a ladder."

"Do you really want to use any of their plants? They could be hexed. Part of the trap."

"The sunflowers were Holly's," I said. "She did the back fence plantings."

That seemed to convince him. He left, and I waited, shivering but hopeful.

He came back too quickly to have created the ladder. "Something weird is going on at that back fence. It's shaking. I don't want to go near it until backup arrives."

"There's no time! Try sending down a cage spell for me. I'll climb in and—"

"I can't. Didn't you think I'd try something like that already? There's something blocking magic at the top of the well." I saw flashes of light. "It's too strong. If I— Demon's balls, the fence is moving. It's like something's trying to break out. Or in? Yes. It's pushing inward."

"The goblins!" I rubbed my hands together. "I think they hate Clem's magic. They might help. Try to help them get in."

"How? I can't see them."

"Pull up the flowers. Ruin as much as you can. Trample them, cut them, whatever. The enchantment is keeping them out."

Darius hurried off. A few seconds later, I heard shouting and screaming. Rupert's voice? His garden was coming down.

More screaming. Another flash of light, then an explosion. I paced and splashed, infuriated to be so helpless.

"Alma!" Darius shouted down. "There's something coming out of the cooler!"

My trembling became so violent I imagined the walls were beginning to shake. No, I wasn't imagining it. The walls really were moving.

Inward.

"What time is it?" I cried. "Darius, please, just tell me. What time is it?"

"Eleven fifty," he said. "We've got ten—"

"The walls are coming in! Get me out, Darius, get me out!"

I pawed the bricks, feeling cracks as wide as my fingers forming between the seams. Dirt trickled through. Pebbles fell and went *plink-plink* in the water around my legs.

I turned my attention inward. My heart thudded against my ribs. If I could concentrate on the deepest source of my natural power, maybe I could buffer myself, or float...

The pebbles became chunks of stone. I flung my arms over my head to protect my skull from the collapsing well.

"It didn't work, Clem!" I shouted. "Let me out! Maybe he'll come to save me next time!"

Time had run out. Maybe I should've called. Maybe Raynor could've saved me.

The walls bent, moved together. There was no more light. I was going to d—

FIFTY-FOUR

When I drew my next breath, I found myself lying on dry earth. Sharp rocks prodded my bare arm and hip. My entire body was trembling with the shock of near death.

I was alive. I was out of the well.

It was night, but there were lights somewhere, nonmag and magical, above me and to the side. The light was blinding after the hours in the darkness. Squinting into the distance, I saw deep shadows from plants, fountains, arbors, fences.

I was in the fairgrounds. I rolled over and saw Darius flung out on his back next to me on the ground. His eyes were closed, but his chest was rising and falling with rapid breaths.

Thank Brightness. My stupidity hadn't killed him.

Floating ten feet off the ground in a magical cage was Rupert—rather, Jake Barber. He'd collapsed into a fetal position and wasn't moving. I didn't know if he was alive or dead and couldn't bring myself to care.

The garden was gone. It was just like it had been the first day I'd arrived: a bare plot of scraped soil; dry, sterile, and ugly.

There was a pile of fabric and something else in the

shadows a few feet away. Head swimming, I sat up and crawled over to it on my hands and knees.

My clothes. And shoes. Even my jewelry and bag. Too stunned to question my good luck, I put them on with unsteady hands and then staggered over to Darius. If he was badly hurt, I'd need my focus beads to help and defend him. Oxygen mask on yourself first and all that.

His breathing had steadied. I couldn't see any blood or obvious injuries.

I put my hand on his heart and pushed a healing spell into his body using my newly restored focus beads. "Darius, wake up."

His eyes opened. They darted sideways to look at me. "What's happening?"

"Not sure. Garden's gone. Rupert—real name Jake—is still in the cage. Possibly dead." I started to help him up, but he was able to rise by himself.

He reached into his pocket and extracted a handful of bark and leaves. "Someone did something to my phone." He flung it away in frustration.

"The fae did that," I said. "Lost mine once that way. Never did get it back."

He cursed, then bent down and used a stick to prod a slab of melted plastic. "This must be the cooler. What's left of it."

I went over and scanned it. There was the taste of fairy fire, something I'd only ever sensed once before at a museum of medieval antiquities with my father. It had also clung to the remains of a cage.

"The gnome escaped." I looked past him at a dark, bulky shape about three feet wide and tall near the fence. "What's that?"

Brushing himself off, he looked where I pointed. "What's what?"

It was in the shadows of the back fence. I couldn't make out its details. "You don't see that?"

He bent his knees and held out his hands in a dueling stance. "No. Might be the gnome."

I got up and walked closer.

"Careful," he said.

As if I needed the reminder; I was clutching handfuls of beads in both fists. "It looks like..." I stopped, too horrified to believe what I was seeing, let alone say it.

There were several goblins in what seemed to be a group embrace. At the center, like the hub of a bicycle wheel, was an object that gave off a power I'd felt before, both at the scene of a local car crash, Clem's backyard, as well as under a redwood tree at my own home.

But it wasn't right. It was... It was too small.

"Oh," I whispered.

It was just a piece. I saw a short limb, the back of a hand, small fingers.

Darius came up beside me. "What? What do you see?"

"It's an arm," I said. "The gnome's arm. There are goblins, the ones from the school, holding it up. They helped her get out."

Darius was silent a moment. "That's sick."

"It's got power. I can feel it."

Darius sprang into action, pacing and sending scanning spells around us. "We've got to get more witches here. This is bad. If only part of the gnome is here, that means—"

"That means Clem's got the rest of it," I finished.

"How...?"

I'd never imagined a gnome could be captured. But to sever its spirit into pieces and then capture it, separated from itself, was a horror that was hard to believe, even though the proof was right in front of me. The goblins were making a noise I couldn't decipher. It was a cross between a hive of bees and a baby crying.

Then I heard her.

Rather, I *felt* her.

FIFTY-FIVE

Darius spun around, showing he'd sensed her too. Clematis Mallory wasn't one of the mysterious, invisible fae but a very real, very familiar human witch.

I felt her pushing something. Something with wheels. And making no attempt to go unnoticed.

The power coming off her was as loud as a siren, an assault on my magical senses.

"Yin to yang," Darius mumbled, coaching me to take a defense pose he preferred.

I remembered the code name but not what it stood for. It was probably the mirror approach—he took her left, I took her right—but it didn't really matter. Even during uncomplicated operations, plans always fell apart before the second hex.

"Got it," I said.

While I reinforced my defensive boundary spells, Darius lit a magical torch and aimed it at the sound of wheels rolling over gravel.

Clem approached pushing a baby stroller holding a large square object. The box, made of wood and iron, must've been heavy; the wheels were leaving deep grooves in the path. Despite the effort to push the stroller, she looked calm.

Cheerful.

Darius and I didn't look at each other, but I felt us sync our energies at shoulder to hip, preparing to defend or attack in unison.

"There's gnome energy coming off that box," he muttered.

Given how much of it was spreading around the stroller, I was sickened to conclude it was more than just an arm this time.

"I didn't call Raynor," I said, not even bothering to raise my voice. She didn't deserve the effort. "You've lost."

"Oh, you called him," Clem said. "You didn't mean to, but you did."

I thought of the bubble wrap. How I'd thrown the package. Was it possible I was lying to myself and I'd actually submitted and made a call? Or that she'd made me do it when the well had collapsed?

I searched my memories.

No. She was lying. I was sure I'd held firm.

"You didn't need to use a nonmag machine," Clem said. "He's a witch. And so are you. I knew he'd respond if your fear was great enough."

A pit opened in my stomach. She might be right. All my determination not to call him might have been for nothing. My suffering, nurtured over hours, enhanced by magic, might have been enough to act as a beacon.

"Isn't it interesting?" she went on. "Witches know a lot about magic, but we totally forget about other mysteries of the human experience. Nonmags call it being psychic. It's good to be humble sometimes. You learn more."

I was disgusted by how she was apparently in the mood to have a friendly little talk. Maybe decades of being a bitter recluse made anyone hungry for a chat.

"Why would he respond to me?" I asked. "He's not my boyfriend. Never has been."

Clem pushed the stroller to the edge of the empty garden plot and bent over to secure the little plastic wheels. "No, it's worse than that. He wouldn't care about you at all if he *had*." Her tone was deceptively light. "My young body meant nothing to him. Or any of the many, many bodies he had after mine. He's a devil. Once he's had you, he forgets you."

Go for the box, Darius said to me in a charm whisper that only I'd be able to hear.

I glanced at the goblins holding the severed arm. Clem hadn't looked toward them once, reassuring me that she couldn't see them. She wasn't demon marked.

I'd have to find a way to use that—or them. The goblins had worked to free the arm; surely they'd want to liberate the rest of the gnome as well.

I wasn't sure, but it made sense.

How could I communicate with them without her hearing? She currently wielded enormous power, and I'd been freezing at the bottom of a well for hours and was still tired.

Now, Darius whispered.

It wasn't what I wanted to do quite yet—I thought we needed the goblins' help—but I couldn't let him down. Holding my power in a shape that would blend with his, I touched my bracelet, reached inward for my power and my anger, and struck.

Our attack bounced off the heavy box with only a faint sizzle. Clem let out a sigh and looked at her wrist, where she wore a smartwatch. Apparently her relationship with nonmag technology wasn't as hostile as she'd pretended.

"He's on his way. He didn't know about the deadline, so he won't give up now that it's passed," she said. "Turns out it was good you didn't call him. All he knows is that you were freaking out. His poor little friend. We'll wait here until he gets here."

Again, Darius said. *This time at her.*

I drew upon my power and did as he prompted. But just

as it had with the box, our hex bounced harmlessly off Clem's protective spells.

I hadn't ever used the silent charm whisper so didn't trust myself to try it now, but I gave Darius a look that any nonmag could interpret as *This isn't working.*

He raised his eyebrows with the universal retort *Fine, what's* your *idea?*

I jerked my head toward the fae gathering only I could see. He nodded.

To prevent her from being suspicious, I would address the goblins without talking to them directly. Like Rupert, she had an ego that was starved for stroking.

"Who captured the gnome?" I asked. "What creature has that kind of power?"

"Creature," Clem said with a laugh. "You know it wasn't a creature."

"Then what?" I asked. "Was there some kind of malfunction? A spell vortex from too many witches living in one place? You were smart to take advantage of it, I gu—"

"The sum total of power from the witches living in Elwin, myself excluded, wouldn't be enough to knock over a feather."

"So how'd it happen then?" I asked.

My obtuseness was breaking through her facade of cheerful calm. "Me, you idiot," she said. "No other witch on earth has mastered the mysteries of the gnome the way I have. And none ever will."

"Maybe the gnome likes the box you made for her." I felt encouraged by the crack in her temper. "They like small spaces, they like wood—you got lucky."

"I spent decades learning, researching, practicing, and perfecting the craft. Decades. There was nothing lucky about it."

I watched the goblins out of the corner of my eye. Although they were still huddled around the hand with their backs to me, one or two green eyes were looking Clem's way.

They were afraid of her. But they were angry. And now they had the freed gnome—well, part of her—to, uh, lend a—

"The gnome has been freed," Darius said, gesturing at the remains of the cooler, then around at the desolate earth. "You've lost."

A small smile curled one side of her mouth. Without moving, she cast a ball of light around her head that expanded outward with each breath until it was large enough to encompass all of us. The night shadows fell away. My garden and everyone—everything—in it was now as well lit as a Broadway show.

In the flood of light, I could now see the details of the box and just how deep into Shadow she'd fallen. Although the exterior of the box was made up of wood—plywood, not my favorite—there was a window, several inches square, covered with steel chicken wire. And inside that...

"I'd intended on fulfilling my mission at my house, but this is better," Clem said. "Seventy-five percent is more than enough to be my own side. I don't need anyone to help me. And there's nothing strong enough to stop me."

Seventy-five percent. That's what she called the semi-immortal spirit she'd hacked into pieces and imprisoned in a cage. As if a gnome was no different than the battery charge level of a tech gadget she claimed to despise.

I could see the gnome's face. Deeply lined, it was pale gray, as thin as a human corpse. Her hair, whatever color it had once been, had fallen out. She stared out at nothing with bleak, weary eyes.

The emotions raging through me were so intense I had to turn away. Teeth gritted against the rising bile in my throat, I fought for calm, tapping into the redwood bead I'd carved under Willy's gaze in my backyard.

I was burning with the urge to strike Clem with all my power. Immediately.

No matter the cost.

FIFTY-SIX

'd been fired from the Protectorate for having an Incurable Inability to kill. Now I was feeling eager to test that diagnosis.

But a small piece of me that wasn't controlled by rage held me back. With so much power on Clem's side, I'd lose if I attacked her directly in a temper. And so would the gnome.

I took a ragged breath, held it for a moment, then let it out as slowly as my anger would allow.

I had to be smart. I had to be deliberate. In my state of mind, with the forlorn gnome's face still in my field of vision, it was going to be very difficult.

Darius's hand bumped mine. I looked up, saw concern in his eyes, and clasped the hand he offered. Resolve and strength poured into me. Clem could light up the night with the gnome's magic, but Darius and I had Brightness on our side.

"Jake up there inspired me," Clem was saying. "He reminded me how nice it would be to have an audience. I deserve some acclaim for once. And the world should see justice done to him."

I squeezed Darius's hand and released it. Feeling that

my rage was now on a leash, although a fragile one, I was able to respond in a flat voice. "To Rupert? I mean Jake?"

Her swagger faltered a split second. "Nice try. You know who I mean."

"I don't," Darius said. "I'm in favor of justice. Maybe we're on the same side."

She snorted, shaking her head, and squatted down to the basket under the box in the stroller. "Raynor's career has been nothing but accolades. But nobody knows who paid the price for all that. Soon they will." She took out a stick as long as her forearm and waved it at Jake's cage. It snapped open, dropping the gardener to the ground.

He didn't move. His sparse gray hair had reverted to thick, wavy brown, and his physique had gained at least twenty pounds of muscle, now straining under the smaller clothes of his disguise.

Clem frowned. "Is he dead?"

Darius and I didn't answer.

She looked offended. "Was killing him necessary? He was only doing what I told him to do. There's really no point trying to fight it. The harnessed gnome energy is bigger than anything even Raynor could come up with."

"We didn't touch him," I said.

She shook her head. "The *Protectorate*. Such a misnomer. Just a gang, really. Gang of killers. Of course Raynor, famous demon murderer, would rise in the ranks the way he did."

"We didn't touch him," I said again.

Clem thought we'd been the ones to break the cooler open. That other fae could've been strong enough to overcome her magic hadn't occurred to her.

Maybe it hadn't occurred to them either—until they'd done it.

I glanced over. More of the goblins were turning their faces outward, listening and watching.

It would be a risk to expose my allies that she was

unable to see, but I needed to act big. My intuition was sure it was the right move.

"The fae are powerful when they band together," I said. "They crushed your magic. They can do it again."

Clem waved the stick at Jake's body. It jerked and flopped to its side. At first there was no sign of life, but a moment later a faint groan rose from his parted lips.

"Wake up, Jake," she said. "Did you hear what she said? She said fairies did this to you. What an insult. Don't tell me the great Jake Barber is going to just lie there and take it."

She spoke with the calm, faintly sarcastic tone she'd had when we'd met. The one that had made me like her. Identify with her. Admire her.

Big mistake.

I looked directly at the largest goblin who had turned completely away from the floating gnome hand and was watching me with two bright green eyes.

"The fae can free the gnome," I said. "The fae *will* free the gnome."

The goblin didn't move, but its eyes glowed brighter.

"No fairy would lift a wing to help a gnome," Clem said. "That's the beauty of it. Gnomes have lived apart from other fae for millennia. They think they're better than everyone else. Fairy, demon, human. Gnomes only respect other gnomes."

"You're wrong," I said. "Under extreme circumstances, with the right enemy—like you, Clem—fairies will rise up to help their own kind, even one they don't usually like."

"That's your play? Trying to scare me with..." She hesitated, then smiled that bored, ironic smile. "With fairy tales?"

The goblins had moved closer. They carefully cradled the gnome arm between them.

I turned quickly to Darius. "Watch for my sign."

He gave me a sour face—I really did need to learn the stealth talk thing—but nodded.

The goblins readjusted the arm until it was protruding ahead of them like the figurehead of a ship. Slowly but steadily they moved closer, closer, closer to the box in the stroller.

I braced my feet on the ground, reached out to all my beads, metal, and herbs, then pitched my voice low and loud. "When they free the gnome, you'll see what justice is."

Clem sighed. "Oh, please cut it out with the—"

The goblins rushed forward. They pushed the arm into the box, then swarmed around Clem's head and chest while they keened in a high-pitched chorus of bee/infant voices.

"Now," I told Darius, but he'd already moved forward, casting an unbalancing spell at Clem's feet. It was a classic move, though simple; it didn't rely on overcoming an opponent's magic, just their physical form.

I added my own hex to his, adding a sideways twirl to Darius's horizontal one. Clem spun around in a twist but after two spins was able to block our spell. She landed on both feet, hair wild, and reached for the box.

The goblins let out a uniform screech and mobbed her face. A moment later there was a billowing mass of dark powder around Clem's head.

No, not powder. It was heavier than that, like sand or soil or...

Compost. It was compost.

She cried out, flapping at the cloud of dirt and throwing spells at the fae she couldn't see. She managed to knock three goblins out of the air. They rolled on the ground, disappearing for a moment under the soil, then immediately sprang up and resumed swarming.

"Again!" Darius shouted.

Just for a moment I was tempted to tease him for not speaking in his magic whisper. I would later, if we survived. My own boundary spells were being chipped away. It wasn't coming from Clem, bowing under the weight of the attacking fae, but from the box, still doing her bidding.

The arm was dislodged. The gnome inside, looking more alert than she had earlier, tried to reach her own severed arm, pushing her tiny fingers through the chicken wire. But the cage held her back. The arm fell away, sinking like dandelion fluff to the ground.

Clem came back into her power. Regaining her balance, she flung a pain spell at my face.

"Cover me," I told Darius, dodging her hex and rushing forward. The blasts coming from the box grew stronger as I moved closer. I felt my shielding spells thin, waver, crack. A sharp pain shot through my left ankle.

I pushed on, falling to my knees next to the arm.

Clem smiled, perhaps thinking she'd broken me. She couldn't see what I was reaching for. She couldn't see what I lifted gently, whispering apologies for my kind. She couldn't know how a fierce, triumphant energy flooded me where the being's limb touched mine.

Staggering to my feet, I pushed it into the box.

"Wait," Darius said. "What are you doing?"

Clem was furious with what I'd done. Lunging forward, she blasted me aside with a hex that burned the hair off my arms. "No!" she cried, embracing the box.

She must've detected something happening in her cage that she didn't like.

I rubbed my singed arm, hoping that was proof I'd made the right move. I hadn't known why the goblins had tried to put the arm in the box, but they'd freed it from the cooler—and therefore me from the well—so they clearly knew something.

I hoped they knew that a whole gnome would be too powerful to contain.

At first there was no change. Clutching the box, Clem continued to hurl hexes that knocked massive, terrifying holes in my boundary spells. She flipped Darius once, but he landed on his feet and flung a boiling-water hex at her face. Her power held, however, and she deflected it with only a nod.

As long as the gnome was under her power, we were in trouble. Within sixty seconds, one of her hexes was going to break through my boundaries and strike flesh, bone, or vital organ. There might be another tragic death by cardiac arrest in Elwin.

I looked at Darius, who was sweating with the strain of defending himself. Eyes blazing almost as intensely as when he'd been under the moonstone hex, he clenched his platinum necklace between his teeth and continued to fling offensive spells at Clem. But he, too, was breaking under the onslaught of her gnome-enhanced offense.

But then...

The sky broke open. Clem's illumination spell went out. Lightning, zigzagging out of the darkness, struck the box. Blinded by the flash, I fell to the ground, not sure who had struck whom.

Another crack landed near the stroller and sent it into the air. Deafening and violent, fingers of white light whipped around my head, tearing at my hair, singeing my fingers. I was knocked over, my arms flung outward, and landed sharply on the ground.

Wrapping an unsteady protective spell around my face, I risked opening my eyes.

The stroller was on fire. The box—gone.

Standing beside the blaze was a figure. Small, wearing a hat with a slight point at the crown, she met my gaze.

Once again, my world went dark.

FIFTY-SEVEN

Throbbing pain in my left ankle woke me up. It was dark, I was on the ground, and a cold sea breeze was cutting through my clothes.

I was getting tired of waking up cold and confused. Wincing with pain, I rolled over onto my hands and knees. I was fairly sure I was still in the fairgrounds. I saw a faintly lit building in the distance that might've been the school.

At least I still had my clothes on.

"We need to find her," Darius said, poking me in the arm. He got to his feet. "We can't let her get away."

I looked around, suddenly wide-awake, but didn't hear any sign of Clem or the gnome. It was too dark to see much more than shadows.

My ankle wasn't strong enough to support me, so I settled on the ground with the injured limb stretched out in front of me. I felt strangely relaxed.

My innate source of magical power seemed strong, much better than I'd expected after the fight with Clem. I thought of the creature in the box, all the power, all the suffering. Was she free now?

Without needing to use my focus beads, I threw a brightening spell high into the air.

As it rose, it illuminated a wasteland. Every garden

exhibit at the fairgrounds—every flower, shrub, or annual; the fountains, pergolas, rose arbors, and gazebos; all the decorative metal sculptures and lights and signage—all of it was gone. Every inch as far as my light reached showed soil that was as bare as the moon.

"Demon's balls," Darius whispered.

I looked behind me and saw there actually was one object that had survived. On the ground about ten feet away was a human-sized figure. Whether he was alive, I couldn't tell.

I pointed. "Rupert—er, the great Jake Barber—is lying over there by the fence. He still hasn't moved."

Darius glanced at him, then turned away dismissively. "We have to warn Raynor. She's out there hunting him again." He took out his phone and frowned at me. "Why aren't you getting up?"

"Hurt my ankle," I said. Then noticed what he was holding. "Hey, your phone is back!"

He hesitated. "Right." Another pause. "It was bark and leaves before." He said it as if he wasn't sure if it had been a dream.

A long, slow breath came out of me. I smiled. "She's free," I said, feeling a great peace come over me. "She's free."

"You can't be sure of that."

I looked around. The destruction had been intentional. And only one creature would've felt that angry. "I'm sure," I said. The return of my magical strength must've been her way of thanking me. I was touched and awed.

What a creature.

Darius resumed typing into his phone. "What we need to be worried about is Clematis Mallory being free. We've got to get everyone out there looking for her."

With the gnome liberated, I wasn't worried about Clematis anymore. My ankle was throbbing, my body was shivering, and my heart missed Seth with a fierceness that brought tears to my eyes.

I was tired. I wanted to go home. I wanted Seth to come home.

While I was bent over my sore ankle, throwing myself a pity party, Darius was talking to somebody on the phone. Holly. Telling her what had happened. What Clem looked like. The possible corpse of a garden designer. Maybe because he was trying to avoid being flirtatious, he was coming across a bit officious and robotic. That was my humble, ex-partner opinion anyway.

He really was smitten with her. His sudden love wasn't a hex from Clem or even Holly, as I'd feared, but my doing. In fact, he should thank me. The healing sachet I'd given him had not only protected him from Clem's hexed rock, it had mended his broken heart just moments before meeting the right woman.

"They're two minutes away," Darius said. "Raynor. Holly. Other agents."

"OK." My entire leg was throbbing now. Something was probably broken. I'd have to wait for a real nonmag doctor before I started playing around with powerful healing spells, which might do something counterproductive to the tissues and bone. I took a tiny bag of home-roasted oak leaves out of my pocket and sprinkled them over my ankle. It wouldn't be as powerful away from my kitchen, but the pain eased a little.

I decided to lie down and wait for the witch cavalry. But when I leaned back, a sharp, lumpy object jabbed me between my shoulder blades.

My yelp brought Darius over.

"What happened?" He had a fistful of silver chains, ready to hex whatever it was.

"Nothing. Fell on a rock or something." I rolled to one side, gasping as my ankle turned with me. "I'm going to need a doctor. The kind on TV with a white coat and an X-ray machine. Don't let Raynor try to fix this with just a gold earring and some snorting herbs, promise?"

Darius bent down and lifted the object that had poked me in the back. His tone became strange. "It's not a rock."

"What is it?"

He didn't answer, just kept looking at the thing. It was only a little larger than his restored cell phone. I reached up to take it from him.

"Wait!" He pulled it out of my reach. "It needs a scan. It might be dangerous." He set it on the ground and began weaving a Protectorate spell of analysis and interpretation.

I moved my own light over to see the object better. It looked like a garden gnome. Squat and round with pink cheeks and a red cap. Not a real one but the kind that were mass-produced for nonmagical people and sold in big-box stores.

My stomach fell. Had all our efforts led to this—the poor thing freed, only to be turned into a statue?

Then I saw its face.

Her face.

"Is it...?" Darius trailed off.

I should've been frightened. If she could do that to one witch, she could do it to any of us.

But... I smiled.

It was so... so right.

"Yes," I said. "It's Clem. Clematis Mallory is now..."

Darius made a noise I suspected was a stifled laugh. "A statue. She turned her into a tacky statue."

We were still staring at it, both of us vacillating between horror and satisfaction, when thirteen motorcycles roared into the now-desolate field and surrounded us.

The largest figure, leading the pack, dismounted first.

"Alma!" Raynor shouted, running over. Before I could stop him, he bent down and lifted me in his arms. "Thank Brightness you're all right."

FIFTY-EIGHT

"Thanks," I said, giving him a hug. It wasn't too bad, being rescued by a witch with action-hero good looks.

He was scowling at me. "Are you hurt?"

"Ankle might be broken," I said, "but otherwise fine. You?"

Darius cleared his throat. He was holding up the gnome statue in the grip of small, foldable silver tongs agents always carried with them. "We believe this is the perpetrator, but you'll have to bring her—it—back to Diamond Street to be sure."

The little eyes of the figurine, fixed on Raynor, seemed to glisten.

"Old friend of yours," I said.

Raynor looked at me, then back at Clem. The stone face didn't move but somehow expressed an incandescent, helpless rage. It began to vibrate within the grasp of Darius's tongs.

Raynor stared at it in distaste. "How could a witch be transformed like this?"

"She kept a gnome captive," I said. "It got out."

Raynor nodded, then looked down at me, still in his arms. I assumed he'd loaded up on both magical and nonmag treatments to enhance his strength, because he didn't seem to be under any strain.

"Clematis?" he asked.

I realized it was going to hurt him to learn the truth about a woman he'd thought was a friend. A witch he'd trusted enough to send me to for help.

"Yeah," I said quietly. "She's been nursing a grudge against you. Since way back when."

He took a moment to absorb that, but nothing showed on his face. "Why attack you?"

"Bait. She wanted me to call you, bring you here."

His eyebrows arched toward his bald dome. "Did she really?" He scoffed, turning back to the angry statue. "I suppose she heard about you from Percival Tuff. I think he had a bit of a crush on you."

I thought of how Percy gave a lot of women that impression. "You can set me down now."

Raynor, still staring at the statue, got a calculating look on his face. "Maybe I don't want to. Maybe I want to keep holding you."

The statue spasmed violently, broke free of the tongs, and fell into the dirt.

"Yeah, that's Clem," Raynor said. He signaled at Galen, an agent who was even larger than he was, to come and get me. As if I were a bag of landscape gravel, I was hefted from one embrace to the next.

My ankle hurt too much to stand without help, but I wriggled one foot down to the ground and managed to stay up by leaning on my new beast of burden. Across from us in the growing crowd of agents, Darius and Holly were shaking hands. Her back was to me, so I couldn't guess if his enthusiasm was reciprocated.

Raynor took a larger set of tongs from another agent— we were surrounded now—and picked up the Clem statue. "Get me an iron box," he said. "There should be one in the tank case on Bike Three."

Agents ran to do his bidding. Less than a minute later,

Clem, shimmying and thrashing, was locked inside the box. A stainless-steel chain was wrapped around it three times and clasped with a gold ring.

Raynor gestured for them to take it away, then turned to Darius. "You said there might be a corpse."

An agent called from the fence. "Over here, Director. He's not dead yet. Should I help him?"

Raynor, to his credit, hesitated less than a second. "Um, yes. Yes, of course. We'll need to build a case against Mallory."

On a last-name basis now, I noticed.

"I'd like some help too," I said. The agent I was leaning against had loosened his grip, making it obvious he wanted to unload me. "Could somebody, like, maybe bring me to a hospital now?"

FIFTY-NINE

"She'd been trying to capture me for weeks," I said. "But I was too stupid to notice."

The showdown at the Elwin fairgrounds had been just twelve hours earlier. Dash—I decided I'd call him that from now on—had driven me to the hospital in my Jeep and then, hours later, on to San Francisco.

I'd rolled into the Diamond Street office in San Francisco on a new knee scooter. My fractured ankle was bandaged, my pain treated with herbs, and I was ruminating about all the mistakes I'd made.

For the first time, I was being a harder judge on myself than were the Protectorate agents interrogating me. I sat in a ground-floor room of the converted Victorian house with my foot elevated on a chair while two witches asked me questions and recorded the answers with a floating glass ball that hovered around my mouth. Darius was being interviewed separately.

Holly was one of the agents asking me questions. She poured me a cup of springwater-laced lavender tea—my third—and shook her head. "From the very beginning, you suspected there was fae power behind the Shadow in Elwin. My team and I were too busy watching the school."

The second agent was an older woman with long,

straight white hair who hadn't said a word. She kept busy drawing little smiley faces wearing hats in the corner of her notepad. I was tempted to apologize for swearing. Every once in a while she looked up, caught my eye, and smiled. She reminded me of a lonely grandmother my father had relied on for free babysitting when I was a kid.

"It's good you were focused on the school," I said. "What was happening there was a huge crime. Since it was kids, I'd argue it was worse than what Clem tried to do to Raynor."

"Mallory murdered Percival Tuff and Nerissa Pike," Holly said. "And she almost killed you too."

A memory of being trapped at the bottom of the well flashed through me. I shuddered. "Yeah."

Holly seemed too compassionate to be a spy. It was strange to be looking at her in her Protectorate uniform of long black T-shirt over jeans, as sleek as a retro tech mogul. Instead of the straw sun visor, she now wore a generous array of gold jewelry and a double strand of pearls that my father would've coveted.

Darius had told me on the drive that she was a Quartz-level agent who had used her gardening expertise—her family owned a nursery and landscaping business—as the keystone of her undercover identity. She'd never met Rupert before this year's Elwin show; it had been a lie they'd mutually agreed to tell for their own ends.

"I should've been more suspicious of him," Holly said. "But I confirmed he was working for you, with Zoe Thornton's backing. Knowing your connection to Director Raynor, I thought it was perfect."

"It was," I said. "The kids are safe now. You caught Jill and Bruce."

She got a funny look on her face. Clearing her throat, she adjusted her pencil. "Bruce was working for us."

"Ah." I thought of his child's drawing. The teeth, the fear. "That's good. I'm relieved."

"He broke it all open, actually," Holly continued. "His

kid told him, then he told Lacoste. Lacoste told his handlers in New York. They roped me in."

"You admit Lacoste works for the Protectorate?"

After a glance at the other agent, Holly nodded. "That's confidential, of course."

"Everyone shuns him," I said. "He's miserable. He's feared and loathed. Is that fair? The Protectorate could clear his name, but instead, they use him."

"I agree," Holly said. "But it's not up to me. His situation long predates my employment with the Protectorate."

I wished Raynor was there so I could talk to him about Lacoste's demon mark. Only those of us who carried it really understood, and I couldn't expose our secret to anyone, not even Holly.

And there was the other agent in the room, who still hadn't said a word.

"Let's get back to Clematis Mallory," Holly said. "You were on her trail from the beginning."

"I wasn't on her trail," I said. "I was after a gnome."

"Precisely," Holly said. "Her gnome."

"No. *She* was the one behind everything. It's not fair to blame anyone but Clem. Why didn't I suspect the bitter loner giving out painful boils to strangers?" I pushed the tea away. "That should've been an easy one to see coming."

"Nobody saw it. Why should you have?"

I met her challenging gaze. Was Holly covering her own mistakes, or did she really think it would've been impossible to have identified Clem earlier?

"It was all there," I said. "She'd been after me for weeks."

Holly looked through her notes. "You'd only been in Elwin since Friday."

I looked at the door. I'd hoped I'd reached the level in my non-career where I only had to explain myself to Raynor.

As if reading my mind—for all I knew, she could—the older woman got up with my mug of tea and poured it out into a potted fern that looked neglected. Well, it had before she'd given it a drink. The magically laced tea perked its fronds up immediately. I wondered if it was the agent's way of showing me that she, too, cared about plants.

Holly watched, frowning, then turned back to me. "He said he would've been here if he could."

"Is he OK?" I asked.

Holly stifled a yawn in her fist. "Long night," she said. Then she reached under the table, lifted a purse, and took out a sleeve of peanut butter sandwich cookies. "Why wouldn't he be OK?" She offered them to me.

"He's being interrogated too, isn't he?"

Holly slumped back in her chair. "If that's what you want to call a few friendly questions between Bright witches just looking to establish the truth."

I took a cookie, then two. "That's what I call it, yes." As I chewed, I looked at the floating glass ball that was recording my words. In the past, Raynor would control which of my words made it onto the official record. This time he wouldn't be able to do that.

"As I said, she'd been after me for weeks," I continued. "She must've heard about me from Percy—Percival Tuff."

Holly nodded, so I went on.

"We'd met in Silverpool back when he left the Protectorate." They'd know all about that. "I think she met him in Elwin, heard he was ex-Protectorate, and immediately started manipulating him. I think she saw him as her ticket to finally getting to Raynor. She played with him, testing out her power by getting him to hit on women in a bad way. That's just a theory of mine though. He didn't seem predatory when I knew him, but I'm not positive. Anyway, I think she realized there were limits to what she could get him to do. What she really wanted to do was kill Raynor. She'd nursed a grudge for decades."

After two peanut butter cookies, my mouth was dry. I looked around, regretting the plant got my tea. Without a word, the older woman got up, poured plain water into my mug, and returned it to me.

I nodded my thanks and continued. "She learned I knew Raynor and created this big theory about me being the key," I said. "She wrote me a letter pretending to be Percy, trying to bring me to Elwin."

"When was this?" Holly asked.

"About a month ago, I guess. I didn't see the letter until a week before the show. It got stuck here at Diamond Street."

The older woman shook her head.

Holly said, "Yeah, the agent who hid the mail works in LA now."

"I think Clem wanted Raynor to see it. The idea of him touching her envelope and paper—and not knowing it was from her—probably appealed to her vanity. She loved feeling stronger and smarter than everyone else," I said. "Otherwise, why not send it to my house? She knew where I lived. She showed up there two weeks later."

Holly sat up. "What? When?" She looked through her notes. "There is no mention of Mallory in Silverpool."

I hesitated. Out of respect for Willy, I would share as little of his story as I could get away with. "There is a gnome who lives in my backyard. He makes himself visible to myself and several of my visitors." That was vague enough, I decided, and it might be written in my file already. "One morning I could see that his home in the tree on my property had been damaged, and he was missing. I believed he was hurt. Seeking advice, I reached out to Raynor. He told me an old acquaintance of his was an expert on gnomes and to go visit her and ask her educated opinion."

"Clematis Mallory," Holly said, nodding. "You think she was the one who interfered with the gnome on your property?"

I was sure of it. She hadn't had the power to take me captive directly, which suggested she'd been unable to travel with the gnome's largest... portion. The thought still made me sick. But she'd had enough power to drive Willy out of his home.

"Yes," I said. "She was the gnome expert. I believe it was all part of her plan to get to Raynor through me. Maybe she'd thought at first she could capture me in my own home. When she discovered the gnome on my property..." I paused, not wanting to expose my belief that Willy had fought to defend me, which might make my story too incredible to believe. "They came into conflict. She drove him out of his home. I think her plan then was for me to seek her out for help since she was the only gnome expert around. On Clem's home turf, where she was most power-ful, she'd be able to capture me."

"But she wasn't able to capture you." Holly looked at her notes. "You visited Elwin for the first time on June 8. That was..."

"The day before Percy was killed," I said. "She manipu-lated me into staying in town until midnight. Then she gave me a stick from her apple tree, pretending it was to help Willy—"

"Willy?" she asked. "Who's Willy?"

SIXTY

"My gnome," I said.

I felt myself flush. In some ways, I'd been as possessive as Clem. "No. He lives in my backyard. He's his own person. I mean, creature. Entity."

Holly's eyebrows rose. "He gave you his name?"

"That's what I call him," I said, backtracking. Holly nodded, satisfied the world was more as she'd imagined it to be, where a gnome would have to be hacked into pieces and locked in a cage to share their secrets. "Anyway, the stick was probably supposed to hex me. She would've dragged me into her house and then tried to get me to call Raynor for rescue. But... Well, I've got powerful self-defense spells. I'd used some before the drive home to keep me awake and safe from fae on the road—they must've protected me without realizing it. She hadn't used strong enough magic. She'd thought I'd be an easy mark."

"She was obviously wrong about that," Holly said.

I smiled, thinking of Darius's words. *You like being underestimated.* "I think that was why she killed Percy. She'd failed to catch me twice. It made her angry. She sent a second letter to me, pretending to be Percy—the note said 'help'—and then killed him. She couldn't wait, or I might find out right away he hadn't sent it."

"Twice?"

"When she hurt the gnome in my backyard. She'd been going for me."

"The gnome interfered on your behalf?" Holly asked, clearly incredulous.

"He's like that." I hadn't had a chance to talk to Willy yet, but I needed to thank him properly. I'd helped him out of the tree, but his shame had been too great to tell me what had happened. Gnome pride was the energy that fueled their kind. I hoped he'd feel better to learn the gnome who had overpowered him had been forced to do so.

"All right," Holly said. "Frustrated twice, she writes a letter to you, pretending to be Tuff asking for help, then kills him."

"Yes," I said. "That's what I think."

"It takes about a week for Dash"—Holly cleared her throat—"Agent Ironford to find the letters and bring them to you. When you hear Tuff was killed, you decide to go up to Elwin, using the garden show entry as a cover."

"Right."

"Therefore it was Clematis Mallory who entered you in the show?"

I nodded. "She wanted me to stay longer than I had the first time. But when I showed up, Darius was with me. So she hexed him."

Holly flinched. "The moonstone."

"Clem saw us on the beach. She must've seen me pick up a rock and give it to him, so she hexed one and set it in my path. I was an idiot to pick it up, and even worse, I gave it to Darius. He walked around with it in his pocket for hours."

"Yet he didn't attack you until later in the motel," Holly said.

"I'd given him a healing sachet when he said he had a headache. And then he took it off in the room to take a shower, and the hex was able to finish its work."

"That must've been an excellent sachet," she said.

"We've got the moonstone. It has no fingerprints that suggest recent manipulation."

I shrugged. "She's good. The gnome was in her power. Who knows what else she could've done?"

Gaze locked on mine, Holly raised her eyebrows. "If not for you."

"I was stupid. I walked right into the third attack. Literally. I parked my car outside and went up to her front door by myself. I might as well have wrapped myself in pretty paper and put a bow on my head."

Holly ran a finger over the notes in front of her. "You spoke to Director Raynor first. Told him of your plans. He agreed and notified Agent Ironford."

"It was stupid."

"And when Mallory attacked you," Holly continued, "you shape-shifted into a cat, escaped, and discovered the dead body of Nerissa Pike. Your continuing investigations corrected the misconception that she'd killed herself because of the exposure of the children's biomatter crime. In fact, we now have evidence Mallory was in the house. There's magical residue of the box she used to contain the gnome. Do you have any theory as to why she'd want Nerissa dead? Why take the risk when she'd just attacked you and you'd escaped?"

"Nerissa was a busybody," I said. "Her niece, Marta, had seen me visiting Clem. Asked me why. I bet she told Nerissa. Nerissa would've wanted to know why I'd been to the house."

"But Mallory could've evaded her questions. Just as she did with Protectorate agents."

"Nerissa had learned mind magic from Percy," I said. "Maybe she caught Clem at a weak moment. She'd just attacked me, and I'd escaped. Perhaps she'd been running around the neighborhood trying to catch me, and Nerissa stopped her then."

Holly nodded. "We've been learning how often Nerissa had been using the mind techniques. She'd begun a political action committee. Some were pushing her to run for office."

"I'm sure Clem had been wanting an excuse to kill her anyway," I said. "After Percy, what's another death? She was probably starting to enjoy it."

The second agent dropped her pencil and used her gold charm bracelet to cast a feel-good spell over the table. It was the sort of magic used with small children.

Holly and I exchanged brief, amused looks, then the ball hovering next to my mouth suddenly turned bright red. A second later, it let out a whistle and went dark. The older agent stood up, plucked the ball out of the air, and put it into a leather satchel she lifted from the floor.

"Well, Alma, thank you so very much for your time," the woman said. "I do hope your ankle heals quickly. I suspect a chat with that loyal gnome neighbor of yours will be most restorative."

Holly looked at the woman with as much surprise as I was feeling myself.

"Thank you," I said.

"We're done?" Holly asked.

The white-haired woman smiled at me, making dimples form in her round cheeks. "I'm sure Alma is eager to get home."

I smiled back at her. "I am." But there were a few outstanding issues I was curious about. "What's going to happen to Rupert?" I'd heard he was alive, but no more.

"Rupert?" the older woman asked.

"Jake Barber," Holly said. "He's being taken to LA. Given his involvement in a plot to kill Director Raynor, as well as the deaths of other connected persons, he's unlikely to have much of a future in garden design. He'll be sent to Death Valley, I imagine."

I actually felt a pang of compassion for the old man, then reminded myself of the muscled dude I'd seen at the end of the confrontation in Elwin. "Just how old is he?" I asked.

"Thirty-two," the other agent said. "We'd almost caught him last year when he used Shadowed magic to levitate a water feature at a garden installation at a tech company in Sunnyvale. But he covered his tracks with, we now realize, some help from a captive gnome."

"He cold called me," I said. "He said he'd heard about Zoe's offer. I was stupid to believe him."

"Oh, Zoe Thornton did contact him," Holly said. "Rather, she contacted Jake Barber. She hadn't known he was Shadowed. It hadn't been proven, and he did have quite a reputation for brilliant work."

And Zoe had her reasons for distrusting the Protectorate's beliefs about who was Bright or not. Nevertheless, I was still angry at myself. "What's going to happen to his husband?" I asked.

"Oh, he's not married," Holly said. "And his girlfriend is cooperating with the agents at their house right now. She's shown them where he stored some Shadowed stuff in a crawl space under their bedroom. She was eager to get rid of it."

I was disgusted. He'd lied about everything.

"We would've found him earlier if Mallory hadn't been giving him such effective magic to hide himself," Holly said. "That disguise was way too good for one witch to do by himself. I never suspected."

It had taken me way too long. I rubbed my eyes, suddenly exhausted. If Darius wasn't free to drive me home, I'd get Raynor to pay for a ride. Seth was home. I didn't care about whatever delicious surprise he had for me, I just wanted to see him as soon as possible.

Holly adjusted her pearls. "How about me?"

The woman gave her a serious look. "I'm so sorry, Holly, but you'll have to fly to New York for another round of questioning. But it can wait for"—she looked at her watch —"seventy-two hours. That'll give you time to recover a bit before you make the trip."

I looked between Holly and the other agent. I'd thought Holly was in charge, but now I understood better.

The sweet-looking old lady was a VIP.

"I beg your pardon," I said to her, bowing my head with respect, "but may I have the honor of knowing your name?"

She stepped closer and patted my hand. "Don't be so formal, child. Call me Cathy." She lifted my mug—the one I'd used to drink two cups of tea and some plain water—and slipped it into a plastic bag. That went into the satchel as well. She caught my eye and said, "Never can be too careful, can we? Don't worry. I'll keep it safe. Better than leaving it to the underlings in this building. They still have a little staffing problem Raynor has to weed out."

I gaped at her. *Cathy?* "Who are you?"

She just smiled at me, gave me another pat, and left the room. I turned to Holly with a question in my eyes.

"I thought she was a visiting Emerald interrogator," Holly said. "From Boston. But now I wonder."

I wondered too. I thought of Raynor's hunt for a new Protector of Silverpool. Was Cathy here to interview for the job?

Or be persuaded to take it?

It was too soon to make assumptions, but I liked her.

You liked Rupert too, I reminded myself.

The door opened, and Darius came in. He gave Holly a professional nod and then turned to me. "Ready? I'll drive the Jeep. Hopefully I can get a ride back to San Francisco with a Flint if Raynor lets them follow."

I looked with regret at my bum ankle. I would've rather driven home myself, but at least with Darius driving I could nap or zone out on my phone.

During the journey to San Francisco that morning, I'd read social media posts about Elwin. The witches of the gardening world were enraged by the destruction of the fairgrounds, and news had already spread about Clem. An angry mob had gone to her house, and a series of confused posts had then described an unidentified force pushing them away. The discussion shifted to when to recreate the show, with a loud majority demanding the blue moon of midsummer.

I would be sure to not be there.

"How about I follow you on one of the bikes and give you a ride back?" Holly asked. "I'm done here. Well, until they pick my brain in New York. They'll want to know everything before I leave."

Darius, stunned by the offer, seemed to have trouble getting out his next word. "Leave?"

"I'm quitting special ops. Didn't you hear? I'm joining you guys here at Diamond Street."

SIXTY-ONE

When we got to Silverpool, Darius didn't linger any longer than the ten seconds it took to park my Jeep and help me get out with my scooter. Then, pulling his helmet on as he ran, he joined Holly on the motorcycle. The two of them drove off without even a wave.

Or maybe they did wave. I was too busy looking at Seth to watch two Protectorate agents start a romance.

He stood between our houses in the same spot of sunshine where we'd said goodbye over two weeks earlier. His hands were folded in front of him, his expression pained.

"You're hurt." He strode over. "Why didn't you tell me you'd been hurt?"

"It's only a hairline fracture. The scooter is just to get people to be extra nice to me."

He put his arms around me. "I should've been there. Are they dead?"

Given what had happened, that was a complicated question. "Is who dead?"

"Whoever did this to you."

I thought about Clem, shrunken and petrified, trapped in a box, held indefinitely in Protectorate custody. "Worse."

He buried his face in my hair. "I should've been there."

We held each other for a moment, me on one foot, knee on the scooter, then I broke away.

"I need to talk to Willy." There were still unanswered questions. How had Clem captured the gnome? Was the creature going to be OK? Was there anything I could do to help her recover, make amends for witches or human beings?

Seth put his hand on the brake of my scooter. "I need to tell you something first."

I looked at him, worried. "What happened? Were you too late? Is the baby a changeling?"

"No, the baby's fine, but—" He leaned over and kissed my cheek. "I want you to meet someone. Don't worry, he's cute. You've always liked dark-haired men." Grinning, he ran a hand through his black hair.

I didn't smile back. "Who is it?" I glanced at his house. "He's in there?" I'd been through too much in the past week to enjoy a surprise.

"Come on. I'll carry y—"

"No. I can get there by myself." I turned the wheels and rolled across the road to his driveway. Unlike mine, it wasn't cracked and overgrown with weeds. At the bottom of the steps leading up to his front door, I paused to let him help me hop the rest of the way into the house.

He brushed a kiss across my lips. "Don't worry, demon's daughter. Everything is going to be all right."

I squeezed his arm, then looked past him for the visitor. A cousin wouldn't be too bad. His adoptive parents might have had extended family that Seth had met and invited home. That could be fun. Awkward, considering he was a fairy interloper who'd killed their true kin, but maybe interesting. Illuminating.

A tiny black puppy came tearing out from around the corner, slipping and sliding on the kitchen tile floor. He began yapping and whimpering, wagging his tail so violently he rolled himself over.

Seth bent over and picked him up. "Alma, this is Fergus." The dog wriggled over in Seth's hands and began frantically licking his face with his tongue.

I was overjoyed the way any reasonable person would be when confronted with a puppy. But...

I had to ask. "Did you steal him?"

Seth hid his face in the writhing puppy. The little guy lunged for his shoulder and began chewing on his ear. "I had to."

I thought of the family in Minnesota, welcoming a new baby, then coming home from the hospital to discover their adorable puppy was missing. "They're probably afraid—"

"Don't worry, I replaced him with a substitute. They won't know the difference." Seth extracted the puppy from his ear and held him out to me. "Especially when you consider the sleep deprivation and excitement of their first baby and that they'd only had Fergus for a little while..."

"But why?" I inhaled the puppy smell and felt all the worries of the universe fall away. "You must've had a good reason."

Seth didn't answer right away. I watched him play with his hair, twirling a long strand over his forehead the way he did when he was thoughtful. "My mother, it turns out, was able to break into the house. She'd gotten in before I arrived."

The puppy nuzzled my neck, making me laugh—despite the bad news Seth was sharing. "What happened?"

"Fergus here did his best, but it wasn't enough. He... he took one for the team. Yes. That's what we'll say. He was a hero."

An uncomfortable feeling crept over me. I pulled Fergus away from my head and held him at arm's length. Unable to stop myself, though I usually avoided using magic under Seth's roof, I used a powerful scan on the dog.

All I detected was playful, joyful energy. The spirit of love and wonder. Curiosity, eagerness to learn, hunger.

Affection. Need for more contact, as much as possible, always and forever.

"He seems wonderful," I said.

"Of course he is. That's why I brought him home to live with us." He nuzzled my temple, lowering his voice. "He's ours."

I studied the dog again, but my magical senses told me nothing.

So I tried my brain. "It's a changeling?"

Seth shrugged. "Well— Yes." He cleared his throat. "Fergus, you could say, is my brother."

Fergus wriggled to get to Seth, so I handed him over. I wasn't sure how I felt about a canine changeling. It had been rough for Seth, so why would it be easier for his fae brother?

But Seth didn't look depressed or worried. He seldom did, but still.

"What about the... the puppy's spirit?" I asked, fearing the answer. His mother was cruel, and any puppy forced to live under her would suffer even more than a human being would.

"Oh, he's still in there. That's the miracle." Seth grinned.

"The puppy and the lake fairy are... sharing?"

"Yup."

"Isn't that impossible?" I asked.

"Apparently not. I tried to evict my brother as soon as I realized he was in there, but... Well... I dreaded my mother getting her hands on him after failing to possess the human baby, and the puppy, of course, would never give up trying to please her, so..." Seth rolled the puppy onto his back, held him in one hand, and rubbed his round tummy with the other. "This seemed best for everyone."

"Are you...?"

"Worried, Alma? Is that what you're going to ask?"

The dog looked like a Lab. Those got big and strong and liked to go outside a lot. If the fae spirit inside was interested in harming people, it would be cute enough to get close and then strike with its strong jaws and sharp teeth.

But Seth trusted him. Seth had lost his human family, his human brother, and his lake fae family of origin. Maybe this fragment of his former life would grow to fill a hole in the human life he'd been forced to lead.

"I was going to ask if you're going to take him outside," I said. "He doesn't look house-trained yet."

EPILOGUE

Two months later, Willy and I sat together under the redwood tree, sharing a box of donuts from the new bakery next to Birdie's bookstore.

Life was finally settling back to normal—or a new normal. As promised, I'd visited Elwin only once more, during the full moon in early July, to deliver a rain barrel of Silverpool wellspring water to the sprites. Otherwise I'd stayed home, avoiding all adventure. Buying a dozen pastries was the most exciting thing I'd done all week.

"The beloved of Birdie is making good cake," Willy said, biting into a walnut bar. He didn't chew, I don't think, because I never saw teeth, but the donut disappeared as if he did.

"I'm afraid Birdie doesn't have a beloved," I said. "She had a crush on Raynor. Director in San Francisco. The big witch without any hair who—"

"I am knowing that one who has also been calling himself Protector," Willy said. "The beloved is making cakes. A better life, I am thinking, for a friend for you, who is here and near me, who is appreciating goodness to eat."

I'd noticed the bakery owner was an attractive man, but how had Willy? Did he know something we didn't?

Probably. I mean, of course. He always did.

"Birdie is going to fall in love with the baker?" I asked.

"He will be wooing her. She will be thinking that there might be a day when he is her beloved." Willy licked a small finger. "He will be making many delicious cakes, I am hoping, to be earning the affections of her."

"Which I'll share with you?" I asked.

He bowed his head. "Loving can be a thing that is not always bad," he said. "You, Witch Alma. Before this day and this year, you were not as happy as you are being since the baby little one came to live with you and the impostor."

"Don't you think you could call Seth by his name now?" I asked. "It's not like he had any control over what happened."

Willy took another bite. Half the bar disappeared. "I am cheerful to be seeing dogs of all kinds here in the dirt under my tree, even if they are also pretenders. They are encouraged to be not opening their liquids over my home, you are telling them."

I found a strawberry-filled donut, considered not having it, then put it in my mouth. "Mm," I said. If Willy didn't want dogs peeing on his tree, he'd find a way to stop them. I'd become more powerful over the years, but that was a skill I didn't think I'd ever learn.

"I am thinking the baby animal will be good at learning," Willy went on. "Do not be telling him not to visit me, for that is not what I am saying."

Smiling, I wiped strawberry jelly off my lip. It was good to learn he liked Seth's puppy brother. I'd hoped he would.

In all the weeks since the disaster in Elwin, he'd refused to say a word about what had happened to him or to listen to anything I had to share. He'd come out and said hello and accepted my gifts and polite greetings—and done something to accelerate the healing of my ankle —but until today, conversations had been abruptly declined.

The new bakery, I'd been happy to learn, was owned by a witch with experience in hearth magic. It was unusual with male witches to pursue the old, domestic ways, but not impossible. His donuts had clearly charmed Willy.

And perhaps, someday, he'd charm Birdie.

"I'd love to know the gnome's name," I said. "She's been through so much. I promise not to share it with anyone if that's her wish. I'll place a silence hex on myself so it doesn't ever come out accidentally or intentionally."

Willy shoved the heel of the maple bar into his mouth. As he seemed to chew, the hat fell back on his head, revealing a bony scalp with white hairs curling down around his ears. Adjusting it back over his forehead, he said, "Lavinia Northwhistle is being her longest real name."

I repeated it silently to myself. "Thank you," I told him. It meant a lot to me to have that one tiny piece of her. Unlike Clem, however, I wouldn't allow myself to contain her. Without any outward show of magic, I sealed the name inside myself for the rest of my life. "Where is she now?"

"She is being in her home, of course, where she should always be," he said. "The witch is now sad as a small rock far away as Livy is wanting. Now there is needing time to wipe away the nastiness of the bad one being there until another is being allowed to stay in the human dwelling."

"Clem said the gnome was a beautiful singer," I said. "I never found out if that was a lie. I hope she can sing again if it was true."

"There is the lack of ability to be stopping Livy from the singing," Willy said. "Even with the ears of others being sad, she is not caring. She still sings. She is singing always."

"You don't like her singing?"

Willy sighed. "Before, it is possible that I was enjoying the music she was making, songs loud enough to hear from Silverpool. That is being true. It is also true that I was very much hating Livy's songs when she was visiting here in the box."

I stared at him, pained. I hadn't heard any hint of fairy song that morning. My powers to hear the fae didn't always include gnomes. "Was it her singing that drove you up into the tree?"

He was silent a long moment. "It is a sad thing to be saying so, but I am saying so. Her songs are where she is having power." He looked up. "They were very long days where I was being in the branches and not the roots, where I am belonging. Her visit, you are knowing, was being very bad."

"It wasn't her idea," I said. "A witch had imprisoned her, forcing her—"

"Of course I was knowing about the box and the other box during the moment when it was happening. All the people were knowing this, even my beloved who is far away."

"All gnomes knew she'd been captured?"

Willy found a powdered donut as large as his face and regarded me through the hole in its center. "All. All is known, all is being known. Of course this is it."

"But you didn't know she was going to attack you, right?" I asked. "You had no idea the witch was bringing her here?"

"As you are saying. The witch was the attacking one. Her little brain was being invisible to me," he said. "Even before, when her brain was larger than her brain is now, in the small rock that is her form since the good events are happening."

I thought as I chewed, trying to interpret. "It was Clem's plan, so you had no idea it was coming." And he knew she was a tiny rock now.

He grunted and took a bite.

I'd thought about asking why he hadn't warned me, but I decided it might offend or even hurt him. If he'd been able to warn me, he would have. He'd protected me as best he could. More than any witch could've ever expected from a creature as special as himself.

"Do you know how Clem captured her?" I asked.

Willy dropped the donut. He got to his feet—no, he

floated to my eye level—and glared at me. A pipe appeared in his hand.

"I'm sorry," I said quickly. "I don't want to know. I meant it literally—do *you* know how it happened? Are *you* safe?"

His eyes softened. Sinking gracefully to the ground, he brought the pipe to his lips. "Is it that in the days of the future you are staying here in the box with your animals and the impostor?"

I glanced at my house. Seth had begun spending more time there. I suspected my magic wasn't hurting him as much as he liked to pretend. Or maybe it had gotten easier with each day we'd been together. "Yes," I said. "I'm staying with Random, Fergus, and Seth. We're all staying."

Willy blew a smoke ring that rose above our heads and disappeared into the ferny branches of the giant redwood tree. "Yes, I am thinking that is true," he said. "If that is what you are doing, then I am being safe, Alma Bellrose."

∾

AUTHOR NOTE

As Willy would say, I am hoping you were enjoying *Hexed in Show*. Perhaps you would also be enjoying a bonus Sonoma Witches short story! Sign up for my newsletter at www.gretchengalway.com/newsletter and get a free prequel ebook, *Death on Witch Street*. It describes Alma's first days in Silverpool.

Having connections with my readers is the magic that keeps me writing. My newsletters contain information about new releases, sales, and fun little details about what I'm working on. I hope you'll join in.

As always, happy reading!

Gretchen Galway

BOOKS BY GRETCHEN GALWAY

SONOMA WITCHES (Paranormal Mystery)

Dead Witch on a Bridge (Sonoma Witches #1)

Hex at a House Party (Sonoma Witches #2)

A Spell to Die For (Sonoma Witches #3)

Charmed to Death (Sonoma Witches #4)

Murder by Magic (Sonoma Witches #5)

Hexed in Show (Sonoma Witches #6)

Dead Witch in the Library (Sonoma Witches #7)

The Sonoma Witches Series Box Set: First Three Novels (Sonoma Witches Books 1-3)

~

OAKLAND HILLS SERIES (Romance)

Love Handles (Oakland Hills #1)

This Time Next Door (Oakland Hills #2)

Not Quite Perfect (Oakland Hills #3)

This Changes Everything (Oakland Hills #4)

Quick Takes (Oakland Hills Stories Boxed Set)

Going For Broke (Oakland Hills #5)

Going Wild (Oakland Hills #6)

Oakland Hills Romantic Comedy Boxed Set (Books 1-3)

RESORT TO LOVE SERIES (Romance)

The Supermodel's Best Friend (Resort to Love #1)

Diving In (Resort to Love #2)

ABOUT THE AUTHOR

GRETCHEN GALWAY is a *USA Today* bestselling author who writes mystery, fantasy, and romance. She lives in Sonoma County, California.

For more information:
www.gretchengalway.com
gretchen@gretchengalway.com